MW01231425

A PLACE TO BELONG

by
Paul Miller

www.placetobelong.com

authorHOUSE™

1663 LIBERTY DRIVE, SUITE 200
BLOOMINGTON, INDIANA 47403
(800) 839-8640
WWW.AUTHORHOUSE.COM

Paul Miller - 1951 - 14 Years Old

First published by AuthorHouse 01/17/06

ISBN: 1-4208-8787-4 (sc)
ISBN: 1-4208-8788-2 (dj)

Library of Congress Control Number: 2005909875

Printed in the United States of America
Bloomington, Indiana

This book is printed on acid-free paper.

Paul & Johnny 1939

Johnny & Paul – About 1941

Paul, Sarah & Mattie – About 1943

Paul, Mattie & Billy – About 1942/43

Paul, Billy, Kitty & Sarah – About 1942/43

Sisters & Billy

Mom & Dad - Pomona, Ca. 1948

ACKNOWLEDGMENT

I am sure; this is probably the most difficult part for any author to put into his/her works. For there are so many people that need to be credited and thanked for their contributions and the author will feel absolutely appalled if someone is left out. So, believe me, if I omit someone, it's not because I'm being inconsiderate, it's more of being totally neglectful and I apologize now.

Two people that have become very close to this story and to me, have contributed so much, that without them, this book would not have come about. All my heartfelt thanks; admiration and respect go out to Colleen Adl and Carol Givner.

I express much gratitude to Gloria Lord and Lori Wall who encouraged me to go forth with my story. Also, thanks to Donna Kehoe for her suggestions, guidance and valued opinions.

Many thanks to all the folks that I had read the rough drafts and give me their honest ideas and opinions, whether I liked them or not.

Finally, to my wife Sherry and my daughter Paige, who I forced to read every word, every comma and every period for three months non-stop, far beyond the call of duty.

Paul Miller

TABLE OF CONTENTS

1.

A PARTY

Party guests hung out the windows and danced their footprints into the snow.

From jitterbug music to the sweet forbidden scent of beer, the living room rolled below me. I crouched transfixed from my unseen perch at the top of the narrow, wooden staircase, bewildered by the topsy-turvy scene.

"Oh, boy, if Mom and Dad could see this! Wow! They'd be madder than heck."

Clumps of big band swinging strangers held their drinking glasses high up above the ever-rollicking terrain made up of blonds, redheads, and brunettes. They held suspicious liquids within their glass confines; the potions tossing back and forth like the rolls of a deep and foreign sea. Necking couples clung to each by their lips and fingertips as the floorboards and walls hummed with the roar of conversation.

There was a man with mountainous shoulders and a blunt crew cut that made his head look like a flat plain. He loomed over a blonde girl with horn-rimmed glasses and a frown that said come hither as much as it said go away. A skinny guy with a rubber mouth jumped around a redhead whose proud breasts pointed like rocket ships at his eyes. He tried to get her to laugh by doing his impression of Jimmy Durante, *Cha cha cha.* She did. A brunette with a wicked smile taunted a chorus of monkey-faced droolers.

The rumble of the party was momentarily broken by the shrill squeal of a woman's laugh. Every head turned to look. One beat later the cacophony resumed with even more gusto, as though that shimmering evening needed to be held tightly, or it would slip away.

The party only added to my sense of vertigo. I was still skewed by the sudden leave-taking of my parents, an event I considered a sign of great foreboding. But I suppose all eight-year-olds feel that way the first time their mothers leave them behind.

The morning after my parents' departure I'd been sitting at the kitchen table eating my oatmeal when my three sisters, Mattie, Kitty and Sarah approached. They stopped shoulder-to-shoulder, arms crossed. Standing in a row like that, they reminded me of soldiers, but those militants wore calf-length skirts, tight sweaters, bobby sox, and saddle shoes. All three twisted their lips as though they were trying to suck a pearl out of a piece of gravel. I guessed I was the gravel.

Mattie stepped forward out of the line. She announced, "We're having a party tonight. Mom and Dad are not supposed to hear a peep about it. You understand?"

I looked from sister to sister. There must have been a measure of tentativeness in their approach, because I asked, "What am I supposed to do while you're having this party?"

Sarah shrugged dismissively and whined in that uppity way of hers, "Take care of Johnny and stay in your room, you silly goof." And she nodded her head as if she was a grand justice handing down a sentence I deserved.

She'd said the wrong thing. I sat up taller and rebutted to all three of them, "Either I get to have fun or I'm telling." And I folded my arms and nodded my head. I didn't feel entirely convincing.

My sisters exchanged nervous looks. I'd upset their plans. A small victory. But then, Mattie's smile became even more vicious. She kneeled next to me, put her arm about my shoulder and all conspiratorial, said, "You know, that's not a bad idea, Paul. How about this. After Johnny's asleep, you can come down, and we'll have something really fun for you to do. How'd you like that?"

It wasn't just the insincere tone of voice that made me suspicious. Since my parents' departure, my sisters had used me as their personal slave. Paul, go to the store, we need milk. Paul, will you drop this magazine over at my friend's house? Paul... Paul... Paul...? Their idea of fun probably involved cleaning ashtrays.

But at eight, standing up to those older isn't a task taken on lightly. They're so much bigger. They dole out fun and pain with such ease it appears miraculous. So I hummed, "Oh, I don't know."

Mattie spoke with greater enthusiasm, sounding more sincere. "Paul, it really will be fun. You'll see. You'll have such a great time, you'll be telling all your friends at school about it. But, not Mom and Dad, right?"

I looked into Mattie's soft green eyes and melted. She knew she was my favorite sister. I usually trusted her implicitly. She'd come through for me when I wanted a baseball glove the Christmas before, the only one who realized how important it was, even if it was the middle of winter. Sometimes, she'd invite me into her bedroom to talk. She'd let me sit on the end of her bed while she filed her nails and asked me about Beverley Hollings, this girl I liked at school, or what I'd been up to with my friend, Billy. And she'd really listen to what I had to say, not just the words, but what was under them. She'd even ask questions, and sometimes provide suggestions, but she'd never ever judge. She didn't love me just because I was her brother. We were friends. Real true friends.

As her boyfriend, Ed, would say, Mattie was some of God's best work with a personality to match. She had curving curls of blonde hair and a seductive come-hither smile that was always compared to that Hollywood heartthrob, Lana Turner. Everyone loved her. I remember one time when a fire engine and three police cars were stopped outside our house to talk to her.

Mother peeked through the lace curtains with a smile that said, "Yep, that's my daughter." When Dad saw what was going on, he ran outside and shooed them away, ranting and pacing like a rabid attack guard.

Despite all the attention, Mattie wasn't a snob. For every admiring look, she'd send out a smile that said, "Thanks for the compliment."

I looked at the eyes of my friend, Mattie. Even though I doubted the depths of her sincerity, there was no way I could turn her down. "Well, okay," I said. "I won't tell Mom and Dad about your party."

Sarah and Kitty squealed at the news. Mattie stood up to join them with an "I told you so" grin.

But their outbursts worried me. Reasserting my miniscule power, I warned, "But only if it's fun. If it isn't, I'm telling."

All three sisters nodded their heads.

Mattie raised an eyebrow. "Oh, it will," she said in a taunting, devilish way.

As I watched Johnny that evening, my ears were tuned with heightened awareness to downstairs as guests arrived. With each rising notch in the volume my impatience grew to match. My imagination conjured up all kinds of hopes and dreams. What had my sisters planned for me?

A dice game between me and Mattie's boyfriend, Ed? A game of kick the can in the basement? Or maybe a high stakes game of Go Fish? I could see myself seated at the dining room table, having to sit up to see the sad faces on the other side of my stacks of plastic coins.

I didn't think it would never happen, but eventually Johnny's eyes closed in sleep and I was set free for fun.

* * *

People had hunkered down, using the stairs as seating. With tentative steps I wove down into that crazy world. I tried to avoid eye contact as if doing so would make me invisible.

As I stepped passed this one girl's knees, she whined to her girlfriend, "What's a kid doing at this party?"

Her derision spurted through me like a spray of ink in a glass of water. I was sent tripping the rest of the way down the stairs. A guy I bumped into called after me with a voice like a bear, "Heh, kid, you spilled my beer," and I ran even faster.

I didn't feel much better on firm ground. My shoulder's caved in as I wove through the crowd, bodies rising around me like trunks of great red cedars, their branches so high they didn't even notice me. This was awful. My sister's had turned my own home into an obstacle course of glasses and wavering drunks.

I turned the corner into the dining room and bumped into a couple kissing. Quickly, I excused myself, turned into the kitchen only to be stopped by a wall of couples jitterbugging in tight spaces, the floor visibly bouncing with their steps.

After a long search I found Mattie in the library. She was in the corner against the window, seated on a soldier's lap, her hands resting possessively on his shoulders. Their mouths were smushed together. They pulled away from each other slightly, and their tongues intertwined like worms playing. I nearly barfed.

"Mattie," I called. She didn't hear me. Louder, I said, "Mattie?"

The soldier's hand crept up the side of her leg, raising her skirt almost to her bottom. As uncomfortable as the sight was, I couldn't tear my eyes away from it. Just above his hand, I poked my sister three times with my finger.

"Mattie!" I yelled.

Mattie disentangled herself and turned to me, body swaying, eyes unfocussed. At my sight, a smile flitted across her lips. "Oh it's Paul!" she said, turned and melted gape-mouthed back into the soldier's embrace.

Angry, I jerked her arm. "What do I get to do?" I said, immediately regretting the whimpering childishness of my voice.

She flipped my arm away without looking. "Paul, go away," she said.

More authoritative, I yanked on her skirt. "You promised, Mattie," I said.

They stopped. Lips like slabs of liver, parted. She faced me again. Her hand went absently to her mouth now surrounded by a smear of lipstick as though she'd eaten a raspberry pie too fast. It was unusual for her to be so sloppy.

"Not now. I'm busy," she said with a sigh of boredom. She leaned back into the soldier's arms and sent him a wicked smile. "Right?" she asked.

The soldier returned her smile. "That's right, baby." They dove into each other again, making greedy, lapping sounds.

This time I jerked on his arm. "Mattie!"

The soldier batted at me, saying, "Kid, get the hell outta...."

But then in a snap, as if suddenly awoken by a cool breeze, Mattie turned to me and said, "Paul, why don't you go downstairs and get me and this handsome soldier here another beer?" Her glance was lopsided. There was something strange going on with her eyes, like two orbs rotating in different directions.

It hit me full force, right at that moment. My exposed naiveté knocking me breathless like a blow to the gut. My sisters hadn't planned anything for me. Fun or otherwise. Not even a lousy snack and a drink. I blinked at her. A bitterness globed onto my heart like some sticky yellow goo that couldn't be shaken away.

She nudged me toward the door. "Well, go on," she said.

My feet stuttered across the floor. Revenge was already burning bright. Parents would be told.

But in that moment I also keenly felt the loss of our friendship. I wondered what could turn my sister so against me that she could be so cruel.

As I headed out of the room, Mattie hollered, "While you're down there, find out where Ed is for me." She giggled loudly, as if trying to show off. I looked back and saw the two of them kissing again. Yuck.

I made my way through the crowd, on automatic pilot. It didn't occur to me to not get the beers. I mean, what else is a kid going to do at an adult party? But oh, the report I would file. I began to set to memory every single detail. My presentation would coat these halls in a wash of sin so shameful; my sisters would have to go to church every day for the rest of their lives.

I arrived in the basement and reached down into the beer case. Just as my finger closed around the stubby bottles, my peripheral vision caught on some movement like a distant flash of lightening you're not sure you saw. Automatically, I looked toward it. I saw nothing, at first. But then, in the crack of the furnace room doorway I saw two figures, flesh, fabric falling. Curious, I stepped closer. They were only half clothed and busy tearing the rest from each other as if it was a hot and steaming day. They collapsed to their knees then fell right to the floor and their limbs began to writhe like a dozen sick snakes. Wow. My eight-year-old gonads stuck me, statuesque, to the spot.

I'd heard the tales from the big boys on the playground. Their hushed whispers explaining the nitty-gritty of how babies were made. My best friend Billy and I had agreed, those guys had made the whole thing up just to see if we were gullible enough to believe it. But here it was, right before my very eyes. For a moment so brief I wasn't sure if it was real or imagined, I had a prime view of the exact point of action, if you know what I mean. It was too weird for words. I gulped. I inched closer, simultaneously bewitched and revolted. The certainty grew that there was no way on heaven or earth my Mother and Dad had ever done such a thing.

A hand grabbed my shoulder from behind and I squawked in surprise.

I spun to see Ed's jovial smile beaming down on me. "What's so interesting there, Paul?" he asked, ducking down and peering in. After a quick glimpse he turned back to me, his eyes twinkling. His hand, wider than my baseball glove, ruffled my hair so some of the hairs pulled. "Thatsa boy," he whispered proudly. "You'll get yours soon enough." He reached into the bucket, grabbed himself a beer, popped it open and took a glug. He winked at me. "One of these days I'll take you for a little trip, we can have a good long talk. You like that? Go camping or something? And I'll tell ya everything you need to know about girls." Too frazzled and overwhelmed to reply I stood there silently, my flushing cheeks burning so bright I was sure I could see their glow mirrored off the concrete walls. Ed nudged me with his bottle. "Your Dad's not the type to be frank with you. But I will be, Paul. You like that?"

I shrugged a half-yes, not wanting to turn him down.

He used his beer bottle to point at the two bottles I had in my hands. "You're starting two-fisted at your age?" he joked.

My tongue was mush. "I was getting these for Mattie," I replied.

Before I knew what was what, Ed grabbed them out of my hands. "I'll take them up to her," he said and headed away.

I ran after him, "Oh no, Ed. I'll do it. She wanted me to do it." I didn't want him to find her like that.

Ed stopped and looked back. "I'm looking for her anyway. Where is she?" he asked.

In that moment I could have told a white lie and not felt bad about it. Mattie and Ed belonged together. Mattie was just being silly tonight. Drunk. But revenge was too tempting, and I replied, "In the library."

He turned and ran up the steps.

Back in the furnace room, it was like the naked couple had evaporated. Given the opportunity, I reconsidered what I'd set in motion. Mattie didn't deserve to lose Ed, did she? I wondered if I could get up to the library before he did. I decided I had to try.

When I arrived at the top of the stairs, shouting came from somewhere in the front of the house. "Go outside! Take it outside!" A fight had started. Chaos ensued as bodies pushed in all directions. I was lifted off my feet, moved one way, then the next. Questions sprinkled the air. Who was it? Where were they? Let's go see. A cold breeze brushed the room from the direction of the front door. I ducked down below adult torso level and made my snaking path out the side door.

A crowd stood in a circle on the front lawn, with Ed and the soldier in the middle, circling with fists held up before their chests. Ed smacked the soldier on the face and the soldier stumbled back two steps. Ed stepped forward, preparing another blow. But just then, Mattie stepped in front of him, clenching fists at her sides.

She screamed, "Ed, no! Stop!"

Ed smirked. "Yea, I'll stop when I smash his dog face flat." He pushed her aside and started at him. Mattie jumped on his back and wrapped her legs and arms around his waist. She was the shell to his turtle. Ed rocked forward and back as his arms flailed, trying to dislodge her. The soldier took the opportunity to run up and smash Ed in the eye.

Two uniformed cops stepped out of the crowd and into the circle, stopping the fight. They stood between the two men and asked who'd started it. Words were spoken that I couldn't make out, and then the soldier darted through the crowd and made his way down the street. Police told the rest of us to go back to what we were doing before.

Mattie crumpled down on the snow beside Ed, tenting herself over his frame as though trying to protect him. Her back rose and fell in sobs. I went over to her, placed an inadequate hand on her back.

Over and over, Mattie cried, "I'm sorry. I'm so sorry, Ed."

"Yea, you're sorry now that he messed up my pretty face." The two of them laughed. I laughed, too, and Ed gave me a brotherly punch to the arm.

I liked Ed. He was muscular like a super hero. He had "MOM" tattooed on one arm, "Mattie" on the forearm, and his ship; USS Maryland BB46 on the other. He could play the drums, tap dance and sing. Yup, a real lady's man. I thought Mattie was lucky to catch such a great guy, and one day soon, he'd be my brother-in-law. I thought that was just terrific.

The next morning the rancid smell of smoke and booze still hung thick in the air.

I found Mattie sitting on Ed's lap in the kitchen. Her gaze was glued to his face as she held an icepack to his eye and ran pencil-thin fingers through his hair as if she had to prove he was really there. His broad palm caressed her bottom in circles. I stopped in the doorway and watched, embarrassed.

"Hi," I said, finally.

Mattie looked up and sent me a mocking, evil eye. "Well, there's the big mouth," she said.

Ed slapped her lightly on the behind. "Oh, leave him alone," he said. "I'm glad he told me."

We were jarred to attention by feet galloping down the stairs. Kitty came sliding around the corner, breathless.

She gasped, mouthed a few words of silence, then managed, "Mom and Dad are coming down the street. They're in front of the Hoover's."

Mattie and Ed jumped up from their chairs. How in the world could it be Mom and Dad? They hadn't had time to go to Florida and back. Not yet.

Like a rabble of keystone cops we made our way into the sunroom to see if it was true. Kitty leaned to pick up bottles as she went, cradling as many as she could in her arms, but she didn't have anything to put them in. So when she got into the living room, she switched to kicking the bottles on the floor under the couch so they rattled across the floor, kalunk, kalank, against each other.

The rest of us looked out the windows, down the street. That was Mom and Dad, all right. Dad with his fedora tilted down on his head, a half a cigar chomped between his teeth. There was something harshly metallic about his chiseled features. He walked slightly tilted to the right, each step a snap. Mother wore her hair combed back, the ends curled up into a small roll. In contrast to Dad, there was not an angular edge to her physique or persona. Even blowing her top she was a muffin.

Ed turned around and gave the room one good long look. There were whiskey bottles and beer bottles sitting on every possible surface. Cigar and cigarette butts littered the floor.

"Kitty?" Ed called. She looked up, her expression desperate. "We can't clean the place up in two minutes. We'll just have to face them."

Her hands twisted back and forth around the neck of a bottle, looking off. She nodded at his wisdom, slumped down onto the couch and hugged a bottle to her chest. She moaned, "Dad's going to make us go to confession and church every Sunday for the rest of the year."

I shriveled my nose at her. "What's wrong with that, Kitty?" I asked.

She sighed and gave me a weary look, "Oh Paul. Just shut up. You don't even know what we're talking about."

Ed said, "You aren't the only ones in for it. Your Mother's going to give me hell about fighting. Then she'll tell my Mother. Then I'll have to listen to those damn lectures from her again." He punched his hands onto his hips and raised his voice to mimic his mother, "Now, Ed, Jesus tells us to turn the other cheek. Don't hit back, love your enemy. Do you hear me, Ed?" He puckered his lips in a petulant pose. We all laughed. He continued with his normal voice, "Yea, shit. What if we told all those Japs and Germans that? We'd be talking Jap, stretching our eyes, and drinking German beer!" The group erupted in one honk of a laugh, letting some of our tensions go. I liked the way Ed talked.

We turned back to the window. Mom and Dad now stood in the driveway, facing each other. .

Dad looked up at Mother and said something. Mom shook her head side to side. Dad started slapping one hand into the other and waving his arms around his head, the lips of his mouth appearing out of control. After a couple of minutes he stopped and Mother started wagging her finger in front of his face. She was really letting him have it. He shook his head several times but didn't speak.

"What is she telling him?" Kitty asked.

Ed looked at each of us, laughed and said, "She's not asking him about the weather." I laughed. Ed laughed. Mattie smiled. Sarah, the gookiest of my sisters, who'd just, joined us, started to cry. She was such a whiner. Mother was always asking me to walk her to the bus stop and wait with her so the dogs wouldn't frighten her.

"Shut it up, Sarah," Kitty said with a grunt.

Sarah cried harder. "I can't help it. We're in so much trouble."

* * *

We stood in one long line in the kitchen, with guilty smiles pasted on our faces watching as Mother pushed the door open. Our shoulders rose up to our ears as they stepped through and turned toward us.

Mother barely looked around. In fact, she didn't really seem to be in the room with us at all. And Dad, he had on a familiar hard stare as sharp as an ice pick. He was caught up in that fury of his that burned with such intensity you knew he couldn't see anything but its red hot glow.

For what felt like minutes, the only sound was our uneasy breathing. Mattie was the first to shatter it.

"Hi," she said with a rasp. "We didn't know you were coming back so soon."

We watched our parent's eyes as they considered the debris. Mother sniffed. We waited for the outburst but, surprisingly, it never came. Mother and Dad just turned away and slipped off their coats.

Mother answered Mattie absently as she pulled off her kerchief, "Your Father and I finished our business faster than we thought we could, so we just came home."

Our ranks grunted an awkward acknowledgment as if that was perfectly obvious. But Ed raised an eyebrow, and Mattie sent the rest of us a glance of disbelief.

Mother smiled, giving us the first truly present look since she'd come through the door. She leaned sideways attempting to look through the line of us into the living room.

Mother continued, "We figured we could start packing and get this place cleaned up for selling sooner rather than later."

The words "pack" and "sell" hit me. I looked from sister to sister; none of them seemed surprised. In nervous unison they chimed, "Ah!"

Mother tiptoed through the bottles. She stopped in front of us, smiling and waiting. Nobody moved, so she asked, "May I get by?"

Kitty and Mattie jumped out of the way. As she walked past Ed she muttered under her breath, "If I'd been you, I would have ducked," and continued on her way.

I waddled after my Mother into the living room. "What do you mean by sell and pack?" I asked.

Mother surveyed the wreckage. "Paul, we'll talk about this later," she said, her voice a sigh.

I put myself in front of her. "No, I want to know now," I said.

From behind me came Dad's rumbling voice, "Paul, your Mother said later, so do as she tells you and shut up."

I looked from one to the other. Not a trace of compromise on either face. So I ran up to my room and slammed the door to. Johnny was still asleep, innocent to the news. I lay down beside him, wiped up some drool that had run down his cheek, and pondered.

Sell? Pack? We were moving.

I didn't want to move. I'd been born in that house. It was all I'd ever known. There was nothing wrong with it. So, why change?

As if hearing my troubled thoughts, Johnny's eyes fluttered open. When his gaze met mine he smiled.

I said to him, "Oh poor Johnny. You have no idea what's happening, do you?" As usual, he didn't answer. "Well, ya know what? Neither do I."

When Johnny woke up, he usually wanted to head downstairs to eat. But this particular morning, he just lay there quietly still, as though not wishing the moment to end. But at length he raised himself and tottered toward the door. I started after him, but stopped myself. Someone else could feed and dress him today. Standing in the crack of the door, Johnny looked back toward me, waiting. I lay back down on the bed with a grunt. I heard the door close and Johnny's footsteps pad down the hall toward the stairs.

Tears rolled down my cheeks, infuriating me and I slapped them away. I wasn't any baby.

Next thing I knew, Mother was sitting on my bedside stroking my forehead. I inhaled a familiar cloud of coffee mixed in with a comforting hint of her honeysuckle perfume.

"Hey, sleepy," she said. "This Sunday is slipping away in your dreams. I have dinner ready."

I sat up, ready to go, but she shook her head.

"I thought this would be a good time for us to have a little chat. Okay?"

I smiled up at her warm face, lay back and nodded.

A gentle smile was on her lips. She said, "We are selling the house."

I sat up quickly, trying to protest. She put her hands on my shoulders.

"And I'm going to tell you why." I grimaced, but did lie back down to hear her piece. "Your Father has quit his job at General Motors and wants to move to Florida."

"Why...?"

"Please Paul, this is difficult enough. Let me explain before you start your questions. Okay?"

"Yes, okay."

"Your Father is tired of the winters in Michigan and wants to live where the weather is not so cold. So that is why we are selling and moving." She stopped, bit her lip.

I'd been expecting so much more because of the way she'd started. "That's it? That's all?"

"Yes, Paul, that's all." She continued, whispering as if to someone far away. "You, me, Johnny and your father will leave Detroit, Michigan. All your sisters will have to find a place to stay. They don't want to move away from here. This is where all their friends and jobs are, and we can't afford to take them with us. There we'll go, down to Florida. Leaving this house — the community we've been living in for almost thirty years — behind forever."

I said, "I don't want to move either. Can't I live with Mattie?"

Mother looked down and caressed my brow. She shook her head and said, "No, Paul. You're too young and besides, they don't even know where they're living yet." She looked away again and sighed. "They don't need another problem."

I squinted at her. "Problem? Is that what I am?"

Mother turned back quickly. "No, no, Paul. That's not what I mean. What I mean is they have enough things to take care of for themselves without having to worry about an eight-year-old boy. They're young and nervous about being out in the world all on their own for the first time."

"Then we shouldn't move away."

All at once Mother threw her face into her hands and rocked forward and back. I felt bad. But her crying didn't last long. Within a minute she sat up, briskly wiped her face with a broad slap of her palm and took in a breath.

"Let's go down and eat dinner now," she said.

"I'm not hungry."

"Okay," she said as she got up and went to the door. "I'll put some away for you." The door shut and her steps faded down the stairs.

Fury over took me. Just because Dad wanted to move to Florida, everyone else had to find a place to live. Why couldn't he just leave things alone? Or go there all by himself?

I lay there all afternoon, thinking very hard. I could come up with all kinds of reasons *not* to move, but none *for* the move. I didn't know anyone in Florida. There'd be no one to play with. I'd have to go to a totally new school.

I'd thought things were topsy-turvy before. Now my whole world was not just turned upside down but inside out as well.

2.

GETTING WHOOPED

The next morning was one of those grisly Michigan days where the wind blows in fierce circles and the cold sucks the air right out of your lungs. My legs plowed through the snow as I headed for the streetcar. The wind blew harder and chunks of cold white wetness fell from the branches above onto my head. I wrapped my scarf tighter about my face and held it there so I could breath. A train whistle moaned off in the distance. In the cold, dark, early morning it had a lonely sound that echoed my mood exactly.

As I walked I continued aloud the discussion I'd been having with God since the evening before, lying awake in bed. So far, he hadn't replied, but I was still hopeful.

"Why do we have to move?" I asked him. Still no answer. "Why can't we just be?" No response. "I don't want to move to Florida. Please hear my prayers and make Dad change his mind?" I stopped and looked up beyond the tree branches into the mottled gray sky, looking for some kind of sign that He'd heard, but somehow I got the sense He wasn't even bothering to listen. It was hard not to get mad at Him at times like these.

I didn't think I had any tears left to shed, but they came flowing again. They froze on my face and eyelids, making it hard to see where I was walking. I stopped and pulled out my handkerchief. (Mother always made sure I had one so I wouldn't wipe my nose on my sleeves.) My lunch and books fell into the snow but I was too distraught to pick them up. I stood there bawling like a baby again. And then, I fell back into the snowdrift with them.

"Oh, God, I want to stay home. Please, please hear me. I know this isn't the way I'm suppose to ask You for something, but I can't help it right now. I'm just trying to say that I'm hurting real bad and I don't want to go. I'll lose all my friends. I'll lose my school. I'll lose everything I know in the whole wide world."

I don't know how long I lay there, but it was a long time. The winter sun finally made its way into the sky. My mittens were soaked through, my hands ached with the cold, and my toes burned freezing.

A thought: I was going to miss the last streetcar. With a start I jumped to my feet, scooped up my things and ran. I came around the corner and there was no streetcar at the stop. The last one for the morning had obviously left.

What was I going to do? School was much too far to walk. If I came in late, Mother Superior would wale the daylights out of me. If I went home, Mother would do the same. I looked around dazed, cold — my nose running full force now. I wiped it on my sleeve.

A Michigan State Police car drove by. The Officer wore a cowboy hat. He eyed me. My bladder went mushy.

I turned and started for home, but wasn't entirely pleased with the destination. Then I remembered Hoover's chicken coop. It was nice and warm in there. I knew how to get in through the woods without being seen. I congratulated myself for my ingenuity and started off.

My pace picked up. I cut into the woods, circled around back of the houses. I walked slowly and quietly to the chicken coop door, looking around to make sure no one saw me. I unhooked the latch, opened the door and went in. Some of the chickens started to cackle and flap their wings. I shut the door and stood still as my eyes adjusted from the whiteness of outside to the murky darkness of the coop.

I had to move slowly or the chickens would start to squawk. Hoover would come out to the chicken house to see what was what. A stool stood against the wall. I moved it close to the stove and sat there. The heat came dry and steady. The ashes had been shaken recently and fresh coal was in the pot. Great; it would last to mid afternoon.

I found a wire rack, moved it close to the stove and hung my wet clothes on it. I sat on the stool and looked at the chickens that were now all looking at me as if they expected a performance.

"Boy, you chickens sure are lucky. You don't have to go to school or walk out in the cold snow, or put on heavy clothes and best of all, you don't have to face Mother Superior. You just nest on your perch there, and let old man Hoover take care of you. Boy, what a life." But they weren't big talkers, those chickens, so I shut up and sat down.

After a while, the heat melted me. My head bobbed as I fought with sleep. Next thing I knew, I woke up with a jerk. Steam rose from my chest like out of a boiling pot and my clothes burned at my skin. I jumped, which wasn't very smart, because the chickens were set to squawking and jumping in circles knocking against each other, feathers flying.

"Stop - quiet - shhhh - stupid chickens shut up." They calmed down and I peeked through the crack of the door to see if old man Hoover was coming. No sign of anyone. So I sat down again, pulled out my Peanut Butter and Jelly sandwich and started to eat. The outer edges of the sandwich were soggy and the middle was completely wet. Mother had wrapped it in Dad's used newspaper. She used newsprint when she ran out of wax paper. Blackened sandwiches were always the result. I didn't like it, but ate it anyway.

As I ate, I asked the chickens, "What would you guys tell your Mother about missing school the way I did today?" I stared at them as if expecting an answer. "Well, let me ask you what you think about this idea: I left my lunch on the streetcar, had no money, so I came home. What do you think? Will she believe that?" Again, they just sat on their perch staring at me.

* * *

"Well, young man. What are you doing home in the middle of the day?" Mother stood in the doorway, her expression so stern it could have cut me into two pieces.

My chicken performance had been Oscar-winning compared to the one I was about to give. Staring at her knees because I couldn't lie to her face, I stammered, "I uh…. The streetcar. I… left my lunch there. And I don't have money, so I came home… for lunch."

"Is that right?" she replied. "Well, tell me then, why did Mother Superior call and ask why you weren't in school today?"

My stomach rose up into my chest and I felt real hot all of a sudden. I looked up at her, hoping to find some remnant of gentility there. Her eyes were hard, mouth clenched tight. She'd caught me lying. I was a goner.

She ordered, "Get down into the basement, take off your wet clothes, hang them up to dry and get your little butt back upstairs, fast."

I did as she said, but tried to linger as long as I could. Eventually her holler came resounding, "Doesn't take that long to get those clothes off."

I gulped and mounted the stairs with slow, deliberate steps. There was one consolation. It wasn't Dad doing it. He used his leather belt.

I reached the top of the stairs and there she was waiting for me. She had rolled up paper in her right hand, legs spread, the apron made from feed sacks she always wore hanging down between her knees. I knew what I was supposed to do.

I assumed the position with hands grasping the chair and braced myself, squeezing my eyes shut tight. Her first whack surprised me with its pepper. She was mad, boy.

The whipping proved to be almost as bad as Dad's. It was the worst one I'd ever gotten from her, that was for sure. When she was done, face all flushed, she said with a voice all fluttery determination, "Now go to bed and no lunch or supper for you."

I crawled into my warm bed, wiping away the tears. I awoke to find Mother sitting on the edge of my bed, stroking my forehead. The smell of chicken soup and bread toasted the air.

"I brought you something to eat," she said softly, her palm caressing my brow. I could see the hurt in her expression, at having to spank me. But I didn't blame her. I'd deserved it.

She shook her head. "Paul, you're only eight years old, in the third grade, and you're already skipping school. I don't understand why. Why did you do it? Where did you go all that time?"

I knew I couldn't lie to her any more. I could feel my insides welling up, choking me. I tried to fight it, but it was too strong.

"I don't want to move to Florida. This is my home. Everyone else is staying here. Why can't I?"

Mother grasped me tightly as she shook with tears. I wrapped my arms around her waist, sucking in that smell of hers, the two of us clinging so tightly you'd think we'd melt into one.

She tried to explain things to me. To an eight year old, it all boiled down to one thing: Because Dad wanted to.

"Eat your soup now and go back to sleep. I'll tell Dad you're sick." She held my head next to her breast, kissed it and, as she left, said, "Paul, it will all work out. It's God's way."

Yea, I mused, after she was gone. God doesn't have to move to Florida. But I did feel comforted now. Mother had a way of doing that

The next morning as I marched through the school door, Mother Superior appeared from around a corner, her black robes tossing in the wind as she blocked my path. Her eyes pierced mine, the sheer force of her will stopping me as the other students continued on in a swirl around me.

"Good morning, Mother Superior," I squeaked.

Her hand grabbed the collar of my coat. She said with a growl, "It may be a good morning for some people, but it certainly is not for Paul Miller!" Her voice echoed off the stonewalls of the atrium.

She hauled me straight up to the top of the marble stairs. She turned me around and positioned me dead center under the arch, as if it were a stage. Boy, I thought, I think there's a man inside that Sister's outfit.

The atrium looming out below us reminded me of a field. She ordered, "Take off your coat. Put your books and lunch on the floor."

What was going on? Was she going to make me spend the day at the top of the stairs? While following her instructions, the Sisters started coming from every direction with students behind them. Sisters arranged their charges in orderly rows. Once stilled, student faces turned up to look at me.

Panic seized me. Mother Superior was going to paddle me in front of the entire school.

When the atrium was filled and the student's silent, waiting, Mother Superior pulled out her paddle and smacked it hard on the rail of the staircase to gather everyone's attention. The whack of it echoed like the blast of a canon. All were silenced. In a husky voice, she announced, "We have for you today an example of the devil's own work. How he can take one of our sheep and lead them astray."

Surely she wasn't referring to me as a sheep?

"We try very, very hard here at Christ The King Church and School to teach you all the good and right things to do in life. The way Jesus taught his followers. The way Jesus wants you to go. To love each other, be honest and follow the Church's teaching."

I searched the crowd and found the familiar faces of my class. Some were fighting the giggles. Others looked at me all wide-eyed as if I really was the devil's worker. Beverley Hollings, the girl of my dreams, with long black hair and skin like cream, stared at the floor. My heart sank a notch.

"Well. Yesterday, the devil made little Paul Miller here *skip school.*" She spoke those last words with a crispness so great they crackled. There were gasps, "oh no's" and shuffling. You'd think I'd tried to assassinate the Pope.

"Well, Paul Miller, in front of all these witnesses today, we are going to kick the devil right out of you." She turned to me. "Lean over and place your hands on the rail, please."

I did and hung my head so my face wasn't visible to the crowd. I kept telling myself over and over, "It doesn't hurt, don't cry, don't cry!" The humiliation of crying in front of the entire school was something I couldn't allow.

I heard Mother Superior get into batting position and take in a breath, ready for the first blow. I recall a silence too profound for an atrium full of primary school kids. The wait for the first whack was interminable. But then came the swoosh of wind as the paddle made its first journey. The room became one massive sucked in breath.

Whap! The first was the worst. I could feel my whole body shudder. It took all the strength I had to control my bladder. I could tell the next one was coming and held my breath again. Whap! The pauses in between were excruciating. Whap! I gasped a breath. Whap!

After the seventh wallop echoed against me, one of the Priests standing behind us called, "Mother Superior? I believe the devil has gone now." A hesitation and then one final, furious Whap! Don't cry Paul, don't cry, don't cry.

Mother Superior announced, "Let this be a lesson to all of you." Then, in hushed tones only I could hear, "You are the first to skip school here at Christ the King, and by God you will be the last! Now pick up your belongings and get to class."

Mother Superior stared at me with wild eyes. I moved slowly. In a strange way I felt both humiliated, but kind of proud, too. Proud at keeping myself from crying. I bet it rankled her that she hadn't managed to get me to cry. The rest of my stay at Christ the King, Mother Superior never looked or spoke to me again.

3.

PREPARING FOR THE MOVE

A couple days later, Beverley Hollings came up to me during recess. She gave me that shy smile that made me feel like melted butter and said, "Come over by the fence where we can be alone. I want to talk to you."

My heart went all-aflutter. When we reached the fence she stopped, turned and gave me an uncomfortable smile. "Paul, you know I like you and I think you like me," she began. "But I talked to my Mother and she said I should stay away from you because you're headed down a bad road. And Mother Superior said I should stay away from you, because you have too many demons inside you, and they could get me, too."

I stood there staring at this girl with the long black hair swaying in the winter air. Red muffs protected her ears from the cold. I know my mouth was open, but couldn't talk. Somehow my brain couldn't put her words together into something that made sense. Only phrases bounced through my thoughts: I like you… you like me… demons… Mother… Superior. It was like waking up after a bad dream and half of it was missing.

"Paul? Paul? Are you listening to me? Are you going to say anything? Don't you want to know why I'm telling you this?"

I shook myself. "Yea," my tongue felt like it weighed ten pounds.

"First of all, I wanted to be your girlfriend before you did… you know… what you did. But I didn't like that, and now I'm going to be Jerry Davis' girlfriend. So, goodbye, Paul." She turned and walked away, her black locks bouncing side to side.

I stood watching as she went up to Jerry Davis. The two of them talked. Once in a while she'd glance my way, flip her head back sharply so her hair would fly around her head. She had the prettiest smile I ever saw. And Jerry Davis? I never did like him. His father owned a furniture store in town. He got straight A's, and Mother Superior was always asking him to do things

19

for her, like clap the erasers clean. What did I care? I was moving to Florida, anyway.

That evening, when we were sitting in the living room after supper, I asked Mother what a 'bad road' was. She told me it was a road full of holes and bumps and curves. "Why do you ask?"

"Well, somebody told me today that I was headed down a bad road."

Mother turned on the couch, and stared at me. "Who said that to you?"

"A girl at school. We were talking at recess, and she said somebody said that because I skipped school I was headed down a bad road."

A smile made its way across Mother's face. She brought me into the fold of her arms and said, "Paul, you did a bad thing, but you are not headed down a bad road."

She explained how when someone says that, it means you're doing a lot of bad or dumb things that can get you into a lot of trouble. Like robbing banks. From what she said it made me wonder if Beverley knew what it meant.

Of course, all Beverley had to do to find out was ask Jerry Davis.

* * *

There were some curious papers sitting on the dining room table. I peeked into the living room. Dad was reading the paper. I could hear Mom in the kitchen humming and doing the dishes. So I walked over and looked. One of them was headed "State Hospital of Michigan, Long Term Care Facility."

* * *

Johnny was older than me by two years but required constant care. There were times I resented him because Mother would show him more attention. But at the same time, I knew Johnny was sick and required all the attention our family could give.

Taking care of him was one of my big jobs. If I took him outside I had to hold his hand or he'd run away. It was my job to sit on a chair in the doorway so Johnny couldn't roam around the house. The room in which we kept him was completely empty. He'd walk around and around, emitting a low moaning, groaning sound, although once in a while he'd manage a short loud "Bahp!" Sometimes he'd stand at the windowsill and tap it with his index finger groaning, "Ahh – Ahh," in a whirling call =.

Once in too frequent a while he'd start howling with laughter. He'd laugh on and on, never tiring, for days on end. It was as if his brain was stuck in laugh mode and couldn't get out of it. And no matter where you went in the house, you couldn't get away from that howl. You'd hear it rambling through the heat ducts, the hallways, in your dreams. It was almost enough to drive the rest of us insane. If he got loose and started running while he was in one of these spells, he'd become so strong that three big men couldn't hold him. I once saw him run into the corner of a wall, split his forehead wide open, stand back, look at the wall and continue that maniacal laugh as though nothing had happened.

I never really understood at the time what was wrong with him. It wasn't until I was older that I was told what had happened.

Johnny had been quite a normal child until one day, when he was three; Mattie took him for a ride in a wagon through a cornfield. A wheel of the wagon hit a beehive, sending it toppling to the ground, a mess of white wooden boxes. Incensed, the bees went for them both. Mattie got scared and ran, her arms windmilling the bees away, leaving Johnny alone. All of the bees transferred to him, and when they finally got him to the hospital he was a mess. Every inch of his three-year-old body had been stung; including the inside of every cavity a bee could get itself into. Doctors said that the venom had burned his brain and there was nothing that could be done. From that day forward, Johnny could not talk; go to the bathroom on his own, eat, dress, bathe, or perform any function that required the use of a normal, thinking circuited brain. He continued to physically grow, but mentally, there was nothing there.

There were times when the two of us connected — when I got the sense that he knew who I was. He would look at me real close, put his fingers on my face and moan softly. It was almost like he was trying to reach across some great chasm, from a different universe entirely, to let me know that he knew I was there.

Johnny and I bathed together and slept in the same bed. Occasionally during the night he'd have convulsions, and I had to hold him so he wouldn't hurt himself or fall onto the floor. I'd call for Mother and she'd come running and hold him until he stopped. While holding him she would rock back and forth, humming and singing, "Oh Johnny, Oh Johnny how you can love…."

I never did find out how that incident affected Mattie. I'm sure it did, but she'd never talk about it. At least not to me. I remember Mother telling me once that Mattie was made sad for a long time after it happened. But we all knew, she must have been much more than just sad.

* * *

With those papers in hand I went into the kitchen and stopped in front of Mother. She was just wiping the counter up from finishing the dishes.

"Hello, Paul," she sang to me. She turned and saw what I held out to her. Her face fell.

I said, "We're leaving Johnny behind, too. Aren't we?"

Mother brought the dirty rag up to her mouth. At the smell, she realized what she'd done, threw it into the sink, tried to laugh at her silliness, but it turned into a sob instead. She leaned against the counter, skirting her head from side to side.

We were losing too much.

I went up to her and she grabbed onto me. The embrace seemed to renew her strength, and she said, "We can't take care of him anymore, Paul. He needs the care of doctors and nurses." I heard the excuse in there, and I knew how deeply it hurt her. She loved Johnny very, very much. So did I. I didn't question her anymore about him. I knew he would be hard to take care of on a trip. And if he got into one of his spells, then what would we do?

That night I lay in bed looking at poor Johnny. He'd always been there, right by my side, since I could remember. I reached over and touched him. He let out a gentle laugh, followed by a long sigh. "I really will miss you, Johnny," I said.

When I awoke the next morning Johnny was gone.

* * *

The world around me, which had always seemed to move with the speed of a glacier, was now racing. But how could I get out of it?

Maybe I could move in with someone else? Like with my friend Fritz.

Fritz's mother was a movie star, working in Hollywood. The hallway of their house was a gallery of pictures of different versions of her. In one, she was a nurse, and in another, a housewife wearing an apron and offering out a serving spoon for you to taste what she's cooked up.

Fritz's Dad was our mailman. He walked up and down the street in uniform; tipping his hat to everyone he met. He was a friendly man, but because of his German accent, rarely said a word. With the war just over, he was ashamed of his native land.

Fritz was frequently sick and in bed. He said it was rheumatism, which made his joints hurt. So, instead of going out we'd play in his room. He had all the best toys and the largest collection of comic books I'd ever seen. It would have been fun to live with Fritz. On the other hand, my Mother wouldn't like it, because they were Lutheran. Mother didn't like Lutherans, although I never knew why.

My best friend, Billy Denton, and his family lived across the street. But, nope, I didn't want to live with them. Their house was such a loud place, a family caught up in a continual screaming match. But still, I was going to miss Billy more than anyone.

Once, Billy and I developed a game where one of us would pull a small tree down. The other wrapped himself around the top get ready and then would scream "Geronimo!" That was the signal for the one holding the tree to let go. The tree would snap itself straight, taking one of us for a whipping ride.

One Sunday, Billy and I were behind Maze's grocery store. We looked in the wire container where Mr. Maze threw all the stuff he'd eventually burn. We sifted through the mess and, at the bottom, found some rotten fruits and vegetables. Billy and I looked at each other, grinned, looked at Mr. Maze's freshly painted garage – and started throwing.

And wow! You should have seen those colorful explosions. The tomatoes were the best. They'd hit that pure, white paint and splatter like a sunset. We laughed and threw just about everything that was in there.

"Are you boys having fun?" Out from the side of the garage came Mr. Maze.

I shouted, "Run. Billy!" and the two of us headed for our sanctuary in the woods.

When we got to our special spot, we were catching our breath, laughing like hyenas. Then we heard a familiar whistle, Billy's Dad calling him in. After that, Billy and I couldn't play together for two weeks and we had to repaint Mr. Maze's garage. Not only the back where we threw all those vegetables, but the whole garage. We didn't think that was very fair. But we did it anyway.

Another time, the police brought us home in a police car. The car pulled to a stop in front of our mothers talking in the street. Billy and I slid down, hands covering our faces. The cop leaned out and asked, "Do these belong to you?"

"Oh Lord," exclaimed my Mother, "what did they do now?"

"Mr. Edwards called about someone in his orchard, throwing apples. When we got there, these," he said, pointing back at us with his thumb, "are what we found."

Mother grabbed me and pushed me towards the house, yelling, "You're only seven years old and the police are bringing you home? Get into that house, young man. And just you wait till your Father gets home."

Three weeks later, Billy and I found a pack of cigarettes and some matches between the back of the school and the coalhouse. "Hey, Billy, ever smoke a cigarette?"

We went through the whole pack in an hour. To hide the butts and matches we threw everything on the coalhouse roof. We were sitting there looking at each other, not moving and feeling rather green. I was about to throw up. Billy stood up, turned around and threw up all over the side of the coalhouse. I looked up so as not to see him. And I saw —

"Billyyyy," I screamed as loud as I could. "The coal shack is on fire!" Again we ran into the woods. We watched from afar as the smoke got thicker and blacker puffing into the air like an angry dragon.

Billy said, "Paul, after this, I don't think we'll ever be allowed to play together ever again."

Yep. I sure was going to miss that Billy.

4.

A TRIP TO BOSTON

A "For Sale" sign was stuck, lopsided, on our front lawn.
   I recall sitting in the window staring at it, twisting in the wind, trying to wish it away. It attracted a parade of strangers who tracked snowy, salty boots all over Mother's clean floors. Mother gave them over-anxious smiles as she played tour guide to the house quirks, like the basement door that didn't close right and the attic door that needed an extra push.

ALL these folks marching through put their noses in closets, poked at the plaster, and opened and closed the windows to test the mechanisms.

I hated every single, last one of them.

Not too long after the parade had started Mother announced that the house was sold. The moving date would be in a matter of weeks.

Mother arrived in a cab filled to bursting with stained and bruised cardboard boxes from the grocery store. When she found one of us idle, she sat us in front of things to pack with a box and a list. She marked and herded boxes like a dog cares for sheep. One set for Sarah, another for Mattie, another for Kitty. Other boxes were for storage, containing the things that would be sent to us in our future home down there in glorious Florida.

I stopped eating oranges.

A hollow spirit invaded once familiar rooms, as though our times in them had been sucked out and we'd been forgotten.

What few toys I owned were sold or given away. I did manage to hold onto my baseball glove. And at least my bicycle, that chariot of freedom, became Billy's, who'd always admired it.

The day for our move arrived. Everything I owned was contained in one small suitcase. I felt naked.

At our family parting, everyone but Dad hugged and cried. It was the first time I could remember my sisters hugging me. We weren't a physically affectionate family. I suspected Mother told them to do it, and I appreciated the warmth, even if it wasn't totally sincere.

With Mother on my left and Dad on my right, we started our walk down the street away from the house, suitcases in hand. I noticed the absence of keys jangling in my father's pocket. Billy stood behind a tree across the street. He sent me a final, forlorn, wave. The moistness around his eyes made me cry even harder.

Dad snapped, "Stop your sniveling, Paul, and get moving, or we'll be late."

I stepped in time, wondering if I'd ever be allowed to cry again.

* * *

We went through the train station doors and I was floored. I'd never realized how wonderful a train station could be.

First, I was mesmerized by its tremendous size. The windows, taller than any tree I'd ever climbed, were placed so high no man could see out of them. The vaulted ceilings, rimmed with gold, were so grand; they dwarfed me like nothing man-made ever had before. On the walls trains had been painted in broad sweeping strokes as if in motion, smoke pouring from their stacks. In the center of the station was a square box as big as a truck with a clock on each side; it hung down from a wire that went way up into the ceiling. I tilted my head back and squinted, but my eyes couldn't see up to where the clock's wire originated. When that clock chimed the hour, it sounded like a big church bell that made the hairs on the back of my neck stand at attention.

At the back of the station there were doors so big, an elephant could walk through them. Above each door a sign; Track No. 4, Track No.5, Track No.7 & 8. These went on and on as far as I could see. The air was thick with coal and diesel fumes. Dirt and soot clung to everything, giving it a dark, drab look.

It was an alive and vibrant place to be. People were everywhere. They sat or slept on benches with newspapers tented over their heads. Kids screamed and cried, running in circles. Mothers and Fathers gave chase, scolding. Soldiers, Sailors, Marines and Air Force men looked smart in their pressed uniforms. There were Priests, Nuns and people with funny looking scarves tied about their heads and faces. Even different colored people. I had seen black people a few times on the streetcar before, but never so many at one time, in the same place.

I walked with unconscious steps, turning in a circle of complete awe. I was energized by it, almost to bursting. What a wonderful, secret, alive place.

I liked how the announcements echoed against the walls of the station:

The Union Pacific Los Angeles Blue Streak, now boarding on track #7 through door #4. Please have your boarding pass ready...Last call.

The Chesapeake and Ohio overnight special to Cincinnati boarding on track #2 through door #9. Last call.

New York and New Haven Silver Bullet now arriving on track #6.

I stood there, wide eyed, listening intently.

Now boarding on track #2, through door #5. The Pennsylvania Rail Road's East Coast Special to Toledo, Cleveland, Pittsburgh, Philadelphia, New York, Boston and all points in between. First call. Please have your boarding passes ready.

My parents straightened at the last announcement. Dad jumped to his feet, grabbing his bag.

"That's us," he said. Mom grabbed her bag and followed.

Well, I was confused, to say the least. I had been listening, after all, and the announcement didn't say anything about Florida. But off my parents raced, paying no mind to me. I picked up my suitcase and hurried after them.

My feet were wheels, spinning, and my parents were twenty steps ahead. After driving my legs as hard as I could, I finally made it so I was in between the backs of their heels. We walked down long concrete walks and passed rail cars spewing steam.

I thought, *Wow. How do they get all these trains inside this building?*

As we went, I called, "But Dad, the guy said this train is going to Boston," he kept walking. "It's going to Boston, Dad. Boston!" No response.

I looked at Mom. "Mom, are we going to Boston?" I saw her shoulders tense. My voice edged up a notch. "But you said Florida, and now it's Boston." Nothing. My voice came out a squeak, "Why aren't you answering me?"

Mom's head turned and she shook it, ever so slightly. But it was a quick move, done so Dad wouldn't see. Just as quickly, she turned back and kept walking.

That was it. I screamed, "What in the world is going on? Just tell me! Are we going to Boston?"

Dad stopped with a spin, flung his bag to the ground. He snapped his left arm into the air as if about to strike. I was stopped in my tracks but didn't cringe. I did gulp, though. I bit my lip, looking to the wooden platform painted green, stained to black. He was angry, but I was sure he wouldn't hit me. Our spankings were always announced. He threatened, but never hit us in the face. After a tense moment, I heard the twist of his shoes, saw his case lift, and off we headed along the track again, a family of three charging forward into the unknown as my mind buzzed. *Boston? Why are we going to Boston?*

The Conductor directed us to our car. We settled down in four seats that faced each other. Mom and Dad sat on one side, me on the other. I gazed out the window watching the people coming and going for a few minutes, letting Dad cool down.

After what I thought was an appropriate pause, I turned in my seat and looked at him. He was looking down at the tips of his shoes, grimacing. I clasped my hands together, and in the quietest, most earnest voice I could muster, asked him, "Dad, please tell me. Why are we going to Boston? I thought we were moving to Florida."

Dad looked up with that cold blank stare that burned like dry ice. "It's your Mother's idea. She wants to see Adam and his family before we move." Adam was my eldest brother. He lived in Boston.

I looked over at Mother. She gave me one of those quick smiles that faded as fast as it came. I looked back at Dad. He stared out the window; his head hung, hangdog like, his eyes gone all slitty. He was in one of those moods. Don't talk, don't answer. Don't even think too loud cause he'd hear and threaten a swat.

From outside came the call, "All aboard," and the train lurched forward.

We gained speed, traveling through the backside of the city. The sun was fading, sending a doleful light across buildings and trees. I'd never seen my city like that before. I could take it in all at once. It was much more than streets, buildings and people, a singular friendly beast, sighing before my eyes.

Mom brought out homemade sandwiches, pickles and cookies. From a colored man carrying a case that hung from straps around his neck, Dad bought coffee for them and milk for me. We ate in silence. Dad was still sulking.

These moods were regular events our family learned to negotiate. When they descended you dared not talk or laugh. Sometimes I got the feeling there was something not quite right about those tempers of his. Other times I assumed I was to blame for them. He hated me, of that I'd become certain.

He'd rejected me, but to be spurned by your own maker, your own Father, that was incomprehensible. It made me wonder what was wrong with me? It bothered me so much I always tried to squeeze myself into the conversation. As usual, he ignored me or gave me a look that said, *Get lost, kid.*

My feelings toward him were a mixed-up muddle I struggled and wrestled with. Most of the time I just plain didn't like the guy. I couldn't help it. I wished he'd go away and never come back. But then, the dark cloud of guilt would settle in. Kids aren't supposed to wish for such things. He was my Dad. I was supposed to love him.

Other times I became the puppy, begging for attention. "Hey, look I'm here, touch me, say something, throw me a bone." I yearned for him to open himself to me, to see that only he could make my spirit to take flight.

At home, I could get out from under his dark cloud easily. I could take care of Johnny, do chores, or homework. But now, here we were, just the three of us on a train heading for Boston. Escaping from his moods would be pretty much impossible.

I couldn't settle, ants, doing their little line dance up and down my veins. Dad came out of his sulk noticing my jumps and scratches. Mother slapped my knee and told me to keep still.

Dad went between the cars for a cigar. I wanted to go, too, to get up, to move, but Mother wouldn't allow it. Instead, she settled me down for the night, with a heavy coat as my blanket.

But sleep didn't come. The seats were hard. I was bounced around. The air smelled like sulfur from the coal. When the train passed a crossing the bells would clang, and the train whistles would hoot and whine at the passing night. I thought back to my walks to school, hearing a train whistle off in the distance, so lonely and lost. Now I was aboard one of those sad trains.

Just down the aisle was another family. They had a little girl about my age with long, silvery hair. I'd noticed her walking to the restroom earlier, the tent of her pinafore dress bouncing as she walked. Now her head rested on her father's lap, a book propped on his knees. His voice was a whisper as he read her the story aloud. How I yearned for such closeness, such normalcy.

Were we abnormal? I knew my father was strict and religious, but was religion so harsh, so patently unemotional? I'd heard the priests speak of love, sacrifice and honor. Why did our existence seem so devoid of those things? There was something else going on in our lives, an unfathomable mystery that I feared I might never understand.

At great length, to the gentle, drifting tones of that little girl's father, I fell asleep.

* * *

The Dining Car had tablecloths, linen napkins and colored waiters who stood tall and smiling in sparkling white jackets. I'd never had such high service before, with the waiter bowing down to pour me a glass of water, let alone at breakfast. I drank the water like I'd never tasted it before. When the food came, all steaming hot, I dug in with gusto. I didn't notice my Mother's impish smile until I'd scooped up the last of the eggs, and she said, "Paul, I don't think I've ever seen you eat so much breakfast before." And you know what? She was right.

My days on the train were spent exploring. The best place to be was standing between the cars. I'd open up the top half of the door and lean out so the cold wind slapped me in the face, and I could watch the countryside tumble by. Sometimes the air stream would bring the smoke of the engine down into the open window and you'd have to close it fast.

We pulled into station after station, every one teeming with service men. I watched Mother's face, as she looked at them with longing and wonder. My twin brothers, Jimmy and Dick, were still overseas. Dad would look over at her but say nothing. I wondered if he was sad, too. He probably did care, but couldn't show it. Somewhere within that opaque shell, there must have been a heart. There had to be.

Late in the afternoon on the third day we pulled into New York City. It appeared to me as though the train was moving right down the middle of the city streets with people standing at crossings waiting for the train to pass. I asked Dad if the train really did go on City streets. He stared at me, as if trying to wish me away.

I turned to Mother and asked her the same thing. She said that in certain sections of town the train had to run on the streets because there was nowhere else for it to go. She knew this, she told me, because she'd lived in New York as a little girl, into her early teens.

"I didn't know that. How come you never told me before?" I asked.

"I guess I never really thought about it much in the last few years," she said, brushing back her brown curls and looking out the window. "Your Father lived in New York, too."

"You did?" I asked, looking over at him. His expression remained a stare. He said nothing. Ever hopeful, I asked, "Did you live right in the city, Dad?"

His expression didn't change. If it weren't for the occasional blink of his eyes, he would have looked statuesque. After a few quiet seconds of waiting, Mother answered for him, "Yes he did, Paul. But he doesn't like to talk about it." Yet another in a long line of subjects he wouldn't talk about.

I tried to imagine Mother and Father as kids my age living in New York City. My imagination conjured Mother as a laughing, playful little girl with friends and dolls. But Dad? All I saw was a sad and lonesome boy with an expressionless face, no laughter in his heart and no compassion for anyone. He stood in the shadows, waiting. For what he waited, I couldn't dream of.

I didn't ever want to be like him, in any way, shape or form. I wanted to care about people.

I asked him, "When will we get to Boston, Dad?"

"Tomorrow, late," he replied. I was surprised he replied at all.

* * *

The waiter approached our table with a smile that twinkled. He asked if we were ready to order.

"The chicken dinner, please," Dad, said.

The waiter leaned down, slightly. "I'm sorry sir," he replied. "But I just served the last one not two minutes ago. Could I get you something else?"

All of a sudden, in a move that made the rest of us jump, Dad threw the menu to the table with a spit and started to pout and sniffle like a five-year-old. Mother stiffened. Sent a nervous smile to the waiter.

"He'll have the burger. You like burgers, don't you, John? That will be very nice," she said. Dad still pouted, his lower jaw jutting forward, his eyes stuck on the table as if glued there. The waiter nodded and stepped away, looking over his shoulder as he went. With the waiter gone, Dad noticed something out the window. I saw one of those rare smiles alight his face. It scared me.

5.

A BOSTON ADVENTURE

The cab pulled up in front of a two story brick building. A tall slender man standing at the curb jerked the cab door open, leaned down and screamed, "Hi Ma! Hi Dad! And this, this must be little Paul?" It was my turn to pout. I despised being called *Little Paul*.

My brother, Adam, seemed more like a distant cousin or uncle to me. He was some twenty years older. He'd left Michigan for the army when I was three and a half and never came back. In fact, this would be the first of only three encounters I'd ever have with him. The other two would be funerals. One not too far in the future.

Mother and Adam hugged and kissed and, much to my surprise, Dad shook hands with him. Adam's large arm landed on my shoulder and I felt a squeeze. The contact made me want to pull back, but I didn't.

We walked up stairs and went through a dirty door, its number so faded it had almost disappeared. Two boys several years younger than me sat on the floor playing with toy trucks. A round chunky woman stood at the sink, Adam's wife, Ann.

After hugging Mother and Dad, Ann came towards me. I cringed, not wanting the hug and kiss I thought were coming and was relieved when all she did was rest her hand on my shoulder and say "Hi."

* * *

"Paul, come here," Adam called to me from the apartment door. I put down my baseball glove and moped over. Standing on the threshold was a boy my age. He had red-hair and so many freckles that if you looked at him real close he looked like one big freckle.

Adam said, "Paul, this here is Bobby Kelly." The boy cringed at the name.

"Everybody calls me Buddy," he said.

"Hi, Buddy," I replied. He smiled.

He said, "Some friends and me are gonna play ball. Do you want to join us?"

Did I? Without answering I ran to couch and grabbed my glove. I'd play ball anytime.

Buddy led me through the project to a ball field. His friends were polite, offering me to have first ups.

"What's first ups?" I asked. They laughed and told me it was first to bat. I felt myself flush and kicked at the dirt.

My showing wasn't very good. I struck out. I was sure they thought I was some kind of crappy ball player. I did better in the field and at my second ups, smacking the ball for a solid double. We played through the afternoon until suppertime. As we headed towards home they told me that they usually played outside until the streetlights came on.

"That is, if there's no stupid black out," one of them whined. The war was about a year over, but the air raid sirens would sing out some nights and all the lights of the city go black.

After supper, the boys and I played my favorite game, kick the can. It involved running. I've always been a fast runner. We played and played, until way after the streetlights came on. Boston was turning out to be not half bad.

Next morning, Buddy came knocking on our door. It was the anniversary of Paul Reveres ride through Boston. A man dressed like him was scheduled to ride a horse along the historic route. Did I want to come and watch?

We went to a square jammed tight with people. They lined up along the sides of the street, talking, laughing, eating hot dogs and candy apples. The excitement in the air was palpable, as everyone craned their necks toward where the rider would eventually come. Buddy and I had to stand on our toes to see.

When we thought the wait would never end, we heard the crowds around the corner froth up with excitement. There was the distant cry of someone yelling, the lightning fast clip clop clop of a horse. Then, it was as if all of us watching were holding our breath together. And then, from around the corner, a black horse darted into view. The rider held a tricorn hat up in the air, waving it around, standing on his stirrups, yelling, "The British are coming! The British are coming!" And we yelled back, clapping, cheering him on.

Oh, how I wanted to be that man. To play a part in changing the world, making it a better place, somehow, someday. I looked into Buddy's face and saw the same desire reflected in the flush of his cheeks.

Buddy and I spent the rest of the day together. Playing in the city was different than playing in suburban ravines. We wandered down street after street, through alleys, across courtyards, and at one place, even cutting through a building to the other side. We ended up back at Buddy's complex where his Mother fixed us something to eat.

Buddy's had long red hair and freckles just like Buddy. I liked the way she talked. Instead of saying yes, uh-huh or yep, she would say "Aye" or "Ah yes, laddy." We sat around and talked about the differences between Boston and Detroit. We talked about different words and their pronunciation; like 'park' in Boston is more like *pahk*. *Car* is *Cah*. Jeans are *dungarees. First at bat* is *first ups*. We went on and on laughing the whole afternoon away together. When the sun's rays arched mournful through their kitchen window, Buddy's mother suggested I go home; it was getting to be suppertime. Buddy asked if I wanted to go out and play kick the can again, after.

"Yea, I sure do."

I met Buddy and two other boys, Tony and Tommy, after supper. But instead of starting to play, they headed out of the courtyard. I asked where we were going.

Buddy turned to me and asked, "Do you like to climb?"

"Yea," I replied. I looked around. I didn't see any big trees anywhere. They saw me look and laughed.

"We don't mean trees. We climb buildings," Buddy said.

"You're kidding me." Again they laughed.

"No, we mean it," Buddy said, "After it gets dark we mean to climb the Library." He pointed at a building off in the distance. It stood five or six stories. I felt myself gulp but didn't want to be seen as a coward, so I said nothing and kept following.

Billy and I used to get on top of his Grandmother's chicken coop, and she was always kicking us off. "You little hellens, get your butt's off there right now!" she yelled as she came down the back porch steps waving a broom. But that was my only building climbing experience.

As we got closer the library's shadow loomed over us. I asked, "Has anyone ever got to the top?"

"Not that we know of," Tony said.

34

"You want to try it out, Detroit boy?" asked Tommy.

"Yea, sure I do, Boston boy," I blurted. I was a good climber. If they could do it, so could I.

* * *

Billy and I could shinny up a tree as fast as squirrels. Well, almost.

This one time, when we were six, we were chasing each other around the woods. Billy started to climb this large, straight maple tree and I was right behind him. We were laughing, and he was hollering, "You can't catch me."

And I would scream back, "Oh yes I can."

But then, all of a sudden, Billy started screaming at me, "Go back down, get down! There's a hornets nest up here and they're getting mad!"

I started climbing back down the tree. Billy was right on top of me. I looked up and, at that precise moment, right in front of my very eyes, Billy's foot slipped and his right leg impaled itself on a dead branch just above the knee. The branch broke through his skin and slid into his leg. He screamed. The hornets buzzed around us in increasing numbers, so fast they sounded like a big electric saw cutting through wood.

"Paul, help me!" Billy screamed. Then he repeated my name over and over, "Paul! Paul! Paul!"

I had to think fast.

I climbed up and got my shoulder under Billy's butt and with all my might, pushed up. My eyes were now right even with his leg and the branch.

I screamed at him, "Billy, pull your leg up. Pull it up!" I watched as he pulled his leg off the branch. Billy's blood squirted and gushed and I got a sick feeling in my stomach. Billy was screaming and crying so loud now that he drowned out the hornets. I felt a wet warmth traveling over my shoulder. Billy'd wet his pants. A similar wet warmth formed a river down my left leg.

I hollered up to him, "Okay Billy, I'll get you down. Okay, Billy. Okay, Billy." I don't know how many times I said it, but it was all my mouth could manage.

When I got to a clear opening in the tree I jumped. I rolled myself on the ground to get rid of the hornets. Billy was still making his way down, mostly with one leg.

I hollered at him, "Billy one more branch and then jump." He did just as I said. I wrapped an arm under his shoulders and pulled him up. We ran three-legged to a pond nearby, jumping in to get rid of the hornets. We snuck out moments later and I took my tee shirt off to wrap around Billy's leg. It was bleeding badly now. The two of us exchanged looks. His face was chalk white. If we were scared before, now we were terrified.

We made our way through the woods, screaming and screaming, hoping someone would hear us, find us, help us. When we arrived at the road Billy's mother, my mother and several other people were there. Billy was taken to the hospital and had several stitches. Mother took me home and put baking soda on my stings. I had 23. Billy had 31.

Dad walked into the kitchen as Mom was working, saw the stings and grunted like something was stuck in his throat. I looked at Mother and she just smiled. Even when I was six, Dad couldn't show concern when I was sick or hurt.

* * *

It took us thirty minutes to walk to the Library.

"Wow, this building is huge," I said. I counted six stories. "How do you get up there?"

Buddy told me, "There's a brick wall in the back that you can climb on and get to the first floor. Then you walk around the building on the ledge right outside the windows. I've got to the third floor complete, but the fourth floor, it's harder."

Tommy took off on a run. "Let's go," he cried. He jumped up on some blocks, pulling himself up. Then Tony, then Buddy, and then it was my turn.

Getting up on the wall and onto the first floor ledge was simple. I looked down and figured it was about as high as the middle of a small tree.

The others were way ahead of me and I tried to catch up, but wasn't sure of my balance. My feet didn't feel secure. In a tree your foot is wedged between two branches. On the ledge your foot was either all on the ledge (if you were between the columns) or half way (if you were going around the column), and your foot never had that feeling of something securing its side. Your hands could never wrap around a solid object, like a branch, either. You could only grasp with fingertips and fingernails. It sure was different. But I wasn't about to back out in front of those Boston kids.

After getting around three sides, my confidence started to build and I picked up some speed. As I headed to the starting point I could see that everyone else was already up and going fast along the second floor. My first reaction was to catch up. But, then I remembered what Buddy had said earlier.

No one had ever reached the top, and he'd never made the fourth floor. So, I decided to take it nice and easy. In fact, I decided to try and go higher than the rest, right to the top. I was going to prove that a Detroit boy could do better than they could.

Getting onto the second floor was not quite as easy as the first. There were places to step up, but they only went up three-quarters of the way. Then you had to rely on the strength of your arms, swinging your leg onto the ledge until your knee or your foot caught. After making it up there, I paused to catch my breath.

I looked down. It was like being at the top of a big tree. Perhaps it was the height that kept them from going above the third floor.

I skirted around the second floor pretty fast. As I came around the fourth side, I saw Buddy up on the third floor, Tommy was standing at the corner of the second and Tony was climbing down to the first.

"What's the matter?" I asked.

With a slight giggle, Buddy said, "Tony's afraid to go higher. Tommy says his arm hurts." The giggle turned into a mild chuckle.

"Hey, Tommy," I called up, mockingly, "if your arm hurts, don't go up. You're going to need your arm to get you down." There I was, speaking with such authority.

"Yea, you're right Detroit boy," Tommy said. "I'm going down with Tony."

Buddy called down, "Hey, Paul. I'll wait for ya. We can do the third floor together."

The climb to the third was the same as the second, but this time, as I flung my right leg up, my knee smacked the edge. That leg swung back down with such force that it hit my other leg and my body swung back and forth like a pendulum. My fingertips scraped along the ledge. Very carefully, trying to keep calm, I lowered back down to the second floor to inspect my knee. It wasn't gashed or cut, just skinned, but it hurt and was bleeding pretty good. I took out my handkerchief, wiped the blood and held it on the skinned area for a minute. I was sure glad my Mother made me carry it.

"You hurt bad, Paul?" Buddy hollered down.

I shook my head. "Naw just scraped it. Go on by yourself. I'll be up as soon as the bleeding stops."

That wasn't what I really wanted to do. I really wanted to climb down and go home, but I was too proud to admit it.

The skinned area started to burn, and it hurt to bend my leg. The image of Billy's bloody leg popped into mind and I figured, if Billy could climb

down that tree and run out of the woods with such a severe wound, then I
could certainly climb up one story of a building with a scraped knee. I tied
the handkerchief around it, pushed my pant leg down and pulled myself up
to the third floor. Ah, Billy would have been proud.

Buddy was waiting for me. "Let's get going," he said anxiously.

He turned to head off, but I stopped him. "Doesn't anyone ever come
around and check the building, like a guard or cleaning man?"

Buddy squinted. "Once a cop shined his flashlight on us, but we got
away," he said.

"Hope a cop doesn't catch us on the third floor!" I said.

A blank look crossed Buddy's face. He'd never thought of that before.
After a few seconds I shrugged. "Well, let's get going," I said.

Buddy didn't say anything. He just turned and made his way along. I
followed, keeping a little distance between us.

I looked down for the first time since the third floor. It was probably the
highest I'd ever been. The sight was breathtaking.

"Wow, you sure can see a lot from this high up, Buddy."

But he didn't reply. He just kept on moving in silence.

With each floor the pigeon droppings got thicker, sticking to the bottom
of shoes like a pasty gum. I scraped the bottoms off across the edge of the ledge
to get them clear a couple of times. It was becoming more than annoying.

We reached the starting point and I looked up, getting ready for our next
jump. But Buddy turned to me and whispered, "Let's go back down, okay?"

"Why?" I asked.

"I'm too tired to go another floor," he said, looking away.

"Let's just rest here awhile, and then we'll go up," I offered with a tone
of confidence.

But Buddy shook his head. "I don't want to," he said. "I'll wait for you
here."

"Buddy, is there something scary about the fourth floor you're not telling
me about?"

There was anxiety in Buddy's voice. "No! I... I mean, I don't know. I've
never been up there." A silence passed between us. The wind sang against
my ears.

I thought Buddy was right, that we should both go down, but pride
wouldn't let me. I had to prove something. Yea, I realized how dumb that was.
I was about to move to Florida and these Boston boys wouldn't even remember
me. But for a reason that was a mystery to even me, I found myself saying,

"Buddy, you go down and I'm going to try the fourth. Keep your eyes open for cops or anybody else for me, will ya?"

Buddy nodded, "Okay, Paul. Be careful. I don't know what's up there."

"Oh, I'll be careful all right. This is too high to get clumsy." I stood up and checked the handkerchief. My knee was hurting more. I pulled my pants up around my waist, took a deep breath, and climbed up the corner until my hands reached the fourth floor ledge.

The ledge on the fourth floor was smaller than the rest. It felt just a little more than half as wide. I was sure Buddy had known about this and wondered what else he wasn't telling me.

It took three tries before my right leg caught the ledge and I could pull myself up. I stood up on the ledge and realized it wasn't flat like the others. This one sloped downwards, away from the building, forcing you to lean in to hug the bricks. But the building was angled inwards, probably to allow rain run off. My feet were going one way, but my body needed to lean further in another. Neither angle was much in itself, but put the two together and it made for a climber's nightmare. It felt like my feet were slipping away from the building, and there was nothing to grab onto.

"Paul," I said to myself, "your Mother didn't raise a dummy. Go back down. Go home and have a glass of milk and cookies." But still I didn't.

The wind blew harder up there, pushing at me in whipping slaps from odd angles. My fingers were raw from the concrete. Two fingernails had broken past the quick, bleeding. I took a deep breath and forced my left foot to take a step. I thought for a moment that my left foot was smarter than my brain, because it hadn't budged at first. But finally it inched its way with the right foot following.

How was I was going to get all the way around moving inch by inch?

I looked down and couldn't even see the ground. It was so far and so dark. I looked straight out and realized how high I was. A cold chill went up the back of my neck. I froze in place.

I found myself thinking the oddest thing: "Step off. Into the air. Try it. Maybe you can fly." As much as I recognized this as craziness, the thought was ever so strangely tempting. Then, when I'd sloughed those thoughts off, a cloying claustrophobia came down and I choked, gasping for breath, despite all the air around me. I was trapped. For the first time, I realized I was terrified.

I stayed like that for what felt like hours, though it was probably just minutes.

A wraith of a voice came whispering up from below. Buddy. "Paul? Paul? All right? Paul! Answer me!"

"Yea, yea, I'm all right." I said. But the sound of my own voice was so high pitched I barely recognized it.

Buddy called, "Down. Get down. "

Yea, Paul, why don't you?

I took a deep breath and inched my way backwards. I managed enough courage to go about half way on the first side. But just as I was about to go around another column, I heard this funny cooing noise. As my foot hit the ledge, a whole mess of pigeons took off. I screamed and again became frozen in place. I could feel my hands squeezing the building so hard I thought the cement would crumble. My heart was beating so fast and hard that I kept swallowing to keep it from coming out my mouth.

Then, if anything else could go wrong, that's when it did. In a high-pitched wail the air raid sirens blew and in an instant the city faded to black. It was like a curtain had descended, life sucked out of the streets.

A warm flood traveled down my left leg. But that was the last sensation I can remember. My body shut down. I could not remember feeling, hearing, seeing, smelling or even breathing. I shut my eyes and prayed, *Oh, for an eraser to wipe away this stupidity.* I opened my eyes again. But the city was so black; having them opened was the same thing as having them closed. For a few seconds I thought I might be blind.

The sirens still screamed and I thought, *the war has been over for almost a year now, so why do they keep blowing those stupid sirens!?*

At length, some sense came back to me. I realized that with the sirens, if Buddy was trying to call up to me, I wouldn't be able hear him.

"Well, Paul, what are you going to do now?" I asked myself. I couldn't go forward. Or backward. I certainly couldn't go up or down. But, then a thought occurred to me. I could go straight!

I positioned myself about half way around a column and with my right foot kicked at a window. The glass was hard, and my foot just bounced off. That might not be a good way to break the window anyway, I figured. The glass would come down and cut me.

It took me several minutes to reach down and remove my shoe. I took the shoe by the toe and swung it as hard as I could at the window. I could hear the glass crack so I hit it again and again and again. I worked my way in front of the window and felt the hole. It seemed big enough for me to get through. I still had the shoe in my hand and used it to knock out pieces all around the frame, clearing as much glass as possible. When I thought it was clear, I slipped my shoe back on and stepped inside.

I didn't know how far it was to the floor or what was under the window. But I remember hearing the glass hit the floor, how it shattered and stopped. So I knew it wasn't hitting on anything on its way down. I sat on the sill, swung my legs inside and lowered myself by hanging onto the window frame and then the sill. The glass cut at my hands like razors. I hung there for a few seconds and then let go. It was not far, and I hit the floor and found myself standing. At the feeling of real, solid mass beneath my feet I felt a wave of thankfulness like I'd never experienced before. But I wasn't out yet.

I felt my way through to where I thought the door might be. There were a lot of small tables, desks I guessed. I reached the other side and felt my way along the wall, and yes, yes, there was a door. I pulled on the handle. It was locked, but locked from the inside. I undid the bolt and jerked the door open. Red emergency lanterns lit the hall so I could see the way. I found the stairs and I think I only hit every fourth step on my way down.

Bursting through the door at the bottom I found myself at the back of the building. I started to run, but it was short lived. The street was still totally black.

Amidst the wail of the sirens, "Paul, is that you?" It was Buddy's voice.

I shouted, "Yea, it's me!" We found each other and kind of touched and laughed with relief.

But then it all hit me. I sat down, my body quaking so hard you'd think munchkins were attacking me from inside with a jackhammer. I didn't want to cry in front of Buddy, but I couldn't hold back.

Buddy asked, "It must have been bad up there, huh?"

I couldn't answer.

It took several minutes for the shaking to stop. Buddy sat by me with patience.

My composure somewhat regained, I said, "Yea, Buddy. It was bad up there." I turned to him. "Promise me you'll never try the fourth floor. In fact, I think you guys have to stop doing this. Did you ever think about falling or getting hurt up there? "

"Never thought about it. Guess we didn't think anything would happen."

The sirens stopped, the all clear sounded and lights came on all around us. Their sudden brightness made us blink like moles.

"Come on," Buddy said. "Let's go to my house. My mother will get you cleaned up before you go home."

Buddy's mother asked us what happened, and Buddy asked her if it would be all right if he told her later.

At the sight of my hands she said, "My, you look like you tangled up with a Bob Cat, you do."

She was right. My hands looked awful. Broken fingernails, fingers raw down to the hand, palms cut and scraped. There was a V shaped gash on my right arm just above the wrist, and my right knee was skinless.

When finished she turned to Buddy and said, "Now, Buddy, you walk Paul home and don't stay but come right back yourself. You understand that, laddy?" I thanked her and we left.

On the way Buddy wanted me to tell him everything that happened up there. I told him without saying how scared I was. I didn't have to. He knew.

I walked into the apartment with both hands thrust deep in my jacket pockets. Dad and Adam were asleep on the couch; snoring so loud I don't know how they didn't wake themselves up. Mother looked at me and could tell right off something was wrong.

"Paul, come into the bedroom with me." She shut the door, turned and said, "Let me see your hands." I pulled them out; she cradled their bandaged messes and asked me who'd done it. I told her, and she took the bandages off.

She gasped at the sight, "Oh, my Good Lord, Paul, what did you do?"

I replied, "We were running down this alley when the blackout came. I tripped over something and landed on a bunch of glass with my hands and skinned my knee."

Her eyes probed mine, doing uncertain circles. She didn't believe the story, but I was praying she wouldn't probe further, because it would only make me lie more and I hated lying to her. It made me feel dirty and sick. This was one time it didn't bother me that much. I didn't want her to know the truth. It would hurt her so.

Dad chose that moment to stick his head through the door. He grinned at me, looked at my hands and said, "What did you do, clumsy? Fall down?" Without waiting for a response he shut the door.

I looked to Mother and started to cry. Her arms pulled me in, she rocked and hummed, 'Oh Johnny, oh Johnny, how you can love. ' I went limp and cried like a baby, finally safe and secure in my mother's arms.

At breakfast the following morning Dad announced that we were leaving for Florida the next day. I shrunk in my seat. I certainly wasn't looking forward to the train again.

Dad looked over at my bandaged hands as he chewed on his toast. "So, what did happen?" he asked.

I grimaced, "Fell down, like you said."

A broad grin appeared on his face that said, "Yea, I knew it," like it was some kind of competition, and he knew everything. Nothing I could ever do would be good enough. He felt it was his job to make sure I remembered that. But why?

Buddy dropped by after lunch, and we went down to the courtyard to talk. He'd told his mother everything, and hadn't left anything out.

"Everything?" I asked.

Buddy replied sheepishly, "Yea. I can't lie to my mother. I try, but she knows."

"What did she say?"

Buddy grinned. "She said that 'you laddy's have no brains'." You had to agree with her on that. "She made me put my hand on the rosary and swear I'd never do it again. She said it was good that I didn't leave you. She was proud of me for that. She likes you. She says you and me are 'like two laddies out of the same pod'."

I felt my face flush a bit. "I like your mother, too. And I think you would like my mother if you got to know her."

I told him we were leaving in the morning. I was going to miss him. He said he would too. He gave me his favorite pocketknife. He wanted me to keep it so every time I used it I'd think of him. I took his knife and for years after, until it got stolen, I did just that.

6.

FLORIDA HERE WE COME

A roly-poly conductor, with a smile as broad as his face and a laugh in every word he said came waddling down the train aisle, punching everyone's ticket. He wore a smart blue jacket with brass buttons that sparkled with his every turn, just like his smile. When he arrived at our seat he noticed my bandaged hands.

"Hey there, big guy. Looks like you wrestled with something nasty."

Dad couldn't say it fast enough. "He's just a clumsy kid. Tripped over his own feet and fell on a bunch of glass."

The Conductor frowned at him, but looked back to me and asked, "Did it cut you up bad?"

Again Dad blurted out "Naw, just a couple of scrapes. But he likes the attention the bandages give him."

The Conductor looked at my Dad and shook his head like something wasn't right. And I looked at Dad, too. His viciousness — there was something amiss about it. This was not the way a Father should be.

The Conductor gave Dad a dismissive glare but winked at me. "Don't let them cuts get infected now." He tipped his hat to Mother and continued on his away.

I was watching Dad when the Conductor tipped his hat. An angry look crossed his face and his eyes darted towards Mother. Mother's head had snapped quickly away from the Conductor's direction and her face froze, as if captured in time. How odd.

The sky was bright and sunny when we arrived in St. Petersburg, five dull days later. A warm wind kissed the air with summer. The Florida towns we'd passed had impressed me by how fresh and clean they'd looked, as though polished to gleaming. This was such a joyful place compared to my home up North where everything was dingy gray. We stepped out of the train station into the street, and I had to take off my jacket. Here it was, April, and the sun was warming bared arms. Perhaps buying a house down here wasn't such a bad idea after all.

We went to the Greyhound bus stop. Dad strode to the counter and bought tickets. We found a bench outside in the sun, sat down and started to wait.

"How far is the house from the station, Dad?" I asked. Dad shifted his weight but didn't even look at me.

Mother explained, "We're not going to that house right now. We're going to a motel outside of town to meet your Uncle Reno and Harold Sadowzki."

"Who is Harold Sa…, ahh… Harold, Mother?" I asked.

She smiled. "You know Harold, Paul. He's married to your cousin, Penelope. You remember her, don't you?"

Yes, I remembered. I couldn't stand that family. Penelope was so homely she made the Hunchback of Notre Dame look cute. The kids were dirty with snot always hanging out their noses like green flags. Harold was twice as homely as Penelope with thin red hair that looked like a bundle of string all tangled up. He had a red nose the size of my fist and large welt-like bumps all over his face. To top it all off he stunk like a chicken coop at cleaning time.

"I don't understand," I said. "Why are they coming to Florida?"

Mother's eyes quickly checked Dad's. Dad ignored her.

"Mother?" I asked. "Are they coming by train or driving?"

Mother's face was flushed, but her voice was stern, "They're driving, Paul. And don't ask me any more questions." She pursed her lips together and looked out in the direction the bus would come, arching her palm above her eyes to shade them. Being brushed aside so easily irked me.

I turned to Dad. "Why are we meeting them?" Dad's lips hardened, and his stone features turned to me. The stare was a blank mask. But why? My question had been a simple one, hadn't it? So when his silent glare continued longer than felt natural, I asked again, "Dad, Why are…."

All at once he yelled, wagging a finger in my face, "It's not for you to understand the decisions I make. You just do as you're told, boy. Do you hear me?" Then, yelling so loudly it echoed around the terminal, "Do you hear me?"

All faces turned in our direction. Mother shrunk down a notch.

"I wasn't…." I tried to explain.

He jumped to his feet and started to pace, His arms flew into the air with a flurry and he started to shake, "Shut it, boy! Shut up!" he yelled over and over again.

The young couple sitting on the bench nearby became nervous. The woman pulled her sweater tighter. The two of them stood up and shuffled away.

Mother reached down and jerked my arm hard, as if to say, *don't say anymore*. Made me mad how she skirted around the volcano of his moods instead of facing them, confronting them. I wished she'd had the nerve to say, "Shut up John!" then smack him. I bet Mattie would do that to Ed if he got like that. Mattie had spunk.

*   *   *

The bus headed into the countryside. We traveled down a highway that had nothing but orange and lemon groves in long, pretty rows going off as far as the eye could see.

"Can you just pick them off the tree and eat them?" I asked.

Dad looked over at me, a rare smile alighting his face. He said, "You can, but I don't think you'd want to eat the lemons." He chuckled out loud. I exchanged smiles with Mother. It was nice to hear him laugh for a change.

"Mom, what are those tall skinny trees called?" I asked.

"They're Palm trees, Paul."

So that's what they looked like. They were kind of funny looking. They'd be hard to climb. No branches.

The bus stopped in the middle of what looked like nowhere. The bus driver announced, "The Fisherman's Motel."

Dad stood up. "This is us," he said.

We stood on the side of the road as the bus drove off. Blowing sand colored the air white. Not a car was in sight. Besides the shabby white cabins of the motel across the street there wasn't much of anything anywhere. Nothing as far as you could see in any direction.

Dad went into the office as Mother and I waited, our hands tenting our faces to keep the sand from blowing into our eyes and mouths.

"Mother, do you know why we're here?"

She snapped at me without looking, "Like your Father said, don't question him!"

I sighed and shook my head. "But Mom, you said we had a house rented or you bought one or something. Didn't you? Why can't we go there? Go home?"

It was Mother's turn to sigh. Then, through gritted teeth she said, "Paul, stop asking so many questions. Please." When she ended a statement with 'please' you didn't ask anymore, because the next step was a swat.

Dad came out of the office and motioned for us to follow. We went to the last cabin. The door had handprints and dog prints all over it. Around the knob it was so dirty you'd think it had been painted black. Dad shoved the key in the lock and pushed. The hot air inside rushed out and hit us the way it does when you open a hot oven, but this smelled of rotting fish. We stood on the threshold, peeking in. A bare bulb hung from the ceiling in the middle of the room. There was a double bed and one scraggly chair in a corner. Dad turned on the light with a quick tug of a string.

The walls had drab, dark green wallpaper, ripped and falling. I pulled one corner up to find more paper. I pulled that up and found another layer. Dad hollered at me to stop destroying the place. I kept my sarcasm to myself.

The bathroom toilet, sink, and a shower were so dirty and rusty I thought for a minute that they were brown. The mirror over the sink, hanging from a rusty wire on a nail, was small and cracked. Dad flipped the light on and cockroaches as big as half a cigar scurried, trying to hide. The three of us jumped and shrieked. Mother starting to pray. Dad cussed up a storm.

"I ain't staying here!" I screamed.

Dad screamed back at me, "Damn it, Paul. Shut your trap and start killing them."

Dad and I stomped, swatted, hit, flushed, and swept out bugs as Mother sat on the bed, singing the Lords Prayer and Hail Marys. After thirty minutes work, he judged our work done.

Dad loped into the main room, hands on his hips. He pulled out a half cigar and lit it. Filling the room with a familiar smell of home.

Without even glancing at Mother he said, "Kitty, stop praying for a minute and pull the bedclothes down. Let's see what's there."

Mother's eyes popped open. "Oh Lord," she said. But after a deep breath she stood to do what he said.

We were surprised. The bedding looked quite clean, no bugs around.

Dad opened up both windows and a breeze started blowing through. It helped with the heat but didn't do much for the smell.

Dad went to the office to ask a question.

I looked at Mom, busy setting out our toiletries on the bureau. Pursed my lips. "Mother," I began, "I know you said don't ask, but I can't help it. I gotta wonder why we're in such a crummy place way out in the middle of nowhere."

Mother sat down on the bed beside me and shook her head. "Paul, I don't know much either. All I know is that your Uncle Reno told us to meet him here. He's stayed here before and said it was nice." She said, holding herself, looking around to the corners of the room.

"Nice? Maybe for cockroaches," I burst with a half laugh. "But, I still don't understand, why do we have to meet him?"

She looked at me and said, "He told your father that he knew about a small farm out this way that might be for sale, and your dad wants him to show it to him."

Finally some real information. I asked her, "Why couldn't you have told me that a long time ago, instead of me trying to guess?"

With a scolding tone she said, "Your father didn't want me to tell you. I don't know why."

I slouched down, puzzling over the likes of my father.

I couldn't for the life of me picture my father on a tractor, picking an orange from the tree and sniffing at it. A farm would mean that I'd be put to work like when he made me work in the strawberry patches back in Michigan during the summer. Transplanting, weeding, picking, selling them door-to-door with my little red wagon. "Strawberries for sale, five, ten, and fifteen cent baskets." That was my sales pitch as I walked through the neighborhoods. I always sold every one. And when I got home, I gave Mother all the money, and she would give me five cents for candy.

Dad returned. There was a small grocery store up the road about a mile. "I'll go up there and get us something to eat," he said.

"Can I go with you?" I asked.

"No, you'll just slow me up," he replied.

Slow him up? I could run all the way there before he got out of the parking lot. He didn't want me to come along, afraid he might have to talk to me.

Just nine in the morning but it was already hot. Mom sat fanning herself with a piece of cardboard.

After a few minutes of waiting I asked, "Can I go look around?"

"Okay," she said. "Just don't go on the highway."

All there was as far as the eye could see were palm trees, pine trees and tall grass. It felt good to get out of the stuffy room. But what could a kid do in a place like this? I had no idea.

I knocked on the office door. A gruff voice hollered out "The door opens. I ain't opening it for ya."

I came through slowly, carefully. Behind the counter was a hairy man, wearing one of those undershirts with a strap over each shoulder. He sat in a chair reading a newspaper with a half-smoked cigarette hanging from his mouth. A small fan blew on him, making the whole room smell of smoke and something I couldn't identify. I kept my hand on the door in case I wanted to run.

Without looking up, he said, "What do ya want, kid?"

I didn't know how to put what I wanted into words.

"Well, damn, speak up, boy. What do you want?" He shouted. His brows arched towards me, like huge and hairy caterpillars crawling across bone.

"I just wanted to know if... ahh... is there anything for a kid to do around here?"

He turned himself all the way around in his chair and looked at me with small, beady eyes. "Off in the back of the cabin, the one you're staying in, a few hundred feet down a path, you'll find a fishing hole. Has some pretty big catfish in it."

"Oh, okay. Gee thanks Mister," I said. I wanted to get out of that room, fast. I pushed at the door, and he hollered at me, "What ya going to fish with?"

"I ... ahh. I dunno."

Indicating with his chin, he said, "Behind the office there are some jiggy poles you can use. Make sure you bring them back. And don't break 'em."

"Ah, gee. Thanks mister. I'll take good care of them."

Just as he said, around the back I found a whole bunch of bamboo poles fixed with lines and hooks ready for fishing. I sized them up, as if I knew what I was looking for, and picked one out.

"Yea, this one will catch a lot of fish," I said aloud and headed for the 'fishin hole'.

I easily found the small path behind our cabin and went down it, carrying the 'jiggy pole' over my shoulder. The spirit of Tom Sawyer visited me. Caught up by it, I grabbed a long weed from the side of the path, cleaned off the bottom and stuck it in my mouth. If only I had a hat.

As I bounced along the path I said, "Come on, Huck. Let's go down to da fishin' hole and meet old Jim and catch us sum dinna for tonite!" I started to whistle. Even thought of taking my shoes and socks off and going bare footed.

Frogs chirped and croaked in song along the path. The smell of rotten fish became more potent as I went. I rounded a big clump of some kind of vines, walked up a small incline and there, down a marsh-lined path, was the 'fishin hole'. It was a small thing, not much more than a high falutin' puddle, really. I found it hard to believe you could get big catfish out of it. But what the heck.

The frogs leaped for safety as I neared the edge. Plop went one, splash, another. The pond's surface had a blanket of green stuff, felt like, floating across its top. Couldn't catch no fish in there. That office man was crazy.

The sun burned hot. I found a shady spot, sat down, laid down the pole. "Just a hole full of water," I said aloud with disappointment.

Out of nowhere boomed a voice, "Well, ya gonna fish, or hope dey just up and come right up and bite you?" It was a deep voice, framed by laughter.

I jerked my head, looking over my shoulder to see who it was. And there, coming up the path, carrying bamboo poles and steel buckets was a massive black man. He was old, with skin like folds of weather-beaten and cracked leather. He wore bib overalls with the left shoulder strap unhooked and hanging down loose across a barrel chest. A beat up straw hat sat towards the back of his head. His boots were in tatters and the shoelaces dotted with knots where they'd been broken and tied together again.

"How did you know I was going to fish?" I asked, breathless.

The man nodded to me. A smile as welcome as the brightest sunshine cracked across his face, He spoke slowly. "I weren't far behind ya. I could hears ya and Tom Sawyer a talkin'." His tones held the gentle rolling timber of thunder, resounding through the air. He saw I was embarrassed, laughed, and said, "No need to be ashamed of dat boy. I play talk to myself all da time."

"You do?" I asked.

"Oh yea. I pretends I is a rich man and I tells my butler and my maid to fetch me supper, bring da shiny car around, and draws me a big hot bath a water ready." He laughed. It was a laugh that came from deep inside his heart. It proved contagious, making me laugh, too.

"That's funny. What else do you pretend?" I asked.

"Oh, I pretends all kinds of things. I pretends I's can talk to da birds and all da animals dat comes here fer a drink of water."

"Do they hear you?" I asked, challenging.

The man sucked in his lips and leaned back, eyeing me. Then, in a quick move, he leaned forward and made small steps toward the water, clucking and calling, "Hello der ducky duckies. I's your big friend calling to yas." The man waddled his big butt like a duck, making me laugh. And all at once several ducks squawked and took flight from where they'd been hiding in the swamp grass, doing circles over our heads and heading out into the sky. The man stood up and harrumphed disappointment. "You see, I's talks ta dem, but dey don't always dos what's ya wants, do they?"

I laughed, and he turned to me with a wink. He continued, "That's okay. Cause dey's ducks. Dey're doing what ducks do." The man moved closer, leaned down toward me, his voice a serious whisper. "Then, other times, I looks up into dat big blue sky way up dar," his eyes, chestnut brown dots on white orbs the size of billiard balls, rolled upwards. My gaze followed. He continued, "And I's talk to da man dat lives in dat big white shiny mansion up dar."

"You mean, God?"

He nodded his head knowingly and the great orbs of his eyes spun toward mine, "Dats what folks call Him. Does you believe in God?" He held out his palm, as big as a dinner plate, towards me.

"Yea, I guess so."

The man popped to his full height, and burst, "Ya guess so?! Ya guess so, boy?" His voice raised in volume. But he wasn't scary at all. He had a presence that was both powerful and gentle at the same time. "You jist look around you, boy, and asks yourself; Who do ya think made all dese things? Looks at da bee a buzzin on your head. Who doz ya thinks made dat bee? Man? Boy, man duzzin even knows what a bee really doz. Duz you?"

"Yea, I think so," I answered sheepishly.

His voice raised in excitement. "Look at da trees around ya. Duz ya knows what dey all duz fer ya and da big whole world?"

"Well, I know some things they do."

"Da fishes in dis here hole, duz ya know what dey **duz** fer ya? Da frogs?"

"Yea. I think so."

He leaned down again with his hands on his knees to be closer to me. His nostrils were almost as wide as my mouth. He said, "Ya take da frogs now. Dey's not only food. But did ya ever lies in yer bed at night with a nice cool wind a blowin in thru da window and jist listen to dem frogs a croakin?"

"Oh, I sure have. I sure have." Many a summer night Johnny and I would lie in bed, listening to the frogs from the woods and staring at the stars. In moments like those, I felt that even Johnny could understand what was going on. He would lie there next to me with two fingers in his mouth, smiling at me. We'd drift off to sleep that way. It was very comforting.

A wider smile crossed the black man's face. "Well, boy, who duz ya know dat could takes a little bitty frog and has it do all doz things to ya? That man called God, that's who."

"I never thought of it that way."

He pulled back, aghast. "Why not?" he asked.

I shrugged. "In school they always talked about being good and praying to God and how He will smite you if you do bad things."

The man nodded, "Yep, dats all true, too. But I thinks God is a Good Fella and wants us all to be real happy, and enjoys, and loves, all da things he makes for us.

"Ya starts a looken at da good, nice, clean things in dis big old world. Like at night, all dem big bright shiny stars dat comes up and race across da heavens. Da perty flowers. Sing songs of all da birds. Da puffy clouds, like cream whipped fresh. And then there's da rain that makes everything grow big, and strong, and smells so good. All da different and beautiful animals in da world. Who else could'a made all dat. Nobody but God. Now boy, duz all dat makes any sense to ya?"

It sure did make sense to me. I'd never thought of God as a 'Good fella' before. He'd always been this imposing bearded Man with a stern scowl, a cold judge sitting up on a great white throne passing sentence to people as they lined up before Him. Not someone with feelings and a sense of humor. Everything this man said rang true.

The man nodded his head, as if I'd said yes. Then he got all-conspiratorial, leaning in closer to me. He said, "But, now there is one animal dat I have to take out of dat 'beautiful' part. Dats da Moose. I thinks dat was God's first time at tryin to makes an animal, and He jist done messed it up." He took in a deep breath so his face became all bloated and made a sound like a Moose. The two of us laughed so hard that tears flowed.

I'd never talked with a black person before. Matter of fact, I'd never had anything to do with a black person in my entire life. But despite this lack of experience, I felt perfectly comfortable. I could listen to him all day. I liked the way he talked.

He looked at me for a few seconds. Then, he leaned forward and in a soft voice, said. "Ya looks like a smart boy. But ya also looks like a very sad boy. Are ya? Are ya real sad? Do yuz wants to talk about it?"

I could feel my face flushing with discomfort. "I'd... ... rather not," I whispered.

The man leaned back again and placed his broad hands on his knees, "Dats all right, dats all right. Maybe some time ya wants to talk to me, feel free. I is a good listner. My ears dey old, but dey can hears real good."

His name was Noah, he said, like from the Bible. He lived not too far away and came to the fishin' hole about twice a week to catch fish and take it home. After he told me this his eyes rolled up toward the sky and he said, "Jist another gift from Him up dar in dat big white mansion."

I could hear Dad calling me. I said goodbye to Noah, and he told me to 'think real hard' on what we talked about. I told him I would, and meant it.

*   *   *

Dad stood up, took off his hat and scratched his head.

"God," he said. "I can't believe they drove that damn thing down here."

An old, black 1928 Ford drove into the parking lot. Sitting behind the wheel was Uncle Reno, and in the passenger seat, Harold.

Uncle Reno was half-Lithuanian, half-Maltese, married to my mother's sister. He was stout, had kinky jet-black hair all around the side of his head, none up top. His head would sort of jerk back when he talked and his voice was low, gentle and slow.

I didn't know Harold very well and, to tell you the truth, I didn't want to. Just looking at him, I could smell the chicken coop.

Dad walked across the parking lot looking the car up and down, still scratching his head. "What took you so long?" I heard him ask.

Uncle Reno pushed his hat to the back of his head and sighed. They'd had trouble, he said. The car broke down. No one knew how to fix it. If they did know, they couldn't get the parts.

Dad bit into his sandwich and shrugged. "Well, why'd you drive it down here in the first place?"

Uncle Reno said a guy down here said he might be interested in buying the car. So he'd told him that next time he came down he'd drive it. "Sure hope he still wants it. Don't want to drive the damn thing back!"

Dad led them to the cabin. They were already booked in to the cabin next to us, but not paid for. Dad and Harold unloaded the car while Uncle Reno went into the office. They'd brought a lot of cooking stuff. Uncle Reno was an ace cook. It looked like we'd be in for some good hot meals. And sure enough, that night Uncle Reno made a pasta dish that was so good I had two heaping portions.

Before putting me to bed that evening, Dad told me that he and Mother were going to town and would be gone for a couple of days. I was to stay at the hotel with Uncle Reno and Harold. The arrangement was fine with me. As long as Uncle Reno kept cooking.

Early the next morning, Mother and Dad boarded a Greyhound Bus. Soon after they left Uncle Reno announced that he and Harold were going in search of car parts. They wouldn't be very long. I wanted to come too, but they wouldn't let me.

So there I was, all alone with nothing to do. I found something to eat. I walked out to the road, which Mother told me not to do. I walked a little ways down one side, crossed over and walked back. Then I went in the other direction.

It was a hot and sticky day. A swim would've been good. I thought about the fishin' hole, but it was too dirty. Around the back of the motel I found a pile of rocks. They were just the right kind for throwing, not too big and not too small. I scrounged around in the wire incinerator and found a bunch of cans and bottles. Not too many bottles, they usually broke in the fire. I set them on an old tree about 100 feet away and started throwing. I was having a good time until the man from the office appeared by the side of the building.

"Leave those rocks alone, kid. They're for some work I'm planning to do." He disappeared as fast as he came.

Boy, every time I found something fun to do, somebody stopped me.

"Well, Tom," I said, "ya'll want to go down to da fishin' hole, see what we kin catch fer suppa?" I grabbed my jiggy pole and the two of us waddled our way down to the old fishin' hole. I was, of course, hoping Noah would be there. But I doubted he'd come two days in a row.

I arrived at the water's edge and no one was there. I found a shady spot and sat down. Got my jiggy pole fixed up and started to fish. I sat way back and after a while sleep came down.

Next thing I knew, the big mitt of a gentle hand shook me awake. Noah's broad mug was smiling down over me, so big it was like a big black moon, blocking out the sun.

"Yus can't catch da fish by sleepin'!" he said with a smile.

I sat up quickly. "I didn't think you'd be here today. You told me you only come once or twice a week."

"Well, yous is right. Dats what I done said. But, I neva told you dat I didn't come two day in a row, now did I?" He let out a chuckle.

"No, sir, you never did."

Noah had a sad look on his face and said, "Paul, I sat here a watchin and a listenen to ya while yous was asleep fer a whole bunch of minutes. Yuz is not resten at all boy. Ya is a moanin and a shakin' and a talkin' to ya self. Whatsa madder with ya boy? What's ya all tied up in a buncha knots fer?"

"How did you know my name is Paul?" I asked him.

"Well, I can sez dat I jist guessed? Or tell ya da truth. I hear ya Daddy a callin' ya." He said.

"Oh, yea, yesterday."

"Ya want ta tell me, or ya jist wanta fight with it inside of ya, all by yerself?" He asked me sadly.

I was embarrassed again. But I also felt Noah would understand things nobody else would.

"Noah, my Mother and Father sold my home, our home, that I was born in. All my friends and family lived there. When I asked them why, all I was told was: *Because Dad wants to get out of the cold weather and live in the South.* My friends were all I really had. I didn't want to move. And now every time I ask a question about why or where we're going, they either don't answer me or get mad."

Noah sat back, thinking hard. He grimaced and looked up at me. "Yea, I knows, Paul. Seems sometimes da parents, dey jist duz what dey wants to do and fergets about the chillen. But sometimes, too, dey duz things dat dey know far down, lots of time from now, will be da best thing for the chillen. Ya know God did a lot of stuff dat people did not understand. How do ya think da people dat was with Moses felt, when Moses takes dem all over the desert fer forty years? Bet dey thought *dat dern fool is lost again!*"

I could see, plain as day, Moses walking around in circles saying, "Where am I? Am I lost again?" And it made me laugh.

"Yuz is named after somebody in da Bible, too," Noah said.

"Yes, I know. Saint Paul," I said, full of pride at knowing.

"Well, ya knows, the Lord had to knock him on his butt ta gets his attention." I smiled. "Dats true ya know. God had lots a talks with Paul and he jist not listen. So God sez, 'I makes him hear Me!' And 'Whop'." Noah slapped his big hands together. "God knocked Paul right from his mule." I started to laugh again. Noah's cheeks jiggled and tears popped from his eyes.

"I is telling ya dat, God duz things in strange ways. Dat we do not always knows why. Might be, He is tellen yer Daddy to move cause He gots a chore He wants ya to do down da road. Stuff happens, Paul, and ya knows not why. But God knows. Always remember dat."

We laughed and talked all the afternoon. He made me feel so free to talk about everything and anything. I didn't want it to end, but finally, Noah stood up. "I has ta go now. Maybe we meet agin."

"Do you really have to go, Noah?"

"Yea. And look," he said, showing me his buckets. "I has no fishes to take home. Oh, Mama gonna be mift wid me. Oh my, oh me." I watched Noah as he waddled over the hill and out of sight.

How I wished Dad and I could talk like that.

Uncle Reno and Harold still hadn't returned by suppertime. I went to their cabin, retrieved a couple of camping chairs and set them up in a shady spot. I sat on one and put my feet up on the other, waiting. Wasn't long before I fell asleep. The cough of Uncle Reno's car braking in the parking lot awoke me.

"You hungry, boy?" hollered Harold.

"I sure am," I hollered back.

"We'll fix up some supper real quick fer ya, boy," Harold mumbled like he had marbles in his mouth. They'd been drinking.

As usual, the meal was delicious. We cleaned up, I said goodnight and went to my cabin but wasn't sleepy because of the long naps.

I was sitting on the bed in my underwear looking at a newspaper when there came a knock on the door. Before I could get up, it opened and Harold squeezed through the crack.

"I just wanted to make sure you're all right and settled down for the night." His goofy face was so red he looked like he'd spent the day at the beach. He had a lopsided smile and his eyes fluttered open and closed. The trunk of him wavered back and forth as though blown by the winds of his thoughts.

I shrugged. "Yea, everything's all right."

He shuffled across the room in baby steps, sat down on the bed next to me. A whiskey cloud enveloped me. I slid away from him. He slid closer.

"So, uh," he said. "You liking Florida?" his hand reached toward me. His warm palm, covered in dirt, like a farmer's, petted my leg with clumsy repetition. I jerked my leg away and slid even further across the bed. He moved closer. The claw of his hand snapped around my leg, squeezing it so it hurt. Another smell bruised my senses. Something sweet but like manure. The contents of my stomach curdled.

"Don't go away from me, Paul," he said. "I just want to help you get a good nights sleep." His other arm reached over. It grabbed my head. He pulled at me.

"Get out of here," I screamed. "Leave me alone!"

I dug my nails into his spongy arms. I batted my fists in a whirlwind until he let go. I jumped off the bed and ran toward the door. I pulled it open and jumped out into the night air. At the top of my changing vocal chord range I screamed at him, "Get out of my room!"

But he didn't move. He just sat there on the bed grinning at me. He patted a spot on the bed beside him, motioning for me to come back.

I ran to Uncle Reno's room. He was sitting in the lounge chair, reading the newspaper.

I yelled at him, "Get Harold out of my room. Now!"

Uncle Reno didn't even look up. From behind his newspaper he said, "Oh, Paul, don't get so upset now. Harold just likes little boys. He won't hurt you."

Shocked, I stood there almost naked in a parking lot, wavering in some non-existent wind.

"Go back to your room now, Paul," Uncle Reno called from behind his paper.

A thought occurred to me. I asked, "What if I was your son, Richie? Would you tell him to go back to his room to be with Harold who won't hurt him?"

The newspaper lowered. Uncle Reno's face was a mask of shock. After a few moments he got up, went to the door. He looked toward our cabin and hollered, "Harold? Harold, get back over here and go to bed. Now!"

I backed away from the door and watched Harold come out of my room, grinning from ear to ear. He smiled at me stupidly, as he went in and the door closed behind him. I raced back to my room, shut and locked the door.

I fell in the torn up chair. My chest rose and fell so fast I went faint. I was shaking so hard the chair rattled on the carpet.

"Mother," I whispered, hugging myself. How I wished she was there. I was sure she'd beat Harold's butt with anything she could've put her hands on.

I must have cried myself to sleep because the next thing I heard was Uncle Reno's car starting up. When I opened the door they were pulling away. I put my pants and shoes on. All the camping equipment was gone. Their cabin door was open. They'd cleared out. Hadn't left anything. No food, nothing.

I was glad they were gone.

I walked around outside for a while, as though looking for something. There were no cars in the parking lot. Indifferent music wafted from the motel office. An occasional car zoomed by on the highway. Other than that, the only sound was the wind.

But then, all at once, it hit me. I was out in the middle of nowhere. Mom and Dad would be gone for two more days. I had no money. No food. No nothing.

I dove into a run down the path towards the fishing hole, hoping to find Noah there. I arrived at the water's edge puffing. All I found were the frogs. My insides churned and twisted.

I screamed out, "Noah! Where are you?" My voice was absorbed by the swamp. No response.

I stayed at the fishin' hole the rest of the day, but Noah never showed up. I thought through everything we'd talked about. I tried to remember how he made me see things in a simpler way.

Sitting at the edge of the fishin' hole, I looked up into that vast dome of the sky and swallowed. I took a breath, blinked, and said, "God, I'm in an awful mess. I don't know what to do." My chest began to quiver. Sobs shook me. I bundled my knees into my chest. Through the tears, I wailed, "What am I supposed to do? Can you help me, please, sir, God? Help me?" I took in a deep breath. Then, the funniest thing happened. It was like a warmth sparked inside me and grew and grew, filling me. I knew with all certainty, in that moment, that I'd been heard. Not because of the warmth. That was a by-product. I just sensed someone… something had heard me. And for the moment, anyway, my part of the planet became a few shades brighter.

That day, that afternoon, I started talking to God the same way I'd always talked to Billy. But with more respect and dignity, of course. No introductions were needed, no summoning him up, no waiting or forms to fill out.

I headed back toward the motel, amazed at how calm I'd become.

It wasn't surprising that Mother and Father weren't back yet. My stomach burped and whined. I hadn't eaten in one full day. I scoured our room and found half a sandwich and half a can of flat soda. I inhaled both so fast they were immediately forgotten. The sun faded in the window, casting a sad shadow across the bedclothes. I took a shower and went to bed, hoping for my parent's early return the next morning.

The cough of a car starting woke me. I jumped out from under the covers, looking out the window. Nothing. I got dressed, went outside and sat in a chair in the shade of a tree by the highway. What an endless ribbon it was, going on to everywhere. But no one seemed to be coming to this stretch of it.

What was I going to do? What if my parents were dead; killed in a bus accident? What if they went off and left me? How long do I wait? What if the man in the office kicks me out? I could go back to Michigan and live with… I didn't even know who I could live with.

I had to calm down. To think straight. I decided to talk to God again.

"God," I began, "I know I asked you just yesterday for strength and courage to face this problem, but, to tell you the truth, I don't know what to do. I'm sitting here in this chair and it's like I can't get up. And if I do get up, what do I do? Which way do I go? How do I eat? God, you really got to help me. I'm one lost and frightened kid!"

As if on cue, the man from the office opened up his screen door and hollered at me, "Hey, kid, get over here."

I got out of the chair, its limbs creaking with release. I walked across the parking lot toward him. His cigarette went up and down between his lips. I was sure he was going to ask me to leave.

He grunted like an ox and scratched at his belly. The cloth of his t-shirt was soaked through and yellowed.

He said, "Noticed your parents ain't here. The other guys left. How come you're alone?"

I wasn't sure what to tell him. "Ah…. my Mother and Dad went to look at a farm they want to buy. I guess they should be back today."

"Well, okay," he said as he puffed on his smoke without touching it. It jumped up and down as his eyes bore down into mine. He didn't believe me. At length he asked, "You got anything to eat?"

My foot kicked at dirt. I couldn't look at him. I shrugged. "Naw. They forgot to leave me anything."

He grunted again. "Well then, y'all come back in a few minutes. I'll have something fixed up for ya."

"Okay. Great. I'll be back." I bolted to our room. With great speed I washed my hands and face and sort of combed my hair with my fingers.

When I arrived back at the office he was sitting behind his desk again. He nodded his head toward an open door. "There's something for you in there," he said.

On a table in the other room was a bowl of oatmeal, toast and a glass of water. It wasn't Uncle Reno's pasta, but it was food. It felt real good to have something in my stomach besides air. I thanked him and thanked him. He told me to come back later if my parents still weren't back.

I headed to the fishin' hole again. Noah wasn't there. My imagination started to run wild all over again. What if this… what if that…. By mid afternoon nothing was straight anymore.

Hungry and resigned to being alone, I headed down the path. But as I went, coming over the rise was Noah heading towards me. I ran to him, throwing my arms about his generous waist.

Noah's thick fingers caressed my head. "Hey boy, things not all dat bad, are dey?" He asked me. I wiped my eyes and told him I was so glad to see him. "If yuz glad ta see me, yuz should holla and a scream, and jump up and down. Not cry."

"Yea, I know. But I can't help it." I told him what had happened to me since I'd last seen him, how my mind had been running.

"Well, first, ya Mommy and Daddy must think ya a very strong boy ta be left all by yerself. But dey should see dat ya has food ta eat and dat ya kin call somebody if something was ta happen. But I thinks dey come back soon."

Then he looked at me out of the corner of his eye, sizing me up. "Boy," he began, "has ya talked to God like we said da last time? Ya gots to remembers, der is a reason for all things, and things happen for certain reasons. God will not give ya more than ya can takes. He won't do dat to ya. And ya got ta thinks, dat things can always be worse dan dey is. You lets dat sink deep into yer head and keeps it dar fer ever. Can ya do dat, Paul?"

"Yes, sir, I sure can and will. It's deep in my brain and I'll save it and remember it always."

We talked on for a long time about people in the Bible, why things happened the way they did. With just about every character, Noah had a way of turning them into something 'real'. Not just a story, but almost like you could reach right into their lives and be with them.

When the sun started to fade on the horizon, Noah said he had to get home. When he was on top of the rise, he turned to me and said, "Paul, ya dun got me in trouble agin. I ain't got no fishes. Mama gonna get me good dis time. God be with you." The big man waved and walked over the hill.

Somehow I knew that would be the last time I saw Noah. I felt sad, but knew that inside he'd never be gone. He taught me more about human feelings and the every day things of the world in that short time frame than I had learned in all my years in school. He enjoyed life itself more than anyone I'd ever met.

I returned to the motel settled down, but very hungry. I hated to ask that man for more food, but had no choice. I knocked on his door, he hollered at me to come in. He said, "Guess you want something to eat again, eh boy?"

"Yes, sir."

"I fixed up a batch of chili, and there's some bread on the counter in the kitchen. Go help yourself."

Three bowls later I was full. He gave me a bottle of orange drink and a couple of cookies. "I'll save these for later," I told him. "I sure do want to thank you for the food. It was really good chili, best I've ever had."

He grinned at me and said, "You only got one more day paid on the room. So your folks better come back tonight or tomorrow."

"Oh yea, they'll be back by tomorrow for sure," I said, ever hopeful. I thanked him again for the food and went back to the room for another anxious night.

Before long I heard the bus stop on the highway. I ran out the door to see. The bus pulled away and there stood Mother and Dad. I ran to them, grabbing Mother with both arms, nearly toppling her.

"Where have you been?" I cried.

Dad looked around, perturbed, "Where's Reno and Harold?"

I wiped away my tears. Said, "They left two days ago."

Mother gasped, "Oh my Lord."

Mother began unpacking their overnight bag as Dad went for a shower. When the water was running I turned to her.

"I have to tell you something, Mother," I said, my voice hushed. "Something bad." I told her what Harold had done, how scared it made me.

She tossed her hair back. "Oh come on now, Paul. You're imagining things." Then she turned back to her unpacking.

"No, Mother. You have to understand. He wanted to do things to me. Terrible things. I know."

She snorted a small laugh. "I don't think so, Paul. Harold has a boy. He just wouldn't do something like that."

The shower in the bathroom stopped. Mother turned to me, leaned down and said, "Do not mention this to your father or bring it up again. Please."

I was puzzled. Couldn't she tell how distressed I was?

She leaned in close and whispered, "How dare you say those evil things about your family. You stop all those wicked thoughts and get them out of your head." She gave me a hard glare. "I want you to ask God for forgiveness. Say three 'Our Fathers' and three 'Hail Mary's' when you're saying your prayers." She stood up with one big stretch and said she was going to take a shower.

As I watched her gather her night things, I didn't know if I should cry, get mad, scream, or just forget it ever happened. I kneeled by my bedside, but didn't say any Hail Mary's. When I climbed between the covers I felt a numbness, as though drugged.

The next morning Dad told us to pack. The bus was coming in an hour. I was still churning inside from the night before. The drugged-up numbness made everything around me surreal.

"Where we going?" I asked.

Dad didn't even look at me. He hissed, "You'll see when we get there."

"Why can't you tell me now?" I asked.

"Paul?" Mother warned.

"No, Paul," I said. "Dad, why do I just have to 'see when we get there'? I want to know. I want to know something. Please?" Dad rumbled at my words.

Mother grabbed my arm, shaking me "You don't talk to your Father that way! You understand me, Paul?"

I jerked my arm away. "I don't understand. Why should I? Why can't you two understand me, once in a while?"

It was no surprise when he rushed across the room at me. What was a surprise was the hard swat across the face with the back of his hand. It knocked me to the floor, and I could feel the sting of his knuckles on my cheek.

He pointed down at me. "You shut your damn mouth and don't you ever raise your voice to me or your mother again! Never! You understand that, boy?"

I didn't reply. I didn't even look up.

He walked over and kicked me in the left side, hard. I crumpled.

He leaned down and yelled, "Answer me, boy! Do you understand that?"

I didn't want to answer, but was afraid he'd kick again. So I struggled in a breath and wheezed, "Yea, I understand."

I could hear Mother whimpering and Dad's heavy breathing. I could feel his cold stare even if I couldn't see it. Holding my side, I struggled to my feet and went to the bathroom to clean up. Mother moved to follow me, but I shut the door and locked it before she could get in.

She knocked and told me to open up. I didn't answer. She stopped. I heard her footsteps fade away. I cleaned the blood off my face and stopped my nose from bleeding. I looked in the mirror and the right side of my face was starting to swell. I was going to have a shiner.

When I came out of the bathroom, they were gone. Why did it not surprise me that they wouldn't wait? I grabbed my bag and walked out the door.

I found Mother and Dad standing at the highway waiting for the bus. I walked up behind them, set my bag down and said nothing. They didn't acknowledge me being there. If I'd felt alone before, now I felt like an outsider. I didn't feel like I belonged to them. I felt no caring whatsoever.

But if I didn't belong with them, if my own parents didn't care, where did I belong?

7.

NO MORE QUESTIONS

The bus whizzed down the highway towards St. Petersburg.

The motor had a monotonous, numbing hum. Citrus groves spanned out in rows off into infinity on either side, giving the impression of endless hallways to nowhere.

That's where I felt I was heading, through a deep, dark tunnel to nowhere. I tried not to allow the shroud of mystery maintained by my parents overwhelm my thoughts, but it was hard.

Certainly I hoped we weren't heading for another dull train journey, bumping across the country, but I wasn't about to ask. That had become a decision, firm in my mind. No more questions. They were ignored or chastised, anyway. So, no more. No more questions unless absolutely necessary. I was resolved.

As the bus bumped along, Dad peeked over the chair with this curious grin waiting for me to ask. He sensed a change. The fact that it visibly bothered him held a revenge I allowed myself to enjoy. It was a kind of power, wasn't it? The only kind of power I had. By the sixth peek, downright agitation screwed his face into knots.

"How come you're not asking where we're going?" he asked. I couldn't let the smile I felt inside show. I looked out the window, didn't reply. His face flushed, his jaw tightened and after a couple of seconds, he turned back around in his chair with the petulant huff of a child.

The bus pulled into the Greyhound terminal in downtown St. Petersburg. We collected our things and Dad hailed a cab. Twenty minutes later we stopped in front of a white stucco duplex. It looked dirty the way a kid does after playing football on a wet field. Each half had a screened-in porch with a door slouching toward the center, giving the impression of a challenging smirk. It was framed by bushes like rags.

The place had a mildew scent, like clothes that weren't quite dry.

Mother pointed with her chin, "You take the room on the left, Paul."

In the room were a bed with bedside table and a lamp with furry little balls dangling down from the rim of the shade. A dresser stood in the corner. Everything looked clean, but it felt dirty.

Welcome home.

I shut my door, threw my bags in the direction of the dresser and jumped on the bed. I overheard my parents mumbling something about the place not being worth the money she was charging. She was ripping them off, and we wouldn't be staying long. We were just moving in and already they were thinking about moving out. What in the world was going on?

* * *

Over the next few weeks my parents left me alone for days on end. I had no idea where they went or what they did. I was given money to go to the store and food was left in the icebox, but no explanations.

I'd established my rules. Knowing wasn't necessary to survival, but that didn't mean it didn't drive me crazy.

Why they thought an eight and a half year old boy could manage on his own, I'll never really know. I had a roof over my head, sure. Back in Detroit, when I was five, they'd leave me baby-sitting Johnny. But that was at home. I could always run next door in an emergency. Maybe they thought I'd handled being alone so well at The Fisherman's Motel. Or, maybe they thought I was mature enough. Or, maybe they weren't thinking at all.

There was a desperate huddled quality to them as they ran out the door. As if chasing, or being chased. At the same time, I sensed they were searching for something. Was it a farm? Another house? I didn't think so. Their looks were too despairing and needy. As if their very lives depended upon this mysterious search of theirs. They'd return more exhausted and disappointed each time.

All the while, I was experiencing a spiritual transformation. Over the course this month, I found myself using God and Noah interchangeably. Then God became a big black man wearing bib overalls, sitting in a rocking chair, high up on a cloud. And I talked to him, one on one, like he was the bestest friend in the world. Cause he was.

I became adventurous, staying out late nights, going down to the main streets, by all the bars and hotels. I'd watch people drinking, fighting, cops arresting people and hauling them off. I watched women dressed up real fancy, walking through hotel entrances; arms interlaced with service men escorts. It took me a while to figure out what they were doing. I recalled that party and what I saw in the furnace room. Wow! I felt my face flush and I laughed out loud. Then I recalled what my Ed had called these women, "Ladies of the night".

I looked up to where I pictured my imaginary Noah to be. He was looking down, seeing what I saw, rocking back and forth on the tip of the moon. "So, Noah," I asked, "what do you think about these ladies?"

Noah's broad laugh echoed in my thoughts. "Think about da moose, Paul. Think about da moose."

One night, I was leaning up against a building when, coming down the street towards me was the largest, toughest, lady I'd ever seen. She was tattooed and had a large black belt in her hands that was buckled together. She opened it in the shape of a big O, and then pulled the ends out sharply so the belt would make a loud snap, like a firecracker. On each side of her was a broad-shouldered man. Two others followed behind. All four were just as big and mean looking as she was.

Much to my chagrin, the lady spotted me, stopped. The men stopped too. She stepped towards me. I had to crane my neck, she was so huge. My legs told me to run, but my brain said stay.

With a voice like gravel she said, "Hey, kid. What in hell are you doing in a place like this at this time of night?" I was immovable. She reached for my chin with the leather strap, I jumped a step back. She shifted her weight from one foot to another in a move like a man.

"Answer me, boy!" she barked.

I felt myself shaking, tried to force out some words, but nothing would come.

One of the men in the back chortled, "The kid can't talk."

Out of the corner of my eye I caught a soldier and a lady of the night going into a hotel. "I'm waiting for my Dad," I said.

The lady cracked a surprised smile, looked back to her muscled escorts and laughed. Her men joined in her chuckle.

Her eyelashes batting, all demure, she turned back. She said, "Yea, and we're all waiting for our Mother's to come and take us home." She crouched down with her hands on her knees, pouted, "Well, where is your Daddy, little boy?"

I ignored her mocking and said, "He and this lady went into that hotel over there." I pointed to one of the hotels across the street. All their heads turned to look. "He told me to wait out here while they talked about something."

The lady jerked up with a hoot of laughter. Her escorts howled. The whole lot of them started laughing so hard, slapping each other, pointing and hooting at me, I was sure they were about to fall over. Eventually their laughter subsided.

The 'lady' reached down with an open palm, patted me on the head and said, "Good going kid. You'll do all right!"

And with that, they continued on down the street howling and batting at each other playfully.

I looked up into the starlit sky. Noah was lying on the Big Dipper, his hat overtop of his face, his jiggy pole dipping into in the Milky Way. "Noah!" I called up to him. "I don't think that woman was a woman...."

Noah tipped his hat back and looked down. "Like I tells ya, Paul. God make all kinds."

I was awoken that night by the caress of my Mother's soft hand on my forehead. I hugged her tight, glad they were home.

The next morning at breakfast Dad announced, "Paul, get your stuff together."

I knew what that meant. We were leaving again. I packed in ten minutes without a word.

When Dad saw my bag sitting at the door, he eyed me. "Don't you want to know where we're going?" he asked. I didn't answer.

Dad turned to Mother and with a mocking tone, said, "Guess he doesn't care where we're going anymore."

Why should I care? Didn't matter anyway. I'd keep to myself and follow.

I was to pay a dear price for this decision, to close off, protect myself. It was paid with a hollowness as I learned to keep my crying inside.

8.

TWO CAMPS - ME VS. THEM

I wasn't really surprised when the cab took us to the train station. When we arrived, Dad went to the counter and bought our tickets. Rather than be upset, I watched the people rushing around. There were so many foreign tongues being spoken. I tried to guess what they were saying.

Then I noticed Mother and Dad watching me and whispering. They stopped at my stare and Mom leaned down to speak to me.

"Paul, would you like to know where we're going?" she asked.

I shrugged, "If you wanna to tell me."

Dad, who loathed being ignored, said, "Don't tell him, Mary. Let him guess." But I didn't answer. "Aren't you going to guess?" he taunted.

I sucked in my lips and shook my head with an adamant, no.

Dad huffed with indignation. He pushed back on the bench and crossed his arms, ignoring me with great purpose.

Mom sat back, too, but slowly, eyeing me. Our eyes locked. I bit my lip. I shook my head as if trying to say, I have to. She sighed with a heaviness like an ocean tipping and swaying.

An announcement came over the loud speaker: "Now loading on track #6, Southern Railway's Express to Jacksonville, Atlanta, Chattanooga, Cincinnati, Toledo, Detroit, and points in between."

Dad grabbed his suitcase, stood up and stared down at me without saying anything. I tightened myself, holding in the surprise.

I said, "My guess is we're going to Toledo. There, how's that, Dad? Did I get it right?"

Dad's jaw seemed to gnarl in a circle. Neither of them acknowledged my remark. Mother picked up her case and they headed for the gate. I followed.

I may not have been registering surprise, but thoughts bounded like pinballs on steroids. Were we moving back home again? I mean, to Detroit?

Had something happened? Were my sisters okay? Did my parents even know what they were doing?

One thing I did know for certain. I was in for a four or five-day train ride. I couldn't wait for breakfast.

* * *

Something had changed between them. They argued in whispered exchanges with occasional furtive looks my way to make sure I couldn't hear. And when I got too close, they'd abruptly stop talking. Dad was always the one doing most of the talking. Mother would shake her head and frequently burst with exasperation. The only thing I could figure out was that they were talking about something or someone in Detroit.

The train pulled into Detroit's station around five o'clock on the fifth day. I was excited about the prospect of seeing my friends and sisters again. But when we got in the cab, it didn't head anywhere near where we used to live. Instead, we headed downtown.

The cab stopped in front of a sad hotel with two shades of paint flaking from its sides. Wooden steps sloped down and creaked as you climbed. Dingy drapes fluttered ragged out of open windows.

Dad went up the step ahead of me. I'd promised myself not to ask any more questions, but this was more than I could bear. "What are we doing at this dumb hotel?" I asked in a burst.

Mother stopped on the stairs. Dad turned back, sneering. "This is where we're going to sleep, stupid."

"But, why don't we just go home? Or to Mattie's or Kitty's?"

"We don't have a home here anymore, remember? And the girls, they don't have any room for us." Then he shook a warning finger at me so I had to step back. "And we don't want them to know we're here. Do you understand that, boy? Does that answer all of your dumb questions?"

Confusion and anger burbled. Questions teemed. But I'd been noticing how much better I felt when I didn't ask, so I shut my mouth again. If I didn't ask, I didn't get ridiculed.

Mother and I took a seat while Dad went to the front desk. A lamp in the corner kept flickering as though it couldn't make up its mind what to do. There was an elevator with an iron gate. I watched as two people struggled to open it. It squeaked like a rusty hinge. They had to use themselves as a winch to push it open, and when the elevator ascended it did so with a horrible, grating growl.

I turned to my Mother. "Mom, why?" She knew what I meant. But her back stiffened. She didn't answer. I rolled my eyes and turned away from her, saying, "You're getting just like Dad, you know. Not answering me."

"Watch your mouth, Paul. You yourself are getting too big for your britches lately."

I turned back to her, imploring, "Well, if you would tell me something about what we're doing once in a while, I wouldn't have to keep asking. Mom, I don't understand what's going on. What are we doing?"

She stared at me. I watched her eyes as they studied my face. There was an emotional blankness there. The gears of her thoughts were working overtime, just like mine. I wanted to shake her, to scare it away. But then she looked towards Dad and my urge became redundant.

I sighed deeply. "Mom?" I said. She didn't move or respond. "Mother, are you ever going to answer me?"

She turned to me again with the same, blank stare, as if I didn't exist.

Dad arrived beside us. "Let's go."

We took the elevator to the sixth floor. I watched with restrained amusement as Dad struggled to open the steel gate the way the others had.

Our room was number 621, but the 1 was hanging upside down. I reached up to set it right but Dad hollered at me to leave it alone, said it would probably fall off and we'd be charged for replacing it.

The room stunk of smoke and booze. A swirling map of spill stains adorned the carpet. Dad turned the switch on a lamp, but it didn't cast much light. The room felt claustrophobic, with dreary, slumping furniture. There was just one bed, a dresser with a mirror, a chair in the corner by the window, but something was obviously missing.

"Where's the bathroom?" I asked.

The question aroused Mother's attention. She looked around, dismayed. "No bathroom?"

Tossing his hat onto the chair, Dad shrugged and said, "The bathroom's down the hall. These old hotels don't have one for every room."

Mother emitted the smallest of gasps at this news. It was so deep and fast, Dad and I turned to check she was okay. Her eyes scanned the surroundings and her hand flew to her mouth. I knew what she was thinking: How could we have sunk so low? This was a place for the dregs of society. Not us. We were good, middle class people.

I sank into a chair "Dad?" I asked. "Could you please tell me why we're here?"

His reaction was out of phase with reality. Jerky, intense, he turned to me. "If I wanted you to know, I'd tell you," he snapped.

I shook my head, not understanding. "What's the big secret, Dad?"

Mother hung her head and shook it from side to side.

He pointed his finger at me again. "It took a long time for your face to heal from the last blow I gave you. You want to try for the other side this time?"

I sighed. "Why do you have to hit me every time I ask a question?" Dad started to pace. He was boiling inside something fierce. But I continued anyway. "Why can't you just tell me why we have to stay in such a dump?"

Next thing I knew, me and the chair were falling to the right and my face stung. . The chair was flung aside and another punch was on its way. Mother's shrill screams piercing the air made his fist stop. Out of one eye, I could see his sneering smile, like he'd won some kind of game.

Blood ran down my cheek. I pushed the chair off and ran out of the room, holding my eye. I wandered blind down the corridor, arm outstretched, probing for the bathroom. I found a door half open and went inside without bothering to close it behind me.

I poured water on my face as fast it came out of the faucet. There were no towels, so I had to use toilet paper to wipe my face and that just made it worse. It came apart in little pieces and stuck.

The door swung open with a creak, bumping gently against my hip. I jumped and spun. A man with dark hair and a pinched face entered. When he saw me, he jumped. He asked what had happened. I told him I fell down the stairs.

"Oh," he said. He threw me a towel. "Soak it in water, rinse it out and hold it on your eye and cut for a while. Do it several times and it'll feel better." He backed out and left me alone. I did as he suggested, gasping through the pain as I held the towel to my face. The bleeding stopped and it did start to feel a bit better. But it still hurt real bad and I could hardly see out of the eye.

When I was all cleaned up, I sat down on the toilet and burst into tears, even though the salt made the wounds sting more. The extra pain was almost a validation, telling me it was okay to cry. I allowed the sobs to grow into hiccups that rolled through me like thunder.

As the minutes turned to over an hour, the realization grew that what hurt most was neither of them had come to see how I was. What kind of parents were they? And my father, the way he'd reacted. It was so weird, so intense. I mean sure, his pride had been damaged. But there was something else going on, too. If only I could figure it out maybe I could do something about it.

When I felt ready to face him again I walked back to the room, turned the door handle, but it was locked. I knocked. Nothing. I checked the number. It was 621, with the upside down 1. I knocked again. Nothing.

"God, can't they hear me?" I knocked harder and yelled, "Open the door." No answer. I put my ear up against it and listened. The silence was too complete. They'd gone. Left me. I turned my back to the door and sank to the floor. A hollow feeling coursed through me like a wave, and the tears came yet again like the torrent of the saddest day.

This hollowness was such a total experience. Like being erased from the inside out. Beyond caring. Just a nothing. A zero. A piece of rotting flesh. This isn't a feeling you want to be acquainted with, or think yourself capable of. It is a despair that overtakes you, settles in and changes your very nature in the process.

I must have cried myself to sleep, because next thing I knew, someone was shaking my shoulder. I snapped awake, realizing where I was. The man from the front desk was leaning down over me. He had friendly eyes and a face with skin like the roughest of sandpaper.

"What are you doing sleeping out in the hall?" he asked.

I searched for something to say. "I went to the bathroom and I guess the door got locked and I couldn't get back in," I replied.

Dismayed by what I said he asked, "Where did your folks go?"

I shrugged, tried to smile. It hurt. "Oh, they… they went out to see about getting us something to eat."

The man fumbled a set of keys from his pocket. He pushed one into the lock and said, "Son, I don't know why you told me what you did. But these doors have to lock with a key. They don't lock by themselves." He eyed me. I looked to the ground and shrugged, went through the door. He stayed on the threshold, leaned down so he could get a better look at my eye. "That's a nasty looking eye you got there. I'll bring you up some ice. It will help the swelling go down."

"Thanks."

A little while came a knock at the door. Standing on the other side was a boy about my age. He had the eyes of a trickster and a mischievous smile. A hat hung low over his right eye and his black jacket was torn in several places. He handed me the ball of a towel.

"My dad said to give this to you." He said. He grunted, uncomfortable and shifted his weight.

"Thanks," I said and took the package. It chilled the tips of my fingers. With a toss of his head, he asked, "What happened to you?"

I shrugged. "Fell down stairs." The story was starting to feel real.

But he chortled and rolled a shoulder. "You can tell the grown-ups that, but I don't believe it."

I looked up, "What do you mean by that?"

He said, "I've had a few of those myself. That's what I mean."

I laughed a little, but regretted it. "Oh, it hurts to laugh," I said. He laughed, too.

He told me his name was Anthony Manzoni, but everybody called him Tony.

"Your dad is the man at the desk?" I asked.

"Yea. We live here and that's his job. That's how he pays the rent."

The way he said it made me curious. "If he just gets enough to pay the rent, how do you get money for food and things?"

Tony looked down at the floor for a few seconds and then back up at me and asked, "How long you and your folks staying here?"

I shrugged. "I don't even know why we're here."

"Well, if you stick around, maybe you and I can get together and do some things."

"What things?"

Tony sucked in his lip. "You ask a lot of questions. No wonder your old man smacks you. And I better get back down there before I get smacked, too."

I closed the door behind him, wondering if he was right. Did I ask too many questions? Wasn't asking questions a good thing? The way you learn?

I lay down on the bed and placed the package of ice on my eye. A comforting, cold numbing spread through the flaming tissues of my face. Melting ice formed rivers down the sides of my head onto the covers. At first, I didn't care. But then I realized Dad would figure out how it got wet and moved to the chair. By the time all the ice had melted the throbbing had dulled. I curled up on the floor in a corner. It was cold. I thought about taking the cover from the bed. Then I considered how Dad would react and forgot the cover real fast. Instead I pulled my coat over my torso and spread a sweater out over my legs.

I was just fading into sleep when I heard a key in the door. I pretended to be asleep, listening as my parents got undressed and into bed without even looking at me. I felt myself sink into that hollow feeling again, my senses drowned by it.

In an attempt to get away from it, my thoughts turned to Noah. I imagined he was there, that I could whisper into his ear. I asked him what it all meant, what I was supposed to do, how I could handle this. "There is a reason for everything, Paul. You gotta trust. Trust. It will all become clear one day. Just hold on." I faded into sleep to the soothing tones of his memory.

* * *

Mother's gentle shake and her voice humming woke me. She had some breakfast ready. I wobbled up, rubbed my eyes and cringed at the painful wound I'd forgotten.

I looked up and saw Mother taking in the purple balloon of flesh that was now my eye. She grabbed onto me. Her body convulsed as she held me.

Dad said, "Leave the kid alone and let him eat. He'll live."

Mother backed away without saying a word and quickly retreated from the room.

On the little table by the bed was a glass of milk, a pear and a donut. I hadn't had any supper the night before, so I was very hungry. Dad watched as I ate. What was going through his mind?

The door opened a sliver and Mother sidestepped into the room, her glance downcast. Her eyes were swollen and her nose cherry red.

Dad noticed. Snipped, "Oh, Mary, stop it. Just get your damn clothes on and let's go."

I started to ask where they were going, how long they'd be gone, but stopped myself. Mom pulled a suitcase from behind the door, placed it on the bed and started packing. Dad threw two dollars at me and leered, challenging me to ask. I didn't. Mother zipped up the bag, came across the room and hugged me.

While I had the opportunity I whispered, "Why?", into her ear.

She squeezed my arm as she stepped back, keeping her face turned away from Dad to hide her tears. All she said was, "Don't get into any trouble, Paul."

I looked out the hotel room window and waited to see them go. They walked down the street and disappeared behind a corner.

I fell down on the bed, looking up at the ceiling, trying to think this through. I was so confused, frustrated. My mother, and me the two of us were becoming ghost-like — barely there. Perhaps only memories of real people. We were allowing ourselves to be ground into nothing by him. How could I let this happen?

I didn't understand why Mother was so afraid of him. And why did they leave me alone like this? But most of all, what were they hiding from me?

In a quick move I turned over and hit the pillow. It felt good. I hit it again. And again. I started to pummel it and scream and scream until I was crying again.

Someone pounded on the wall next door. A voice called, "Hey, keep it down in there." I don't know why, but it made me laugh. But laughing hurt my face and that made me laugh even more.

I grabbed onto the pillow, pulling the marshmallow of it to my chest.

Could I run away? That was a possibility. But do you know what kept me from doing it? The fact that it would make Dad happy. I didn't want to make him happy.

A loud knock on the door startled me. It was Tony. He said he saw my folks leave and wanted to know if I wanted to go out and do something. I told him I couldn't because my head and face hurt too bad.

"Do you want some aspirin?" he asked. "That'll make your head feel better." I thanked him for the offer. The aspirin would help. But I didn't feel well enough to do anything. He looked disappointed. "How long do you think your folks will be gone?" he asked.

I shrugged. "I don't know. They took a bag, so I figure two or three days."

This seemed to make him happier. "Well, we'll go out tomorrow night then. Okay?"

I smiled. "Yea, tomorrow night," I said.

Tony started backing down the hall. "I'll get the aspirins and be right back," he said. He returned in no time. As he handed over the half bottle of aspirin he told me that he'd really think about where and what we'd do tomorrow night.

The next night at precisely six o'clock Tony knocked on my door. I didn't want to go anywhere, but knew he was looking forward to it, and the diversion would do me good.

Tony squeezed in through the door and glanced around the room as if looking for something, slapped his hands together and asked, "You got a black or dark shirt or a jacket you can wear instead of that light colored thing?" he asked.

"Yea. But why?"

"The light colored shirt will show in the dark, and where we're going you don't want to be seen."

"What are you talking about, 'don't want to be seen'?"

Tony shifted his weight from one foot to another "You know Paul, you ask too damn many questions!"

"But that's how I find things out."

"It's not that I won't tell you. I will. But not right now. Okay?"

I changed shirts and put on my dark brown jacket and turned to Tony for approval. He smiled, nodded and off we went.

We left the hotel through the back way. After walking a couple of blocks Tony told me we were going about four more blocks. Then we'd get on top of a building.

I stopped in my tracks. "Oh no! Stop right there. I'm not climbing no buildings! No sir!"

Tony thrust his hands onto his hips and gave me an acid glare. "What's the matter, afraid of heights?"

"No Tony. I'm not scared. But I ain't climbing no buildings. And that's that. I'm going back to the hotel." I turned on my heels and started away.

Tony ran up beside me. "Wait a minute Paul. We're not climbing a building. We get up there by walking up the stairs."

I stopped, blinked at him.

He asked, "What are you thinking, that we'd climb up the outside?"

"Yea, that's what I thought you meant."

He started to laugh. He stepped aside and started to laugh even harder.

"But, Tony, you don't understand. That's what I did with these guys in Boston, you see?" I told him the whole story. He was stunned.

"Now I know why you wanted to go back," he said. "But that's not what we're doing. We're going to go into this old deserted building and go up to the roof and then across several buildings to where the black people live."

"Why? What for?"

Tony shrugged. "Because their stores are easy to break into."

I started to back away. "I don't want to break into no store, Tony. I'm sorry." I was surprised he could even think of such a thing. "What if your Father found out you did this? What do you think he'd do to you?"

"Who do you think taught me how to do break in without being seen in the first place?" He said with a laugh in his voice.

My mouth fell open and I stared at him. He was lying to me.

Tony looked around the street. He came in close, real conspiratorial, putting his arm around my shoulder.

"Do you remember when we first met; you asked me about other money and how did we get it for food and stuff?"

"Yea, I remember."

"Well, this is how we get that money. Me and Pop go out about three to four times a month and rob some stores. Mostly in the black sections of town because they blame it on their own people and the cops never come looking for us white folks. Understand now?"

I stared at him blankly. Did I believe him or not?

"Oh, come on, Paul, we'll just hit one small place and come back. You'll be safe. I've done this lots of times."

"How about I just watch you?"

"What, are you scared? Afraid Daddy might get mad at you?"

"Yea, I am. And I don't want him hitting me anymore."

Tony stepped back and tapped the back of his hand gently to my chest. "Hit him back," he said with an authoritative nod.

Hit him back? I'd never thought of that. I said, "I can't hit my Father."

"Why not? A kid in school hits you, what do you do? You hit him back. And if you hit him pretty hard and it hurts, he'll leave you alone. Right?"

"Well, yea, but that's a kid. We're talking about your Father."

"No, not my Father, Paul. Your Father."

"I know that. I just mean… you know what I mean."

"Pops used to beat me up real bad. He still lets go once in a while, especially when he's been drinking. But not too many times since the night I took a baseball bat and hit him so hard on the back of his legs that he couldn't walk for a week. Damn near broke both his legs. He's left me alone since except, like I said, when he's been drinking."

I imagined myself taking a baseball bat to my Father. I saw the bat hit, Dad turn around and kill me, broken legs or no broken legs.

Tony put a hand on my arm and said, "Next time he starts on you, grab the nearest thing you can get your hands on and let him have it. He'll leave you alone." I nodded but didn't reply.

Tony started away, and I joined him. "Come on. Let's go. It's getting late," he said. As we walked he told me, "One thing Pop and I usually do is blacken our faces. But we won't do that tonight."

We went into an empty apartment building and up the stairs. On the second floor something ran across my feet. It made me jump. I told Tony.

"Just a rat. These old places are full of them."

Several rats later and three more flights of stairs we reached the roof. I looked up into the sky, loaded with stars. The air was crisp and cold, an early spring night in Michigan. I wasn't cold; I was too scared and excited at the same time to be cold. As a matter of fact, sticky sweat radiated around my neck and underarms.

Tony walked over to the edge and crouched down. I joined him.

"Okay, here's what we're going to do," he began. "We're going to walk along the roofs of these buildings and when there's a separation, we jump to the next one. We repeat this about four or five times before we go back down to the street. Got that?"

"Why do we go across roof tops?"

"Because up here we can't be seen."

I nodded. "I don't know about this jumping between buildings thing."

Tony repeated the nod and asked, "Paul, if I were to lie down flat, could you jump over me from head to foot?"

I shrugged. "Of course I could."

"Well, that's about how far the gap is between the buildings. Just a small alley way."

"Oh, okay that sounds all right," I said like I'd done it a hundred times.

"Now you watch me on the first time to see how far I run before I jump."

I nodded with complete confidence and thought back to Boston when I told myself to go home and didn't. Here we go again.

Tony went about twenty feet from the edge. He started running and jumped before he reached the edge so he would clear the wall that rose up there. He landed well onto the other building.

He turned and waved to me. "Okay, you try," he said.

I gulped down my fear and walked to the point where he started. I took off into a run and jumped. I flew through the air, my eyes stuck on Tony, trying not to notice the void I passed over, and landed. I felt a gasp of excitement, the sudden energy of thrill. This was easy. I'd cleared both walls and landed on the other building with plenty of room to spare.

We followed that pattern three more times before we entered a building to go back down to the street. Much to my surprise people were living in it. We took each floor slowly, twice holding up on the stairway because someone was coming or going.

At the ground floor we went out the back door. Tony told me that our destination was a small grocery store on the corner. We made our way down the side of the apartment building to the back of the store. The door had a padlock the size of my fist. Tony took a steel bar out of his left sleeve. It was about twelve inches long and had one pointed end. He inserted it in the opening of the lock and pushed the bar down fast and hard. The lock snapped right off. We went in.

There was just enough light coming through the windows to allow us to see where we were going.

"Probably won't find any money in here, except small change in the register, but we can take cigarettes and other small items that will fit in our pockets. Don't take anything big because, remember we have to jump those buildings."

"Okay. I gotcha."

We set to work. Tony was right, no money in the till, just a few pennies and nickels, which of course I stuck in my pocket. "What do we want cigarettes for?"

"I'll take them home to Pop."

"Why do you call him Pop?"

"I don't know, always have. Why?"

"Just wondered. I never knew anyone that called their father 'Pop' before."

I stuffed my pockets with cupcakes, bananas and, oh, yes, some candy. What a thrill to think these were mine for nothing.

"Okay," Tony said quietly, interrupting my grabbing spree. "Let's get out of here, we've been in here long enough."

"What do you mean, long enough?"

"Well, if anyone saw us come in, they had enough time to call the cops and the cops had enough time to get here. So you leave before all that happens."

"Your Dad taught you that?"

"Yea. That's why I've never been caught."

We slipped out. Tony put the lock back on and closed it like it was locked.

"Another thing your Dad taught you?" I asked as we scooted down a side alley.

"Yep," Tony replied. "If a cop drives by and shines his flashlight, it still looks locked. Only the owner will know when he opens the store in the morning. And by then, we'll be home sleeping." Clever. I would never have thought of that. But then, I wasn't in the habit of breaking into stores.

"Hey, what you white boys doing here?" a far away voice hollered.

I felt Tony's hands in my back, pushing me forward "Run, Paul," he whispered. "Run like hell. Don't let them catch you!"

We took off down the street towards the hotel. I heard the pit-pat of shoes hitting asphalt behind us. How many were there? Hard to tell. Over ten. The cupcakes and bananas shoved in my pockets fell out like a breadcrumb trail but I was past care. I just wanted out of there.

"Tony, they're gaining on us. We've got to go faster." I passed Tony.

He hollered, "Paul, don't leave me behind!"

"Run faster, Tony. Run!" I kept running and after a short time, I looked back and Tony was gone. Half of the black kids were gone, too.

"Oh, God, no, they got Tony!" My heart raced as fast as my legs carried me. I smelled the salt vinegar of my sweat, covering me in a haze. My mouth was dry. I came to an alley, turned down it. I thought I'd lose them in the dark. I swerved, made my legs go faster. At the end of the alley I found myself pounding fists on a twelve-foot brick wall. There was no way I could get over it. A dead end.

I spun. There they were. A mob, their feet stuttering to a halt not ten feet away. My legs shook; my heart was ready to come out my chest. My breathing was getting faster and I could feel myself sweating so bad my clothes were soaked through. My bladder let go and the warm piss ran down my leg.

The light of a flashlight struck my eyes. Between it and the sweat I was blinded. Interrogation time.

At first they didn't say anything. But I could hear their cumulative breaths, hard and heavy.

One of them said, "I asked you a question back there, White Boy, and you didn't answer. What you doing in my neighborhood? You gonna answer me now — *boy*?"

My tongue was glued to the roof of my mouth. And even if I could get it loose, I probably couldn't say anything, I was shaking so badly.

The voice continued, "Guess the white boy can't talk. Maybe we can help him."

They started shuffling closer, saying things like, "Yea, let's help the poor white boy talk."

"Maybe he don't know English?"

"You right, maybe he a white Russian and don't know no English."

The light was kept tight on my eyes so I couldn't tell how close they'd come or how many there were. I sensed they were just beyond swinging distance.

In one mad epiphany, I thought I could make a mad dash and surprise them. I took a breath and took off for the race of my life, but didn't get very far.

They jumped me. My cheek skidded across asphalt. I felt a fist hit the back of my head and then a kick to the right side of my ribs. It took my breath away. Next, I felt my shirt buttons pop, hands wrestling with my fly and the chill air bite flesh as they pulled my clothes off. As they pulled at my jeans, my bareback was dragged one way, then another across the asphalt. One side of my shirt was pulled out from under me, turning me over like a loaf of bread, and then dragging on my chest in another direction.

One of them said, "We gonna cut you up bad, White Boy. Real bad. Teach you not to come into our neighborhood again. You got that? You understand that you white Russian?"

They dragged, pushed, playing with me like a toy.

I felt the solid pressure of hands holding my shivering flesh to the ground. And yet, my emotions were the essence of stillness. I was an observer, waiting, incapable of changing the trajectory of the moments ahead, except to make them worse.

Another voice suddenly piped up, "Maybe he ain't Russian. Maybe he a Jew boy." A few of them roared with laughter.

Another screamed out, "We can find out if he a Jew boy. Jew boys have the skin on their dicks cut off. And if he don't, well then maybe we make him a Jew boy." Their laughter grew. It echoed in circles around my head. Two hands fumbled at my waist, pulled my underwear off.

In what I thought were my last moments alive, I cried out, "Oh God. Please help me, help me. Let them leave me alone."

My cry must have surprised them, because they stopped.

One of them said, "Hey, the boy can talk English!"

Another said, "We got all his clothes. Let's go before the police get here."

"What? I thought we was gonna carve this white boy up, Jesse?"

"He's all tore up already." The light scanned the length of me. "Look at him. He's blood head to toe."

My underwear hit me in the chest as I heard their footsteps heading away. One of the reluctant ones kicked me in the left side of my ribs as he passed. It took my breath clear away again.

As they went around the corner I heard one of them say, "Oh, Jesse. Man, you done took all the fun away."

I managed to get my underwear on. I lay silent trying to ignore the pain. I looked to my left, right; they'd taken my clothes with them.

I tried to get up several times but every joint and part of my body ached. I had no idea how I was going to get back to the hotel dressed in just underwear. I remembered running past a trash dumpster when I came down the alley. Maybe they'd thrown my stuff in there.

I made my way to it. Just when I was trying to figure out how to get up high enough to look inside, I heard a whisper from around the corner, "Paul? Paul? Are you in there?"

"Yea, yea, it's me!"

Tony came around the corner. He ran up to me. "We got to get out of here before they come back." Then finally, he really looked at me. "What happened to all your clothes?" I didn't have to answer. Without so much as a blink, Tony took his jacket off, draped it over my shoulders and gave me his shoes. He said he had heavy socks so he could walk all right.

"Come on, Paul. We've got to get the hell out of here, fast." I almost found that funny. Fast? I wasn't going nowhere fast.

We made our way along. He explained that he'd gotten away in the alleys. He lost them and hid, but knew they'd caught me. He could hear their laughing, like they'd caught a trophy.

We had to stop several times because it hurt so much to walk. There were splotches of my blood on Tony's cheek, covering his hands.

We came to a streetlight and Tony took a better look. At the sight he became visibly upset.

"Good God Almighty, Paul. They beat the shit out of you. You're all raw skin top to bottom!" He paced in front of me, almost too scared to look. "Them black son-of-bitches," he cried. "Those dirty bastards. I'll kill them. Kill them."

"Tony, forget them. Just get me home. Please?"

Tony stopped pacing. Came over, put an arm around me. "Yea, yea. You're right. We'll go to my place so Pops can fix you up. He's good at that."

We stumbled into the apartment. Tony's Dad was sitting in a chair, reading the paper. He saw me and the pages fluttered to the floor.

"Good God." He crossed the room and did a circle around me. "You look like you've been through a combine!" He motioned us forward. "Bring him into the bathroom, Tony," he said and raced ahead of us.

As we made our way, Tony reassured me, "Pops knows how to fix wounds. He was a medic in the war over in Europe."

Tony's Father made me sit in the bathtub so he could wash me all over with soap and water. The soap made every inch of me burn. He patted me dry with a towel and lay me down on the floor. He went away and, moments later, came back with a powder container.

He looked down at me, said, "This stuff is going to burn when I put it on. But it helps heal the wounds and stops them from getting infected. It's going to hurt bad, so just bite your lip and hang onto Tony. Okay?"

I nodded. He kneeled down beside me and raised the container over my left arm. A powder, like icing sugar, dusted out as he shook. It floated down through the air like light snow but hit my wounds with the pound of a heavy hammer. My body jerked at the shock of it. I wanted to scream but instead, did as he said. The treatment was so painful I would have preferred dying.

He leaned back on his heels when he was done, looked me up and down. He said, "It'll stop hurting after a while, Paul. We'll let the wounds dry a bit and then I'll put bandages on the deeper cuts. It's best to leave the others open to the air, they'll heal faster."

Through watery eyes I nodded. He clicked his tongue and continued, "You got three wounds I think should have a butterfly bandage put on. They're pretty deep." He clicked his tongue again, looked off, stood up and hurried away.

He continued working for three more hours. When he was done he gave me some aspirins and told me to go to bed and sleep as long as I could. Tony put a pair of his pajamas on me. They were way too big, but that's really what I needed for all those cuts and skinned areas.

As we left, I took Tony's Dad's hand and said, "Thanks Pops. Thanks a lot."

He smiled, nodded his head and said, "You're young and healthy. You should heal quick and fine."

Tony put me to bed and said he would take the key so he could lock the door and come up in the morning to check on me. But before he left, he sat down on the edge of the bed. I could tell he was struggling for words. He stared down at his twiddling thumbs and kept sighing. After a moment he looked up and said, "Paul? I'm really very sorry I got you into this mess. I should never have taken you up there… I just wanted to show you how brave I was. But you know what? You turned out to be the brave one."

Getting up on my elbows, I said, "Tony I'm not blaming you for this. I didn't have to go. I'm just glad that you didn't desert me. That you came back and helped me. Now that's bravery."

Tony nodded and sniffled. He hugged me and left the room. I heard the key turn in the lock and his footsteps padding down the hall. His tears surprised only in that I couldn't shed any. It was as though my emotions had been shut off.

I lay back on the bed and closed my eyes.

Next thing I knew, the key was turning in the lock again, waking me. Tony entered backwards, holding a tray of food. I moaned and groaned and everything hurt as I moved for the first time in hours. Even my hair hurt.

After breakfast I took the pajamas off so we could look at me. There wasn't much good skin left.

"Your Dad's right," I said. "It does look like I fell into a combine."

I told Tony what one of the black kids said about cutting the skin off my dick to make me a Jew boy. We both laughed.

"They might not have stopped at the skin!" I said.

"They probably would have taken it home for a trophy," Tony said. We laughed harder.

Tony asked, "Do you think your folks will be back tonight?"

"I don't know. What's this, the third night?"

"Yea."

"Either tonight or tomorrow." That was depressing, in a sense. Their time away had developed a schedule.

Tony gave me two aspirins and said he would be back around suppertime if my folks hadn't returned. I slept all that day and into the early evening, fading in and out of sleep. A key entered the lock, twisted. I sat up. Tony backed in with another tray of food.

"This is the third time I've come up today," he said. "You sure are a sleepy head."

We jumped at the sound of three sharp knocks on the door. Tony and I exchanged glances, looked toward it. Tony crossed the room and opened the door.

His father sent the two of us terse smiles and hurried towards me. "I wanted to check those wounds to see if any of them are getting infected," he said.

I took the pajamas off and we looked me over.

He said, "There's only one I'm concerned about — your left eye. And that's not even from the fight." Fight? Even the fight was no fight. "All this sleep you're getting is the best thing for you right now, Paul." As he headed for the door I told him how much I appreciated what he was doing for me.

Tony's Father stopped at the door and turned. He pursed his lips and bounced his chin. "Your Dad would do the same for Tony, I'm sure," he said. I wasn't about to contradict him. He smiled, disappeared and Tony closed the door again.

"Tony, that supper was really great. Had all the things I really like." There'd been meat loaf, mashed potatoes, corn, green beans and a piece of apple pie. "Did your Dad make all that?"

Tony sat back down on the edge of the bed beside me. "Yep, he's a good cook, and he likes doing it, too."

"Maybe you and him should open up a restaurant. Bet it would be good."

Tony shrugged. "We talked about it, but you got to have money to start. Maybe someday." Tony picked up the tray, said goodnight and left.

I wasn't all that sleepy so I looked at some comic books Tony had brought up. I went to the bathroom and came back and crawled into bed. I hadn't been asleep very long when I was woken up by the sound of a key in the lock. I sat up wondering why Tony was coming back so soon. But it wasn't Tony.

Dad switched on the light. Mother came in behind him, put the bag down and saw me lying there, all scratched up. Her hand went to her mouth and she muffled a scream as she ran across the room. Her hands passed over me, as if they were eyes, afraid to touch me.

Dad looked down his nose from behind her. "What the hell did you tangle with? A mountain lion?"

"Paul, Paul," Mother whispered. "What happened to you? Tell me, tell me what happened? Who did this?" Every inch of her was quivering.

I'd already decided the story I'd use. I told them, "The boy that lives here with his Dad? His name is Tony. Well, he and I was out playing kick the can the other day, and these black kids came along and just started to beat on us. Tony got away but I didn't. And they took all my clothes and that's how I got all torn up from the cement, and they kicked me a couple of times, too."

Mother's arms wrapped around me and she held me hard, rocking back and forth. For the first time since the beating I cried, too. I felt myself open like a dam and the tears poured forth, unstoppable. I didn't want her to let me go.

When I looked up. Dad was leaning back against the wall, looking away, picking at his teeth. Our outpouring made him uncomfortable. He felt my glance, eyed me quickly and looked even further away. As if in answer to my inquiring eyes, he said, "None of my business."

Mother jumped up out of my arms, turned and screamed at him, "None of your business? It certainly is your business." She pointed at me. "Somebody just beat the hell out of your son." Then she pointed at him, stepping towards him. "You sorry ass for a Father, John Miller. Jesus is gonna get you for this. He's gonna get you good. You mark those words, John Miller. And let me tell you something else. You touch this boy again, and I will call the police on you. You hear me, John? You hear me?"

His arms were up in front of his chest like she was sticking him up. "Yea, yea," he said. "Stop raving, old lady. You'll have a hemorrhage."

She stabbed her finger into his chest. "No, you'll be the one that'll hemorrhage if you ever touch this boy again."

Dad sidestepped away from her and mumbled something under his breath as he walked out the door.

I was so proud of Mother at that moment. Finally she'd stood up to him. Boy, I almost thought the beating was worth it, just to see that transformation.

Mother came over to the bed, sat down beside me and wrapped her arms around me again. I grabbed on and held tight.

"Paul," she said. "I'll never leave you alone like that again. Never again. I promise you."

After a big long hug I pulled away from her. I looked up into those eyes I knew so well and asked, "Mother, where did you and Dad go? Why were you gone so long?"

Mother smoothed an unruly lock of my hair. She shook her head, "That's not important right now. The important thing is that you get better."

"No, Mother. It is important. I have to know what it is —"

The door opened and Dad entered. He had a knack for coming in at the wrong time. But I still wanted an answer.

I pulled away from her and looked from one to the other. "I'll ask both of you."

I saw Mother send a wincing look toward Dad. "Now, Paul," she said. "You need to rest."

Dad stopped at the end of the bed. He punched his fists onto his hips and glared at me. "What is it you want to ask there, Paul?" A challenge.

But I was incapable of saying anything. A long silence ensued. Dad said louder, "What is it Paul? What do you want to know?"

I looked to Mother. She shook her head just the slightest bit. I bit my lip. "Oh, nothing. Nothing important."

Dad huffed and smiled. "Well then, if you two have nothing to say I guess it's time to get to bed. Paul, I'd suggest you get down on the floor there so I can go to sleep."

Mother flew at him again, stabbing her finger into his chest. "Paul is not getting out of that bed, and neither am I. You're the one that's going to sleep on the floor. That child is not going to lie on that cold hard floor in the condition he's in! You understand that, John Miller?"

Dad was taken aback. He tried to laugh like her fury didn't bother him. He sneered, "Sure. I'll sleep on the damn floor. Give you and your little baby the bed."

Dad tried to act like his pride wasn't battered. Getting ready for bed on the floor like it was a perfectly natural thing for him to do, spreading his coat out over his feet. Just before lying back, he looked over at the two of us. "By the way," he said. "You better get a good nights sleep. Because we're leaving here tomorrow."

Mother sat up in bed and glared at him. "Oh no, we're not. We're not going anywhere until this child is better."

Dad looked down at his feet, fuming. He said, "Oh, shut up Mary and go to sleep." He lay down on the floor and turned away from us, onto his side. I could hear him muttering and mumbling to himself.

Mother turned out the light and let me cuddle up next to her. I fell into the flannel smell of her, intoxicated by its warmth. She giggled and rubbed at my hair. Her whisper caressed my ear, "Serves him right."

9.

A TIME FOR HEALING

The next nine days was a roller coaster ride of arguments and profound silences against the brown backdrop of our dumpy hotel room.

To pass the time Dad would go to a bar, come back drunk primed to argue. It would always start with his manic pacing. Back and forth in front of the bed. Back and forth in front of the window. A haze of anger roiling about him like a dust cloud.

Through gritted teeth he'd seethe, pointing his finger at Mother, "I want you to order Kitty to go to Church every Sunday. She only listens to you. She can spend three hours at a movie show," Dad railed on, "but doesn't allow one hour a week for her faith? Her soul is at stake. Eternal damnation. She must attend confession."

Mother countered, "Oh come on. You're so strict with everybody else and look what you do yourself. Coming in here drunk every night. I honestly don't understand it, John."

He'd pound the wall and turn to us. "Drinking does not go against the teachings...."

"It does if you spend all our money, John Miller."

The worst was when it turned to tit-for-tat, the two of them one-upping each other the way children do. You do this. You do that. You don't do this. You don't do that. I'm gonna... gonna... gonna....

When arguments reached a peak, the two of them would stop, turn to me and say, "We're going for a walk," and quietly step out the door. I'd watch them from the window as they traced a line back and forth in front of the hotel. Dad doing the talking as Mother's head skirted from side to side. A few times she'd stop, throw her hands up, turn toward Dad and start lashing out at him with everything she had.

* * *

On the tenth day we checked out and grabbed a cab. Much to my surprise our cab didn't stop in front of a train or bus station. Rather, it stopped in front of a pretty, yellow house with window boxes just sprouting red spring flowers. The front door swung open and a familiar face appeared, ghost-like on the other side of the screen. My gangly sister Sarah pushed through the screen door. She ran down the steps to meet us, her face pruned by sheer intensity. Her skirt looked brand new, her bobby socks were too neatly folded above saddle shoes and her hair bounced neat under the restraint of unadorned barrettes.

"There you are," she exclaimed, pulling the car door open for us. "We were waiting for you forever. You said one o'clock. Gerry had to go to her hair appointment."

I watched with amazement, questions buzzing like ants over a picnic, as they pulled our bags out of the trunk and Dad paid the driver. I knew Sarah was boarding with a woman, Gerry Blanche, while she finished her senior year in High School. I guessed we were staying here for a while. But I didn't know how these arrangements were made. Sarah had never come to the hotel. Last I'd heard, our presence in Detroit was a secret.

Sarah led us into the house and stopped in the foyer. I peeked into the living room. There was a blue couch like one I thought Queen Victoria might have, wingback chairs and a Persian rug. A bowl of fruit tempted me from the dining room table, through an archway. I felt like I'd arrived home.

Sarah stood in the foyer, rattling on to Mother and Father in that whiny way of hers with her fingers flying through the air. She told us all about the thinking her and Gerry had done about where they were going to put us. The basement reeked of mold and wasn't heated. The back room had sewing bits and pieces stuffing it to overflowing. The attic room was too hot.

She led them into a room with one small double bed and when I tried to follow them she glared at me and said I was sleeping somewhere else.

I sat in the hall waiting as Sarah showed my parents around the bedroom that had been prepared for them. The bed was fresh-made and towels laid out. The conversation turned to school, and Sarah sat on the bed and rattled on about this teacher she didn't like.

"Can you believe he'd do that to me?" she whined.

When she was done she told Mother and Dad that she'd let them get settled and breezed right past me calling out how she'd get some tea on.

"Sarah?" I called.

She stopped, and looked down. "What?"

"What about me?"

Sarah stopped, just for a breath, as if changing direction. Then she rushed up, her hands reaching up to undo her hair barrette. She stroked at her silvery blonde hair, like spun sugar. She carefully clipped it back together. When she arrived in front of me, she said, "Now, listen to me, Paul. I don't want you to upset Gerry. Okay? You are guests here. So please, be on your best behavior. Do you understand that?"

I wanted to swat her. My sister, acting like my mother. How dare she?

I asked, "Where am I staying?"

She harrumphed and waved her hand up in the air. "The attic room," she said dismissively and proceeded to lope down the hall, yelling as she went "You behave, Paul."

We were sitting at the dining room table when the front door opened. An older woman in a smart dress suit entered and rushed across the room toward us. She was older, but there was a youthful vigor to her movements. An eagerness sparkling from the eyes, as though she rejected the humdrum. Whatever the moment, she'd make it into something spectacular and, most of all, fun.

A welcoming smile in her voice, she said, "Well, I'm so glad to see you've gotten yourselves comfortable. Do you need anything?" My parents said they didn't. She turned to me. "I'm happy to have you here, Paul. I got an apple tree out back that's perfect for climbing. And from what I hear, you're a good climber." I fell in love with her right that minute.

We stayed with Gerry for eight, wonderful weeks. It was so good to stay somewhere that felt like home. In lieu of rent, Mother kept the house, cooked, washed and ironed clothes. Dad performed maintenance work, including painting the woodwork around all the windows. It was late in the year so I wasn't put into school. It was boring being by myself all the time, having nothing to do. I did meet two brothers who lived four houses down. We played some baseball and talked, but never really became good friends like me and Billy or me and Tony.

Gerry worked at a department store. She was such a generous lady with a great sense of humor. Over dinner we'd talk about our day. Sometimes she'd get so excited telling us a story, she'd stand up and act out the temper displays of her irate customer, going through all the antics. She'd mimic a

customer fingering some fabric, "You call this quality? I call it garbage."
She'd come back with, "I don't know, sir. I'd call it a sweater," and all of us
would laugh.

* * *

Dad looked up from his dinner with a self-satisfied smile. He said, "Paul,
Mary. I've decided we're moving to California next week."

Mother got up and ran to the bathroom. I looked over at Dad. He wore
a smug grin as he watched her go. When she was upstairs he sniggered as
though he'd pulled a fast one on her and won. He dove back into his dinner
with such gusto you'd think he'd won a prize.

Gerry and Sarah looked down at their plates, willing their absence. This
wasn't their affair.

"Why, Dad?" I asked. "Why do we have to move to California?"

Dad was digging into his chicken by the time I asked. Between mouthfuls
he said, "Because that part of the country is growing fast."

"But —"

"This isn't our home, Paul. We can't stay here."

"Can't we buy a home here, in Michigan? Get an apartment?"

Dad threw his fork onto his plate, but wouldn't look up. "No. We're
moving to California, and that's that!"

I pushed away from the table, making the chair legs squawk across the
hardwood floor. I ran through the kitchen, out the back door and fell onto
the grass under the tree.

Noah was up there, sitting on a branch. He leaned forward, resting his
elbows on his knees. He cocked his head, as if in question.

"Why?" I asked him. He shook his head, but didn't answer.

I continued talking to him. Here we were, moving again. Would it ever
end? And why were we moving? Our family was here.

The door opened and Mother appeared. She made her way across the
lawn with measured steps, head bowed. She sat on the grass next to me. We
sat, silent.

At length, I turned to her, asked, "Did you know about this before?"

She shook her head. "I did know it wouldn't be long before he decided it
was time to move on. But I didn't know when."

"I don't understand. Why do we have to move away? Do you want to
move, Mother?

"No, of course not." I'll bet she didn't, with her daughters and two grandchildren here in Michigan.

"Well, then, let's tell him we won't go."

Mother shook her head sadly. "I'm afraid we can't do that Paul."

"Why not? Doesn't majority rule? Two of us don't want to move, so we don't move. Right?"

"I'm afraid it doesn't work quite like that. Your father is the man of the house. We must follow him, do as he says."

"Mother, that was back in King Arthur's days. This is 1948. People don't think that way anymore. What we want should matter for something."

Mother's words came out stiffly, as if she was trying to convince herself. "Paul," she began, "when I married your father, I promised to obey him. That's the teachings of the Church. I intend to honor those teachings and my oath. That is my duty."

"But Mom, all I'm…."

She looked at me, sitting up taller, an unhappy decision marking her face. She said, "I'm sorry, Paul. That's the way it has to be." She tried to smile. She touched the back of my neck. I pulled away from her with a shake. She got up and walked across the yard, disappearing into the house. I admired her faith, but couldn't understand why we had to be made so unhappy because he wanted it that way.

Dad enjoyed making us unhappy. That was becoming clear. But what an absurd idea. How do you enjoy someone's pain? Sometimes I thought that maybe I was just too young to understand. But most of the time, I knew I was a human toy even if I refused to accept it.

Noah was looking toward the house. I said to him, "Noah, I know you told me that parents do things that children sometimes can't understand. But for the life of me, Noah, I can't believe my Father's decision to move to California. Me and Mother don't want to go, and the rest of the family doesn't want us to go. Its just Dad. Please, my head is about to explode, help me figure this out."

Noah leaned out from behind the leaves, looked toward the house, but all he'd say was "Ya Mama won't let nuttin bad happen. Ya gotta trust. She loves ya very much. As long as ya with her, ya be all right."

We spent the next few days saying goodbye and finishing up projects around Gerry's house. Mother carried her rosary wherever she went. A few times I came across her sitting on the living room couch, the dust cloth on the coffee table, a solitary bead being twisted between two fingers as she mouthed words, lost in prayer. Was she praying for strength or insight? I didn't know.

The house was somber the morning of our departure. No one spoke over breakfast. When we gathered by the front door, our suitcases standing at attention by our feet, that's when the crying started. First Mother hugged Sarah and both of them started to cry. Then Gerry hugged me and she started to cry. Then I felt the tears. I turned to wipe them away and noticed my father. He had this blank look on his face like nothing was out of the ordinary. He couldn't understand why we were so upset.

Mother cried all the way to the train station. Dad and I were silent. I was preparing myself for another long train ride. If it took us five days from Florida, I figured it was going to take twelve, maybe fifteen days to California.

Here we went again.

10.

CALIFORNIA, HERE WE COME

Our train was part of the Union Pacific Line. Its cars had a sleek design, with silver aerodynamic lines that made it look like it could speed along like lightning. It even had one of those dome cars with windows all around where you could sit high up watching the landscape whiz by.

The conductor came down the aisle asking for tickets. When he got beside our seats, he leaned down to my level, studied me with eyes like an old dog's and asked, "Hey, little boy, is this your first train ride?"

"Yes, sir. First time," I replied. I don't know why. It just came out. It startled even me.

The conductor smiled back, nodded his head and said, "Well, you enjoy the ride and if there is anything you want to know, just ask."

"Why, thank you, sir," I replied. "I have one question already."

The conductor smiled and leaned down closer to hear. "Well, let's hear it."

I jumped up in my seat, excited. "Can I go between the cars and open the top of that half door while we're moving?"

The conductor clicked his tongue with a shake of his head. He said, "You're not suppose to. But I guess you can once in a while. Just don't hang out too far." He did a gentle karate chop to my neck. "Don't want that little head of yours getting chopped off."

"Oh, no, sir. I won't lean out too far. Thank you very much."

The conductor nodded his head, tipped his hat to Mother and went to the next seat.

I looked over to my parents. Mother was staring at me with surprise and Dad had a stern, quizzical expression.

"You're getting to be a pretty good liar," Dad began. He launched into a lecture. Lying was a sin. God would strike you down for telling false stories.

"Dad," I interrupted him. "When you're standing in a dark alley at twelve o'clock at night, and the biggest, ugliest, roughest looking woman you've ever seen with four huge men behind her, walks up to you, snaps a black belt right in your face and asks you a question, you'd better find out real fast what she wants to hear. And, if you don't answer her right, you can be in big, big trouble. Or if a gang of boys asks why you're in their territory, you better answer them. Lie, tell them stories, give them your watch, or whatever you have to do, so you don't get the crap beat out of you or... well... something worse. Yes, I'm a liar, a storyteller. Whatever I have to do to survive or get what I want. But I'm not hurting nobody. And that's where I draw the line."

Dad stared at me for a moment as if trying to decide how to react. Without a word he stood and left the car.

I checked Mother. She was still staring at me; lips parted slightly.

I took a deep breath, leaned forward with my elbows on my knees. I looked at the floor of the train, trying to decide how to put what I had to say. Then I looked up, put a gentle hand on her knee and said, "Mother I'm sorry you had to hear that. But you know how I'm feeling? I'm feeling, he has no right to tell me about what God will do if I lie or tell stories. Not when he goes around treating us the way he does. I'm sure God doesn't like that very much. I'd think God would punish someone for mistreating people more than for telling a lie."

Mother pushed back against her chair, shaking her head. I leaned forward even more, looking up into her taut face. "Mother, are you all right?" I asked.

After a moment she wiped her eyes, took a long drink of her soda. She set the soda down, sighed and said, "Paul, how do you know about things like that?"

I shrugged a shoulder, like it was nothing. "Just stuff I learned from people I met on the street."

Mother looked out the window and shook her head. "Paul, you scare me. You seem to know too much for a nine and a half year old boy." She seemed so detached, so far away.

"Mom, are you okay?"

She caught her breath. "Yes, I'm all right. But, lately Paul," she looked me in the eye, "I don't think I really know you. You're a different person."

It was my turn to look out the window. "When you get left alone and have to do things for yourself, I think it makes you think and act differently." I sent her a quizzical look. "What do you think I do when you go away for days at a time? Sit in the hotel room by myself, staring at the wallpaper? I've done a lot of thinking, Mother. I don't think God likes it when a father knocks his kid around every time he says something."

"Paul, your father has his reasons. Someday he'll tell you. But please don't hate him — don't push him aside."

"Mom, I can't take this getting beat up all the time."

"I know, I'll have a talk with him. And Paul, I meant what I said about not leaving you alone anymore."

I nodded but didn't say anything.

* * *

The scenery from the dome car was fan-tas-tic. The sun made the mountains look different with each angle change of the passing day. I'd never realized rocks had so many colors. I'd always thought of a desert as nothing but sand, but the desert we passed through was filled with plants and flowers of all descriptions. I spotted rabbits or small dogs, which Mother told me were foxes. At night the heavens transformed into one giant Christmas tree of lights from horizon to horizon. They made me think of Noah.

If Noah had been along, he would have looked out at those majestic mountains and said, "Paul, why dus ya think God made all doz big mountains? Duz ya think He dun made them for the peoples to ski down, or duz ya thinks to catch the snow fall, or for all da birds and animals to hunt and live on, or duz ya thinks He made them for all da people to looks at and drink in their beauty?"

And I'd reply, "Well, I don't really know Noah, but I'd guess God made them for all those things."

And Noah would slap the armrest of his chair and say, "Ayyy, ya thinks right boy. He done made doz mountains, da waters, da forest, da desert, all dos things for all dos reasons. Da ya know what, Paul, He done did one upright fine standing job."

I just loved to hear Noah talk.

We arrived in California on the morning of the seventh day. The sun was shining bright and hot on row after row of orange and lemon trees as far as the eye could see. For hour after hour that's all there'd be. It looked like a farmer's dreamland. I assumed that was why we were here.

We pulled into Los Angeles in the early evening. It looked so different from Michigan, Illinois or New York. It was like Florida. Fresh, clean, new.

So many colors and stucco houses. There weren't any old buildings like in Detroit or Boston. I noticed that there weren't many tall buildings either. So I asked Dad why.

He said, "California has earthquakes now and then, just like Michigan has tornadoes. Just something you have to learn to live with." I didn't like the sound of that. But he had answered my question without getting angry. That was progress.

"Dad, can we go to Hollywood and watch them make movie pictures?"

"You can't just go there," he said. "You have to get a pass to go into the studio."

"Well, can we get a pass?"

"I don't know how to do it. I'll have to find out."

I was amazed. This was first time I'd ever heard Dad say he didn't know something. I was beginning to think that Mom's discussion with him had worked. That finally, we were becoming something like a real family.

Our cab pulled up in front of the McArthur Park Hotel. A polished Bellhop took us up to our room on the fourth floor with a park view.

The next morning, Mother and Dad said they were going to try and find a house for us to rent. They wanted me to stay at the hotel.

Mother said, "We'll only be gone for the day, Paul. We'll be back by dark. I promise you that."

After they left I got dressed and headed for the park.

The park had a lake full of ducks, geese, swans and lots of pigeons. You could rent boats and row around in the lake. A sidewalk ran all the way around the perimeter. There were even picnic tables. I thought it was great. Detroit didn't have anything like it.

I bought some peanuts and fed the animals, but once you started that, they were all around you. I wanted to rent a boat and row out on the lake but didn't have enough money. I decided to ask Dad if I could do it tomorrow. Maybe we could go together.

I was sitting on a bench about midway on the lake when a group of ten kids, seventeen or eighteen, came towards me. Something about the way they dressed made me feel uneasy. Each wore a uniform of black pants, leather jackets, boots with long chains hanging from their belts that swung down to their knees ending in their pockets. Before they got too close I headed away.

One of them hollered, "Hey kid, wait a minute."

I wasn't sticking around to find out what they wanted. I took off running.

Another voice hollered after me, "We ain't gonna hurt you. Don't run."

My legs automatically went faster and faster. I was not gonna get caught again. I was not gonna get beat up again. I was not.

. From across the lake I could hear someone holler, "What you white boys chasing? A scared little rabbit?"

I stopped to look. Across the lake was a group of black kids. They too were dressed in a kind of uniform with white tee shirts and bright scarves wrapped about their heads. Some carried billy sticks.

"What business is it of yours what we chase?" screamed a white kid.

The black boys called, "No business of ours what you chase. But you white boys think you are big and tough when you run down a little white boy all by himself. See we don't do that with our kind. We help and protect our kind. We don't eat them, like you do." The black gang roared with taunting laughter.

One of the white kids screamed back, "We wasn't going to eat him. We were waiting for you black boys to get here so you could come over and eat us." Then the white kids laughed and slapped at each other.

The black boys replied, "We would, but you white boys don't have anything to eat but a little wiener and that just ain't very filling!" Then the black kids laughed again, beating each other around.

The white boys called back, "We'll come over and get yours, because we can use them at our baseball games for bats."

Now both sides were screaming, laughing and pushing each other around.

Their laughs were interrupted by the sound of a whistle. Cops appeared from every direction and the gangs took off running. And me, I ran for the hotel as fast as I could.

Mother and Dad arrived back with some supper for me. They'd been to a couple of towns but hadn't found anything. I felt a part of the information loop, even if the news wasn't good. Mother admitted they'd have to try out the other direction.

The next morning, after breakfast, Mother pulled out a bag, opened it on the bed and placed her white, folded nighty into it. A cold swelling crept through me.

"Why are you packing a bag?" I asked.

She stopped, looked up at me and sighed. She turned and sat next to me on the bed. "Where we have to go, it's far away, Paul. Dad and I think we might have to stay over night. The day trip might not be enough time for us to find a place."

The swelling was a choking mass in my chest. "But you promised."

"Yes, I know, Paul. But…" I was listening so hard I couldn't hear what she said, but she finished with "…I'm sure you'll be all right."

"Why can't I go with you?"

Dad came out of the bathroom tucking in his shirt. "What's the matter, baby. Afraid to be alone?" he said. He put his hands on his hips and continued, "If the big boys come after you again, just run a little faster or learn how to stand and fight."

"John, stop talking to Paul like that."

I looked from Mother to Dad and back again. They didn't know, didn't care, and didn't realize how much this meant to me.

Dad tried to reassure me. "Hey kid," he began, "we'll only be gone one night. Just stay out of trouble, stay in the room, and like your Mother says, don't go any further than the park."

But a black pall had taken over the room. My parents were leaving me alone again.

"Why can't I go with you?" I said, hating the rattle of baby cry in it.

Dad replied, "You can't! We cover ground faster without you and I don't have to pay your bus fare." He turned to the chair and scooped up his jacket. With another thought, he added, "And I don't have to listen to your stupid questions."

The acid of the word burst. He had no bloody right to call me stupid. We looked at one another from across the room. He was a heartless, terrified thing, peeling away at me the way one does a banana, until there's nothing left. I refused to allow that to be done to me.

Through gritted teeth, I said, "My questions aren't stupid, Stupid."

He gave me a wide-eyed glare; his nostrils flaring like a horse's. He ran towards me. His right hand pulled into a tight fist, raised above his shoulder, aiming directly at my nose. I refused to flinch. To take it. Tony's suggestion made me aware of the chair just to my right. My fist widened to grasp at it.

Mother jumped to her feet, screamed, "John, don't you dare!"

Dad's fist stopped a foot from my face. His lip curled and he seemed to growl at me. He brought his arm down. His fist changed to a wagging finger. "That's why I don't want you to come along." He reached in his pocket and threw two dollars on the dresser. "Here. Don't buy anything you might choke on." He had on that grin that said he thought he'd been funny. He started for the door. "Come on, Mary. Let's go before I lose my temper again."

Mother bent down, kissed me on the cheek. Quietly, "I'm sorry, Paul. But this is the way it has to be." They walked out the door and I fell back onto the bed.

The air of this room that had seemed so bright and cheery just the day before had lost its luster. I lay there for a long time pondering the questions crowding my thoughts.

Could I run away? It was tempting, only because on my own there could be certainty. No raised hopes that are dashed moments later. Or, so I thought. Most of all, I yearned for Noah's presence, for his calming words. I tried to conjure him, but it was as though I couldn't find him. As though he'd never been there, and that thought was the worst of all.

Mid-afternoon I went to the park and bought a hot dog. I sat on a bench to eat and had to keep chasing the dang pigeons away. I noticed a boy roaming around the lake, throwing stones at the ducks and swans. He was clean looking with dark hair, about my age. He had an easy, aimless quality and a curious eye. He spotted me, smiled and came towards me.

He sat next to me on the bench, looked around, tossed a crumb of bread from his hand down at the birds.

"Hi," he said. He introduced himself as Mike Ford and shook my hand, but the grip was leery.

"You live around here?" I asked.

"Yea. I've been in that hotel over there for three months now." He pointed at the hotel where we were staying. "I hate it," he added.

"Three months? How come so long?"

"My Dad's in the Navy, he's at sea. Mom's trying to get into the movie business."

"Can't you live in a house instead of a hotel?"

"The manager is my Mom's cousin. He gives us a good rate." Then he eyed me. "What about you? You and your folks just got here a couple of days ago."

I jumped in surprise, "How'd you know that?"

Mike shrugged. "Told you, the manager is my Mom's cousin. I know who comes and goes in this dump."

"I thought it was a pretty nice hotel."

Mike sighed and said, "When you've stayed here as long as I have, it's a dump!"

His Mom worked nights at a restaurant downtown. After she went to work, he usually came to the park for a while, but he didn't stay too long. The 'big boys' came out in the afternoon and took it over. I told him that I'd found that out.

"Did they get you?" he asked.

"No, I ran away."

"You're lucky they didn't. The white boys would beat the hell out of you, take all your clothes, money and leave you out here naked. The black boys, they'd have done the same except they would have raped you, too."

"Raped me?" I asked.

His eyes became curious slits. "You don't know what rape is, do you?"

I squirmed on the bench. "Well, yea, kinda, I think..."

Mike shook his head. "Don't feel bad. I didn't know what it meant either until I came down here. I met a kid that was staying in the hotel at the time, and he and I got to be friends. He told me he watched ten black boys rape two white boys across the lake." Mike pointed to a wooded area. "Two black boys would hold them, while one stuck his pecker in the white boy's asshole. Those white boys were screaming their heads off something awful."

The image sickened me.

Mike continued, "Jimmy — that's my friend — he said the two white kids were plain out of their minds when the cops found them. He didn't know what happened to them. Never saw them around here again."

I asked him, "Did you ever get caught by them? White or black?"

"No, Jimmy helped me out there."

We talked for quite a while. I told him about what I'd been through over the past few months. I found it hard to believe how long and how short a time it had been. I'd been nowhere and everywhere. A limbo world that didn't seem to have an end. He listened with rapt interest to my tale of scaling the library in Boston. There was envy in his smirk as I told him about learning the basics of thievery in downtown Detroit.

He was from Iowa and wasn't sure whether he liked California or not. He missed the snow and friends. Sometimes he wished his family would move back there. I understood the sentiment exactly.

The sun tilted toward afternoon. Mike said it was time to get going.

"Would you like to come to my place and have something to eat?" he asked.

Their hotel room was like an apartment with a small kitchen, living room and two bedrooms. Mike heated up some of his mother's homemade soup, spread peanut butter across bread and poured two glasses of milk.

When he was done eating, Mike pushed his bowl aside and leaned forward on his elbows. He asked, "What do you want to do tonight? Your folks aren't coming back, so we can stay out late."

"What do you want to do?"

At the question he fidgeted with his spoon in the bowl and didn't look at me. I waited for an answer, but nothing came.

"Mike, what do you want to do?"

Mike started to clear the table, putting our bowls in the sink. He turned to me and just stood there, looking at the floor. Either he didn't want to tell me or didn't know how.

"You don't have to tell me, Mike. I can think of something for us to do."

He looked up. "Yea, like what?"

I shrugged. "Well… like you know, go downtown and watch all those weird people. Or, how about we sneak into a movie?"

His voice full of sarcasm, he said, "Oh yea, that sounds like real fun!"

He waved for me to follow. We went into his bedroom. He opened the closet door and struggled to pull out a suitcase from the back. He lay it down on the floor and unhooked the clasps, but then hesitated, looked up at me and said, "You got to promise me you will not tell anyone, and I mean anyone, what I'm about to show you."

Curiosity was proving a strong force. "I promise you, Mike. I'll never tell a soul, so help me God."

Satisfied, he unlatched the clamps, untied the strap and threw open the top with a flourish.

The suitcase was like a pirates treasure chest, overflowing with money, guns, pieces of silver, rings, jewelry of all kinds, wallets, purses, hunting knives, fancy leather gloves….

Mike stood up and stepped away from it. He wore an admiring smirk, the glitter of the treasure reflecting in his eyes.

"Mike, where in the world did you get all this?" I asked.

"Remember when we were at the park talking, and you told me about that boy and his Father, how they robbed stores and stuff?" I told him I did. "When you were telling me that, I knew I could trust you and I thought that maybe you and I could team up."

"This stuff didn't come from stores?"

"No, it came from people's homes. That's what I do. Late at night I go around neighborhoods, find empty houses, break into them and steal stuff. Nothing real big. Nothing I can't put into my pockets and sell later. I don't take people's pictures or stuff that might have sentimental value."

I pointed out some of the objects in the case. "What about a ring or a necklace, or even this gun. It could be special."

Mike looked aside with a grimace. He shook his head. "I don't look at that stuff in that way. If it is, well, then I'm sorry, I didn't know it."

He sold his stuff to his mother's cousin, who sold it to other people for more money. So they both made money on it.

Mike stood up and crossed his arms, eyeing me. "So, what do you think? Want to go with me?"

"No, I don't think so, Mike. Last time I almost got killed."

"You don't have to do anything the first time, if you don't want to. Just come along and watch me."

I smiled. "Yea, that's what Tony said when we were heading out."

"Paul, you strike me as a guy who likes to try adventurous things."

I had to agree with him. "But I've also learned that if I get too close to the fire, I get burned."

Mike sighed. "Paul, I've been doing this for two months now, and I haven't even come close to being caught."

"Yea, I heard that before, too!"

Mike looked disappointed. "I'm not going to force you. But if you do, and we do get caught, I'll tell them you had no idea what we were doing."

Our eyes caught. Mike smirked. I laughed. Mike laughed. We laughed harder. We were going to do this.

Mike slapped me on the back and said, "Now, I want you to go upstairs and....."

"Yea, I know. Get a dark shirt on!"

* * *

The similarities between Mike and Tony's methods were spooky. We exited the hotel through a service door so no one would see us. As we made our way down the street, he explained how he never hit the same neighborhood twice. We'd walk about a mile into an area and pick out a house. We walked straight for a few blocks, then turned right for a couple of blocks, then left, then right.

"How do you remember how to get back if you keep walking like this?"

"You have to keep track of your path and don't take the same way back. If anyone saw you going, at least they won't see you returning. That way, the cops can't put you at the crime scene at a certain time."

"Boy, you got everything worked out to the T, don't you?" We laughed and picked up our pace.

We spotted a house that was dark with the porch light on, no car in the driveway or in front. We walked around the corner and up the alley at the back.

Mike nodded his head. "No dog, no lights, looks like a good choice. Now just follow me, and be quiet!"

We crouched down low to keep in the shadows and walked up on the porch to the back door. Mike tried the door and it was locked. He pulled out a long screwdriver and shoved it between the door latch and the jamb. He jerked the screwdriver hard against the jamb and the door popped open. We waited a few seconds to see if anyone heard us or was coming. It was quiet, except for my heart which I thought could be heard on the next block.

The door led into the kitchen that smelled of cooked cabbage.

Mike looked at me. "I thought you were going to wait outside?"

I was taken aback. "I guess I forgot." He smiled, turned and headed down the hall. I followed.

We went through the kitchen into the dining room. We surveyed the living room, went through the two bedrooms. All we came up with was some change on the kitchen counter and some jewelry.

"Let's go," Mike said. "There's nothing here. Couple of old people with nothing."

I asked him how he knew they were old.

"Smell the cooked food, look at the stuff in the bathroom, the pictures hanging on walls. They're all of young people. Young people have pictures of old people, old people have pictures of young people."

We got out to the alley and went in the opposite direction. We walked down two blocks of alleys and saw another house that looked empty.

We followed the same procedure and found less than the first. On the way back, Mike asked me what kind of people lived in the second house.

"I think they were old, too." I had seen the pictures, the dishes, and the clothes in the bedroom. Mike agreed with me.

"Were you scared?" he asked.

"Yep, scared to death, especially coming out. Kept thinking the cops were going to shine a bright light on us or neighborhood kids would be waiting in the bushes." We laughed, and Mike said I was still thinking of Detroit. He was right. So why, I wondered, was I doing this again?

We got into Mike's room and dumped out what little loot we had. Mike laughed and said I was bad luck, smallest amount he ever came back with. The money from the first house added up to sixty-seven cents, some jewelry Mike said was cheap, and a few pieces of silver.

"About twenty bucks total," Mike said.

"Wasn't worth the trip or the risk of getting caught," I said.

Mike mentioned how you always hear about these old people and how they have money stuffed in a jar or in their mattress. I pointed out that we could search better next time. We agreed it would work well if one of us looked for stuff like we did tonight and another looked in jars and behind dressers and places like that. That way we'd spend the same amount of time, but look in different places.

"Paul," Mike said, grasping my arm, "you're a born robber."

The title didn't sit comfortably. As if in reaction, all the excitement caught up with me and I was suddenly exhausted. Mike asked if I wanted the money. I told him I could use it, so he gave it to me.

As I was washing up for bed, I looked at myself in the mirror and saw something I didn't like. "Oh Noah," I said to my reflection, "Now I really am heading down a bad road."

The next morning the shame and guilt had vanished, but I found myself hoping for Mother and Dad's return so I wouldn't have to do it again. I regretted opening up my big mouth, getting him stirred up.

I went down to the park and got a hot dog and a drink and went to what was turning out to be my favorite spot. I sat down, bit into my dog, enjoying its salty smooth chew, and thought about the sixty-seven cents from the night before. I pulled it out of my pocket and one by one threw all sixty-seven cents into the lake as I asked for forgiveness. I stole the money, but I didn't use it for myself, so I felt that would help.

I gazed out on the lake and saw Noah lying back in a boat, his hat down over his eyes, with the line of his jiggy pole in the water and the other end held firm between his legs at the knees. He tipped his hat a little, looked over at me, and said, "I guess dis is one of doz times dat a 'yea but' comes in ta play. Is dat right, Paul?"

Oh, man, I wanted to hide behind a tree.

Mike came bouncing down the walkway toward me. He sat down beside me. "Hey partner, how ya doing?"

He slapped me on the back and laughed.

"Pretty good," I said without much enthusiasm.

Mike rubbed his hands together enthusiastically. "Tonight we'll go out and do what we talked about. Maybe find a bundle."

I couldn't look at him as I said, "My folks are supposed to be back today. If they are, I won't be able to."

Mike slumped down. "Oh damn. I forgot about your parents."

Mother and Dad did come back that day. They told me that they'd rented a little house in Pomona. That we'd be leaving first thing in the morning.

Mike was upset when I told him. But he knew there was nothing we could do about it.

We said our good-byes and I had to promise him again that I wouldn't tell a soul about his suitcase. I told him to be careful — not to get too cocky, because that's when you get caught or worse.

He looked at me and said, "You mean that, don't you?"

"Yes, Mike, I sure do. You be very careful."

11.

DON'T LEAVE ME

I distinctly remember the polished radiance of the town of Pomona that first moment when I stepped off the bus.

What created this seeming incandescence, I don't know. Perhaps it was those rays of sun, wide-open and endless chasms of light that turned the whole world a few shades brighter than you think it possibly can be. The lawns weren't just plain old green. They were expanses of faceted emerald. In fact, all the colors were much more than mere colors in that place. Each color was an event. A blue was deeper than the sky. The house down the street was painted a yellow that shimmered a welcome smile. The red of a passing car sizzled and hissed. What a wonderful, vibrant place.

In truth, I think the reason I saw this brilliance was because, as my Mother told me, this small town, just fifty miles east of Los Angeles, was where my parents had bought a brand new house, a home, for our whittled down family of three.

Across the street from the bus station was The Fox Theater. On its marquee the words, "Opening Soon." Oh, what marvels of Hollywood I saw myself enjoying with my parents and with the friends I was going to make.

I followed my parents down a small suburban street not daring to ask which house was ours. They marched ahead of me, up the path to a white stucco box with a red door and black shutters. It sat as if bare naked, not a plant to frame it, on a square of fresh-sown sod, rows still marked by brown scratch lines down the length of the property where the carpet pieces met up. Dad put the key into the lock and I pushed around him, rushing through the door, leaving my suitcase on the pathway behind me.

My shoes slid across the floor as I looked around the bare rooms. So many smells. The plastic of fresh linoleum, paint drying, windows recently wiped with vinegar. This was ours. The walls were white. There were black

and white tiled floors. It was wonderful. I ran down the main rooms' length
and looked out the window into the yard.

I turned to my parents. "Can we plant a tree out there?" I asked.

Mother smiled at me, rocked back and forth on her heels. "Of course we
can, Paul."

Dad was smiling, too.

I poked my head into the kitchen. It was small, but I could already see
Mother standing before the stove wearing her apron, shooing me away from
cookies. I slid back towards the front door and ran into the first bedroom.

"That's your room, Paul," Dad said.

Something in the sound of his voice stopped me, my former exuberance
echoing like a drum, fading to nothing. I looked up, saw him watching me.
There was caring in that gaze. He couldn't show he was happy, but I could
tell he was. We didn't have any furniture yet, but we were all home.

Home!

* * *

That couldn't be a school, could it? Four tin-gray Quonset huts, like
halved cigars, were arranged in a circle with a grass courtyard in the middle.
More like some otherworldly, space-alien command post to me. Certainly not
like any school I'd ever seen.

With the principal's hand warm on my back I was escorted to my new
classroom. I'd missed so much the year before I had to start fifth grade over
again, one of the many left over symptoms from the crummy year I'd had.

I was pushed forward to stand before the assembly of tanned Californian
students. There was something strange about them. Like they were too perfect-
looking or something. My new teacher, Mrs. Camp, introduced me to the
class. "Everyone," she sang, clapping her hands, "welcome our new student,
Paul, to Westmont."

The class replied, in chorus, as if they'd rehearsed it many times, "Welcome
to Westmont, Paul." I flushed.

Mrs. Camp indicated the last desk in a row. I made my way there, shirking
under their orange grove smiles. I slithered into my desk, trying to keep my
head down. Flossy blonde curls danced in the uppermost quadrant of my
vision. I saw them disappear and I heard the girl before me turning sideways
in her seat so she could look at me. With some reticence, I looked up.

Eyes made of green fire met mine. She was the most beautiful girl I'd ever seen. Three times prettier than Beverley Hollings. And then some. I choked at her attention.

She gave me a smile. In tones that twinkled, she said, "Hi, my name is Gray Navarre." I introduced myself, all a-stutter. She giggled in reply, "I know who *you are. Mrs. Camp just introduced you, silly.*"

"Oh yea, I forgot."

* * *

The school buzzer wrinkled the air. I cringed. The other students leapt up, forming long lines at the door. Mrs. Camp watched them file out, as if counting.

A presence remained, beside me. A boy my age with a wily smile. His black hair was one unified set of waves going up and down toward the back of his head. He shoved his fist toward me to shake.

"I'm Jack Carbone, Paul. Ya wanna play ball?"

"What kind of ball?" I asked. My glove was at home.

Something about the question affected him quite strangely. He intermingled his fingers from both hands, put them to his open mouth, closed his eyes and shook his body all over by tightening his muscles. When he was done, he replied, "Basketball," as if it was obvious.

I looked him up and down. "Why'd you do that?" I asked.

His eyes widened, as if he hadn't a clue what I was talking about.

So, I mimicked him, though not in a mean way, intermingling my fingers, putting them in my mouth and shaking. "That," I said.

He looked off, as though the question had never occurred to him before.

"I don't know. When do I do that?" he asked, thinking. "When I'm kinda excited, I guess." He gave me a smile, his eyes direct, unflinching. "Does it bother you?"

"Nah," I said with a shrug. "I'm just curious. Let's go."

* * *

Jack dribbled the basketball close to the ground with an enviable mastery. Bat, bat, bat. He approached the hoop and in a fluid series of hops, skips and a jump, transferred the ball from one hand to the other, his figure one tall reaching S-shape, performing a lay-up. The ball bounced off the backboard, but didn't go in. He scooped it up from its errant path and tossed it my way. My turn.

The dimpled ball was foreign to my hands. Too big.

"Go on," Jack encouraged, noticing my tentativeness.

I began my dribbles, long drooping beats. Tried to move my hand closer to the earth to gain control, but the increased speed made it harder for me to coordinate my movements. I took my first steps towards the hoop, but a figure ran into view, and suddenly, the ball wasn't there anymore. Whoever it was had stolen it away from me. Two beats of the ball later and the figure jumped. The ball went up, made a graceful arc and came down through the hoop. They caught it, turned and faced me with a big smile.

Much to my surprise, the master basketball player was a girl with sandy blonde hair gathered up in pigtails. She had eyes that sparkled and cheeks that stuck out like pink ping pong balls.

Jack intermixed the fingers of both hands again, put them to his open mouth and shook all over, giggling.

"Hi there, Paul," the girl announced more than said. She looked to Jack as if expecting something from him. "Aren't you going to introduce me, Jack?"

I knew he must've liked her from the way he looked at her. By the way Dee Dee looked at him, I could tell right off they belonged together. A pair.

She shrugged and came toward me. "I'm Dee Dee Johns. I'm new, too."

Gray appeared at my side. A princess. She clasped her hands before her, raised herself onto her toes and lowered again with a sigh, giving me a demure look. And that was it; our gang of four was formed.

* * *

Dee Dee had moved to Westmont only two weeks before, but she was the kind of girl who didn't like to sit still. She happened to live right next door to me. So of course, the two of us shared the walk to and from school. As it turned out, Gray lived a few doors down from Jack. So they shared their walk as well. The four of us found this irony very funny.

Jack's Father bought one of the first television sets in the neighborhood, and everyone wanted to come over and watch. Since I was Jack's best friend, I got to watch the most. My parents got very upset with me. They couldn't understand what I did there all the time.

Gray invited me to come to the Methodist church on Thursday nights when they showed movies out on the lawn. Jack and Dee Dee would come along too and we'd sit watching movies, holding hands. That is, until Gray's Father, who was the Minister, walked by, sending stern looks from under bushy eyebrows at our intertwined fingers. Our hands would flinch and pull away, as though suddenly burned by a hot element. But as soon he returned to his seat at the back, our arms would reach out and our fingers would fold into each other again, fitting so tightly, as if they were made for each other. The tingling sensation of another's touch made us giggle. What a lucky young man I was.

Soon I was walking Gray home. The two of us would hold hands all the way. Then we'd reach her street and we'd each jump away, walking as far on the other side of the sidewalk as possible, to appease her Father. When we reached her house, there he'd be, standing with his arms crossed at the top of the stairs. On my way home, at the half waypoint, I'd meet Jack, who'd walked Dee Dee home. We'd stop, laugh and talk about the girls.

It was so good to have friends again, friends that I didn't have to say goodbye to. To have a structure in my life, to feel like I belonged somewhere, to not have to guess at the rules of the game. For the first time in a year and a half, I was happy. Happier perhaps, more grateful, than I could ever remember being.

Then one day in the middle of November, 1948, when we were walking home, I noticed Gray wasn't talking much.

"What's wrong, Gray?" I asked. She looked away from me, shook her head. "No, come on. Tell me please. I want to know."

Gray stopped but wouldn't look at me. "I just found out this morning, Paul. My father, he's accepted a position in a church in Germany. We're moving to Germany, Paul."

We faced each other. Tears streamed down her face. She bit her lip and looked off.

"Gray, please look at me."

Her eyes came to mine and she exploded into sobs. She nosed into my arms grabbing my shoulders. Her frame quivered under my arms.

"I'm sorry, Paul. I really like you, and I want to stay being your girlfriend."

My chest choked up. Words eluded me. My mouth became so dry my tongue stuck to anything it touched. All I could do was look at her.

We walked the rest of the way in silence, squeezing hands. When we reached her street, I tried to let her hand go, but she wouldn't let me. She held onto mine until we were at her front walk. Her father's dark stare made her pull her hand away. I waved to him and tried to smile, but it was a weak façade. I wasn't feeling very generous toward him.

Heading back down the street, that terrible empty, lonely feeling came creeping. Why was it that every time something good came along, it was taken away? Why?

I turned the corner and there was Jack coming towards me, a bounce in his step. When we met, I tried to pretend everything was okay, but he knew. We sat on the curb for a good long hour, kicking at the stray pebbles, discussing the sad facts as if we could do something to change them.

Thoughts wouldn't let sleep come that night. I lay there for what felt like hours, watching the shadow of the moon creeping across my ceiling. But then I checked the clock, and it was only midnight. I snuck out the back and went over to Dee Dee's bedroom window and tapped on it like I'd done so many times before. The blind fluttered. Dee Dee peered out with slits for eyes. When she saw who it was, she opened the window and leaned out to talk.

"Gray never said anything to me," she said after I'd told her.

"It just happened."

We talked for several minutes until Dee Dee's mother hollered, "Dee Dee, what are you doing up? Are you talking to Paul Miller?"

"Yes, Mother."

"Tell him to go home. It's late."

* * *

The day of Gray's move, Jack and I sat on the curb in front of his house waiting for her family to drive by. We talked about a lot of things. Things we did, things we might do, things we would like to do.

"Jack," I said. "Do you ever ask yourself sometimes why things happen the way they do? Why is there so much sadness? Why people are angry all the time over nothing? Why did we have to have the war that just finished?"

Jack sent me a quizzical look.

I asked him, "You lived here all your life?"

"We moved here when I was six from Los Angeles. I started school at Westmont in the first grade."

"Well, I guess I started thinking about those kinds of things because of what I've been through. Sometimes I think that life is like... well, it's like trying to push a one hundred pound stone up a hill. You push a little, and it starts to roll back on you. You stop it from rolling by putting a stick under it, shake the dust off yourself, catch your breath, and tell yourself, 'okay, lets try it again'! You push with all your might and it moves a little and then starts to roll back on you again. You just keep doing this over and over and over. You know what I mean?"

Jack shrugged. "Yea, get a smaller stone," he said, giggling. I laughed too.

"It's just hard to believe, you know? How is it I meet a girl with the nicest, prettiest, softest smile I've ever seen, and she seems to think I'm pretty okay, too. And after two brief months, the damn stone is rolling back on me again."

Jack got up and went into the house. He came back a minute later with two Coca-Cola's and we sat, drinking them in silence.

Finally, the moving van came driving down the street. Jack and I stood to meet it. Gray's father had the decency to stop in front of us so we could say goodbye.

Gray rolled her window down. She reached out her hand to me and I grabbed it. We both squeezed real hard. Her eyes filled with tears. Gray's parents and brother didn't even look at us. Either they were pretending the situation didn't exist or thought we deserved the privacy.

I heard Jack say goodbye and walk away.

Gray and I said our quiet good-byes. We let go, I stepped back from the car and they drove off. And I stood there watching until long after the car had turned the corner.

I thought to myself, "Paul, you got to push the damn stone a little harder next time."

* * *

Every Thursday after school, the coach would have activities for kids that wanted to stay. Sometimes we played baseball; sometimes we had races, or kick ball, or gymnastics or whatever we wanted to do. After the activities, I'd go home and make my favorite sandwich — two pieces of white bread, one with butter, one with mayonnaise and lettuce in between. I'd take the sandwich and a cold glass of milk and go sit under the tree in the back yard.

I'd sit and think about Gray, what she was doing, if she had a new boyfriend and what her home looked like. I figured out the difference in time between California and Germany and tried to picture what Gray would be doing at that hour. It made me sad and happy all at the same time.

Dad had been put on a schedule that made him work late into the evenings, giving Mother and me precious time without him. After my bath we'd sit on the couch and talk about all kinds of things.

"Mom, do you remember the time when we were on the train going through New York City, and you told me that you and Dad lived in New

York? Dad didn't want to talk about it, and you said he might tell me someday. What is it that he doesn't want to talk about?"

Mother's brow furrowed. "Yes, I remember," she said. "I also know he'll never tell you, so I will." But she tensed for a minute, as though she didn't feel comfortable with the tale. But then she let out a great big sigh and said, "Your dad's parents lived in an apartment on the sixth floor in New York City. One day his mother told him to go down to the store and get some stuff for supper. Well, your dad didn't want to go, he went into a rage. So, his mother went instead and your dad stood at the window watching her. As she crossed the street, a car hit and killed her. He blames himself for her death, and doesn't like to talk about it."

I tried to picture Dad standing at the window watching as his Mother crossed the street. I saw a kid with a self-satisfied smirk on his face. When the car hit her his face became blurred — nothing, no sounds, no crying, no grief at all. I turned to Mother and asked, "Why did you marry him if he was so bitter and angry all the time?"

"He came to my room one night and held a gun to my head and said that if I didn't marry him, he'd kill himself and me. I had no choice."

"Oh Mom, he wouldn't have killed you," I said.

"How do you know that? I didn't know." She started to cry and I felt bad for questioning her judgment.

"I'm sorry Mom. I didn't mean to …"

"There was something else, Paul. He also said he'd kill my parents if I ever told them about this. I couldn't take that chance, Paul. I just couldn't."

"No, I guess not."

I was stunned, but at the same time I accepted it, found it totally believable. All those blurry bits of their relationship came into focus.

Mother continued, "Paul, it's been a horrible life with John Miller. Your Father is very jealous. I can't look or talk to another man without him accusing me of infidelity. That's why we moved to Florida. Why we went back to Detroit. Why we came to California. He was convinced I was having an affair with a man in Michigan and he was going to get me away from him before I made a fool of myself. Then he became convinced there was someone in Florida."

"I noticed you and Dad arguing but."

"Jealousy. He'd come after me, and after me. Anything would set him off. The stray eye of a stranger standing by us at a bus stop. The conductor on the train. He's even jealous of you boys, his sons. Do you know that he came after Jimmy one night with a knife?" I did know this. I'd been standing on the stairs watching that night. Mother continued, "Jimmy and Dick both left after that. They went into the Army. Adam lives in Boston because the distance makes him feel safer. Your Father accuses the girls of every sin in the book. He hated Johnny and what he had become and couldn't wait to put him in a hospital."

"What about me?" I asked, even though I could guess the answer.

"Paul, you weren't supposed to happen. You were a change of life baby. Your Dad went on a three day drunk when he heard I was pregnant again. If it wasn't for the teachings of the Church, you wouldn't be here right now."

"What do you mean, I wouldn't be here?"

"Well, he talked about me getting an abortion," She started to cry again.

I knew what that meant. My own Father wanted to kill me. I'd always known that he didn't like me. That he'd be happier if I wasn't around. But to want to kill me? This upset me so much I got up and went into the kitchen to get a glass of water. I wanted to hit him so hard he'd go flying to kingdom come. And then I'd say, "You deserve more than that, you rotten bastard."

I went back to the living room and sat down next to her again. She'd calmed down and was watching me.

She said, "Paul, I'm telling you all this now so you'll understand. Everything I've told you, those are just a few of the reasons I'm leaving your father. I can't take it any more."

I sat up in my seat, excited. This was what I wanted, too. How happy we'd be without him. That's all I could think of. How happy we'd be.

Mother continued, "I'm going to go back to Michigan. I want to be with the kids and grandchildren. But I only have enough money for me right now."

"You can't leave me here alone with him. He'll kill me, you know that —"

"— Paul, I can't afford to — "

"—You can't do that. He'll beat me to death —"

"— I'll work hard to save —"

"— You're not leaving me! You're not! You're not!"

Mother grabbed my wrists and held me still. Her gray eyes locked onto mine. "There's no other way to do it, Paul. I don't have the money for both of us. I promise you, I will send for you as soon as I can. I promise." The same old song, like a skipping record. We can't afford you. As though I was to blame for being born at all.

I jerked away from her. "By the time you send the money I'll be dead."

I wouldn't look at her and she didn't say anything. I said, "Why can't you wait until we have enough money for both of us?" I turned to her, excited by the idea. "I can help, you know. I'll make some money, too. Then we can both get away, together."

She leaned forward on her knees. The way her back moved up and down, she looked as though she was being beat up from the inside out. "No, I can't take it any more. Not any more, please."

I put my arms around her and cried with her.

Her sobs subsided and she looked up, her face smeared and worn. She said, "Do you remember last Sunday night, when that car had a flat tire in front of our house?"

"Yea, I remember."

"Well, your father was convinced that that man was my boyfriend. That the man had willed his car to have a flat tire right there, just so he could see me."

I smirked at her. "But, that's crazy. That man had two kids in the car, and his wife."

"I know that. You know that. But John Miller, he doesn't know that. He's getting worse, Paul. Every day he's getting worse. He's gone too far."

"What do mean, too far?"

"He started beating me the other night. He was screaming at me, demanding that I tell him who my boyfriend is. He said he was going to find him and kill him and then he'd kill me. He's never said that before. He's scaring me."

"Let's call Michigan. The girls will send us the money."

"I already called Sarah. She told me to hang on. She's coming out in a couple of weeks for vacation. What I thought I'd do is go back with her."

"No, no. You're not leaving me alone. You're not going to leave me with him. You can't do that to me."

No matter what I said, Mother wouldn't listen. She insisted that her plan was the only way. I went to bed, thoughts whirling with scenes of Dad beating me, yelling, "Where the hell is your mother? You know, you bastard. I know you know, you good for nothing bastard. Tell me!"

12.

A VERY SAD HOUSE

I was terrified. As I sat through classes the next day I repeated a promise to myself. Tonight, during our talk, I was just going tell her: she was not leaving without me, and that's all there was to it. I'd hide in the baggage car if I had to. But she could not leave without me.

It was Thursday, my favorite day, so I tried my best to enjoy it as much as possible. I stayed after school for extra activities and enjoyed the release of running and concentration needed to participate in a game of baseball.

When I finally walked into the house I could smell cooking, which was curious, because no one was usually there when I arrived home. There was a half eaten meal on the dinning room table. I checked in all the rooms, but no one was there. Very curious.

I made my favorite sandwich and went outside under the tree to eat. It got dark and still no one came home. Mother was always home before dark. I went out on the front porch and waited.

Eventually a car pulled into the driveway of Dee Dee John's house. A minute later, Dad came around the front and headed across the lawn. He went into the house without saying a word. I followed.

"Where's Mother?" I asked.

He sat on the couch, pulled out his paper and opened it up, so it formed a wall between us. "Hospital," he said, as though she were at the beauty parlor.

"Why? What happened?"

"She got sick today at her job and fainted. She was rushed to the hospital and she's still unconscious. They'll call the neighbors when she comes to."

"Why did she faint?"

He lowered the paper with a grunt. "Damn it, Paul, I don't know. Not even the Doctors know."

I sat on the front porch and prayed for Mother to get better. It had been so long since I'd talked to Noah. I guess when things are good, when you're feeling safe, you don't need that kind of someone to talk to.

Shortly after nine o'clock Dee Dee ran out of her house, cut across the lawns.

"The hospital called," she said, panting. "She's regained consciousness. They want you there right away. Get ready. My Dad's getting the car, okay?"

We arrived at the hospital about half past nine and were met by two nurses and a Doctor. The Doctor walked up to Dad, put a hand on his shoulder, pulled him aside. I saw the Doctor whisper something into Dad's ear. Dad looked up, his eyes widening. He ran around the Doctor, into the room where Mother was and threw himself across her bed, screaming, "No God. No, you can't do this! Mary, Mary come back. I'm sorry, I'm sorry."

What was going on? I'd shut down. Nothing made sense. What was happening?

A nurse put her arm across my shoulder and said, "I'm very sorry." I looked up at her. She must have seen the puzzled look on my face. She bent down and held my face in her hands. She said, "Paul, your Mother has died. She had what is called a 'cerebral hemorrhage'."

Dee Dee's Father, Mr. Johns came over, put his arm around me and said, "Paul, I'm so sorry." Breath wheezed in and out of my lungs. Faster, ever faster. It was as though nothing was getting in. I couldn't breathe. Nothing was getting in. I sucked harder. Harder. No air. No air.

A Nurse's voice, far away, "Want to go into the room with your Father, Paul?" A hand pushed at my shoulder. My steps stuttered. Another push, towards the room. I refused to move. No, not there. Not in that room. Please.

Muffled voices boomed and echoed around me, their words incoherent. Figures, like ghosts in double time, swam about me. They were facing me, words like gobs of nonsense. I remember thinking to myself, *you have to cry, Paul. You must cry. Cry Paul, damn it. Cry. I put my hands to my face and pretended to cry. A white-clad figure grabbed hold of me, trying to comfort. I was hemmed in. Caught, choking. Let go, please.*

I broke away and ran outside, fell prostrate onto the lawn. I remember rolling over, looking up into the sky. Was it true? Was she gone? Why couldn't I cry? Why could Dad? How could he cry, after all he's done? Why wasn't he laughing?

I'd begged Mother not to leave me and she did. She left me all alone with him. How could she do this to me?

The drive home passed in silence. It disgusted me how Dad sniffled, wiped his eyes. When we arrived he went to the John's house to visit and I went home.

I walked into the house, sat on the couch. Mother and I were supposed to sit there that very night and talk about going to Michigan. The house walls were suddenly so odd. So pointless. They held nothing but empty space. There was nothing to do but wait. But wait for what? How long? Why bother?

Then the house became very cold. I started to walk around it. I know it sounds odd, but I became afraid of it. I ran outside and sat on the curb. Then I picked up stones and threw them at the house as fast and as hard as I could, screaming at the top of my lungs, "I hate you." I did, I hated that damn house.

I went to the neighbors and knocked on the door. Mrs. Johns let me in and asked if I'd like something to drink or eat. I told her no and sat down in an empty chair.

Dad had his usual smirk on his face. He asked, "What's the matter? Scared the house is haunted?" It infuriated me that he'd guessed right. I stared at him without reacting. I wanted to call him every rotten name in the book. Every damn book.

Mr. Johns told me that he'd take Dad to the funeral home in the morning to make arrangements. They'd talked to Sarah. She was going to get an early flight. We'd pick her up at the airport tomorrow afternoon.

When Dad and I left that evening, Mrs. Johns hugged me and said, "Paul, if there is anything I can do, just ask."

Dad went into his bedroom and shut the door. I could hear him crying and talking to Mother, but could not understand the words. He'd said nothing to me. He hadn't even touched me or said 'I'm sorry' or anything.

How I hated that man. I prayed for God's forgiveness for doing so, but I couldn't change how I felt. I hated him. Hated him.

I lay wide-awake in bed for a long time. It was Thursday, May 19, 1949. Thursday couldn't be my favorite day anymore, damn it. This Thursday had been the worst day of my life so far.

What I'm about to tell you I've only told to a handful of people. I suppose at one time or another a lot of people have had some sort of a supernatural or spiritual experience that is inexplicable. Many choose not to discuss it. Your wits can get muddled at times of extreme emotional distress. But knowing that, I still have to say that I believe it did, really — happen.

I discovered myself wide-awake. It was three in the morning. I sat up in bed. The door to my closet was closed, but there was a bright light inside that streamed into the bedroom out around the edges. Something was in there, an energy. The doorknob turned, the door opened and the light floated out into the middle of the room, radiating in pulses from the center. Mother came out of that light, sat on the edge of my bed and we hugged. She kissed me on the cheek and said, "Everything will be all right, Paul. Do not be afraid." Then she stood up and backed into the light waving to me.

I hollered at her not to go, to stay with me.

"I'm sorry, Paul," she said. "I have to go." She disappeared into the light, the door shut and the light was gone. I sat there blinking at the closet door. I felt no fear. I whispered for Mother to return to me, but nothing happened and I suddenly, inexplicably, fell back into a deep sleep.

In the morning, I jumped out of bed and opened the closet door. There was nothing but the shoes and a suitcase standing up in the back. Nothing else.

Dad was already gone, which was good. It meant I didn't have to face him. I dressed and went next door. Mrs. Johns asked what I would like for breakfast and I told her it didn't make any difference, whatever she had.

In addition to Dee Dee, the Johns had one little boy of five, and a baby girl one year old. I was standing at the playpen, playing with the baby when the five year old came up to me and said, "Your mommy died last night, didn't she?"

His words gutted me. The sobs catapulted from me. Mother was dead. Gone forever.

The little boy backed off, terrified. He cried in confusion. Mrs. Johns ran into the living room apologizing. I ran outside, sat on the curb and let myself cry it out.

Mother was dead. Gone forever. Mother was dead. Gone forever. The words repeated.

Dee Dee came out and sat beside me. I felt her arms wrap around me and I·threw my head onto her shoulder.

* * *

I enjoyed the ride to the airport. The change of scenery helped my mind stop dwelling.

This was my first time at an airport. It sure beat the heck out of train stations. Sarah's plane was two hours late, but I didn't mind. I spent the time watching the planes take off and land, people loading the baggage, trucks pumping fuel, pilots looking over the plane, kicking the tires and all the passengers getting on and off. I'd dart from one area to another to another, captivated by everything.

Someone looking exactly like Sarah appeared at the terminal door. No, wait a minute. It was Sarah. But, wow. She wasn't a gooky, teenage sister anymore. In fact, she was pretty. She was dressed in a blue dress suit with high heeled shoes, and a hat that was angled just so. She carried a suitcase in one hand and her handbag rested in the crook of her other arm. I'd never thought of my sister as a grown up before, but there she was, a real lady.

We hugged and cried, cried and hugged and then got into the car for the trip to Pomona. Sarah talked about the plane trip; how her ears would pop and how the stewardess gave everyone gum to chew. She told me how from way up in the air cars looked like toys. The land spread out under you like a patchwork quilt.

Dad and Sarah headed into the house ahead of me. As he entered, Dad turned to me and said, "You stay out here. I want to talk to Sarah alone."

I sat on the porch and waited, and waited. Finally fed up, I knocked on the door and asked if I could come in. "No, you stay outside! I'll tell you when you can come in." But I was bored. I said that if I couldn't come in, could I have some money to go to the show? Dad's footsteps pounded towards the door. He came rushing out wagging his finger at me, "Your Mother just died, and you want to go to the damn show? What's the matter with you? Don't you have respect for the dead, boy?" He turned and went into the house and slammed the door.

A few minutes later, Sarah came out, gave me a dollar and told me to go to the show. I went and watched two movies. It was good to get away from everything. Afterwards, I headed for home and didn't hurry. Why should I?

I got home just before dark but no one was there. They drove up in Mr. Johns' car a while later. They'd been to see Mother.

"You could have gone too, if you didn't go to the damn movie show!" Dad said.

Sarah turned to me and said, "The funeral is tomorrow, Paul. Do you have something to wear?" I told her I did. She said she was going over to the Johns' for a visit.

She went out the door; I went into the dining room and sat down, looking out the window. I heard Dad's feet scuffling along the floor and looked up. He was leaning against the wall at the corner where the living room met the dining room, his head lowered, snarling at me.

"How dare you," he said. "Do you have any idea how you embarrassed me in front of absolutely everyone?" He came further into the room. "Everyone?" he screeched and kicked at a chair's legs, making it fall on its side and slide across the floor. It was an absurd gesture. He raged, pacing, his arms windmilling about, "You show no respect for anyone, you heathen. You're a disrespectful stupid kid. How dare you go to the movies? The movies!?! Everyone in town saw you there. Stared at you there. You ignorant, sinning wretch. How dare you embarrass me like that? How dare you? Now, go to bed you thankless, sonovabitch. GO TO BED."

I wasn't about to question that order. I ran to my room and shut the door.

Jimmy and Adam arrived sometime during the night. I hadn't known that more family was coming. Why hadn't Dad or Sarah told me?

We left for the funeral home early so we could visit with Mother before the service. Several people were already there when we arrived. I had no idea who they were or where they'd come from. I sat off in a corner and watched everyone crying, hugging Dad, telling him how sorry they were for his loss.

His loss? Oh God, if they only knew the truth.

When the attention of the crowd turned away from the casket and everyone moved to the Foyer, I got up and walked over to her. "Mom," I said, "I don't know if you can hear me or not. I don't know if you are here with me or off with God doing some of His work or what. But I've got to ask you. Were you really going to move to Michigan and leave me alone with Dad? I'm glad we had all those talks together before you died. Almost makes you think that God arranged those moments for you and me because he knew you were coming to live with him. But I don't know what's going to happen to me now."

Mr. Johns appeared beside me. "There you are," he said. "Come on, we're going to the church." I looked at Mother one last time. I kissed her on the forehead and said goodbye.

At that time Catholic service was still held in Latin, which I didn't understand. It was an hour-long mass with communion. I cried because you're supposed to cry at a funeral mass, right? But by that point I felt all cried out.

The ride to the cemetery was quiet. The services at the grave, short. We went back to the Johns' house where food was set out. Over the next few days Sarah, Jimmy and Adam spent most of their time with the Johns. I could tell they enjoyed each other's company. But eventually Adam and Jimmy left. Then the day came for Sarah to leave, too. Dad pleaded with her to stay. I begged her to take me with her. But she told us she was in love with a man back in Michigan; that they were going to be married. She couldn't take me with her. She had no place for me to live, and didn't have the money to get me there.

I remember standing on the train platform, hearing the sniffing off the engines as though they too had something to cry about. The Johns and my Dad were busy saying goodbye to my sister, their faces puffy. When I got the chance I pulled Sarah to the side and said, "You have to take me with you."

Her eyes fluttered shut, bored at hearing me ask again. "I can't, Paul."

"You don't understand. Dad's going to get me. I know it."

"Oh, don't be silly, Paul."

"No, no. He will. Please, you have to take me with you."

"It's too late for that, Paul."

My body quivered and twitched. She must have noticed.

"You okay?" she asked.

"No!" I yelled. The others looked over, nervous. Dad sent me a steely stare. "He's going to kill me, Sarah."

I looked up into her face. Her forehead crinkled up as though she thought I was nuts. But finally she saw something in my face, my eyes.

With hesitancy, she said, "If anything goes wrong, go over to the Johns' house. They'll help you."

Infuriated, I turned away from her. She returned to the others. I listened as their feet shuffled with the exchange of hugs. Good luck. Have a nice trip. Write us soon. So smarmy sweet it turned my stomach.

Sarah's voice beside me said, "Goodbye, Paul." But I wouldn't even look at her. She walked away from me with a huff.

I watched the train pull out of the station and continue off into the distance, until it went completely out of sight.

Mother was gone. Sarah was gone. I experienced that familiar and profound sense of solitude. The sensation was very much like being stained inside and out. And boy, when I looked to the future, it sure did not look good.

Dad had already started back on his own. I walked home slowly. When I arrived I didn't want to go in. I sat on the curb and tried to put the puzzle of my life together, but I couldn't do it. None of the pieces fit.

Someone walk up behind me and sat down beside me. It was Dee Dee again. She put her arms around me and pulled my head to her shoulders. She said she watched me for a long time and didn't know what to do or say. "So, I'll just hold you and hum a little if you can stand it." She started humming, rocking me back and forth. It felt so good to be held, to be touched by someone who cared. I felt the tension in my body go.

After a long time, after it had been dark for quite a while, she turned to me and asked, "Can you go into your house now?"

"Yes. Thank you."

"Go get something to eat, take a bath and go to bed. You'll feel better in the morning."

I turned to her. "Dee Dee, do you know what a cer - sarebi - what my Mother died from?"

"Cerebral hemorrhage. My Mom said that it's like a lot of blood vessels in your brain that burst. And, well, it's like the brain drowns. Does that help?"

"Yes, yes it does. Thank you."

I found Dad sitting on the couch reading the paper. He folded an edge to peek at me. I felt so exhausted, so lost; I didn't know what to do. So I found myself just standing there.

Dad threw the paper down and jumped to his feet. "Okay now. I want you to tell me who your Mother's boy friend was." He screamed, "Right now! I want to know now!"

I looked up at him. His anger just tired me. "Dad," I said, "she didn't have a boyfriend." I sat down in the lounge chair.

"Don't you lie to me, you little brat. I know she had a boy friend. I saw them together. They were plotting against me. They were going to run away together. Right? I'm right ain't I? Tell me who he is. I'm going to kill him."

"Dad, I'm telling you the truth. She did not have a boyfriend. There was no one but you. No one in her life but you and me. I promise Dad."

Dad turned away, running his hand through his hair. "She taught you how to cover up and lie for her. Didn't she?"

"No Dad, she didn't do that stuff."

"You're lying," he raged. "You know how I know you're lying?" He was throwing his arms all around. "I found a note in her purse. She was going to meet this guy last Sunday night, but she couldn't get out so he staged a flat tire in front of our house." Dad straddled the chair I was sitting in, leaned down so his face was just inches from mine, screaming as loud as he could. "Right smack in front of our own damn home! Can you imagine that? Can you see that Paul? Can you see that?"

Oh how dumb I was! I came back at him. "Dad, you're imagining things! You need help. You're sick. You need to see a doctor."

Dad backed away from me. The muscles of his face spasmed. His arm pulled back and he hit me on the side of my head with the back of his hand.

A look came over him, as if this physical contact was deeply satisfying. So he hit me again and again. His hand moving back and forth, from left to right. He'd hit me with his palm, then the back of his hand, then again and again. I struggled out of the chair and ran into the bathroom and locked the door. He banged on the door, screaming at me to open it. I stood there grasping the sink, watching the door nervously as it bulged and shook with his blows. I went to the window. Could I squeeze out that little opening?

"I ain't through with you yet," he screeched. "Open the damn door or I'll break it down. You hear me? You hear me? Open the door you little son-of-a-bitch! That's what you are, a little *sonovabitch*!"

Fifteen minutes of ranting later, he gave the door one big bang and walked away. I could hear him mumbling to himself but couldn't understand the words. Then the back door slammed to. I turned the lights off in the bathroom and looked out. He was in the backyard smoking a half of a cigar.

I turned the lights back on and looked in the mirror. My face was covered with cuts and my nose was bleeding. Both ears were red and hurt bad. I placed a cold washcloth on my face. It burned. One tooth on the upper right side was loose.

How could I go to school like this? What could I say?

I had to get away from him. If I stayed, he really was going to kill me.

Maybe I could make up a name for Mom's supposed boyfriend? Tell Dad the guy lived in Montana. But then, Dad was liable to drag me to Montana, find some guy and kill him.

I went into my bedroom and put a chair up against the door. Maybe I shouldn't sleep here. But how could I get out? Where could I go? A kid of eleven years old is supposed to be thinking about his baseball team, his girlfriend, and his bike. This wasn't fair.

As soon as I was sure Dad was sleeping, I went to the kitchen and got some ice for my face. The next morning I was awoken by Dad's pounding. "Get up and go to school, you lazy good-for-nothing," he yelled. I told him I wasn't going to school today because of my face. He didn't reply. He left the house shortly after that.

I tensed when Dad through the door early. He acted like I wasn't even there. But it was better than being beat up and hollered at.

* * *

For a few weeks our life took on something like normalcy. Words were rarely spoken. Whenever I heard the tick tock of a clock it reminds me of this time. Dad and I maintained the schedule we'd had when Mother was alive. Work, home, Church on Sunday.

Then one day, we sat at the table reading. Dad the news section, me the funny papers. I held the paper out in front of me with my arms stretched out, so my view of him was blocked. All of a sudden, something came through the paper and hit me hard above my left eye.

I felt my head spinning. I looked to the floor, saw Dad's shoe next to my chair. I looked up and he was standing across the table from me, his face flaming. He breathed heavily. He looked terror-stricken.

"Are you going to tell me who your mother's boyfriend was this time?" He pointed down at the shoe on the floor. "That shoe was just an opener for what you're going to get if you don't tell me, you little *sonovabitch*."

Blood dripped into my eye. I couldn't open it and if I opened my right eye, it made my left eye hurt. I pulled out my shirttail and held it to the wound.

Dad grabbed my shirt close to my neck, pulled me to standing and threw me across the floor. "Tell me you little shit, tell me before I beat the living hell out of you."

I waved my arms in front of me, blinded. "I told you. There was no boyfriend. Stop thinking there was. You're making yourself angry. Stop it."

He nudged my hip with his foot. "I'll stop when you tell me who the dirty bastard is!" He picked me up again and threw me like some bowling ball back across the floor so I knocked over the chair.

I hit the wall and kept moving. I jumped to my feet and ran out the front door, down the porch and out onto the driveway.

Dad stood in the doorway. He yelled, "Get back in this house, you ungrateful *sonovabitch*. N O W!"

I didn't answer him. I walked around the back of the house, turned on the hose and let the cold water pour over my face.

I heard the front door and froze. Forced my right eye open. Dad appeared on the sidewalk. I ducked, ready to run. But he kept heading down the street toward town. He didn't even look for me. How could he turn his emotions on a dime like that? It just wasn't normal.

I had to do something.

Mrs. Johns who opened the door. At the sight of me her hand shot to her mouth and she gasped, "My God, Paul, what happened?"

It was hard, but I told the Johns everything. How Dad was behaving, his paranoia. Everything. It was difficult not to be embarrassed. Like we were less human somehow because of my Dad's problem. But they understood.

When I was done, Mr. Johns stood up and said, "I'm calling Sarah right away. And Paul, you're staying right here in our house until we find out what we're going to do. Is that okay with you?"

I nodded. But how shameful, needing to go to a stranger's house for protection.

Dee Dee sat next to me and put her arms around me. So comforting, to be held.

Mr. John talked to Sarah for a long time. Sarah was going to get with the family, discuss the situation and call back this evening. In the mean time, I was to stay away from Dad.

Dee Dee and Mrs. Johns decided to go to the store and took me with them. We had a good time — they even bought me an ice cream cone. When we arrived back at the house Dad was standing on the Porch talking to Mr. Johns.

Mrs. Johns turned in her seat, told me, "Paul, you stay in the car until I find out what's going on". They got out of the car and walked up to the porch. After a brief discussion Dad and Mr. Johns walked to the car.

Dad stopped at the window and glared at me, but continued on without saying a word.

Mr. Johns opened the car door and said, "Come on. Let's go inside."

Sarah had called. She'd told them to get me on a bus to Detroit as soon as possible. Mr. Johns said he'd go down to the bus station the next day and get me a ticket.

I asked him what he'd told my dad. He said, "We told him that we knew what he was doing to you, that we'd called Michigan for instructions. If he objected to any one of these steps, raised a fuss about it, we'd call the police and have him charged with cruelty to children."

"What did he say?"

"What could he say? He just walked away."

I stayed with the Johns for three nights. On Wednesday, they took me to the Bus Station. The bus was waiting to be boarded when we got there. Mr. Johns gave me my ticket. That's when I noticed him.

Dad was standing at the sidewalk staring at me, a cigar hanging out of his mouth and his hands in his pockets. What was the connection he felt to me? Did he need someone to hate? Or did he really love me? He was such an utter mystery.

Mr. Johns said, "Your dad doesn't have a car, Paul. So he can't follow. But just to be on the safe side, the police will escort the bus to the county line. Does that make you feel better?"

"Yes, it does. I'm sorry."

"You have nothing to feel sorry about, Paul. None of this is your fault. Your dad is sick and needs help."

"Yea, I know he does, but... I feel like I'm the cause of all this trouble for everyone and it's making me feel, I don't know, bad or something."

Mrs. Johns grabbed my arm and shook. "No, Paul," she said, "Don't feel guilty. You're the victim here. Please, don't blame yourself. Okay?"

"Yea, okay." But inside I couldn't help it. I did feel guilty. There was something wrong with me. I should have been able to do something.

Dad stood there watching, motionless as the bus pulled away. I felt so sorry for him. What was he going to do with the rest of his life? He had no one. Maybe I could turn my life around, start over, and push that stone up the hill all the way. But what about Dad? How was he going to push his stone up the hill?

13.

BACK TO MICHIGAN

The weaving, tedious trail of the cross-country bus was tolerable only because I thought my destination was true home.

We went through rag-tag towns where the bus stop was not much more than a bit of dirt worn to a shine at the side of the road. The big city stations were back alley buildings stained by diesel soot. They stank like urine. But it was still good to get off and stretch. The bus rumbled me to my bones.

The station halls held a cloying grayness with a rush and wait atmosphere. The people waiting in the line-up to purchase tickets shuffled with nervous feet. Clumps of travelers slumped on benches and upturned suitcases. A chorus of customers sipped coffee at the lunch counter, while a waitress with features frozen in a cynical grimace leaned forward to hear orders. Behind her a cook, his white smock smeared with brown grease, flipped grilled cheese sandwiches with one hand as he rubbed an eye with the other.

They were microcosms of impermanence, these bus stations. I could be fascinated by them because I considered myself to be a tourist passing through. When the journey was over, I'd be back where I belonged for good, welcomed by family and in the company of old friends. After a major detour, life would be firmly back on course.

I imagined I'd live with Sarah and Gerry in their pretty little house. I saw myself waking up in the room my parents had stayed in. Gerry would let me climb that apple tree. I'd mow the lawn every Saturday, and every Sunday after church we'd have a roast beef or ham dinner, just like before.

In between the bus stations was a rural panorama replete with history. We'd come over a hill, and the driver would point out a spot and tell me about what had happened there. As the journey continued, the sense grew that my country was a familiar cloak, wrapping itself about my shoulders. It was mine. And all of ours. A place formed not just by mythologies, boundaries and laws, but mixed into the very earth we traveled. I saw it in the face of a Latino man leaning under the hood of his over-heated pick-up stopped in the middle of the desert. He nodded to us as our bus flew by. I saw it in the shoulders of the woman raking a gem's nest of fall leaves. At the sound of our bus she turned to watch and waved her arm with broad strokes as if she was paid to. I saw it in the scurrying steps of a Chinese family outside a restaurant in a small town, too busy to notice our passing. A placard on the sidewalk read, "Now Open." You could almost hear the earth sing from the essence of these people. They belonged here. This country, this land, was all of ours. Traveling it was a renewing experience.

Five days later the bus pulled to a stop in Detroit. Relief and excitement exploded inside me when I saw Sarah standing on the platform. She was on her tiptoes, covering her eyes with a gloved hand, looking for me through the shaded glass. When the bus door opened I was the first one to run down its steps. I landed in her embrace, nosing my face into the crook of her arm, tears welling up. Passengers flowed around us.

She broke away from me, pulled my chin up so we were eye to eye. "It's okay," she said. "You're home now." I wrapped my arms around her again, rocking her back and forth, craving the physical contact to prove her words true.

Mattie appeared beside us. "Hi there, Paul." She hugged me too, but there was a reticence to the embrace that bothered me. "That must have been one awful trip," she said.

"Where's Ed?" Sarah asked.

"He couldn't find a parking space," Mattie replied. "He's going to meet us out front." Minutes later we were piling into Ed's car and heading for the suburbs.

Once under way, Sarah turned to me. "Paul," she announced, matter of fact, "we've decided that you're going to be living with Mattie and Ed."

I caught my breath. Why wasn't I getting any say in the matter? Mattie and Ed had three kids. Didn't Jimmy live with them, too?

"But I thought I was going to live with you and Gerry."

Mattie turned in her seat and squinted, hearing the disappointment in my voice.

"No, that can't happen, Paul," Sarah began. "I'm getting married in a few weeks and moving. And the apartment Barry and I have chosen is just a one-room studio. Our family can't afford to pay Gerry for you to stay there. Mattie has offered her home to you, I'd be grateful for her generosity, if I were you."

My consternation must have registered. Mattie said, "We're happy to have you, Paul. It'll be just like old times."

"Yea," I said, without enthusiasm. I didn't want to start an argument or hurt anyone's feelings.

I sat back and marveled at the suburbs passing, recognizing bits and pieces. Mr. Maze's grocery store, where Billy and I threw tomatoes against the newly painted wall. The alley where me and Fritz played kick the can. The woods where we'd catch frogs. It all looked just the same. But how could I have endured so much and these streets have changed so little?

We turned the corner onto our old street, Grandview Avenue. We passed the home where we'd lived as a family without comment. Mattie and Sarah didn't even turn their heads to look. Blue draperies hung in the living room window now instead of white lace. A little girl not much younger than me bounced a ball on the front lawn.

We stopped just down the street in front of a squat, yellow cottage. I was shown to my room in the attic. I looked at the studs of the slanted ceiling, the little window that didn't open, the double mattress sitting on the floor and sighed. I'd be sharing this bed with my brother, Jimmy, another family member made refugee by our father's early retirement.

Standing next to a wall of cardboard storage boxes that leaned so badly I was sure they were about to topple, Mattie pointed to a bureau next to a wall. "Jimmy cleared out the bottom drawer for you," she said. "Get unpacked, and then come downstairs for some tea."

The last bit didn't sound like a suggestion.

                                    *   *   *

I found Mattie at the kitchen table, biting a nail as she studied a piece of paper. Her back stiffened as I stepped into the doorframe.

"Come on in, Paul. Have a seat." She got up and brought tea things over from the counter.

I slipped onto the chair across from where she'd been sitting. As I watched her putting the plate of cookies down, I noticed how she'd withered. The Lana Turner shine of earlier days had faded. The wear of more than a few bad days had taken its toll.

"Where are the kids?" I asked. The house was quiet to be home to children, one six months, another just under two.

"With Jim and Ed, out at the park," she said. I didn't know that this was unusual. Her hands shook as she poured my cup of tea. She put down the pot, picked up her mug and sucked on it. The brew had an immediate, calming effect on her. Then her eyes lowered to the piece of paper.

"Paul, you know that we're glad you're safe. That you couldn't stay with father anymore."

The bass drum of my heart pounded at my chest. "Well, yea," I said, displeased by the trembling tone in my words.

She angled her head slightly, and sent me a half smile. "But, things are already tight as it is, Paul."

"Yea. I know," I said, tracing a finger along the pattern on the linoleum table.

Mattie turned the piece of paper around and slid it across to me. "Here's what I want you to do, to earn your keep," she said, almost swallowing the words before they could get out.

On the paper was a list that was much too long to read in one go. Wash dishes, make breakfast, vacuum….

Mattie's finger entered my frame of vision, pointing. She rattled on, "It's just that, Paul, with the extra expense, I know we can't afford a baby sitter anymore, so, you're going to have to do that. Because I do need to get out sometimes. And the other things; well, you should do something to earn your keep. So, you see, our basement does need to be cleaned out, so I thought that would be a good thing for you to do. And…." Her words became a blur. I looked up. Her lips moved fast, like cards being shuffled.

I spoke loudly, stopping her, "You didn't want me either, did you?"

Mattie stopped in surprise. She blurted, "I already have brother Jimmy."

I looked to the floor. Nobody wanted me. She reached her hands across to mine. I backed out of their reach.

"They're not giving you any money to help out?" I asked.

Her arms slithered back across the table with a flick. She looked down into her lap. "They said they would."

"But you don't believe them?"

She shook her head. "Jimmy will," she said. Her chest rose high with a breath and lowered again. She looked up at me. "I'm sorry, Paul," she said. "I know you never wanted to end up in this situation. None of us did. So, let's just try and make the best of it, okay?"

I smiled as hard as I could and nodded my head, trying to reassure her. She was so unlike Mattie, so nervous. It didn't wear on her well. I wondered if there was more to what was going on than I knew about. I was just staying here with them, that wasn't such a big deal, was it?

She noticed my untouched tea mug. That disturbed her. "Why aren't you drinking your tea?" she asked.

"I've never had tea before," I said with a shrug. "Could I have some milk and a butter and lettuce sandwich with mayonnaise?"

Her brow knitted into mounds of confusion for a moment, and then she looked up at me, her eyes wide. It was as though she was seeing me for the first time as the eleven-year-old boy that I was. When she fell forward in tears, I came around beside her, standing not much taller than her seated figure. I hung myself over her and patted her back. My poor, Mattie. But those pats didn't feel like they offered anything. I was at as much of a loss as she was.

*   *   *

The doorbell sounded exactly as I remembered. I listened to the footsteps knocking about inside the house. I couldn't keep the giggles at bay and tittered into my fist. The door swung open with a whoosh and Billy's mother stood there, dishrag balled in her hands. She saw my face and jumped with a gasp. She called over her shoulder, "Billy, there's someone special here for you at the door." She stepped away, as though to deal with me further would take the pleasure away from him.

Billy's head popped into view at the end of the hall. Blonde tufts of hair stuck up from the crown of his head. Red cheeks puffed up like balloons as he grinned. . He pulled himself around the corner and ran toward me, calling out, "Paul! It's Paul! You're back!"

I stepped aside so he could come through the screen door. It opened like a whip and slammed behind him. Billy kept on running, right past me, across his lawn, calling out, "Come on, let's go play, Paul. Let's go play."

Who was I to question such an order? I gave chase, running down familiar streets. What a joy to be home again.

Billy stopped with a spin when he arrived at our neighborhood park, right in front of a new, multi-colored jungle gym. He spread his arms out wide over his head and exclaimed, "Look at this, Paul. Isn't this great?"

Billy turned, ran for the red bars and reached. Up the ladder he went. When he arrived at a horizontal ladder he turned around and, in a practiced move, slipped his behind between the bars and hung upside down by his knees so his hair stood straight down.

"Look at me, Paul. Look at me!"

I walked up to his upside down face. "Hi there, Billy. Looks like you've changed a lot."

He puckered his lips as though tasting something bitter, not understanding my meaning. But undaunted, he reached up for the bar, grabbed it firmly and let his legs fall down.

"Bet ya can't go from one end of this ladder to the other without falling," he said. His words slurred together slightly, child like. "I'll race ya. Start timing me." He rocked his body back and forth. On his fourth swing he let the momentum send a free arm to the next ladder bar.

"I think you'll beat me, Billy. My arms aren't as strong as they could be. I haven't been climbing many trees like I used to."

Billy let himself fall to the ground. He turned his upper torso to look at me. "You haven't?" he asked. "Why not?"

It struck me as such an odd question; I couldn't for the life of me answer it. In fact, he hadn't asked me anything yet. About where I'd been, what had happened to me? It hurt that he didn't think of it. But I brushed that aside.

Billy tapped me on the arm. He suggested, "How about we play space ship on that, over there?" He pointed towards a series of raised platforms. It surprised me that the idea didn't appeal. I hadn't played pretend games since I'd left Detroit.

"I don't know," I replied.

Then I saw something intriguing across the field. The gaping maw that was the sewer output. A round, black hole in the side of a hill that had always terrified me. But now it struck me as an opportunity for adventure. What critters could be found, squirming in the trickle at its bottom? What was hidden around the first corner? Where did it ultimately go?

"I got an idea," I said, now walking quickly across the field toward the hole.

Billy caught up beside me, bouncing sideways like a frisky pony. "Oh yea? What's that?" he asked.

I nodded toward the sewer. "Let's go exploring."

Billy turned to look and stopped, rigid. In that expression I saw a terror that once had been mine when I'd looked at that sewer, only trebled by the thought of journeying into its monster mouth. He shook his head, ever so slightly.

Hushed, he said, "I don't know, Paul."

"I'm sorry. We don't have to do that, Billy," I said. "Let's play space ship, like you said."

But he was spooked. His eyes were magnetized to that dreaded open hole as if it might gobble him up if he looked away. There must be some terrible memory or nightmare associated with it I didn't know about. I wanted to erase the suggestion, but then he looked to the street, to the lights. They'd come on.

"I gotta go home," Billy said without looking at me. "I'll see ya later, Paul." He finally glanced at me. Tried to smile. "Maybe we can play tomorrow, huh?"

"Yea, sure. I'd like that," I said. And off he ran.

How in tune we used to be to each other. As though we had identical heartbeats. But now, somehow, the cadence wasn't there. I guessed it would just take some time to get reacquainted.

The next day I answered a knock at Mattie's kitchen door. Billy was there, smiling.

"Do you wanna come out and play, Paul?" he asked.

I held up the cleaned diaper in my hand. "I gotta finish folding laundry first. But I can in twenty minutes."

Billy jumped and started away. "Okay," he called over his shoulder. "Meet us in the park."

When I arrived in the park thirty minutes later, Billy and some boy I didn't know were already busy at play. Billy stood atop one of the platforms, the other boy hid behind a ladder pole. Each held a piece of wood, and aimed it at the other. I called out to them. Billy jumped down and ran over to me, his hair tossing back and forth across his face with each lope.

"Hey, Paul," he called as he came to a stop several feet away. As excited, as he was to see me, there was a sense of reticence. I was both known and unknown. Perhaps that's the scariest creature of all.

"This here's Roman," he said. Roman joined us. Our three figures formed a wide circle. He was a brown-haired boy with a frown that appeared worn into his features. We nodded politely.

"Whaddya wanna play, Paul?" he asked, almost a challenge.

I shrugged. "What were you guys doing?"

"I don't wanna play that no more," Roman said. "Besides, it's hard to play with three."

Billy burst forward into our circle, waving his arms, excited by an idea. "I know," his voice screeched. "We can play cops and robbers. Me and Paul can be robbers. We can rob a diamond store, full of diamonds. And Roman, you can be a cop. Okay?"

Up until that moment I'd never truly understood the meaning of innocence. My experience with Tony in that black neighborhood store itched at the recesses of memory on one side. Mike Ford, on the other.

Roman stepped forward, nodding his head with excitement and checking my reaction.

I wanted to say yes, but I couldn't.

They were still little kids, playing pretend games. So, as it turned out, I didn't want to spend time with them. I think they were just as baffled as I was.

But of course, they'd always lived right here on Grandview Avenue, so how could they have changed?

* * *

Sarah dropped by with a letter one day and showed it to Mattie and me. It read:

August 1949

Dear Sarah;

Thought you'd like to hear about recent events concerning your father. We have not spoken to him. And based on your last letter, we know you have not spoken to him, either. But we did speak to the police, a reporter, and a doctor involved. I clipped this piece from a recent newspaper for you, just to fill you in. Your father has been admitted to a local Sanitarium. They believe he experienced a nervous breakdown. They expect treatment to take a year and would like you to call them. I've included the number, below. We hope you are doing well. Say hello to Paul. Mrs. Johns.

The clipping, from the Pomona daily newspaper, read:

Local man arrested

A local man was arrested after a violent confrontation, Friday. The man, John J. Miller, apparently knocked on a total stranger's door and accused the gentleman of the house of infidelity with his deceased wife. The situation escalated until threats of physical harm were made. The gentleman's wife was able to call police. The alleged attacker, who works as a janitor at a local college, was taken into custody.

The doctor at the Sanitarium was more explicit. Dad was mentally ill. Knowing this didn't help me forgive what he'd done. Mental illness, at the time, was a matter of mystery only discussed in dark hallways, in hushed tones.

Act like it isn't there and maybe it'll go away.

* * *

"Everyone says Mrs. Fahey is a such witch, but I don't think so," my new friend, Connie, blurted too loudly. We were walking down the school corridor, approaching Mrs. Fahey's door.

"Shh, Connie."

She didn't seem to understand why I was shushing, and she continued, in a loud ramble, "I don't care if she never shaves her legs. Even if it is disgusting, seeing that black hair poking out from her hose and...."

I put my hand over her mouth.

Connie jumped away. "Paul, what are you doing?" Those kinks of red hair looked even more like a halo of exclamation marks than they usually did.

I gestured with my chin. I could see Mrs. Fahey through the door, studying something on her desk. Her attention turned toward us, her back stiff. Connie looked over her shoulder, then suddenly jumped down into a crouch position and ran down the hall. I pursued. There was going to be some fallout from this and I'd have to pick up the pieces. What in the world did this girl do before I'd moved here, I didn't know.

Connie turned the corner and stopped, hand to chest, panting. Her blue, button eyes glanced into mine quickly. "Do you think she heard?"

I shrugged a reply. Her face flushed. Her fingers covered her nose like she was trying to hide behind their bars. "Why do I do that?" she asked.

"You just don't think, Connie. It's like you just blurt every thought you have out loud."

She stopped just before heading out the door. I stopped, too, and looked back at her to see what she had to say next. "Well, isn't that what everyone does?" she asked me with a straight face. I couldn't help but laugh at her. These times, walking to and from school, were the only ones I had to myself. Connie always had a way of surprising me, making those times enjoyable.

I proposed as we walked that I help her with this. How? We decided I'd throw out random words and she was supposed to think first, formulate a picture, and then tell me. And, so we went out the door, got to the sidewalk and I started.

"Mrs. Fahey," I said.

Connie did some footwork to avoid a crack in the sidewalk. Then she said, "Discipline."

"Very good," I replied, and took in a breath to say another, but Connie beat me to it.

"She answers every question you ask her, no matter how stupid, without telling you you're stupid. She's helping me pick courses for college, but I don't know if I'm even going to get out of high school, the way things are going. I'm failing everything. I totally lack discipline."

I'd stopped walking. It was her turn to look back to me. "What?" she asked.

"Well, I agree with you."

"Huh?" she screwed up her nose like a piglet.

"You're doing it again."

Connie rolled back on her heels and twisted her lips. "Oh. Yea." She started to walk again and said, "Okay, I'll try harder."

I waited until we were walking steady again, with Connie jumping over the cracks, the way she always did.

"Superstitious," I said.

Connie narrowed her eyes at me. I always bugged her about this jumping the crack business. She smiled at a thought.

Said, "Crack."

Then she jumped so she'd miss another one and continued on.

I laughed and caught up to her. She was like such a cat. Inscrutable, surprising, demanding. A red haired cat with springs for hair and the darndest smile.

"Math," I said. Connie hated math.

She thought for a moment, and then said, "E."

"That's not a word."

"Well, that's what I'm going to get in it."

"I said I'd help you."

"It won't make any difference."

"It will if you try."

"I'm trying."

"I haven't started helping you yet."

"I just hate it, Paul. I don't think your help's going to do me any good."

"So, you're giving up before we even get started?"

"I'm sorry."

"Okay, let's concentrate again on the words."

"Okay."

I let us walk a few steps before beginning again. Then, I said, "Friend."

Connie stopped, looked at me. A decision passed through her.

She sent her arms wide, allowing her books to fall to the ground in front of her. She jumped over them and ran up to me, grabbing my arms. Her face came pushing into mine.

I felt her lips. They were warm and reminded me of the scent of vanilla. She wrapped her arms around me and my books, squeezing so hard I felt my limbs going numb. Her tongue was wet and tasted of peanut butter. It parted my lips and probed at my teeth. I pulled away, but she wouldn't let go. I yanked my head back, cemented my lips together until she gave up and backed away, covering her face with her hands.

"Connie," I gasped. "That's not the way the game is played."

So she wouldn't have to look at me she picked up her books, one by one. "Shut up," she said.

We walked in silence the rest of the way home. I didn't know what to say. I just wasn't interested in her that way. She knew that. We'd been through this before. I didn't want to hurt her, but I'd made myself clear.

We stopped in front of my house. She gave me that shy smile I knew would melt some guy's heart one day. She said, "I guess I owe you another big piece of cake, huh?" As the school year had continued, her lunch had become bigger and bigger as she included treats for me, not to pay me back for anything, but just because she liked me, thus acknowledging the controversial territory between us.

"You don't have to bring me anything, Connie."

She nodded and sighed. I could tell she didn't want to say goodbye. "Do you wanna come over to our house?"

"Can't. I gotta —"

"—Do my chores," she finished my sentence for me. She shook her head. "You do more work than most adults I know," she said.

I couldn't say anything. I only kicked my foot at the edge of the driveway, but inside I was a ball of pent-up resentment at all I had to do for my keep. But to open up would only get me started. And if I got started, I knew the explosion would be a big one.

Connie picked at the edge of one of one of her books. "My parents are talking about Atlanta again."

Connie's father had a business in Atlanta. He spent most of his time there, coming home every other weekend. This news gutted me. If they moved, I'd be losing two friends, not just one. The only ones I had, really.

"Do you think they're serious?" I asked. Connie nodded her head. "When?"

Connie lifted up her shoulders and held them by her ears. "They won't move me and Mary Lou during the school year. So, July, I guess." Only five months away. I'd barely gotten settled and already the earth was moving under my feet, all over again.

Connie's mother, Rachel, was a potter. She worked in a studio in their basement. Some days she'd invite me in and together we'd make figures, ashtrays, small plates and things. It was such fun, I'd stay even after Connie lost interest and went upstairs, leaving me alone with her mother. Which was fine. I found I could really talk to Rachel. We'd pass the hours chatting idly about just anything. Rachel listened to what I said as though it really mattered. She didn't speak to me as a child. I'd become accustomed to dropping by to discuss my problems.

Before I could say anything else, the door slammed behind me. Mattie charged out, pulling her coat onto her shoulders, yelling, "Paul, where in the hell have you been? I've been keeping the doctor waiting for over an hour. If I don't get there in the next ten minutes, he's not going to see me, and he's going to charge me, and it's going to be all your fault." In too much of a furious rush, she ignored Connie, telling me, "Brucey's been fed. He's playing in the...."

I looked over Mattie's shoulder to see Connie backing down the street, tilting her head to one side, a forlorn frown on her lips.

*   *

Ed rolled his eyes at Jimmy with boozy exaggeration, stabbing his thumb in my direction. "Listen to the big man of the world, here, Jimmy. Telling us two ignoramuses about the way things are." Ed lurched to his feet and crossed to the fridge for another beer.

Jimmy kicked me under the table, kidding me.

Ed held up a bottle of beer. "Want another, Jimmy?"

Jimmy rocked from side to side with indecision. "I don't know. I gotta get to work in an hour."

"Its just beer. One more won't hurt," Ed plopped the bottle down in front of him and snapped off the cap. I always wondered why Ed even bothered asking at all, if he was going to insist. His glance spun to me. "Whatabout the big man of the world, here? Want another one?"

I was feeling kind of loopy. Happy. I'd only had one, but at twelve years old, that's all you needed. I didn't even bother shaking my head, knowing that he'd just plop it down in front of me no matter what I said. I was trying to figure out how I could get out of the next round, cause three would make me barf.

Jimmy slurped at his beer and kicked me again. Sarcasm dripped from his words, "So, go on, Paul. Tell us white-knuckled guys about the black gangs downtown Detroit."

They didn't believe I knew anything about them. All I'd said was that you had to watch out for them, and told them what area I knew they were in. I couldn't understand why their disbelief was making me so sad and angry all at the same time. It was the booze. It'd opened my mouth in the first place, and made feelings well up inside me with such exaggeration.

They didn't know about the gangs; they had never experienced the confusion that comes when an adult tries to take advantage of a lonely, lost, kid. They didn't know much about hunger, poverty and the lengths some people would go to get out of their grip. They knew nothing of the empty, abandoned, sick feeling of not being wanted and not knowing where your future lies, or worse, whether you even have one. They weren't even interested. And what hurt most, they couldn't believe for one minute that a twelve-year-old knew more about that stuff than they did.

The door opened, sucking some of the warm air out with it.

Mattie.

The three of us jumped in our seats, upsetting the beer bottles on the table. Empties toppled and rolled to the floor with a clatter. None broke.

Why hadn't we heard the car? Ed scrambled to his feet, hitting the table with his hip, sending more bottles tumbling. This time we were not so fortunate. Two bottles broke showering dark pieces of glass all over the dining room floor. Mattie entered, saw the beer bottles and her jaw dropped.

She sucked in a heavy breath. "What the hell is going on here?"

Ed stammered, but didn't manage to say anything. Jimmy walked out of the kitchen, mumbling something about getting ready for work. I was on my feet. My stomach felt like it was doing an acrobatic act. Mattie's glance jumped from me to the beer bottles and back again.

She yelled, "He's a twelve year old boy. Ed, you're giving beer to a twelve year old boy?"

Ed came back, "He's going to do it someplace, woman. Might as well be under adult supervision."

Mattie's voice ran up into shrieks, almost indiscernible as language. Her keys went rattling across the counter and rammed against the fridge, falling to the floor. Her coat thrown onto a chair, knocking it over. And he called himself an adult? She wailed. He boomed back that he made the money in this house. She yelled that he spent it all on beer. And besides, it's their money, not his money. On and on the familiar argument went, filling the house with the shattering ring of raised voices, banging of doors, the smashing of anything handy.

The next happened with so little drama I thought I was dreaming. Ed stood up, walked across the kitchen, drew up his fist and smacked her in the face with a pop. She crumpled backwards, eyes spinning in their sockets.

Ed stuck out his chest and pounded his feet like a stallion. He raised a finger, shook it before her face.

"No woman of mine gives me lip like that. Do you hear me?"

Mattie's eyes, still wild, held his finger in their sights, but she didn't reply.

With an abrupt stamp of his foot, Ed shook his hand into a new fist. "Do you hear me?" he yelled.

She nodded wordlessly. With the motion, something inside me deflated. Mattie, she'd always been so chock full of spunk. How could she take this from him?

Ed stepped away from her and went out the door without so much as a sweater on. He pulled the door to with great purpose, using it as an exclamation mark. A pillow of cool air brushed my face. His footsteps crunched away in the snow, probably headed to the bar and would stay until she was asleep.

I tried to step toward the living room, the way Jimmy had.

"Where the hell do you think you're going, young man?" Mattie said, her composure regained. But her voice was tinged with a snide ferocity never heard before. I stopped, bracing myself for her redirected focus. She continued, "If I go down those stairs, what will I see?" I was supposed to have cleaned up a corner of the basement for her, but hadn't gotten around to it. I was cemented still in the moment, incapable of reacting. She huffed, just for the sake of drama, crossed the room flung open the basement door and went down the stairs. Moments later she re-appeared, stopped with two gentle, feminine steps, hanging onto the doorframe, looking out at me.

In a whisper packed with malice, "You expect to get dinner tonight, do you?"

The beer was like a poker into the hot coals of my resentment. I said, "I don't have to do what you say."

Mattie came across to me. "If you want to live here, you do."

"Who says," I yelled at her. "You're not my bloody mother."

"I ask you to do one thing. One thing."

"No, you don't. You ask me to do everything while Jimmy sits on the couch all night drinking beer."

"Jimmy has a full time job, mister. And he pays room and board."

It was so unfair. I tried to stop my face from puckering as the tears welled up and the sobs started. "I can't …I don't....What do I have to do to....?"

I blabbered, falling back against the wall. I let myself slide down against it into a crouching position as the tears took me over. I didn't know how to say that I had a full time job, too. I went to school, and then I came home and worked until it was time to do my homework, but by that time, I was too exhausted.

Mattie stepped back and turned away from me. "You have to do what I tell you to do to earn your keep, young man. But look at what you do instead, you're a kid and you're drinking beer."

"Mattie," I cried.

"What is it," she asked absently, looking in the fridge.

"No, look at me, Mattie. Please?"

She stood erect slowly, turned to me. The look on her face, all the weight of all the worries sloped her shoulders, as though the young beautiful woman I'd known had been erased and a hag propped inside the tent of her worn skin.

I whispered, "I didn't ask for this to happen. It just happened."

Her eyes closed as her bottom lip quivered. The lids of those eyes reminded me of bumpy olives. She sucked in a quick breath. "But I didn't either, Paul. Not any of this," she cried. I knew what she meant. The *this* was Ed's job that didn't pay as much as they needed. Ed and his boozing. The kids and all their expenses.

One of my nails was dirty. I picked at it. "I know."

I shrugged, and looked up at her, hopeful she was really listening to me. "It's just so hard. Seeing Jimmy laze about. Taking orders from you. You're not my mom. It's hard. I just want to be a kid."

Mattie opened her eyes but didn't look at me. As she moved to the other side of the kitchen, she said curtly, "Well, until you're making a living, you better get used to it."

* * *

"You're lying to me, Paul Miller," Mattie yelled across the table. "Where in the hell do you think we're going to find ten dollars? Do you think we have a money tree out back? You squandered that newspaper money. You find a way to pay it."

The accusation stung, partly because it wasn't true, but even more so because I'd asked to borrow the money, not take it. But Mattie wasn't accepting it that way.

The early morning paper route I'd taken on was supposed to make me pocket change. I pulled myself out of bed into the chilly winter air at four each morning. Our attic room was unheated, which made getting dressed a challenge. I managed to get dressing for bed down to nine seconds and the morning dress down to three minutes.

Snow piled up into hedges lining the road as tall as me. Gutters contained gray slush pools whose depths you couldn't discern just by looking at them. I'd try jumping across, but after a while learned not to bother. On mornings like that, eventually I'd get a soaker some way or another. When I did fall, the papers slithered out of the bag like dead fish. The wet snow turned them into gray mush or the wind picked them up and carried them off. I'd be left standing there, watching as the pages fluttered down the street, doing a jaunty jig in the air. As the pages separated, the jig would turn into a party.

After my route, as I rushed to put on dry clothes for school, Mattie's voice rang in my ears. "Do you know how much you're costing me in hot water, Paul Miller? You go through more clothes than a girl. You're going to run us into the poorhouse, inch by inch." I'd take off my thick socks, the kind with a red line encircling the toes. The dye would turn my pruned toes red, as if they'd been bleeding. And for what?

Collecting money was proving difficult. A lot of people would just refuse to pay, claiming they never received the papers. The next day the branch manager was expecting me to pay up my bill. All of it. Or else…

"Mattie, I didn't ask you to *give* it to me. I asked to borrow it."

Mattie gave me that penetrating stare she'd inherited from father. "Well, if you're quitting your paper route, then that's the same thing, isn't it?"

I looked down at the pieces of meat loaf and half-eaten mashed potatoes on my plate. It turned my stomach.

"I'll find something else," I whispered without looking up.

A sarcastic laugh sputtered out. "What in the world are you going to do to make money at your age? You can't do anything."

I looked up to her and said quietly, "I didn't spend the money, Mattie. Why won't you believe me?"

She banged a palm on the table, setting the plate's a-clatter. My nephew, Bruce, burst into a wail. Ed was sitting back in his chair with his arms crossed and his legs long and straight under the table. He had a smirk on his face as he watched us the way one would a movie show. And all the while, the baby screeched and gasped in the bassinet beside him, but it was as if he didn't hear it.

Mattie spat, "If you quit that paper route before you pay off that ten dollars, you are finding another place to live, Paul Miller. Because you're not getting that money from us." Mattie jumped to her feet, grabbed at Bruce. The boy coughed in surprise at the jolt of her grip. His skin spurted scarlet, like a dye bath had just been poured under his skin. His hands knotted into fists and his face became one gaping hole of a mouth making more noise than one would think possible.

Mattie ignored him and pointed at me. "I mean it, Paul. You quit and you are not allowed under this roof. You can't waste your money and expect us to pick up the slack. I won't stand for it. I have enough on my plate as it is." She turned and waddled out of the kitchen, her frame an off-balance triangle with Bruce balanced on her hip. She clucked at him as she went, "It's okay, my weetle Brucey. It's going to be okay."

The subtext of her words struck me. It was going to be okay when I was gone. I didn't belong here.

"Hey, Paul," Ed called. He twisted a ten-dollar bill between thumb and forefinger. A finger went to his lips, telling me to keep it quiet. I always wondered how much money he hid from her. I suspected it was quite a lot.

I shook my head, went over and scooped up the baby. "She's right. It's time for me to move out, Ed," I said. The diaper bulged and I headed off to change it.

Ed grabbed me by the arm and sent a crooked smile. "You've got no place to go, buddy."

"With Sarah, maybe."

Ed laughed at the suggestion. "Believe me, buddy. You don't want to be around newlyweds, and they don't want you either. I can just see the three of you sleeping in that one room apartment. Three little pigs blowing the walls down. It won't work. Listen; don't pay no attention to Mattie. Quit the paper route. Mattie's just uptight. This'll pass. That's the way women are, right?"

I shook off his fingers and headed out of the kitchen. I knew Mattie would never believe I was losing money on the paper route, or that I could get a job elsewhere. Just after eight o'clock, when Mattie was reading Bruce a bedtime story, I slipped out the door and went down the hushed streets to the Baylor's.

I found Rachel working in her pottery studio. She saw the look on my face and said, "Go grab a hand full of clay. I need it worked out." I'd done this before, working the clay by pounding and folding it to get the air bubbles out. In the kiln, air bubbles would expand, shattering every piece. The clay had to be worked hard to make sure that didn't happen.

We worked in silence for a while. The clay felt slippery and wet between my fingers. I liked how the gray of it was almost blue, like a dolphin. I'd throw it down on the table and pound it with my fist, then roll it with my palms into a slim tube. It was like being a kid again.

At length, she looked over. "A little late for a visit, isn't it, Paul?"

I punched the clay.

"Talking can help, you know," she said.

I looked up. There was such caring in her eyes. I'd only seen the like in my mother's. I told her about the argument with Mattie and about my job that was losing money.

Rachel turned back to the wheel. She worked for a moment in silence. Then, with the wheel still turning, her hands shaping the clay, she said, "It's a difficult situation. You must feel resentful when they tell you what to do and how to behave. They make you pay your way because they have to. It must feel so unfair and unnatural. Like you belong nowhere, to no one."

"How did you know?"

Rachel stopped her work, looked over her shoulder. With a smile and shrug, she said, "From some of what you've said, thinking it through. You can never be your sister's son, Paul, and she can never be your mother, but it's no one's fault. Of course, living in it is very difficult. I can just barely imagine the problems." She turned back to her work. "You never told me how it ended up this way. What happened to your parents? Do you want to tell me now?"

Rachel listened to me tell my story with her feet pushing the potter's wheel round and round, her gaze steady on the pot being formed between her deft fingers, pinching.

For some reason I was reminded of Noah. I hadn't thought of him in such a long time.

When I was done she pulled her hands away from the pot and stopped the wheel's spinning. She put her hands on the apron on her knees and looked down between her feet with a big sigh, thinking. In a minute, she looked up.

"Did I ever tell you about my sister, Eileen?" I shook my head, finding the question odd. Rachel looked up. "She has two daughters. One's married. The other's just a year older than you. But you know what?" I shook my head. "They always wanted to have a boy." She smiled. Rachel continued, "Would you, if they accepted, and your family approves, like to live with them? I'm sure they'd love to have you."

What a strange offer. On the one hand, the idea of living in a real home — where I wouldn't be a burden, where I'd actually be wanted — was enticing. But it was weird, too. How could I live with complete strangers? Why would they want me?

"Where do they live?" I asked.

"Not far from here. In Dearborn." She scrunched her nose. "I can arrange for you to go over there for a visit, before we say anything to your family, or you make a decision or anything."

"Sure. That's a good idea."

The next evening we went to visit Rachel's sister and brother-in-law, Eileen and Terry Montayne.

Eileen was like the opposite of her sister, Rachel. She was all fixed up, with red polish on her nails, a dress like a sailor suit, and heeled shoes that matched perfectly. Cinnamon hair fell in neat curls down to shoulders, framing her teardrop face.

Terry was the gruff type who spoke his mind. A suit was propped on him; I could tell he didn't like it. He sat in his chair, giving me a mischievous eye, as if he were trying to crack into my soul just by looking.

Eileen served cake, ice cream, and lemonade. Terry squinted at me and asked, conspiratorially, if I'd like to learn how to shoot a gun and catch pheasant. Well, of course I did. Eileen wanted to know if I liked to go camping. I'd never been.

After the snack, I was led on a tour. They had a big yard and an old barn. There was a front-screened porch that reminded me of my old home on Grandview Avenue. I had to admit, they were a polite and attractive couple. What I liked about them most was that they weren't trying too hard. But still, they were looking me over like a pair of shoes, and I was looking them over asking myself, do I or don't I?

On our way back in the car, Rachel asked, "Well Paul, what did you think of the Montayne's? Do you think you would like to live with them?"

"I don't know," I said. "I just don't know."

Rachel was silent. Then, after a few moments, said, "Paul, how about this. Try it until school starts. If you still feel that way, you can move out. But, I would like you to at least give it a chance. They'd really like to have you."

One ingredient in my decision was that Rachel and Connie would be moving to Atlanta at the end of the summer. But with me living at the Montayne's, I could see Connie a lot until then. Once summer was gone, life in that crowded house, friendless, would be intolerable. This was a chance at normalcy that I just could not pass up.

"Yea, I guess so. I don't have nowhere else to go."

"Okay, good!" Her hand came to my knee and gave it a squeeze.

When we got back to the Baylor home, Rachel asked who we had to call in my family. I gave her Jimmy's number — he was my legal guardian. Rachel called and explained the whole situation. He said something that made her jump in her seat and send me an eye-popping look. Then she looked away at something else he said and shook her head, confused. When the call was over she turned to me and said, "Well, that was a surprise."

"What is it?" I asked.

She pointed at the phone. "I just can't believe what he said," she began. "After I asked, he said, 'Hell, yea, put him somewhere. I don't care.' What kind of brother is that?" Rachel came over to me, reaching out. I let her arms slip around my back and she rocked me back and forth in a nice, warm, hug. She rubbed the back of my head and said, "You have a home, now, Paul. You have a home."

*　*　*

For the first time in a long time I had a clean bed, all to myself in my very own room, just off from the living room. There was a dresser, and all the drawers were for me and a closet with just my clothes in it. It was the end of July 1951, approaching my fourteenth birthday, and finally, I could be a regular, ordinary kid, with a real home to come to and no mass of chores to pay for my keep.

We had a wonderful summer. The Montayne's were a camping, fishing and hunting family. Terry taught me how to fish. In the fall, we went pheasant hunting, and he taught me how to shoot a 12-gauge shotgun. Fall arrived so quickly. Just before Connie and Rachel moved away, I was asked during dinner if the trial period had been a success.

Did I want to stay?

I agreed and was enrolled in a new school.

14.

LIFE RENEWED

I mounted the steps of the bus for my first day of school. I had a brown paper bag lunch tight in my fist. Crayoned across each side was my name in Eileen's neat printing. Eileen said she'd put a secret treat in there. I was planning on digging in to see what it was as soon as we pulled away from the curb. I wore new clothes, new shoes and had a fresh haircut. For the first time in a long time, I felt like someone special.

I looked up to Eileen who was standing in the front doorway, watching me. You'd think I was five years old, going to my first day of kindergarten, the way she was carrying on. An arm was wrapped tight about her middle, as if she had to hold herself together or shatter into pieces. She was chewing on the knuckle of her free hand to keep herself from sobbing, but there was a smile of pride in those gray eyes.

I gave her a final wave and mounted the steps of the bus. That's when I saw him. A husky, shadow of a figure, about my age. He sent a harsh and steely stare my way. The worn and torn shirt he had on could've been one of mine, plucked out the garbage, it was so similar. Intimidated by his glare, I continued to the back. When the bus started away from the curb, he stood up and lurched down the bus' length toward me, hands pushed deep into his jacket pockets, his head hanging low. Without a word he sat sideways in the seat in front of me and sent a leering smile without opening his mouth, giving me a snide all over check.

"Spiffy," he said. I spied some yellow teeth. A vapor, meat smell, wafted towards me. I tried to keep from shirking at it, but it was worse than his attitude.

Yet, the attitude held sway over me. All of a sudden, the new clothes were unnatural; the navy pants with the smart cuffs too adult, the shirt that Eileen had said brought out the blue of my eyes, garish.

148

He continued, "You're new this year, aren't you?"

I nodded.

"I live just around the corner from you. Of course, I can't afford spiffy clothes like that. You're quite the actor, you are." He whistled and looked away, a cool grit in his eye. He was right, and it stung. I was an impostor, pretending to be a normal, suburban kid.

I coughed, nervous. "They're new," I said in defense, regretting immediately that I'd revealed the obvious.

The guy turned to me with mock realization. "Really?" he sang. "I'd've never thunk it. But how could I? You see, I don't have a rich momma like you have. I've never seen new clothes before. Guess that makes you better than me, huh?" He rested his head on the bus seat between us, his eyes steady on mine, challenging.

I coughed again, looked away from him and squirmed. "They're not from my momma."

He gave me a pouty look, like he was puckering for a cartoon kiss. "Your papa, then." I shook my head. He shrugged with frustration. "I don't care who you got them from. Grandma. Grandpa. Who cares? They don't make you special, pretty boy. You hear me?"

I fidgeted for a moment, trying to contain myself, but then blurted, "What's wrong with being special?"

Surprised eyes flashed my way. I'd caught him off guard.

I went on, poking him, "How the heck can you judge someone just because of the way they're dressed? Huh?"

He sat back against the window.

I continued, "So somebody who cares for me bought me some clothes. What's wrong with that, huh? I've never had new before, either. A couple months ago, I was dressed just like you. So, if someone offered to buy you new clothes, wouldn't you take 'em up on the offer? Wouldn't you?"

"Of course," he said automatically.

I leaned back in my seat in victory, watching him, curious to see what he'd do, pretty certain he'd beg off, all apologies, and find another seat. He sat there thinking for a minute, staring at the floor, his face puffed and red, like an overly ripe tomato. A decision settled into him. He sighed, and then looked at me.

"Sorry for pickin' on ya," he said matter-of-factly, with an honesty that was enviable. "I didn't mean nothing. I don't know why I did it. Just to prove I'm cool, I guess. I'm sorry." The ball of his right shoulder squeezed tight to his ear, and he arched an eyebrow in question. "You're not going to hold it against me, are ya?"

I smiled. "Nah," I replied.

He shook his head. "I can tell already, you're a pretty good guy. Why, if some jerk had done that to me, I'd've told him to DDT."

"DDT?" I said, pretending not to know.

He shrugged. "Drop Dead Twice."

I cracked back the going reply to the put down, "What, and look like you?"

His look snapped my way with happy surprise. He laughed and I joined him, but turned away from that awful smell coming out of his mouth. His hand disappeared inside his jacket, bringing out a pack of cigarettes. He offered me one, and I sent a furtive look to the bus driver.

"She don't care," he said. "We just open the windows and it's nobody's business, right?" He jumped up, turned and opened two of the windows with quick flicks. I took one. I didn't really smoke, yet, but everyone did it. If you didn't, something was wrong with you.

He exhaled the first puff in a stream over his shoulder, and then reached his arm over the chair to shake. "I'm Don Carter," he said.

Half an hour later, we were walking up the steps to the school, chatting like old friends. We were just about to go through the doors, when Don grabbed me by the arm and pulled me out of the stream of students. "So, Paul? Whaddya say we skip today? It's just the first day. Nothing important's gonna happen."

I was glad he liked me enough to suggest it. But what if Eileen found out? I couldn't do that to her. I turned him down.

He sent a yellow smile out from under that hung head of his, and he closed his eyes, at my wisdom.

*   *   *

Don had me by the arm, pulling me up the walk to the little pink house where he lived with his Mother and brother. It was a former garage that they rented, tucked behind a more substantial home. He told me the landlady was a frail thing with a bitter mouth on her. She was going deaf and yelled at her cat constantly as she bumped about that house, a place stuffed with doilies and knickknacks.

He burst through the door of his home ahead of me, yelling, "Ma, I got someone I want ya to meet." He sent me another yellow smile and nodded reassurance, but then he didn't know what to do. I smiled back and looked around, waiting as he shuffled toward the stairs. The couch was covered in a floral patterned cloth that had seen better days. All the furniture leaned in a different angle. The scent of boiled cabbage clung to the air so thickly you could almost see the green coating of it on everything but me.

Don jumped, as if remembering something, and pulled out a kitchen table chair for me. "Come on, sit down. Do you want some milk? Cookies?"

Thumps rattled the house as someone made their way down the stairs. "Don, what in the world you yelling about? I was sleeping. And you know I don't...." She came around the corner, saw me and stopped. She was a spindle of a woman, with a salty face, tightened by overwork. She knotted a satin bathrobe dotted in Chinese characters tighter about her waist.

"Ma. This is Paul. He's a new friend."

She sent Don a strange look, and then gave me one even stranger, with a slight, crooked smile. She came toward me with little steps and reached out with a hand that was more bone than flesh.

"Nice to meet ya, there, Paul. No offense. But I work nights and this character here isn't supposed to come banging about the house like an elephant. It's good to meet ya, but I need my sleep if I'm going to put in a good shift. Do come again, Paul." She nodded and headed up the stairs.

Don watched her leave. A wash like pride covered his face. He looked to me again, said, "Let's go out back and hang out." He insisted on bringing the bottle of milk from the fridge and the cookie jar. We sat on the back steps under the fading leaves of a sumac and started to munch.

"Where's your dad?" I asked.

The question made him bristle. "Not here," he said, his voice ominous. He pulled out his pack of smokes and offered me another. I accepted. He continued, "Right this very minute I imagine he's drunk somewhere, hanging out in some bar. We left him, kinda."

"Sorry. I didn't know it was like that."

Don told me about how his father used to come home drunk and just start beating the family up. He'd push his mother around the kitchen. He'd scream at Don for being a lazy sot, punch him about, and toss him around the living room. Don showed me the scar on the right side of his head, just above the ear, from the time his head collided with the corner of a doorway.

Then there was that awful day when Don's father cornered his mother in the kitchen. He pulled out the cast iron frying pan, wacked her with it on her side. He wacked her leg. By that time, Don and his brother were looking for weapons they could use against him. His dad whacked at her hip. Something crunched inside her and Mother was on the floor. This made his dad even angrier. He jumped down and raised the pan high in the air. He was going to bring it down right on Mother's head. Don and his brother came up from behind just then; Don had a lead pipe, his brother, a broomstick.

Don recounted with dismay how he can remember seeing his Father's face, looking up at him, his features tightened to slits, his hands up to ward off the blows. Don smashed at him, holding the hands back, thrusting, pounding, with more force than he knew he was capable of. And in that memory, he recalled how he felt pleasure, satisfaction at the revenge. He could have kept on hitting that bastard, wanted to kill him, but his Mother and brother stopped him. He was glad he never had to see his Dad again, because he knew that if he did he'd probably kill him.

*   *   *

Living with the Montaynes in the summer had been like a vacation, where everything is the way one imagines it's supposed to be. But with the advent of the school year, the elements of fantasy were fading

They tried so hard to make me feel at home. Eileen would spend her nights with me at the kitchen table after dinner. She'd give me a chocolate cupcake and a glass of milk. She'd cook or clean or sew with her little dog, Two, asleep on her lap as I did my homework. Try as she might, she couldn't keep herself from humming as she worked, no matter how much it bothered me.

Our nights wouldn't be all work. I told her about Don and the experiences we shared, and she would always listen to what I had to say. She loved to laugh. Her nickname was "Short", because she was so short. One could get her started laughing by just saying; "Hey, everyone look at Short!" Within twenty seconds she was roaring with laughter. She'd laugh so hard, she had to hurry to the bathroom for fear of wetting herself. And there she'd go, scurrying, holding herself, and laughing all the way. And when she came back, she'd ambush me for a wrestle on the kitchen floor, like we were brothers.

But despite all this fun, living with them just didn't feel right.

I tried to call them Mom and Dad. It caught in my throat like a hunk of salt-water taffy that's too big to swallow. But, most of all, I had a difficult time resigning myself to the fact that, as foster parents, they were allowed to tell me what to do. I couldn't accept it.

*   *   *

The front door opened with a bang. Eileen looked in its direction, fuming. I glanced toward Terry's cold plate of dinner. It was still sitting in his spot at the dining table; I could see it framed in the doorway from where I sat at the kitchen table. This was the fourth time that week he'd been late.

Terry appeared before his plate of cold food, his torso wavering in a drunken wind.

Eileen got to her feet and yelled, "Terry, where have you been?"

Terry's finger spiraled to the plate and returned to his mouth. He spat. "This is cold," he said, making the three words one.

Eileen ran into the dining room toward him. I started to collect my things. I didn't want to be there when they got going.

"Answer my question!" she yelled.

I didn't have to see his curled lip when he replied, "I don't have to tell you anything."

"I had this dinner ready at 7 o'clock. That's two hours ago. Five hours since you finished work. And you couldn't take the two minutes or spare the dime to call and tell me where you were?"

In one big sniff, Terry roused himself to a bloated pigeon with his messy breast feathers plumped out. "I don't have to tell anyone where I am," he yelled. "I don't have time to…."

Eileen poked him in the chest. "How dare you. I slave away getting your dinner ready, keeping your…."

"The piper calls the tune, woman."

"You may be the piper. I won't deny that. But I…."

Terry wiped the plate onto the floor with one swoop of his arm. Eileen shrieked in dismay and fury. Terry headed into the kitchen to grab himself a beer.

And on they went for the fourth time that week. I slipped into my bedroom to escape it, but it wasn't much of an escape. If I hadn't had a project due in school, I would have snuck out my window and gone over to Don's.

There came the smash of something falling, making me jump, but that was common. From what Eileen said, I gathered it was one of the table lamps. This was followed not too long after by a loud bump. Eileen's lounge chair had been upended. Their argument moved upstairs to their bedroom, which I hoped meant he was losing steam. But five minutes later Eileen started to screech so loudly it shook down the walls. I rushed up the stairs; certain that he'd finally smacked her. I arrived in their bedroom to see the two of them doing a tug-of-war with a dress. He stood by the open window, a beer in one hand, the dress clutched in the other. She had the dress by two hands, leaning backwards at an angle. Her heels dug into the floor and her normally feminine mouth was twisted into a knot of determination. All at once she lost her grip and went tumbling to the floor with a groan. Without even looking at her, he threw the dress out the window, a nuisance. He pushed past her and lurched to the closet, hungry for more.

Luckily he was drunk enough that the two of us could corral him out of the bedroom. He became a wolf, holed up in the kitchen, drinking his beers as if they were his right.

I found half of Eileen's clothes piled like a layer of fresh snow across the rose bushes and spruce. I gathered them and brought them back up to her in the bedroom to hang. Each time I passed the kitchen door I gave it a wide berth, wary he might reach out and grab me.

Why in the world did such a joyful woman stay with such a boor of a man?

* * *

Eileen saw what I had in my hand and her eyes popped.

"Paul Miller, you get that...." she began.

I put a finger to my lips to silence her, and she obeyed. I lifted up what was a rubber replica of a dog dropping. I shook it so she'd understand, pointing my thumb out to the garage, where Terry was working. Eileen put her knuckle to her mouth, hunched down and giggled.

She crept behind me and watched with me as he picked up some boxes he had to throw away and headed out to the curb. I rushed into the garage and placed the dropping dead center, then turned to get the lawn mower ready for cutting the grass. The blades needed sharpening. Eileen came from around the front of the house. She went to her gardening boxes full of bulbs and started to root through them, but I knew she was really there to watch the fun. We both knew Terry had a weak stomach for filthy things.

We tried to contain our giggles as Terry came back. He saw it sitting there and stopped. You could almost hear the working gears of his brain. In due time, he went to the corner, grabbed the broom and started to sweep. When he got to the center, he swept around it. Finally, he turned to Eileen and asked, "Would you pick this up, please?"

I don't know how she managed it, but without cracking a smile, she looked, saw what it was, shook her head, and turned back to her boxes.

The sigh Terry gave was like the burp of a steam engine. He went to the back of the garage and started to arrange the tools. I headed out to cut the grass.

At length, he came and got me, told me to pick it up. I told him I'd be right in, but continued to cut the grass. A little while later, when I finally went in, it was still lying on the floor.

I looked at it, shook my head and said, "No, I can't pick that up, it'll make me sick."

By that point, Terry was distraught. He grabbed the shovel and broom and tried to sweep it up. But in the process, it hit the top of the shovel and went bouncing across the floor. Eileen and I started to laugh so hard, but Terry refused to acknowledge what was going on. He flew into a rage, screaming at Eileen that he could smell it, it made him sick, and the next time he tells me to do something, I'd better jump to it right away.

I left the garage, still laughing, returning to mow the lawn, but the lawn mower wouldn't start. I pulled several times and finally checked the tank. Empty. All Terry heard was me pulling the starter, and he came out screaming at me as loud as he could about me not knowing a damn thing about fixing things and abusing the equipment and on and on. I walked away from him, got the gas can and filled up the mower. When it was full, while I was putting the cap back on the gas can, Terry went over to the lawn mower, pulled it, and, of course, it started right up.

"See," he said, "that's how you start a lawn mower, dummy."

The word *dummy* blasted through me. I stood upright and yelled, "Don't you ever call me a dummy. Never. You just can't stand the fact that we played a joke on you. Can you? Can you?"

"You SOB," he said.

I walked away from him and went into the house, sneaking out the back way to go to Don's.

Did bickering, fighting, and nagging hound me? Was this what life was like behind everyone's closed door? Cause if it was, I didn't want any part of real life. It seemed like wherever I went, it was like hell followed.

Don sat on the tree stump out behind his place and puffed on his cigarette as he listened to this new tale, part a series, called Living with Terry and Eileen.

When I was done, he asked, "Why don't you leave?"

I sputtered a laugh. "I got nowhere to go."

One of those ragged smiles twisted his lips. His gaze was faraway and dreamy. An idea was forming. "We could both haul ass out of here," he said in a whisper.

"Where to?" I asked without enthusiasm.

His glare pierced me. "I'm serious, Paul. I mean, why not? I'm so sick of school, it gags me. You got a real nowhere situation you want no part of. Right?"

"Yea. But where would we go?"

Don sucked on his smoke, staring down at the growing bug of the heater as if it could tell him something. Mixed in with the blue smoke of his exhalation came, "Some place warmer. Cause winter's coming, right?"

I shrugged agreement.

"Some place full of opportunity." He nudged my knee. "And beautiful women, bathing beauties, sitting on blankets in bathing suits, begging to be slathered in oil."

The concept was starting to have a certain appeal, but I was still unsure. "But how?"

He motioned up and down with his thumb sticking up. "Thumb to freedom, buddy."

"Where?" I challenged.

Don threw his arms wide, as if it was obvious. "Florida!" he exclaimed, with great enthusiasm.

Now, if it had been any other place, I would have gone right that minute, but it took me until the weekend to agree.

We left early on a Tuesday morning. Our first ride came from a traveling salesman. Once inside, he asked where we were heading, what we were doing. Don told him Florida and the guy gave us a double take. Something was wrong. So Don bumped him on the shoulders and told him we were just joking. We were going to football practice, but our parents couldn't drive us. That seemed to appease him.

Two rides later, we were hungry. We ate burgers and onion rings at a truck stop. We were on our way back out to the road, when Don noticed the neon lights of a saloon in a concrete shoebox building. We went in smoking cigarettes, hunched moodily at the bar and ordered beers with clipped words, as though we did it all the time. And the guy served us. Two beers later we decided to hit the road again. Unfortunately, the first car to pick us up had flashing lights. Ohio State Police. They slammed us in jail and called our parents. In my case, Jimmy.

Jimmy told them to keep me. The police said they couldn't do that. Jimmy called the Montayne's, and Eileen and Don's Mother came down and got us the next day.

In the car on the way back to Dearborn I'm sure not half a dozen words were spoken. That evening Terry and Eileen and I had a little talk. Why did I do it? I couldn't tell them the real reason. I blamed it all on eccentricity, a confused state of mind and, well, 'bullshit'. They said they'd give it one more try, but I would have to straighten up and fly right. No more smoking, no more skipping school, and I had to get my grades up. Of course, I agreed to all. I had nowhere else to go.

I did try, but the world around me stayed the same. Once given the taste of the road, if but for one day, I couldn't let it go. The idea had taken shape.

I didn't belong in this family. Not in any family. There wasn't any real love in the world. Just a story. A myth perpetuated in books, or misplaced, the way Eileen's was.

All that stuff Noah had talked about. It was garbage, as far as I was concerned. Stuff for kids to believe. God didn't have any master plan for nobody. It was all shit, and who cared, anyway? In the end, the claustrophobia wore me down. I was trapped in a box and couldn't see a way out. So, in January 1953, I left again. This time, alone.

15.

WHERE TO?

I left early on a Monday morning. Instead of getting on the bus for school, I walked to the highway. I didn't know where I was going, how I was going to get there, when I did get *there*, or what I was going to do. I just had to go, to get away. I was fourteen years old. I had $16.47 and half a pack of cigarettes in my pocket.

It was very cold that morning, with the wind blowing snow across the road, piling up in wavelike formations on the far side of the shoulder. I wore a light winter jacket, Levi's and tennis shoes. Not exactly deep winter weather gear. But I was determined.

From Detroit, going north only gets you to Canada and more cold. So I positioned myself by the southbound lane under a bridge to stay out of the wind and blowing snow. I stood there with my thumb out for forty-five minutes before a car finally stopped.

The man in the car was alone, heading to Monroe, Michigan. He let me out just short of town where the highway split.

I stood at the side of the road below the sign that said Toledo. After thirty minutes, I was hungry and cold again. I'd noticed a truck stop about a quarter of a mile back down the highway, so I headed there.

After ordering my food, I asked the waitress in a whisper if she knew whether any of these truckers were headed south.

She smiled at me, stood up and hollered out, "Hey, any of you jokers going south?" The place erupted with laughter.

One guy called out, "Not me, I'm not going down to that damn warm weather and sweat." Another said, "Can't go south, sun gives me burns." It was a funhouse in there for everyone but me, let me tell you. One guy asked, "Who wants to know?"

The waitress pointed at me and said, "This kid here. Looks like he needs a ride."

Every face turned to look in my direction and my face flushed. Not one of them said anything. All heads turned back to their business with barely more than a murmur.

Disappointed and embarrassed, I finished my lunch, paid the bill and went out the door. I didn't get five feet toward the highway before I heard, "Hey kid, where you going?"

Off the tip of my tongue came out, "Atlanta." I'd just learned, you can't be on the road without a destination. With Rachel and Connie in Atlanta, it was as good a destination as any.

"I'm headed for Richmond, Virginia," he replied. "But I can take you to the cut off to Atlanta."

"That's great. Thanks."

"I'm that silver and blue rig over there." He pointed at it. "Wait there and I'll be out in a few minutes."

I walked over to the truck and waited. I really wanted to get inside but he'd said, *wait over there*, so figured that meant 'outside'. I didn't want to get him mad.

As the big rig rolled down the highway I could feel the wind making it sway and the driver fighting to keep it under control.

The driver's name was David. He lived in Grand Rapids, Michigan, and drove that route once a week. He had a wife and three kids, and he was trying to get enough money to buy the rig, but he was afraid by the time he got it together, the truck would have too many miles on it and would cost him a fortune in repairs.

David was a quiet man, with a presence so still, every word he spoke was like it was carved out of a diamond. You had to listen. Nothing ruffled him, as if he drove his rig on clouds and he was master. He made me feel at ease from the get go.

The small talk done, he said, "Kid? What you done back there in that truck stop, I'd advise you never to do again." He explained that truckers could lose their jobs taking on passengers. Companies don't allow it.

"Okay," I said.

He asked, "Why are you on the road?" His question caught me off guard. I didn't know what to say.

"You're running away aren't you?"

"Well, yes, sort of."

"It's not good for a young fella like you to be on the road by yourself."

"I thought it would be good experience for me to find out what the world is like."

He laughed and said, "You just might find out that there are more bad things than good, and you won't like some of them."

"What do you mean by 'bad' things?"

"Son, there are creeps out here that look for boys like you. They pick them up and sometimes the boys are never seen again. Do you know what molestation means?"

"Ah, no, sir I don't."

"Do you know what rape is?"

"Yea, I've heard of that."

"It's the same thing but done with a child, anyone under 16."

"What do you mean by 'they are never seen again'?"

"They kill the kids and bury the bodies or burn em up or whatever."

"Why would they do that?"

"So the kid can't identify them, put them in jail."

"Oh yea, I never thought of that."

"So you be real careful."

About daybreak, Dave pulled onto the shoulder and said for me to take the road on the right, to U.S. Highway #1 in South Carolina. He had to keep going straight. He pulled out five dollars and handed it to me saying, "Get where you want to go, and then stay off the highway." I remember the earnest look of concern in his eyes, the sight of the bill snapping in the wind of a passing rig. I thanked him, climbed down, watched his rig pull away and stuck out my thumb.

Three minutes later a white car stopped.

"Where you headed, son?"

"Atlanta."

"Well I'm not going that way but I'll take you to highway #1."

"That's great, a big help, thank you."

After we got under way, the man asked, "What's a boy like you doing out on the road, anyway?"

"I'm just going to visit my aunt in Atlanta for a while."

"Well, where you coming from?"

"Detroit."

"Detroit? Always hated that city. Full of gangsters and black folks. Aren't you afraid to be on the road by yourself?"

I shivered, but forced on a smile, saying, "No, actually. You meet some very nice people on the road." I was trying to maintain the I know what I'm doing façade.

Every ride was both the same and different. There were the chatty ones who wanted to find out all about me. Others who didn't say more than a word. The weather got warmer by the mile. I learned how to wash up in the gas station rest rooms, maintain a polite and entertaining banter for those who wanted it and keep my thoughts to myself for those who didn't.

* * *

He pulled over to the side of the road, told me which road led to Atlanta, then drove off. He'd been a silent one, which I'd been thankful for.

It was so dark, I couldn't see my hand in front of my face.

I started to hike down the road. I was in mountain country, so the air was full of fresh earthy smells, which was great, but the roads were curvy and dark with forests all along the sides past the ditches. It was silent but for cricket song and wind in the trees.

Then, I heard the rumble of a car. I turned and stuck out my thumb. The vehicle's lights appeared in the trees, turned the corner, and the car suddenly screeched its tires as he pulled around me and sped off. I guess he didn't see me until the last second. I probably scared him.

As I walked, I could hear animals scurrying, wondered what they could be. Rabbits, perhaps? Bears, maybe? Mountain lions? Or was I just being silly?

But then, as I walked, I noticed a sound like something making its way through leaves, rustling them. I stopped. The sound stopped. I started again. It started again. I ran fifty yards. The rustling was along beside me, right behind the blackness, in the trees.

A car came down the road. I turned and stuck my thumb out. The car slowed and came to a complete stop next to me. It wasn't until it was up close that I could see it was a Georgia State Police cruiser, and I became nervous.

"Kid," he asked, leaning over, his hand still on the window crank. "Do you have any ID?"

I shook my head.

"Where you headin' this time of night, boy?"

"Atlanta," I replied. "Visiting my aunt."

The officer huffed in surprise. "How in the hell did you get on this road to Atlanta?" he asked.

I shrugged.

"Boy, you got yourself one hell of a path to Atlanta. Watch out for bears, and snakes this time of night. Good luck." He rolled up his window and drove off.

I stared at his brake lights as he continued down the hill.

"Good luck?" That was his idea of helping me? No directions, no ride. Just watch out for bears and good luck? I couldn't believe it.

Once my eyes adjusted to the dark again, I kicked around until I found a good size stick to defend myself with. Even as I did it, I thought it funny. How was I going to defend myself against a bear with a stick?

My thoughts grasped for something to hang onto. They retrieved Noah. What would he think of my situation? I found it hard to imagine. The forest was dark, its shadows felt so mysterious, almost evil. I was scared, I needed hope. "Oh Noah," I said to myself. "Where are you?"

All of a sudden, I heard the sound of a truck struggle up the mountain behind me. I turned around. After quite a long time, I could see lights jumping about in trees until finally the vehicle came around the curve into view. It was an old moving van traveling at about ten miles an hour. When he arrived in front of me the van stopped and someone inside hollered at me to get in. I climbed aboard and before I even slammed the door, the vehicle jerked on its way.

"Where ya'll goin' boy?" the man asked with a deep fried drawl.

"Atlanta, to visit my aunt."

"Atlanta? Whew! How'd you get on this here highway to get to Atlanta?"

"Last ride I had told me to take it," I said.

The man turned and looked at me. "Boy, that man was foolin' you. Ya can get to Atlanta on this road, but it takes fer ever and a day."

"Where are you going?" I asked.

"Well, I'm a goin' to Atlanta eventually, but I gots to drop off some of this here furniture in a little town called Winder first. Y'all can stay with me if you wants. But I'm a tellen ya, it'll take some time."

"Yea, I'll stay with you. I'll even help unload the furniture if you buy me breakfast."

"You done got yerself a deal, boy."

As he drove, he told me how he grew up in the Georgia mountains and moved furniture with his Daddy's old truck once in while. But wasn't sure how long this old beauty would keep rolling.

"Gots a lot of miles on her," he said. His name was Gabriel, but everyone called him Gabe.

We chatted as we plugged along and finally reached the first town. We found the house and unloaded the furniture in twenty minutes. Gabe was so strong; he picked up a lot of the furniture himself. We found a restaurant, ate breakfast, washed up and headed for Atlanta. The scenery through the mountains was a sight of beauty that grabbed at my heart. Trees, creeks, wildlife. I was glad I didn't get to see all of it up close.

* * *

The street where the Baylor's lived was lined with clapboard houses that reminded me of cottages. On the front porches were rocking chairs or church benches, screened in rooms off to one side. I could see myself living in one of them, but knew that wasn't what I was there for.

Trouble was, I didn't know what I was there for. I knew they couldn't take me in. I'd tried that. A friendly voice to help me find the answers? What was I going to say when they opened the door?

I walked back and forth in front of their house for two hours. One minute I'd be pacing, the next I'd be sitting on the curb, head on my arms, thinking or worrying or both. One thing I knew for sure, Rachel was going to be furious. So maybe the best thing to do would be to just continue on my way? But where? To Florida, where it was warm and sunny? To see if I could find Noah? Or off in a totally new direction? To find a place for me in a totally new city?

I dreamed for a few moments of disappearing, never letting my relatives or anyone know where I am. But I knew I couldn't let go that much, which must have meant there was something to still hang on to. Although for the life of me, I couldn't figure what it was. And besides, what in the world could a 14-year-old boy do once he arrived in an undiscovered city?

Finally, I got up and said, "Oh hell. It can't make that much difference." I reasoned that most of the damage had already been done, and I really wanted to see a familiar face.

I knocked on the door. There was a pause that felt eternal. Then stocking feet on hardwood floor. In one swoosh, the door was pulled open and there was Connie, the red exclamation marks of her hair sprouting out all over, just like I remembered. Small eyes, rhinestones of blue, went so wide I thought they would pop right out of their sockets.

Connie shrieked, pushed through the screen door, grabbed me tight and started to jump up and down. She hollered as if declaring victory, "Paul is here! Paul Miller is here in Atlanta!"

Rachel's head appeared at the back of the house. "Paul!" she screeched, and ran toward the door. "Oh, I'm so glad you're finally here," she said. She too ran through the door, arms encased me like a blanket and she rocked me back and forth. She pulled away, brushed back my hair, looking into my eyes as if she was surprised to see I existed. "What took you so long?" she asked. "We were expecting you for days, now."

"Expecting me?" I didn't even know I was heading here. How could they?

"Terry and Eileen called and told us to expect a visitor. And here you are. They're worried sick about you, being on the road by yourself."

"But how did they know I was alone?"

"Well, Paul, now that didn't take too much detective work. All they had to do was call Don Carter."

"I never thought of that."

"That's because you're a kid," Rachel said with a smile, ruffling my hair. We all laughed.

Connie brought me upstairs to the spare bedroom. We hugged again, though briefly. She handed me some towels and said, "You stink, Paul Miller. Go take a shower."

I stood in the stream of hot water and thought about those cold times out on the road, and they made the shower feel like heaven itself. Clean clothes were on the bed when I returned. Mine had disappeared. They arrived later that day, cleaned, pressed and smelling fresh.

Over supper I was told that Eileen was on her way down. She'd be arriving the next day.

"Guess I'll have to get back on the road then," I said.

Rachel reached across the table, took my hand and shook it. "Oh no, you're not. You and Eileen need to talk your problems over and decide what you're going to do. You can't keep running away, Paul. Do you understand?"

"Yea. I understand," I said. But suddenly I felt alone. Even here, amongst my friends. "Excuse me," I said and pushed away from the table.

Comfortable for the first time in days, tucked into bed, I pondered what I could say to Eileen. It was so humiliating, them figuring out where I'd gone. I guess I wasn't quite as smart as I thought I was. But I was too tired to let more thoughts keep me up. Pretty soon I faded into that deep kind of sleep that was a void, so complete it's like God took an eraser to the hours.

My head bounced up off the pillow with a jerk, dismayed at first by the strange environment. It was light out. The clock read eleven. For a moment, I wondered how it could be so light so late at night. Then I realized, I'd slept for fourteen hours.

Rachel was in the living room, waiting for me. She fixed me a big breakfast and we had a talk, just like we used to.

I tried to explain to her what I thought my problems were, and she acknowledged that Terry and Eileen had been having problems for years.

The doorbell rang and the two of us exchanged glances. Rachel went to the door and I stayed sitting at the table, listening.

Rachel screamed with joy.

Eileen.

I stood up and said to myself, "Okay, Paul, be nice and apologetic. Not withdrawn or sarcastic."

Eileen rushed into the room, her eyes puffed out and red. She saw me, stopped, then her arms went wide, and she ran up to me. We talked late into the night, and we agreed I couldn't go back to living with them. I just couldn't do it, and they didn't want me.

Eileen sighed with the weight of that admission, and shook her head. "I'm sorry, Paul." She looked up, concerned. "What are you going to do?"

I swallowed. What could I do? I said, "Maybe I'll go out to California. Live with my Dad for a while." What a damn lie that was. It just came out of me like someone else was saying it.

"How are you going to get there?"

"Same way I got here. Hitchhike."

Eileen grimaced. She didn't like me being on the road. But as unhappy as it made her, she didn't try to change my mind. I guess this was her letting go. She asked if I'd stay on at the Baylor's for as long as she was there. I said I would.

We stayed three more days, but then our presence started to feel silly and burdensome. It was time to leave. We said our good byes, got in the car and headed away.

Eileen pulled onto the side of the road where the highway split in four directions. Our parting was quiet, yet I heard the spit of electricity charging between us. I got out of the car, Eileen handed me a twenty-dollar bill and started to cry. I said goodbye and walked away.

I watched as her car pulled onto the highway and disappeared over the rise. I didn't wonder how she could leave a fourteen-year-old boy out on the street. But I did recognize that empty, hollow sick feeling returning with a vengeance.

I crossed the street and headed for the sign that said 'Birmingham.' I found a little area off the road and sat down and cried. Here I was, all alone again. Was I destined to roam the highways for the rest of my life?

I said to myself, "All right, Paul Miller. It's time to make a decision. What are you doing? Why are you doing it? And don't make up any stories or lie."

Being totally honest with yourself is hard, perhaps, even, the most difficult accomplishment of a lifetime. It's so easy to accept obvious answers, to not listen to your gut, to try and think your problems away.

My mind filled and emptied many times before I finally came up with an answer I could accept as honest.

Continuing down to Florida didn't sit well, though I wasn't sure why. I suspected Noah had passed away by then. It had been four years, and it certainly felt like a long time. And he was so old. I convinced myself that finding him would be impossible. I was too young to remember where we were going, but more to the truth, I didn't think I could muster up the guts to face him.

If going back to Detroit had been my plan, I should have just stayed in the car with Eileen.

Then thoughts wandered to the remaining destination where I knew someone, and much to my surprise, it turned into a possibility.

Dad had spent about a year in a sanitarium getting medical attention. Maybe, just maybe, they'd helped him. And if so, then maybe he could accept me now, and we could start a new, fresh life together.

16.

ACROSS TO CALIFORNIA

By eleven the first night I arrived in Meridian, Mississippi. I didn't want to be on the road late, so I found the Greyhound Bus Station and sat in a seat as far from the ticket counter as I could get. I wanted so badly to lie down, but there were too many hobos and drunks wandering around. Before dozing off I looked at the clock. Ten minutes to twelve. I wondered where Eileen was.

A flurry of activity awoke me. Police walked through the crowd, picking out the vagrants. I spotted a lady sitting by herself, and walked over to her, asked if I could sit down. She smiled but didn't say anything. I sat down beside her. The police passed right by me. After they left, I thanked the lady, went to the restroom, washed up and headed back out to the road.

A painted school bus stopped and opened the door. "Hey gringo, you want ride?" the bus driver asked.

I put my foot on the first step. "How far you going?"

He motioned with his hand for me to get on the bus, a smile sweet like hot peppers. "Come, ride, come come." I got on and took an empty seat five rows back. He closed the door, and we bumped forward down the road.

The bus was loaded with Mexicans, migrant workers, I assumed. The driver kept talking to three men in the seats next to him. From time to time one of these three would look back at me and laugh. It was discomforting. I checked the reactions of the others on the bus. The women were very still. I watched their faces as the driver and men talked. Some would grimace and swallow hard. Some didn't move a muscle and some rolled their eyes and shook their heads in disgust.

The bus made a right turn on a dirt road. I jumped from my seat and ran to the driver saying I wanted to get off. He ignored me and kept driving. I grabbed him on the shoulder and hollered at him to stop. He pushed my arm away. The three men got out of their seats and headed down the aisle towards me. I jerked the door handle, ran down the steps and jumped. Luckily, because of the bumpy dirt road, the bus wasn't going fast. I hit the ground and rolled over and over in the sand and dirt. When I finally stopped I wasn't surprised to see that the bus didn't even stop to see how I was.

*   *   *

A rig passed me, pulled over to the road and braked. I ran after it.

"Where you heading?" the driver asked. I told him. "I'm heading to Dallas," he replied. "Get yerself in." I climbed up the side of the rig and pulled the massive door shut.

"The name's Mack," he said, turning the big wheel of the rig back onto pavement. He was a bear of a man, with the ball of his stomach tucked under the steering wheel. He didn't ask too many questions, just the necessary ones, like where you going, where you from.

Mack could tell I was sleepy, and he told me I could sleep if I wanted to. I said, "I really would like to, if you don't mind."

"No, go right ahead. Roll your jacket up and lean it against the corner of the door and go to sleep."

"How far is Dallas?" I asked.

"From here, about 500 miles."

"Do you drive it straight?"

"Oh no. I'm not one of these road hogs that eats up the highway. I'll go about another 200 miles today and then the rest tomorrow."

"Sounds good," I said and drifted off to sleep.

Mack liked to talk about his family and life in Birmingham, Alabama. I liked listening to him because he sounded so genuine. He really loved them. I asked about those Mexicans on the bus. He told me I was lucky to get away.

"They pick up young kids like you and take them to the fields, make them work. The straw boss pays them and the poor sucker that got picked up gets dumped back on the street with no money. Happens all the time. Sad part about it, they have no one to complain to because the law doesn't care."

"How long do they keep these people they pick up?"

"Depends on how long they go out for. One day, two days, even a week."

"You mean I could have been taken out there and worked for a whole week, get no money and couldn't do anything about it?"

"That's right. That's exactly right."

"But that's not fair."

"Paul, there are a whole bunch of things that go on in this world that are not right or fair."

We rolled on to about nine o'clock and pulled into a motel. While Mack was in the office I tried to figure out where I was going to sleep. Did I dare ask to sleep on his motel room floor? It wasn't that cold during the day, but at night the temperature got down there, so being in the truck would be on the chilly side. Mack came out the motel office door and handed me my own room key.

"Why did you do that?" I asked.

"These rooms only have one bed and they're small. I know you don't want to sleep with me and I don't really want to sleep with you. So don't look a gift horse in the mouth. Go take a shower and get a good nights rest. I'll get you up in the morning and we'll head for Dallas. Okay?"

"Okay Mack. I really appreciate this."

He smiled. "I know you do, Paul."

*   *   *

A dark green car stopped down the road and I ran up to it. The man driving had a ballooned face; with big smile and eyes so small they were black dots.

"How far you going?" he asked, a giggle in his voice.

"California."

"I'm not going that far, but I'll take you as far as I go."

"Okay, thanks." I got in and we drove off.

He was the chatty type, starting with the questions, why, where, how come and when. It started getting dark, but it didn't quiet this man down.

The conversation turned to girls. Did I have a girlfriend? Did I make out with her? Did I like to look at dirty magazines? I tried to change the subject, but he kept going right back to women.

"What about sex with a man?" he said, trying to make his voice seductive.

My muscles turned stiff as rock. It was late. I didn't see any headlights in front or behind.

He reached over. Fingers like slabs of meat grabbed my thigh and squeezed. My thoughts flashed: 'Some kids never come back.' I jerked my leg away and slid up close to the door.

With a sudden move, he swerved and hit the gas. The car jumped forward around a turn, off the main road. He pounded the accelerator. The car spurted down the gravel at full speed. The road wound uphill, back and forth.

"Where are you going?" I squealed. "Stop. Let me out."

His hand reached for me again. I grabbed his hand by the wrist and threw it off.

I screeched again, vocal chords ripping, "Stop! Stop! Let me out."

A perverse laugh filled the cab of the car. He gurgled and said, "I'm not going to let you out until I'm done with you, boy." The dashboard light turned his face a ghoulish green. A mad clown. His attention returned to the road as we hurtled deeper into the woods.

I felt my pocketknife; the one Buddy had given me, through my jacket. I slipped my hand in, pulled it out and opened the blade. But did I have the nerve to use it?

The octopus tentacles of his hand reached over and grabbed my leg again. I was as far over as I could get without going through the door. The fingers probed and reached, grab-by-grab, moving up and up, towards my testicles. I pulled his hand off again.

Fingers were slippery on the knife. I screamed at him again to stop and let me out of this car. That laugh curdled the air and he reached for me again.

We were so far away from everything. Soon he'd be looking for a place to stop. It wouldn't matter how loud I screamed out here. He'd drag me out, and he'd.... My hand drove the knife hard into his hand. He screamed. I thrust again, pulled back. Again, pulled back. He slowed the car. I reached for the handle, threw the door open and jumped out into the void of the black night. The last thing I heard was him screaming, saying he was going to kill me when he caught me.

But his voice disappeared. My body was falling, rolling, bouncing down a hill. Briars tore at me. There went a stump. I put out my hands to stop, but couldn't. My body picked up speed. Would I ever stop? What if the hill ended in a cliff or river?

Slam. I hit a clump of trees and came to an abrupt halt.

I sucked at breath, but felt only a wheeze, and, oh, the entire surface of me, from head to toe, had become pain. I listened for any noise or sign of that jerk, but there was nothing. Guess I was too far down the hill for him to come after me, and besides, he had his own wounds to tend to.

When revenge is deserved, it really does taste intoxicating sweet.

I reached for my handkerchief and put it on my face. The warm trickle of blood seemed to ooze from every part of me. But I didn't dare make a move until light.

Time ticked slow in the total blackness. I don't know if I passed out or not. The grass about me crackled with bugs and things.

I started to cry. First I cried because of the pain, then because of the despair.

"Noah," I called out, "I need you." But there only seemed to be blackness.

What was I calling on Noah for? He's a dead man. Long gone. Forgotten. Meaningless. All that stuff he spouted, just dreams and fluff. And me? Nobody knew where I was or cared. Sarah, Mattie, Kitty, Jimmy, Ed — they didn't care what happened to me. Obviously. They wanted me gone. Out of their lives. I'd be better dead. For everyone. Dead.

I tried to calm myself, crying myself into a dizzy sort of sleep.

As uncomfortable as it was, I stayed in the same position until the sun blushed the sky. My first move was tentative. Just a shift. It hurt so bad, I was sure I'd broken a bone, damaged something internally. I decided to try it nice and slow.

Starting with my left arm, I raised it slowly. It seemed okay except for cuts and bruises. Then the left leg, it moved okay. I reached up with my left hand, grabbed a branch and pulled myself off the tree. I managed to sit up and my head went into spins. I tried to move my hand, but it went to the wrong place. I moved my head. What was I looking at? It was as if I couldn't get my head, eyes and sense of direction to work together. I sat there in a daze for a long time, waiting for myself to settle.

Up towards the road it was at least 200 to 250 feet to the top. There was a path made by me on the way down. How had I not broken my neck? Looking downward, the hill rolled more gently into a valley.

I discovered that my right hand was still clasped about the knife. I picked up a hand full of leaves and wiped the blade clean. That was his blood. I wanted every drop of it scraped off my knife.

Looking over my body in stages, I realized nothing was broken. My ribs hurt when I breathed. My clothes were torn, pock-marked with thorns and briars. There was dried blood on my jacket. Was it mine or the grotesque clown's?

Finally, I got up the courage to stand. Once erect, the question begged, Should I go up or down? I was too weak to go up so, slowly, carefully I headed towards the bottom.

Upon reaching flat ground I heard the light burble of running water and headed towards it.

It was a stream you could jump in one stride, but it was water. I got down on my knees, took my handkerchief, and put it into the ice cold water and then on my face. It felt so good; I splashed water over my entire head.

Something pushed me hard on the behind and my hands reached out to break my fall. They landed in a foot of water. I was wet up to my elbows. I jumped around, and scrambled backwards. Standing there was a white and black cow with eyes as big as my fist. It blinked at me.

I hissed at it and yelled, "You big dumb son-of-bitch, look what you done to me. I'm all wet. Go away! Get! Get outa here! Stupid cow."

"The cow isn't stupid," came a voice from the opposite side of the creek.

I jerked around, jumped to my feet. Not twenty feet from me, up on the far slope, sitting on a horse, was a black man. He continued, "You're in his territory, drinking his water."

I took a couple of awkward steps sideways, taking this in.

The man said, "You look like you been fighting with a bull. What happened to you?"

"I fell out of a car on the road on top of the hill," I said, pointing. "And I, I couldn't climb back up. So, I came down."

The man looked to where I pointed, shifted on his saddle, gave me a sidelong glance. "When did you fall out of this car?" he asked.

"Last night. Some time around ten or eleven."

He gave me a quizzical look. "Tell me, just how did you fall out of this car?"

I struggled for a story. "Well, ah, I…. the door wasn't shut good, and I guess when the car went around the curve fast, it swung open, and well, I …. fell out."

The man grimaced and nodded his head. "Sounds good. But I doubt that's what really happened. Where are your parents? Where do you live?"

"Ah, well…" Where did I live? I didn't live anywhere. I didn't have an address. Was I a hobo? A migrant?

I was homeless.

Nausea hit me. I leaned forward. My stomach retracted in a heave but nothing came out.

The man leaned down. "You don't look very good. Come on. Get on the horse and I'll take you to my house and get you fixed up."

I looked at him, way up there. "How do I…?"

"Give me your left arm and I'll swing you up behind me," he said.

I reached up. He told me to put my foot in the stirrup.

"Which foot?" I asked.

His head turned up to the sky with a great laugh. He smiled down at me. "Boy," he said. "you are a real, live, pale face, city boy, aren't you?"

"Well I, uh. Yes, I guess I am."

"Your left foot, city boy. Come on, let's go. You ain't getting no better standing there soakin' wet."

After a few tries I got on the horse and we set out. He introduced himself as Virgil. But our conversation didn't continue much. Each step of the horse pained my ribs. I yearned to cry out but bit my lip, forcing myself into silence despite the agony.

We approached an old farmhouse that looked like it had been standing for 200 years. A black lady, came out with a broom in her hands and a white apron tied about her waist. She was a dumpling; with lips so black they shined purple.

"What's you got there, Virgil? Don't look like something we want for supper, honey."

"Found him down by the stream trying to take a bath with all his clothes on. I wasn't worried though. Matilda was watching over him."

The lady laughed. It was the kind of laughter that comes from way down and makes you want to laugh too, just like Noah's.

She said, "He was trying to steal milk from Matilda, was he?"

They both laughed at the idea.

With Virgil's help I got off the horse, nearly collapsing to the ground with the landing.

The lady motioned to me. "You come inside, boy, and let's get you patched up."

She pointed through a doorway. "You go into that room right there, take off all your clothes... well, at least what's left of them... and put this on." She handed me a robe.

In a mirror on a dresser. I saw what a pitiful specimen I was; all scrapes, cuts and bruises.

The lady called from outside the door. "Come on, boy, I know it doesn't take that long to get them rags off."

She motioned me to come over by the sink where she had a pan of hot water and a big washcloth. "Now, you just sit down on this stool and I'm going to wash all these cuts and scrapes." She started to work. She continued, "When I'm done with this I'll put some white powder on them. That stuff is going to burn you, boy, so you holler if you want to, but it keeps them from getting infected. Virgil learned this in the big war."

The ritual was familiar, not an experience I relished repeating. She was not very tender in her washing or applying the powder either. I wanted to ask her if she thought I was Matilda, but held my tongue.

"Boy, there ain't much to you," she said with a sigh as she worked. "You need some viddles put in you to fatten you up for market." She laughed again and looked into my face. "What's your name?"

"Paul. Paul Miller."

"Paul, huh? You a tryin' to be like the Apostle, Paul, when he was struck down by the Lord?"

"No, I don't think so."

"You do know that Paul was struck down by the Lord, don't you?"

"Oh, yes, I know that. He was on his way to Damascus when the Lord came to him."

"Well, glory, glory. A white boy that knows the Bible. Maybe you were sent by the Lord. The Lord always sez, I'll come —"

"— Like a thief in the night." I finished for her.

Just then, Virgil walked in. She said to him, "You done picked up a white boy that knows the Bible. Virgil, honey, we got to take good care of this boy. He's a gift from the Lord."

I said, "I'm no gift, I can tell you that. I sure do thank you for helping me, though."

She told me to put my robe back on. "You must be hungry. I'll fix you up some viddles."

"What is your name?" I asked.

"Matilda," she replied.

"I thought that was the cows name?"

She thrust one palm onto a hip and nodded her head. "Yep, it is. But you see, Paul Miller, we have around here what you call a bunch of comedians. When they brought the cow home, they said it looked like me, so they all named it 'Matilda #2'. Now let me ask you, Paul Miller, is that a way to show respect to your Mama and to your wife?"

I looked over at Virgil and he winked at me. "Ahh, Mama. You know we love you."

"Yea, I knows that. But I'm talking respect now, Virgil. Respect."

She fixed me pancakes, eggs, grits, sausage, toast and coffee. When I was done eating, she showed me into a bedroom.

"This here's Tessy's room. I put you in here because Tessy always keeps her room neat and clean. The other two are slobs. You crawl into that bed now and get you some sleep."

I did as I was told. It felt so good to lie flat, knowing I could go to sleep in safety.

I was awoken by a girl's voice, loud and angry.

"Mama, I can't believe you gave him my bed. A white boy! A complete stranger!"

"Oh, Tessy don't let your drawers choke you. He ain't gonna corrupt your bed."

"But Mama…"

A younger voice sang, "Tessy's got a white boy in her bed. A white boy in her bed."

"You shut up Junior, and don't you dare tell the kids at school or I'll murder you. I sure will!"

Matilda said, "Tessy honey, you getting yourself all worked up over nothing. Paul was hurt and needed help, and that included sleep. Now, he…."

"Worked up over nothing? I come home from school, and there's a white boy sleeping in my bed and it's nothing?"

"Tessy's got a white…."

Matilda ordered, "Junior, shut up and go help your Dad with the chores. Right now."

I heard the screen door slam and chair legs squeaked across the floor.

Whom I imagined was Tessy, said, "Mama, I'm never going to live this down. How could you do this to me?"

"Look, honey, when somebody needs help, white, black, yellow or red, it's your duty as a human being to help that person out. The Lord doesn't ask you if the one you helped out was white or black. He expects you to help them and you better, or when you come up to see him, you don't want Him to say, 'Well, I'm sorry but you're black, I can't do anything for you,' do you? Do you Tessy?"

"No, mama, no. I'm sorry."

"Okay, honey, now let's get the chores done and I'll start fixin' supper."

I lay there and thought about what Matilda just told her. It sounded just like something Noah would say.

I got out of bed, but with great difficulty. My ribs hurt so badly I almost didn't want to breathe. When I came through the door, Matilda looked at me and said, "Well, it looks alive, but I'd better check."

I smiled and said, "I don't feel alive. My ribs hurt so bad I can hardly move."

Matilda punched her hands onto her hips. "Okay, I know what to do about that. My daddy had a few busted and bruised ribs in his time." She went into another room and came out with some kind of cloth all rolled up like a ball. "Sit down here and I'll fix ya up."

She wrapped me in that cloth from armpits to naval real tight. "You have to keep this on now for several days. It will help the healing and make you more comfortable. Don't get it wet, or take it off."

"I won't," I said. She continued to work in silence for a moment. Then, I said, "I heard you talking to Tessy, earlier."

Her hands stopped for a moment. "Oh, Paul. You gotta forgive her. She's still a young one, like you. She's learning all the time. She didn't mean nothing by it. She's just thinking selfish."

I shook my head. "I know all that. But that's not what I heard. It was what you were saying. And earlier. Your faith. It's so strong. How do you keep it when things are tough?"

"Are you kidding me?" she exclaimed. "It's only faith that can carry you through the hard times. It humbles you, because you got to trust that there's a reason for it. Sometimes that's hard to do. But being humbled, that's a good thing. Trouble is, most folks only call on God when they're in trouble. It's easy to forget after the bad times and how you got out of them. You need to talk to Him all the time, thank Him for the sunshine he gave you today, the nice flowers out in the field, the good health of you and your family, and, most of all Paul," she patted the table, "for that old Matilda and her good cookin'." We both laughed.

"Thank you Matilda."

"You already did, honey." She finished up and instructed, "Go back in the bed, and I'll call you when supper's ready."

I did as I was told and drifted in and out of sleep. Virgil knocked on the door when supper was ready. At the table, Virgil introduced me to the family and told them my story, and said I'd be staying as long as necessary.

Junior was giggling, Lizzy was smiling and Tessy was embarrassed. I thanked them for all they'd done, especially Tessy.

I stayed on for three more days. During that time, Virgil, Matilda and I talked about a lot of things. Virgil told me how his great-great grandfather had been a slave to the original owner of several thousand acres in this area. After the Civil War the owner released most of his slaves but kept certain ones and gave them sections of land as their pay. His family got 50 acres on the southwest corner, which was this land here. The land has been farmed and handed down to the eldest male in each generation. After Virgil, Virgil Junior would get it. He'd be the 5th generation.

Virgil didn't want to be a farmer at first. He went to live with an aunt in Chicago, and that was where he got his education and Matilda. But, after working in factories and construction, he decided that farming was a better way of life. "So, Matilda agreed to come with me, and she has turned out to be one heck of a cow, I mean farmer."

We laughed.

Matilda said, "See, I told you, there is no respect."

I looked over at her wide, familiar face, and said, "Matilda, there is more respect and love in this house than I have seen in fifty houses. I envy you folks, I really do. And I know, I just know, God is shining his blessings down on you."

Matilda's dumpling form pushed around the kitchen table, sending chairs squawking and Tessy whining. Her great brown eyes overflowed wet as she looked up into my face and pushed back my hair. Her arms enveloped me and the mass of her shook like a jelly layer around me. I felt a choke balling in my throat. If only I could stay. But I couldn't. In that moment I determined to make this kind of loving family for myself, no matter what. These people showed me it was possible. All it took was doing it.

Virgil drove me to the main highway. I thanked him again for all he and his family had done, and I told him I didn't know how I was ever going to repay them for their kindness and generosity.

He said, "The Lord will repay us, not you."

I felt great sadness as I watched his truck disappearing into the distance. They were one great family.

* * *

A young man with a Tennessee tag in a ragtag Cadillac, which was more rust than metal, pulled over.

"Where ya goin', boy?" I told him. "Hey, that's where I'm a-headed. Ya'll jump in hare and we is off."

But I wasn't jumping in too fast. I looked him over. He was a little dirty and rough, but I didn't think he was one of those. How, of course, could you tell?

"Well, come on," he said with impatience, "Get in if your comin'."

I climbed in and hoped for the best.

His name was Carlton. He started talking right away about his 'old lady', as he referred to his wife. She'd filed for divorce and "Just down right kicked him out of their trailer." Carlton carried on about her and her cheating on him and taking all his money, and now she got the dang trailer.

About an hour down the road we passed another hitchhiker. An older man, covered in an overcoat more stain than cloth. I moved to the back and he got in the front. As he did, the smell of garbage and piss filled the cab of the car. Carlton hit the gas and we were off.

Carlton started his story all over again. The wife, the trailer, divorce. The hitchhiker pulled out a bottle of whiskey and asked Carlton if he wanted some.

"Why, hell, yea, man. I never turn down a good drink of whiskey."

The two of them took a drink, offered me some. I refused. They were having a time, getting louder as the car started to weave from side to side in broader arcs. The conversation veered as broadly as the car, until it turned to women. Once latched onto that topic, their talk became more vulgar by the minute. They'd occasionally look back at me and say, "Hey, Paul, you ever try that with a woman?" Or "Hey, Paul, doesn't that sound good?" I'd smile and shrug.

Carlton unzipped his pants, pulled his penis out, shook it around and hollered at me, "Hey Paul, how da ya think the womens would like this?"

I stiffened. One hand grabbed the door handle and I pushed back into the seat, ready to jump.

The hitchhiker turned around and gave me a look up and down. To Carlton, he said, "Do you think Paul knows what that there thing is for, besides pissin'?" He laughed. "Maybe we need to give Paul some lessons. Show him how to use that there pretty dick. Whats ya think, Carlton? Huh?"

This made Carlton uncomfortable. "Naw, I betcha Paul knows."

The old hitchhiker looked back. "Does ya Paul? Does ya know how to use it?"

I pushed my right hand into my pocket, grabbed my knife and pulled it out, hiding it under my jacket. If this dirty son-of-a-bitch made one move at me, I was going to plunge it right into his rotten, stinking neck. He had a good size jugular I could take aim at.

Carlton said, his voice warbling, "Leave old Paul alone. He don't want any part of us. We all will get us some nice pretty female girls tonight in town. Whats ya say to that, old buddy?"

The old hitchhiker said, "Why spend good money on girls, when we got us a nice tender little boy here, all fer free? I don't knows about you, but I don't got no money."

"Ya makes a good point dar buddy, but I — I just don't cowtale to doing it with boys."

"The way I sees it, I paid fer my ride with this here whiskey. Now the nice, cute little boy back here... well, he needs to pay, too. Don't ya think that's just the right and noble thing to do?"

Carlton grimaced. "Right now, I needs to get Bessie some gasoline, or we alls will be hitchhiking." Carlton turned into a gas station, almost hitting the pump. He came so close he had to back up and come in again so the attendant could get to the tank. They both laughed and slapped the seats of the car.

Carlton told the attendant to fill it up and check 'all Bessie's vital signs'. We headed for the rest room; they let me go in first.

In the restroom there was another door that went into the garage area. I made noises, flushed the toilet and went out the other door. There was no one in the garage so I headed for the back of the gas station. Behind the building I found some old junk cars and mountains of trash. I circled around until I found a car that looked like a good hiding place. The bottom of it was rusted out and the rear seat sat on the ground with debris all around it. I slid under, pushing up the seat. As I was about to crawl, a platoon of rats came screeching out, scattering into the bushes. I had to hold my mouth to keep from screaming. I hesitated before continuing. Being in there was the lesser of the two evils. So I slid under the seat and let it down on top of me.

It was a dirty, uncomfortable place to be with the rusty spokes of the seat precariously close to my face. Mold smell mixed in with something rotting. The rats returned to their nest a few times, but I discouraged them by hissing like a cat. It worked, they ran off.

It was two hours later when I crawled out. A man was working on a car in the garage, and the attendant that pumped gas sat reading in a chair. No sign of Carlton or the hitchhiker.

The attendant noticed me and said, "There you are. Your friends were looking all over for you. They figured you ran away again, so they left and told me to tell you to meet them in El Paso." I grinned and said thanks. He smiled back. He said, "I told them when they started looking that I saw you running back down the road, from where you all came. So they jumped into their car and went looking for you. I saw them come back and head to El Paso about ten minutes later."

I was amazed. "You did what!" I said.

He giggled. The other man came out of the garage. He told me that he saw me run around the building up towards the junk and figured I was trying to get away from them, so they thought they'd help me out.

"We see a lot of bad, scroungy looking hombre's come through here and we could tell by looking at them that you didn't belong to or with them."

The other one said, "They were drunk. That old guy is nothing but a hobo. He's probably going to get that guy drunk until he passes out, take his money and maybe his car. Happens all the time around here."

One of them said, "It's kinda late for you to get back on the road again. There's a cot in the office. You stay there tonight, and tomorrow we'll get you a ride to El Paso. How does that sound?" Well, of course, it sounded great. One of them didn't live too far. He'd bring me back a plate of supper.

After they closed the station, I laid down on the cot, thinking. Here was I, being helped again. I sat up, tried to figure out what I could do for these fellas in return for what they were doing for me. Now, I'm no mechanic, and I can't fix cars, but the garage needed sweeping and picking up in a bad way. So I picked, swept, wiped, and brushed up the whole place. And I must say that when I was done, it looked pretty good.

When the guy came with my food he noticed right away. "First time that floor has seen a broom in months."

He left and I locked the doors. I washed up and settled down for a nights sleep. But once my head hit the cot I started thinking about the next leg of my journey. That led me to thinking about the destination. Dad. My heart sank.

In the morning I was brought a breakfast and a big cup of hot coffee. They got one of their suppliers out of El Paso to give me a ride. As I waited for it to show up, I helped them pump gas. I thanked them very much for all they did. They asked if El Paso was my final destination.

"No, I'm really going to California. Los Angeles area."

"Well, instead of hitchhiking, why don't you catch a bus?"

I shrugged at the suggestion. "Because I don't have the money for a ticket."

"One ticket on a bus can't be all that much," one of them reached into a pocket, pulled out ten dollars and handed it to me. "There, I'll bet it's not much more than that." He looked over at his brother and said, "Come on, give Paul some money."

The other pulled out seven dollars from his shirt pocket and handed it to me.

"Now, I know you can take a bus and get the hell off the highway. Am I right?"

I felt my face flushing. Fingered the bills between my fingers. "Yes, you're right." I looked up and nodded my head. "That's what I'm going to do. Take a bus."

We shook hands, and they wished me luck.

17.

POMONA

The bus pulled into the Pomona station two days later as the sun was rising behind me. It wasn't the building I remembered, the one where I'd climbed aboard that bus back in June 1949 as Dad watched from across the street. This was a new building. In a sense I was relieved. It was almost four years later, February 1953, but reliving that scene would have turned me right around, my doubts and dreams remained.

I stepped off the bus, walked out to the street and looked around me. The polished radiance of the town I remembered so clearly from that first day I'd arrived so long ago just wasn't there at all. It was as though the streets had been tarnished by time itself. A proud old dame of a yellow house I used to admire whenever we walked downtown had slumped into a sad state of disrepair. Its window boxes hung awkwardly, the yard was golden crisp and the house was long past due a coat of paint.

The sun opened the sky up as wide as I recalled, making it burn a crystalline blue. But the super brightness made every color gaudy cousins. Green lawns came off as fakery. A red passing car glared. It was a place lacking in shadows to hide in and for some reason, this struck me as a terrible thing.

I stopped before the funeral home where Mother's service had taken place. History started its parade of images. Me, standing next to the casket looking down on her, bursting with fury. Dad hugging Mother's co-workers, our neighbors, soaking up sympathy. Pallbearers shuffling like grim penguins out the door and down the steps. It was all too much. I sat on the curbside and let the sobs pass through. A man stopped behind me, asked if I was all right. I told him I was, but I really wasn't. This little boy had a broken heart and didn't know how to put it back together again.

The closer to Main Street I got the more I recognized. I even went out to the train platform where Sarah had said her goodbyes to us all. How her eyes fluttered shut, bored at hearing my repeated requests to take me with her. How I turned away as the others said their smarmy sweet goodbyes.

A new rush of scenes played out. The disbelief and shock I felt and expression on Dad's face after his shoe hit. Terror as the bathroom door puckered at his pounding fists. The pit in my stomach from seeing him stare as he watched my bus pull away.

It was time to face him. If I didn't do it soon I'd never do it. The regret of that would turn my life into an eternal question mark. If there was anything that could destroy me, that'd be it.

Dad's hotel was on a one way side street dotted with the lower level of retail stores: a barber shop, diner, smoke shop and an offset printer. The hotel entrance was just a crack between two storefronts. I walked past it at first, because the address wasn't on the door. Then I saw the painted sign tacked above. "Palm Tree Hotel" the sign said in a looping cursive script with a blue background and a palm tree holding the words in its curve, as if this was some beachfront resort.

Inside was dark with stairs that squeaked at every step. Urine harassed my nostrils. By the time I arrived in front of Dad's hotel room door, my heart thundered in my chest so loud I was certain it echoed down the halls. I wouldn't have been surprised to see that ball of muscle burst out of my skin and run away on its own hobbled feet of arteries and veins.

I got up the nerve and knocked. No answer. I knocked louder. No answer. I called, "Dad?" a word so weak, despairing, I scorned the sound.

The clerk at the desk told me that yes; he still lived there, but usually didn't get in until six. I walked around town to pass the time. A little after five I went back to the hotel, sat on the steps and waited.

What was I doing? Why had I come? Maybe I needed a sanitarium myself. The situation didn't feel right. I didn't belong here.

Just as I was thinking that, the door opened and a figure walked out of time towards me. The fedora was tilted down on his head the way it always had, a half a cigar chomped between his teeth and a newspaper folded under his arm. He tilted even more to the right than I remembered, each step a snap.

I recall thinking how little and how much time changes a person. I was struck right away by how haggard his features had become. Yet at the same time there was this kernel of him, so distinct and unchanged it was unnerving.

He saw me and stopped in mid-step, holding his foot in the air for such a small beat I don't think anyone but me would notice it. A growl formed on his lips and he continued up the stairs, muttering as he passed, "What the hell you doing here?"

At that point I should have just walked away, but I didn't. I sauntered up the stairs on his heels like a puppy.

"Hiya Dad," I began, the word fudging up my mouth with its distant strangeness. "I was wondering if I could stay with you."

Dad stopped in the hallway, turned on his heels, looked me right in the eye and said, "Bullshit. You never could live with me. Never wanted to live with me. I don't want you living with me, and can't afford you." He sent his arms wide, a banty rooster spreading its wings to show off its sickly form. "Look at me. Look at me, Paul. Living in a dumpy hotel. Damn place doesn't even have enough light to read a paper by." He started away. I continued to follow, as if drawn along by his wake.

He led me down a hall that ended in complete darkness. His rant continued, whah, whah, whah, with his mouth jawing up and down like the pistons of a car running full tilt. The air had a brown taste as if made up of tobacco tar, excrement and double digested booze. The wainscoting was mottled black with grime.

He ranted, "You, your brothers and sisters and your damn Mother all left me. Left me here all by myself. No money, no home, no job, nothing, not a Goddamn thing. Nobody came to see me in the hospital. Nobody cares about 'dear old Dad'. Nobody. You can take that back to Michigan with you." He pointed a finger at me. "And now you come here wanting me to take care of you? Get the hell out of here and don't ever come back again. You hear me? Do you hear me?"

I was being led by a ranting man into Hades itself. I could only take in half of what he was saying.

He got to his door, shoved the key in the lock. He pushed it open but didn't go in. He just stood in the doorway, glaring at me.

I felt very much like one of those butterflies stuck by straight pins through its wings.

This couldn't be true. The sheer intensity of his hatred was impossible. Inhuman, really. My only sin against him was that I'd been born. Certainly I'd been inconvenient, but was that enough to warrant such animosity?

I was trapped. I had no money, nowhere to stay. But not only that, I couldn't just leave after all I'd been through to get here. There had to be something underneath that hatred. It was too intense to be real. I had to test him.

"Dad," I said. "I'll leave. But can I stay a few days to rest up first? I've come an awfully long way."

He squinted at me. His voice calmed. "How long you talkin' about?" As if he was negotiating late payment of the rent.

"Five, six days?"

He gazed down at the floor, twisted his lips and grunted. "Okay. But no longer than that."

"I promise."

He snarled and said, "Yea, you promise. Everybody promised me everything all the time. I never got a damn thing."

He pushed at the door and went into the room. I moved onto the threshold, looked inside and was struck by the squalor. It wasn't more than a closet. Up against one wall was a single bed. It had an indentation in the middle as though a ghost was napping there. A lounge chair, its edges black with dirt, seemed to melt into the floor.

There came a sudden grasping at my throat. The urge to get away overwhelmed me. "I'm going down to get me something to eat," I said. "I'll be back in a while."

He shrugged. "I'll be in bed. You sleep on the chair and be quiet when you come in."

"Anything you want?" I asked, as if I could provide it.

He didn't answer, just turned away from me and pulled the bed covers down. I hurried down the hall, watching only my feet, holding my breath against the stench.

The fresh air was a salve on my lungs. I leaned up against the building outside, panting at the relief of it.

Oh God, he was pitiful. He needed care, that was clear. What a poor, sorry shell of a man. An empty and meaningless story of a life.

His words pinged at me, an unnerving echo of my own. Mother had left me; brothers and sisters didn't care about me. I was abandoned by circumstance and bitter, just like him.

Was this what I was to become? Was this my future? He was the reverse of everything I wanted to be. But that was awful, wasn't it? Not wanting to take after my father.

I had a small supper in the diner across the way and wandered the streets, passing time. The town seemed so much smaller than I remembered. As if it had shrunk two sizes smaller. I guessed this was because I'd grown.

When I finally returned I pushed at Dad's door and was surprised to find it open. I grasped at the gentility afforded this simple act, while at the same time recalling that night in Detroit when I'd arrived back from the restroom with a blackened eye to find the door locked, my parents gone. Dad was good on his word to me this time. I took it as a kind of progress.

He was snoring up a racket. He'd always snored some, but this rumbled the floor. I curled up in the chair but wasn't tired.

And so I watched him, trying to pierce that hard exterior, hoping to find something of his heart revealed by the innocence of sleep. His breathing would stop now and then, for one beat, two beats, three beats, four. It went on so long at times I almost got up to check if he was still alive. But just as I was about to move, he'd cough and the motor of his lungs would rattle again.

I saw pain in that figure. Wear and tear and a pain. There was so much sadness to him.

My conviction remained. This man, my father, and his life were the antithesis of my hopes and dreams, even if I didn't have any myself. He'd been hurt. In revenge, he'd turned his back on all the possibilities for love.

It hit me. That's what I couldn't understand, wasn't it? He'd shut himself off, walled himself away from all love. From my mother. From me?

But why? Isn't that what makes life worth living? Isn't love, in one way, life itself? Maybe the rest of us hadn't tried hard enough to reach out to him.

At length I was too tired to think any more. But the lounge chair was too uncomfortable for sleep. Blinding my thoughts to the creepy possibilities I spread my jacket out across the floor and lay atop it.

I was shattered into wakefulness by father hollering, "What the hell you doing on the floor?" I opened my eyes to see his skull baring down, flesh loose as if it was about to slip off the bones. "I almost tripped over you," he said, snapping upright. He hobbled out the door, tightening the belt on his robe, mumbling down the hall.

I jumped up and pulled on my pants, getting myself ready to talk to him when he returned.

A few minutes later I heard the uneven thumps of his footsteps. He burst through the door with pepper in his step and slammed the door. Without even a glance at me he went to the bed so his back was to me, grabbed his pants and stepped into them.

I sat forward on the chair, looking at the steeple of my fingers to steady me. Keeping my voice as even as I could, I said, "Dad?"

I tried not to let the vinegar of his voice affect me. "I was wondering if you'd let me buy you breakfast. Would you like that? You know, just at the diner across the street. We could talk."

He stuffed his shirt in his pants with a hand like a spatula flipping eggs. He clucked his tongue. "No," he said without even thinking about it, "I eat my breakfast at the restaurant. Get it for free. It's too far. A five-mile walk. You can't come there."

By sheer will, I propped up my smile. It felt fake but was still a smile. "Okay, well I'll see you tonight then. Maybe we can have supper?"

"No, I always eat at the restaurant before I come home. Get it free."

The air hung quiet, expectant. To break the awkwardness of the moment, I said, "Oh. Well, that's good you get to eat free, I guess." So, meals were out.

"Yea, free," he said as he turned to face me. He grunted and stood there, hands on hips, staring at me as if we were two combatants caught up in a challenge.

"What do you do at the restaurant?" I asked.

"Wash dishes," he said and turned sideways. Embarrassment made its way across his features. But then he glared at me again, as if laying down a challenge, waiting for my reply.

I looked into his piercing eyes, determined not to blink or allow him to stare me down. What could I say to break through? I sensed hopes from him, expectations, secrets too mired in the muck for even him to realize what they were. But they were there, solid and full. How could I find them?

"Dad," I said, at length, "I'm sorry for..." But I didn't know how to finish.

He pulled his jaw back and clamped it. Some kind of whorl moved through him, under that shiny surface. He held it back, too proud to let me see. He turned on his heels and reached for the door. "Yea. You're sorry. Lot a fat good that does...."

"Don't go," I ordered, hating the knife of my voice. But it stopped him. "I didn't come here to bother you. I just wanted some answers." He stayed. I allowed my thoughts to flow out of me. "I've never understood why you hated me so much. I mean sure, I left you here. But don't you understand that I had to? You were destroying me. But why? What in the world did I ever do to you to make you hate me so much? I'm your son. And....” words which, up until that point had come out in a stream, slithered away from my tongue's grasp.

Dad tilted his head up just slightly to look at me and then his gaze moved back to the floor. His shoulders were tennis balls up beside his ears. With jerky moves, he backed away from the door and collapsed into sitting on the bed. He turned his head away, clamped his eyes shut. He was crying. But then he drew his mask up again, tight and steely, as always.

“I let you stay here, didn't I?” he said.

A lump like a hunk of wet bread lodged in my throat.

“I appreciate that.”

“You better,” he said with a growl.

I leaned forward with my elbows on my knees. I said, “Dad, none of our family has much. Mary, Kitty, Sarah, everyone's having trouble just making ends meet. But I know that if we got back up to Detroit...”

“You're nuts if you think I'm going back to that godfersaken cold.”

“Okay,” I said, casting my thoughts for other possibilities. “If I got a job and...”

He spat, “I can't live with you.” He turned back and bounced once on the bed, fuming.

“Okay, I'm sorry,” I said.

The air hung silent and stiff, as though made of cardboard. Then, with a jerk, he stood up and headed for the door again.

“I'm gonna be late for work,” he said.

“Just one more minute, Dad. Please?”

He stopped again. He stood at the door with his back to me, his hand on the handle, jiggling it with impatience. What else could I say? All I had left was the obvious.

“What do you want from me, Dad?”

All at once, his form appeared to grow to twice its size. He turned. “Stop it with your questions.” His yell shook the walls. “That's all you ever did to me, is demand answers to stupid questions.” He over-pronounced, as if repeating words he's heard over and over, “A child is seen and not heard. A child does not ask questions. Do you hear me?”

Someone pounded on the wall in the next room, a voice muffled, shouted, “Shut up you crazy old man.”

Dad melted suddenly, and continued, exhausted, almost pleading, “I can't answer your questions, Paul. I don't know. I don't know. So stop asking me, please?” Then, as if the wind picked up and re-furled his sails, “You stop it with the questions or you're not staying one more night.”

"All right, all right," I said, pushing down on the air with my hands as if I could push down the tone of his mood.

He walked out the door without even saying goodbye.

I sat there in the dump of that room, listening to the quakes and shifts of the other tenants, thinking. The picture of my father had shifted over the past few minutes. He didn't mean to be uncaring, a hurtful bastard. He was a man broken, lonely, withdrawn. Yes, perhaps even unstable. But he existed doggedly from day to day, washing dishes at a restaurant a five-mile walk away. God, what kind of a life was that? A tragedy of a life. Almost worthy of opera.

Our family had to do something for him. But what? For now, all I knew was that I had to scare myself up some money to get somewhere else. I left the hotel and headed across the street to the diner for breakfast.

I walked in the door and stopped. Dad was there, sitting at the counter, a smile more joyous than I'd ever seen on his face. A waitress with a sly crooked smile framed by yellow curls stood leaning one hand on the counter, the other on her hip. She was chomping hard and fast on some gum. I stepped back into an aisle and picked up a magazine, pretended to read it, watching him over its edge.

The waitress was saying, "And that mister misery came in through the door and ordered a cup of coffee. Well, I just about walked out the back. Thank god you came in or I would'a had the rottenest day this side'a hades."

Dad beamed. He wasn't the same man who'd walked out the hotel room fifteen minutes before at all.

The waitress started away from him, but he called after her, "Hey Jane," he began, "did you know our mailman got a dishonorable discharge from the Navy?"

The waitress smirked, leaned down on the counter, and replied, "No, I didn't know that. You got a punch line for me?"

Dad nodded. "You betcha. He tried to install a screen door on his submarine."

They both burst into laughter. The waitress flicked her notepad at his arm and poured him another coffee.

Had that stuff in the hotel been an act? And if so, why? I was baffled.

I left the diner and headed down the street.

* * *

I headed out to Westmont to look up Jack Carbone and Dee Dee.

I arrived at my old house and stood at the end of the lawn staring at it. So much pain had been felt within its walls, I was sure the people who lived there were still haunted by it. No one was home at Dee Dee's, so I went to Jack's.

Jack's mother told me that he was still in school. He'd be back around four o'clock.

"So tell me, Paul," she said, eyeing my worn clothes. "What is it that brings you back to California?"

"I really don't know," I said, being totally honest.

She gave me the most puzzled look.

I walked past Gray's old house, wondering what she was up to, so many years later. I went by the school; it didn't look very different. I thought of going in, but thought it would be too weird.

When I arrived back at Jack's house, he was waiting for me on the porch. He ran to greet me shook my hand, slapped me on the back as if trying to make sure I was real. We sat on the curb without missing a beat and talked about old times. I was surprised to learn how many had moved away, including Dee Dee. She was now in San Francisco, living with her father. Jack hadn't changed all that much. He was still shorter than me and had that odd habit of clenching his fists and putting them to his mouth.

He asked why I was back in California.

"I know it sounds strange, Jack. But I can't answer that. It's not that I won't. I can't."

"Are you going to live with your dad?" I told him what had happened since I'd arrived.

"That's strange," he said.

"My father is a very troubled man, Jack. He gets so angry sometimes, it's weird. And one thing I figured out this trip, I do that to him. It's as though he wants me to behave a certain way but can't tell me what that is. Cause if he could, I'd do it."

"You would?" Jack asked.

I kicked at a bit of gravel, watched it bounce into the middle of the street. Shook my head. "I'm too old, now, Jack. If things had worked out differently, maybe my dad and I could've become friends, but he'll never want to be my father, and I can never be his son again." My own words surprised me, but I knew as they came out how true they were.

Jack asked me what I was going to do. But what could I do? I had to go back to Michigan as soon as I could get the money together.

Jack asked, "Can't you get some from your dad?"

I shrugged. "He don't have any money. Guess I'll have to get a job or something."

Jack sat up with surprise. "Job? You crazy? Where are you going to get a job?"

Defeat took over me. "I don't know. But I've got to get out of here in six days."

"How much you got now?"

I pulled everything out of my pocket and counted a whole nine dollars and thirteen cents. "That won't get me very far."

"Well, how much you need?"

"To go all the way back to Michigan? About sixty to seventy five dollars."

Jack shrugged. Said, "I got three bucks you can have." We laughed. It felt good to be with Jack again. It was like we'd picked up right where we'd left off.

He nudged me. "We just got to figure out how to get some quick money, Paul. And there's only one way I can think of to get big, fast money."

"Yea, rob a store," I said sarcastically.

"Don't have to be a store, you know. There's this bike shop downtown, and the owner will buy stolen bikes. Don't get much, but he will buy them. I know that for a fact."

I pulled back, looked at him in surprise. "Jack, you been stealing bikes?"

"Well," he said with a shrug. "Yea, a few, I guess. I need the money."

His parents were in the process of a messy divorce. His dad had already moved to Los Angeles to live with a girl friend. He didn't send them much money.

"Does your mom ask you where the money comes from?"

"Oh yea. I told her odd jobs here and there after school. Seems to satisfy her."

I rolled a shoulder, as if to dismiss it, and said, "I robbed a store up in Detroit, once. My parents had left me alone in the hotel for three days and this guy showed me how it's done. But then I paid for it, boy. I was caught by some black boys and they nearly beat me to death."

Jack blinked his eyes at me, mystified. "How come you never told me that before?"

I scuffed at the ground with my shoe. "I don't know," I replied. "I guess I just wanted it forgotten."

"Your parents left you alone for how long?"

"Three days."

Jack looked off into the air, as if imagining a wild world.

I looked at him out of the corner of my eye. I nudged him. "What's going on?" I asked.

He looked at me and blinked. His eyes reflected a new respect. "Paul, I honestly can't remember ever being left alone for more than a few hours. And never over night. And I'm thirteen."

I laughed. "I bet you haven't hitch hiked across the country on your own, either."

"Oh, no," he gasped with relief.

With a bit of pride, I recounted how I'd learned to break into homes in Los Angeles.

Jack ribbed me with an elbow. "You got experience, boy. You can show me and in the next few days we might make us a nice little bundle."

"It doesn't always work that way, Jack. Lots of times you come out with next to nothing."

But Jack was still excited. "Let's start tonight!" he said.

"Hey, not so fast. We got to think about where, and when. Not just go out and start breaking in any old place."

"Well, what do we have to do?"

"Know any stores here in Pomona that might keep cash in the store?"

"No, just that bike shop. But I don't know what he's got there."

"We don't want to touch him. He probably knows all the thieves in town, so we stay away from him."

"Yea, you're right. How about houses?"

"They're the easiest, but you get the least from them and then you have to sell it to get cash."

"We'll sell it. That bike shop guy, I've heard he takes more than just bikes."

"You sure of that?"

"Not positive, but that's what I've heard."

"If we can sell it real fast, then we might do some houses."

"Hey, let's go in and get some supper and talk about this. What do ya say?"

"Sounds great, let's do it."

* * *

The next day, just before dark, we met in Jack's garage and picked out the tools we'd need. I'd already told Jack about wearing dark clothes. While Jack was at school I chose a couple of isolated places that looked easy. As soon as it was dark enough, we left Jack's garage and headed into town. I had a small crow bar slid up my left sleeve, and Jack had two screwdrivers. One long, one short and stout.

We walked slowly past the first store, looked in and saw no signs of people or dogs. We walked around the block and came up from the back. It was dark, no security lights, no dogs, no burglar alarms. The back door just had an ordinary lock that could be broken by a good hard push, but we didn't want to make any noise.

I pulled out the crow bar and wedged it between the jamb and the door and pulled it hard. It popped right open.

Jack let out a little giggle and his hands went towards his mouth. I giggled a little myself. We entered the store and closed the door.

I told Jack to go through the right side and I'll take the left. "Remember, no big bulky stuff that will show. Only stuff that you can put in your pockets."

"You mean like money?"

"Yea, something like that."

The side I was on had the check out counter and the cash register. The register had only loose change, no bills. I searched under the counter and found a moneybag hidden way in the back. It was heavy. I opened it up and found that it was full of loose change and one dollar bills. "Hey, I got some money. Don't know how much. It's in a bag."

"Great, I can't find anything but groceries." Jack whispered back.

I grabbed some cigarettes and candy and shoved them into my pockets. For a brief moment I was back in Detroit with Tony, going through that store.

I whispered, "Okay, let's get out of here."

"Not so fast," Jack protested. "I haven't looked around much yet."

"No, let's go! I'll explain later. Let's go now!" We went out the back and the opposite way from which we came, me with the moneybag tied around my waist.

"What did you get?" I asked him.

"Just some food stuff. You wouldn't let me stay in there long enough to find something good." I told him why we didn't stay long and he understood.

We went down three blocks and right for two blocks to our next store. The entry door on the back had a big padlock, which broke off real easy with the crow bar. Jack got the register this time, and he pulled all the change out of it and stuffed it into his pockets. Told him to look under the counter for anything. He came out with a box of pencils and a ruler.

On our way back to Jack's house, I asked him why he took the ruler. "I lost mine a few days ago and I need one for school." He smiled over at me. "I don't have to buy one now."

In Jack's garage we got into a corner and pulled out all our loot. The bag I'd found contained a lot of silver coins in it and six one-dollar bills. The coins added up to forty-six dollars. Jack's money added up to fourteen dollars and thirty-two cents.

"$66.32 divided by two equals $33.16 each. Not bad for our first time."

"You're half way to your goal, Paul. Another night like this and you can go back to Michigan. But I sure wish you wouldn't go. Wish I could talk Mom into letting you live with us."

I shook my head. "I've done that Jack, and it's hard living with strangers."

"We're not strangers!"

"I mean, not people from your own family. You know, relatives, kin, things like that."

"I know. Mom won't go for it, anyway. She's got a lot on her hands right now with just me and my sister."

Walking back to the hotel, I could still feel the adrenaline coursing through me like dynamite. How exciting our night had been. I wasn't afraid the way I was before in Detroit and Los Angeles. Maybe I could be a robber.

I turned a corner. Standing in a doorway was an old black man.

How long had it been since I'd even thought of Noah? I felt caught, guilty as charged, heading for hell.

The man glared at me. I looked away. Walking down the street toward me came another black man with chubby cheeks just like Noah's. He glared at me, too. My insides quaked. "Thou shalt not steal — Thou shalt not steal — Thou shalt not..." My breathing became funny. Syncopated. The man passed, glaring at me. I ran across the street.

I was stealing the money for a good cause, wasn't I? It was for Jack and his Mother, for me to get back to Michigan. Weren't those good reasons?

I made myself believe it, even if I knew deep down inside that He wouldn't.

I climbed the stairs to Dad's hotel room and felt doom descending. This was why I had to steal. This was why.

The next night, Jack and I broke into three homes in another neighborhood and got a total of $17. 89 cash, some silver serving plates, a camera, a small radio, jewelry, two watches, one ring, cufflinks and two candleholders. Jack skipped school the next day and we took the stuff to the bike shop. To my surprise and shaky nerves, the guy gave us thirty dollars for the lot. We had no idea if we were taken, because we had no idea what we really had.

Sitting in the back corner of the garage, we reviewed our haul. "Now $47.89 divided by two equals $23.94 and a half cent." We roared with laughter, and Jack said I could have the whole penny.

The third night, Jack said he knew about a house a few blocks away from him. The guy had a collection of guns.

I said, "I don't know about stealing guns. He's probably got those locked up pretty good. And besides, you don't want to hit a house in your own neighborhood."

"I don't care about the neighborhood. And this guy doesn't have the guns locked up. I saw them. Most of them are in his bedroom. Let's at least go over there tonight. If they're not home, we go in. If they are, we go in anyway."

I reached over and smacked him on the arm. "No, we'll forget about it if they're home." Jack shook his head. "Okay," I said. "But I don't like it. I just don't know about stealing guns. They scare me."

On the way over I hoped they'd be home. When we arrived the house was black, not a light peeping from anywhere.

Jack said, "There are big bushes around the back door that hide the house from the neighbors. Let's go in there."

We forced the lock and entered the laundry room. "The bedroom is down this way." We went into the bedroom and sure enough, the room was loaded with guns. Rifles, pistols, I even saw a Tommy gun from the war. We were both admiring the guns when we heard a crack — the front door opened. It felt like my blood stop flowing. Jack and I headed for the closet, got in and shut the door.

We heard the lady scream, "Someone's broke into our house. Oh my God, they broke into our house." She came running into the bedroom and flipped the light on. You could hear her whimpering, "Oh my God, Oh my God."

Her husband said, "I'm calling the police!"

She said, "It doesn't look like any guns are gone." She was quaking, sobbing.

I whispered. "Let's go."

Jack said, "You hold up the window shade and I'll open the window." We slipped out of the closet and I held the window shade up while Jack unlocked and opened the window. There was no screen and Jack climbed out. I slid

myself under the shade and started to climb out the window when the shade
fell.

The woman screamed, "Oh, God, they're still in here!"

Powered by some kind of invisible fire, Jack and I ran to the school.
Halfway there we heard the wail of sirens. We arrived on the school grounds
and sat on a picnic table in the dark, hidden from the road. Panting, out of
breath, we watched as flashing lights passed by, reflected in the trees.

I said, "I didn't feel right about that house from the beginning. I should
learn to listen to my feelings."

"Ah hell," he said. "They just came in on us, that's all. We were lucky,
though."

"Yea, that's for sure. Can I stay at your house tonight? I don't want cops
stopping me on my way back to town."

"Yea sure, Mom don't care."

The scare had shocked some sense into us. We sat and talked for a
couple of hours. The decision was made, that was our last caper, job, heist, or
whatever you want to call it. It was too close for comfort, and I had enough
money to get back to Michigan.

The next day was Saturday and Jack and I went out to the garage after
breakfast and split everything. $57.10 each is what we ended up with.

"Not very much to go to jail for is it Jack?" He agreed.

Jack gave me some clean underwear and socks. At his insistence, I gave
his mother my pants and shirt, which she washed and ironed. I took a shower
and had lunch with them and then we said our good-byes. I hated leaving
Jack. A good friend will always travel with you, but they're also always hard
to leave.

* * *

I looked through the diner window and saw Dad sitting at the counter,
chewing on a soggy half a cigar. I hesitated before going in. We'd not seen
each other awake once since our discussion that first morning. I suspected
he was pretending to be asleep when I came in but I'd done the same thing
to him once or twice in the morning. Now the questions was, could I leave
without saying goodbye?

The hell with it, if I embarrass him, too bad.

I walked through the door, across the diner and sat on the stool next to
him. He stiffened his back and pulled in his lips. He knew it was me without
even turning his head to see.

"Hi, Dad," I said loudly, so others would hear. The waitress, who was putting together a sandwich on a plate, spun her head at the words. Her face widened in surprise. "What are you doing there, Dad?"

He sucked in a breath and held it, caught off guard. He lifted his cup, held it in front of his mouth. After a beat, without even looking at me, he said quietly into his cup, "Just having a cup of coffee."

"I have some good news for you. I'm leaving town tomorrow morning."

"Oh, you have enough money now, do you?" he asked.

"Why? You want to give me some?"

He looked down to his lap. He picked at a fingernail. "I don't have any to give you," he said.

"I know you don't. But I'll tell you what. I'll tell the family that you're doing just great. Have a good steady job, get all your meals free, have a nice comfortable room to sleep in and are still smoking R.G. Dun's. Anything else I should tell them?"

He pulled back and turned to face me. His steely stare met mine for the last time. "No, you smart little shit," he said. "Now get the hell out of my life and don't come back to California again."

"Whatever you say Dad. Whatever you say." I got up, walked out and never looked back.

18.

BACK TO MICHIGAN
- AGAIN

When I arrived on the sidewalk my cockiness disappeared and my mood sank. It was time to leave. Not tomorrow morning. Now.

Since it was late afternoon, I thought I could get a ride before dark on Route #66, two miles from town. I got there, stuck out my thumb and began the wait.

Why did I make this journey to see him? I'd been hoping he would have changed. I'd been hoping he'd be better, that he'd want forgiveness. That I'd get some kind of explanation for all the shit I'd been dragged through. That he'd be sorry for how he treated Mother. But there was not an ounce of regret in that man.

And now, here I was, even more lost than I'd been before.

I had nowhere to go. No one wanted me. I was human garbage. That was the truth, wasn't it? It wasn't even worth crying over, really.

I hated myself for having hoped for the impossible. Why was I even born in the first place? Life was just a stupid, endless mountain and a rock. Why bother trying to push it anywhere? All it gave you was grief and shame and guilt.

I sat down. I can still remember quite distinctly the next few minutes that passed. I remember the landscape before me, a grove of orange trees going off into forever. It didn't speak to me of the joyous wealth of the land. It was an infinity of tedium. I remember the red, then green cars that passed, followed by a container truck. People headed to nowhere. Why even bother having a destination? It was uselessness itself. I remember looking into the future and seeing my life as tragedy followed by calamity. My heart became a black hole; filled with an emptiness that is so complete it has to be experienced to be understood.

Then I looked up from the asphalt. What I saw made me catch my breath. It was Noah, standing on the other side of the road, looking totally out of place with a bucket and a jiggy pole. I stood up, ready to run to him. But a car horn broke my concentration. I watched as the car passed, looked across the road again and he was gone. But as if Noah was standing right behind me I heard in my ear, "Paul, everyone in dis big world belongs ta somebody, somewhere. God, he dun make it so." I spun around to see nothing but California desert.

I stood there for a long time, spinning in one spot, thinking I'd gone over the deep end. When I looked across the street again I saw that there was a man there, but he didn't have no jiggy pole. He was walking through the orange groves, looking at the trees.

Whatever it was I experienced, it brought me some of Noah's optimism. I recall thinking, "You know what love is, Paul. That's what makes you different from him. You may not belong anywhere now, but if you keep loving more than you hate, you will find someplace to belong someday. Maybe, just the work of trying to find it is all there ever will be. But that's no excuse to give up. If you give up, you'll end up just like Dad and never find it. But if you try, you'll eventually end up somewhere." So that's what I decided to do.

I decided that the only place I had to go was back to Michigan. If there was any love in the world for me, it was there with my sisters. And with that decision I realized that you make your own relationships, they don't just happen. Maybe, when it came to my brothers and sisters, I just hadn't tried hard enough.

The trip was going to be a long one. It was early March, which meant a lot of bad, snowy weather ahead. But somehow, I now felt ready for it, as if the despair of a few moments before hadn't existed.

* * *

The wind was blowing hard, the kind that goes right through you. I stood at a blinking light where traffic had to make a left hand turn for Route #66. On one side of the road was a row of stores all connected together. On the other side was a parking lot. About 100 yards on the other side of that was the rail line coming out of California and going somewhere.

I stood there for what seemed to be forever. I'd stopped feeling my feet ages ago. So I started looking around to see if there was something else I could do instead of just getting nowhere. A jeep was parked across the street. I considered stealing it. I walked over, stood beside it, looking around. Nobody anywhere. The keys were in the ignition. But I couldn't drive and didn't want to land in jail.

I went into a restaurant and had a cup of coffee.

"Can't get a ride?" the waitress asked.

"No. No one will stop."

"That is really a bad spot to hitchhike from. They don't want to stop after making that turn. Walk down about a mile and there's another traffic light. Stand at the light and I think you'll get a ride there."

"Thanks, I'll do that."

She was right. I got a ride within twenty minutes.

The driver was a quiet man. After a few miles of driving I got the idea that if I wanted a ride, I better keep my mouth shut. We pulled into Flagstaff around noon and it was snowing fast and heavy.

The driver said, "Better get a ride quick, before they close the roads."

I thanked him for the advice and stuck out my thumb.

*   *   *

I stood at an intersection where the road split. My feet throbbed. I was shaking so hard from the cold that my arm looked like it waving hello, up and down, to every car that whizzed by. I stuck at it for two hours and finally went into a little store with a gas station across the street.

As I entered, the lady behind the counter said, "Wondered how long you'd last out there. What are you doing hitchhiking for, anyway?" I was trembling so hard I couldn't answer her. She came up to me and said, "Well, are you going to say something?"

"Yes ma'am. Soon as I can breath good."

"Are you hungry?"

"Yes ma'am. Starved."

"You look like hell. When's the last time you had a good nights sleep?"

"Four days."

"All right," she said. "Get warm. I'll get you something to eat. I got an empty cabin in the back. It doesn't have a bed or anything, but it's warm and empty. You can spend the night there." She fixed me a hot meal, took me back to the cabin, gave me a pillow and blanket, looked at me and ordered, "Now sleep."

The cabin had an oil space heater in the middle of the room. I curled up in the blanket; lay down by the stove feeling ever so thankful. I slept for fourteen hours. When I got up I folded the blanket, put the pillow on top and took them back to the store. The lady was standing behind the counter when I walked in.

She smiled at me. "Boy, I had to check on you a couple of times. Thought maybe you died out there during the night."

She fixed me some breakfast, packed me a big lunch, gave me five dollars and said, "Now get your ass home and off the road!"

As I was leaving she came around the counter and gave me a big hug. I could feel my eyes start to water. Her eyes were full of tears, too. I went back to my spot on the road and got a ride within minutes. I could see her standing in the store watching me. I figured she must have a kid that was like me or something, to do what she did for me. She was one fine lady. Yet I didn't even get her name.

* * *

I heard a train whistle.. A short distance down from the road I saw a train, inching along. It looked like an option begging to be taken up. I walked down the embankment by the tracks. The train was going so slow I thought it was going to stop. I waited for an open boxcar and jumped on.

I was hanging half in and half out, looking inside. At both ends of the car there were all these men huddled together, looking at me.

One of them shouted, "Come on in boy, get out of that weather. We'll keep ya warm." The laughter bounced against the metal of the boxcar. I jumped off and that was the end of my freight car rides.

* * *

A red Buick picked me up. Said he was going to Albuquerque, New Mexico. Didn't know how long it would take because of the condition of the roads. "If they're not too bad, should make it in around twenty hours."

Not long after we got under way he started talking about girls. He said, "I especially like the young girls. How nice their skin feels and how soft they are…"

I started to panic. I had to get out of that car right away. I lurched forward, holding my gut. I pretended to gag. "I think…I think… Oh geez, I think I'm going to be sick. Would you pull over please?"

He pulled over right away. I got out and told him to continue on without me. I pretended to gag some more, told him I didn't feel very good. He sped off instantly.

When he was gone I looked around. I was out in the middle of nowhere again and it was late afternoon. I started to put my thumb out when I noticed his car coming back from the other direction. I bent over, pretended to be puking. He drove right past me. I felt a shiver go down my back and a flush of pride at the fast one I'd pulled. I was learning to take care of myself, that was for sure.

* * *

"I can give you a lift to Norman, Oklahoma," the transfer truck driver said. I climbed aboard. I was still riled up by what had just happened. Guess it showed, because he asked me if I was okay.

I shook my head, let it hang. I said, "These kids. They gave me a ride, but before we'd gone half a mile they pulled off onto a side road and pulled a gun on me. They took all my money."

"That's too bad," he said. "That happens all the time. They cruise the highway looking for kids like you. Lucky you didn't get picked up by one of those child molesters. You best get yourself on a bus or train."

"I was going to get a ticket for a bus, but I guess I can't, now."

"What about your family? Can they send you money?"

"How can they? I don't have an address or Post Office."

He laughed and told me how the telegraph office could wire money. We arrived at a town called Norman. He dropped me off, telling me to look for signs that said "Telegraph and Telephone Office" or just "Telegraph Office."

I found one in a hotel. In the lobby a lady the size of a football player stood behind the counter.

I didn't quite know how to ask or who to ask or just what I should do. So I was standing there humming and hawing and looking around.

She got impatient. With the tone of man, she said, "What do want?"

I managed, "I need to call my family. For money. For a bus to Detroit."

"Why didn't you say so in the first place?"

I just shrugged my shoulders and said nothing. "The telephones are over there, make your call and give them this number to wire the money to," Handing me a piece of paper.

"I, uh, I don't have any money to make the phone call. And I don't even know their phone numbers."

She leaned forward and cocked her head. "You're one bright kid, aren't you? You know how to dial a phone?" Her voice soaked in sarcasm.

"Ah, yes, I do."

She said, "All right, give me their names and I'll call information." I gave her the Montayne's and Kitty and Danny's.

"You go over there in that first phone booth and I'll ring it when I get them on the phone. How much money you going to ask for?" I hadn't even thought about that. She looked at me with that look that said, 'what a dumb kid.' She said, "Well, whatever you ask for, add a little to it for these phone calls I got to make for you."

I asked her, "How much do you think a ticket on a bus to Detroit would be from here?"

"Kid, what do I look like, a walking encyclopedia?" I wanted to say yes, but held back. "I'll make that call first." She called the bus station and got a price. "$22.75", she shouted at me.

"Thanks, now I know what to ask for."

The first call was to Kitty. They said no, they didn't have the money. I got out there by myself; I could get back by myself. It sounded like a typical Kitty reply. I secretly hoped that one day she'd come to me for something. But at the same time I knew I'd give her whatever she wanted. The Montayne's said no, they couldn't do it.

"Why?" I asked.

"I don't want you to think that every time you get in trouble, or need money, you can just call us and we'll send it to you." I slammed the phone down. I couldn't believe I heard that. I started to cry.

The clerk came over to me and said, "They're all giving you a hard time, huh?" I wiped my eyes and turned away from her.

"Don't be ashamed to cry. When your family turns you down at times like this, it's hard to accept. I know, I've been through it a few times myself. Is there anyone else we can call?"

Mattie didn't have a phone, so I gave her Adam in Boston. Adam said he would send me the money providing I send it right back to him when I arrived in Detroit. I was about to promise anything at this point.

The clerk told me to sit in the chair way over in the corner and curl up and go to sleep. She said she'd wake me up when the money came in. As I made my way across the room her lecture came after me. Running away was never an answer. Being on the open road by yourself is only asking for trouble. Your family's mad at you for that, but it's only because they care. If only she knew the truth. Why do adults always assume the child is at fault?

The next thing I knew the clerk was shaking me awake. She had me sign a paper and gave me the money. I asked her how much the phone calls were.

She shrugged. "Nothing. I'll let the hotel pay for them. You'll need what little money's left for meals." She directed me to station. "You just get off the road honey, and stay off it."

19.

A DECISION TO MAKE

Mattie and a neighbor were sitting at the dining room table drinking coffee when I walked through the door.

Mattie saw me and a slight smile crossed her lips. "Well, look at the world traveler, Mae," she said. "Must have run out of money and decided to come home." I found the use of the word *home* ironic, wondered at it.

We hugged and I noticed her bulging tummy. Pregnant with number five. She'd had such a bad time with the last one she said she'd never go through it again.

"That's what I said, but, you know how things work out," she said with a shrug.

Mattie poured me a cup of coffee and joined me at the table. She wanted to know all about the trip, how Dad was. I told her what happened, how he was still a very angry and miserable person.

Mattie looked into her coffee and grimaced. "I was hoping that year in the sanitarium had done him some good."

I asked her if I could stay with them until I figured out what I was going to do.

"You know you'll have to sleep with Jimmy again. That's all the room we have. Jimmy's been talking about getting an apartment closer to work. Maybe you moving in will make him do it."

I asked where Ed and Jimmy were. Mattie replied, "Where else? Goddamn Palen's Bar, that's where. They spend all their time and money down there, and the kids and I have to do without." She looked to the floor and shook her head. She looked up and said, "That son-of-a-bitch gives me thirty dollars a week and tells me it's for food, clothes, and all the bills. I ask him where the rest of his check is and he gives me all kinds of bullshit. Jimmy slips me some extra money each week. If it wasn't for that, I don't know how we'd make it."

"Does Ed know Jimmy's giving you the extra money?"

"No way! I'm not going to tell him."

"Yea, but then doesn't Ed think you're making it on thirty dollars a week?"

She sat back and smiled at me. "You know I never thought of it that way." She took another sip of coffee, thinking. When she looked up, she said, "I'm going to bring this to a head. I'm getting tired of always getting the short end of the stick." She looked out the window, saw something. "Oh, and look, here comes the drunken duo now."

Ed and Jimmy walked in a minute later, laughing filling the room with a cloud of second hand booze. Ed said, "Lookie here, Jimmy. Little brother is back from his travels."

"Did you bring us any gifts?" Jimmy asked. Both of them burst out laughing, slapping each other on the back.

Ed continued, "By the look on his face, I think he came back empty handed, Jimmy. Maybe we need to take him down to Palen's and fill him up. What da ya think?"

Mattie raised her voice, saying, "That's right. You need a new customer for that Goddamn Palen's Bar. Might as well take Paul down there and break him right."

Ed gave her a hard look. "Just shut up, Mattie," he said. "Don't have to stick up for little brother here. He's a big time traveler now. Knows all about the world. Isn't that right, Paul?"

Jimmy walked out of the room and came back with a new pack of cigarettes. Mattie started to fix supper and Ed got beers out of the refrigerator.

Ed sat down at the kitchen table, slid one of the beers to me and snapped his open. "So, tell me, Paul. Where are you going to live now?"

"I asked Mattie if I could stay here for a while."

Ed almost choked on his beer. "Bullshit. This damn house is full enough; don't need any more bodies in it. Except the one inside here," he said as he patted Mattie's passing stomach. Mattie tossed his hand away and moved to the fridge.

Jimmy leaned forward, tapped me on the arm. "You know, Paul. Ed and I've been talking about you. We knew you'd come back eventually. So we came up with a plan."

I didn't like the sound of this. "A plan?"

Mattie turned around and stood behind Ed. She put a hand on his shoulder and was watching me. I sank back in my seat, expecting the worst.

Jimmy continued, "You can't seem to live with anyone. You hate being told what to do. You can't seem to stay put long enough to finish school. You got everybody so pissed off at you that they don't want anything to do with you. So we came up with three choices for you.

"Now, I want you to think about them, and let us know which one you choose, because you have to pick one. Or else, just disappear from all of us forever, or until you can support yourself."

I looked away from the three of them, shocked. Why were they ganging up on me like this?

I asked, "Why is it everyone wants me to 'disappear'? I'm not even sixteen, for crying out loud. Dad told me to get the hell out of California and never come back. I was stranded in a blizzard, hungry, cold, hadn't slept in days and none of y'all would send me money. The only one that would, I had to promise to send it back as soon as I could. I don't understand this damn family. Do you reckon Dad taught us all to be selfish sons-of-bitches?"

Their three pairs of eyes blinked at me.

After a moment, Ed looked to Jimmy and Mattie. He said, "Wow. He must have got tied up with some of those Baptist people down there in the south. Reckon, Jimmy?"

Jimmy laughed a little and turned back to me and said, "Paul, the thing is, none us can take care of you. We all have full time families. The jobs we have barely pay for anything. And since you don't want to do what you're told, what do you want us to do?"

"Nothing. Nothing at all. I don't like being a burden, you know. That's what y'all seem to think of me as."

Ed pointed at me. "See, see? Didn't I tell you? He got down there in the south and tied himself up with some of those 'holier than thou' folks. *You all* this, *you all* that. Oh, poor Paul."

I wanted to smack Ed right in the mouth. Instead, I said. "Ah, shut up, Ed. What do you care about except music, booze and women?"

Mattie gave Ed a good bat on the arm. "Calm down, Ed. Paul is right." She said, "This damn family don't care about any of their own. We all went our separate ways and could care less about the others. Yea, he sure is right. Dad taught us good." I was proud of Mattie for saying that, felt vindicated.

Jimmy gave a shrug of frustration. "All this talk is not gonna solve the big problem. And that's what, or where, does Paul go? That's what we need to solve here. Not what Dad taught us."

Mattie turned back to her cooking.

Jimmy leaned forward. He said, "Now Paul, as I said earlier, you have three choices you can make. And here's what we've come up with. Number one, we can make arrangements for you to go to Boy's Town in Omaha, Nebraska. Number two, you can join the Catholic Priest pre-school, or whatever they call it, you live right there on the school grounds. Or three, you can join the Navy in your brothers name, Johnny, and me being your legal guardian, I'll sign for you."

Jimmy leaned back satisfied. He slapped the table and said, "There, those are the three choices. You need to pick one, and pick one soon. Any questions? No, I take that back. No questions." He pointed a finger at me. "Give me an answer in two days."

He threw some Boy's Town literature across the table at me and sucked hard on his beer. I could tell he was upset. They were probably all very tired of the subject, "What to do about Paul".

But two days. Two days?

After dinner I read the material on Boy's Town. It sounded interesting. But Nebraska? The next day I visited the Catholic Priest's pre-school. I talked to a priest about joining. He went into a long narration about one's commitment to the Lord, accepting the stringent rules and regulations. Abstaining from sex and marriage. That was too much for me at the time. I knew I couldn't do it. So, that got rid of two choices. But I was having a lot of trouble with number three. Me? Little Paul Miller, a sailor? It sounded like one of those science fiction stories on television. I couldn't go into the Navy. Could I?

I wrestled with the problem for those two days solid. It didn't seem fair. The fact that I didn't belong anywhere wasn't my fault.

On the third day, during dinner, Jimmy looked over at me and nodded his head. He said, "Okay, Paul. Your time is up. We want an answer. Which one will it be?"

I looked at their expectant faces as they waited. I saw a caring in them I'd never noticed before. They wanted me to fit in somewhere somehow. Perhaps that's all a family can ever do. Some families are just better suited to help you get there.

I pursed my lips and nodded my head. I said, "Let's join the Navy."

Jimmy tickled his fingers on the table in celebration. Mattie sat back in surprise, smiling. Ed tousled the hair on the top of my head. "A Navy boy, he is," he exclaimed to us all.

Jimmy said, "We were all hoping that was going to be your choice, but we had to let you make it."

I asked, "Now explain to me, just how is that going to work, me being John J. Miller, Jr.?"

"We'll go down to the recruiting station and sign you up. I have Johnny's birth certificate. You've just got to remember that you're not Paul Miller anymore."

I smirked and said, "Well, I must congratulate everyone. You all finally figured out a way to get rid of that little bastard, Paul Miller." Everyone roared with laughter.

Jimmy said, "I never thought about it that way, but you're right. After today, Paul Miller won't exist anymore."

I did find it funny at first. But the more I thought about it, the more I didn't like it. John, if you remember, was also Dad's name. I was becoming more like Dad all the time. Now, God save me, I had the same name.

Jimmy, Ed and I went downtown to the U.S. Navy Recruiting Station the next day. A big burly sailor stood up from behind a desk to greet us.

Jimmy said, "My little brother, Johnny, here decided he wants to become a sailor."

The sailor replied, "Well that's terrific." He looked right at me. "Do they call you John or Johnny?"

I was stunned momentarily. Was he talking to me? "Ah, John, they call me John." I didn't know if I could get used to this.

"Have a seat right here, John. I need you to fill out some papers. First, what is your date of birth?"

And here we went. Ed and Jimmy had drilled me all the way. "November 19, 1935."

"Do you have a birth certificate?" He looked up at Jimmy, "And are you, sir, the legal guardian and capable of signing for him?"

Jimmy handed him the certificate and said yes he could and would sign. The sailor gave me a bunch of papers and directed me into a room next to his office to fill them out. I'd never seen so many papers, applications, affidavits (what ever that was), in all my life. The three of us sat down to get started.

"Write real nice now, Johnny," Ed said his knuckles coming to his mouth to hide the giggle.

Jimmy laughed and whispered, "Remember now, John, you're 21 months older starting right now."

As I filled out the papers, Ed and Jimmy reminisced about their time in the service. Jimmy had been in the Army for nine years and Ed in the Navy for four.

When I was done I had to take a test. I must have done all right, because the sailor came out and told us that everything was fine. He informed the three of us that I wouldn't be called into active duty for six to nine months. That suited me just fine. But Jimmy and Ed's faces fell with disappointment.

When we left the building they said they were going to see some old friends that lived in the area and told me to go home.

"Where's home?" I asked.

"With your big sister, sailor," Ed said.

Jimmy moved out a week later. Ed was mad at me for separating him from his drinking buddy. From then on he spent even more time at Palen's Bar. Mattie said she'd like to blow the damn place up. All it did was steal husbands and break up families, she'd say.

Then the unbelievable happened. Ed went to work one Friday and never came home again. We checked with family, friends and work. No one had any answers.

Mattie wasn't surprised. She'd always thought he'd do something like this one day. But she always thought he'd be legit about it and file divorce papers. But, then again, by disappearing he didn't have to pay child support, did he?

She said, "That dirty son-of-a-bitch never cared about these kids anyway. All he liked doing was making them." She tried to laugh about it, but couldn't. I could see the bitterness, the hurt. Now she had to have the fifth child on her own and raise them all, all by herself.

I'd always liked Ed. I'd never thought he would do something this cruel. I guess he'd fooled me. He wasn't strong. He was a weakling who couldn't face his own responsibilities. That's what I'd come to realize, that strength was shown in meeting what the world throws at you.

Here I was with four children, a pregnant woman and no money. To add to the misery, Mattie was having a difficult pregnancy. Some days she could barely walk, for the hemorrhoids. She'd lie in bed crying and there was nothing I could do. She had no money for a doctor, no money for medicine, no money for anything. About all the food we had came from the in-laws. I had to do something and do it fast.

I'd reconnected with a friend from school, Keith Duncan. Keith was a good-looking kid with black hair, always combed just right and nice clothes. He could get just about any girl he wanted. He had one fault. When he drank he got mean as hell and wanted to fight anyone, big, small, short, tall, he didn't care. Most of the time he got the shit kicked out of him, too. That's one reason he went through a lot of friends and girls. But he always had a nice car and lots of money. His parents were divorced; he lived with his Mother and did not want to talk about his Father. He'd dropped out of school and about all he did, that I could tell, was work on his cars.

Sitting in his back yard I discussed our situation with him. He said that if I wanted, I could come work for him.

I said, "Work for you? I don't understand."

He shrugged a shoulder. "I have this business on the side. I have one employee already, but I'm always looking for more."

"Business? I didn't know you had a business. What's your business?"

He clucked his tongue. "Can't tell you unless you come work for me."

I sighed. "It's illegal, isn't it?"

He raised an eyebrow. "Like I said, I can't tell you unless you come work for me."

"What are you doing, B&Es?"

"Paul, stop asking. I told you, I can't tell."

"Yea, I know, unless I come to work for you. Can you at least give me a hint?"

"Nope."

"That's it, 'nope'?"

"Yep."

"How long you been doing it?"

"Paul, don't ask me another question, because I ain't gonna tell ya nothing. Okay?"

"Can you at least tell me if you make a lot of money quick?"

"Nope."

"Well guess I have a job then. When do I start to work, boss?"

"Are you sure you want to do this?"

"First, I don't know what 'this' is. Second, you won't tell me anything. Third, I need a job and I need money fast. Yes, yes, I want to do it. Do I have to cut my arm off so we can bleed together?"

"You know, that might not be a bad idea. But, no you don't. You pretty well guessed it. We do B&Es. Not too many homes. Mostly businesses and schools."

"Schools? What do you get in schools?"

"Schools are always collecting for some kind of funds, charities or something. Their office safes are full of money."

"How do we split?"

"Right down the middle. If you come with me and Don, we'll divide by three. Fair enough?"

"Are the cops onto you?"

"No. We move around a lot. Never hit the same area twice."

"When do I start?"

"Tonight. We have a school picked out. Meet us in the rear of Brock's Drug Store at seven. Wear dark clothes, good running shoes and don't be late."

I didn't tell him I was already familiar with the procedure.

For the next four months we broke into at least two places a week. We got really good at it, with every move between the three of us down right to the minute. Keith taught me how to open safes, bypass alarms and case a place to determine if there was anything of value on the premises. We hit mostly commercial stores and businesses. We only did one house during that whole four months. Don, our third person, had heard that this guy had a big collection of silver and gold coins. Turned out to be false. And after that I told them I didn't want to hit any more homes. I didn't like it. They agreed and we never went into a residential area again.

Then we started to spread into different areas. We stole cars, car parts, got into the black market of cigarettes and alcohol. The money was really starting to come in fast. Mattie never asked me about it and I never told her.

We only had one close encounter with the law. It happened in June 1953. We were busting open a safe in the office of an elementary school. There was a terrible electrical storm going on at the time and it knocked the power off, turning the office pitch black. Don found some candles and lit them so we could see to finish the job. Someone saw the flickering of the candle and called the fire department, probably thinking the school was on fire. We heard the roar of the fire engines approach followed by someone trying to bust down the doors. We scrambled out of the second floor office and ran for the fire escape, the way we got in. As we slid down the tube, around the corner came some firemen and hollered at us to stop. We ran across the play field and the cops were right behind us. All three of us were real fast runners. We scaled an eight-foot solid concrete wall, which I never thought I was capable of. But when you're scared and running for your freedom, there's not much you can't do. The experience frightened us enough to stay idle for a couple of weeks.

Then, we were at Keith's house one day when Keith showed me and Don three guns he'd bought for us.

"For us? What do you mean for us?"

"I'm thinking we need to get out of the petty B&E and go big time. Like holding up gas stations, liquor stores and who knows, maybe we'll go to banks someday." He and Don laughed with relish at the prospect.

I stood up. "Well, I guess this is the end of our relationship. Because I'm not going to carry a gun and hold someone up."

Keith came over to me, put a hand on shoulder. "Calm down, Paul. I'm not saying we shoot anybody. We just scare them."

"But Keith, you've got to understand…" I searched for words, couldn't find them. So I said, "The other night when we were chased by the cops, what would have happened if you had a gun and one of those cops caught you? Would you have blown him away so you wouldn't be arrested?"

Keith blanched at the supposition. Considered it honestly, and said, "Yea, probably. It's him or me, right?"

I knew I had to get away from them. I didn't want any part of that. I said to him, "If you think you're capable of shooting someone, then it's time for me to go." I picked up my stuff, wished them luck and said goodbye.

As I walked to the door, Keith said, "You keep your mouth shut about us. You say anything to anybody and you might be the first one I shoot." They both laughed.

I turned back and said, "After all this time, and what we've been through together, do you think I'd rat on you?"

"No, Paul we don't. But you can never tell. It's just something that has to be said."

I went home and counted up what money I'd set aside. I was discouraged when it added up to less than a thousand. I thought for sure I had more than that. With five kids and two adults, it would trickle out quickly.

A couple of weeks later I ran into an old friend, Dave. He told me he was working at the 7-Up bottling company. I applied and started working the next day.

Dave and I worked the midnight shift, unloading and loading semis. It was hard work, and certainly didn't pay anything like what I'd been making, especially if you figured it out by the hour. But the only thing I hated about the job was having to hitchhike back home at five o'clock in the morning. There was no bus that early, and it was too far to walk.

In September I received a letter from the Navy telling me to report for a physical and indoctrination. Most of the day was taken up by what they referred to as indoctrination. They told us we'd receive orders within two weeks as to how, where and when to report. Then at the end of the day a Captain came in and swore us all in. I was then legally and officially a recruit in the U.S. Navy.

I took Mattie's two oldest kids to the store and bought them a whole bunch of clothes for school. They were just tickled, showing them off to everyone who came by.

Mattie lost her house eventually and had to move into a government-funded project. I have to give her a lot of credit. Under bad circumstances, Mattie raised five good children. She never remarried and didn't ever have a boyfriend that I knew of.

Twenty years later Ed popped up at his mother's house. She called Mattie, telling her he wanted to see her. Mattie at first said no, but then curiosity set in. So she and her eldest daughter went to see him.

He was no longer the well built, handsome dancer and feisty character, but a humble, fat, bald man, dressed not much better than a bum. I was told he asked their forgiveness. Mattie not only told him no, but HELL NO! All she wanted was an explanation. He didn't have one. One day he just decided to leave Michigan and went to Iowa. He re-married and had two children, a boy and a girl.

Mattie came home from the meeting disgusted. He returned to Iowa. A few weeks later, word came that he killed his other wife and himself. He had some insurance, which Mattie filed for and ended up getting half. The other half went to the other two children in Iowa, which was fair enough. All those years, everyone speculated as to where Ed had gone. All kinds of exotic places were mentioned, but I don't think anyone expected Iowa.

End of September I received my orders from the Navy. I was to report to the Greyhound Bus Terminal in Detroit on 11 October 1953 for transportation to the Detroit Metropolitan Airport for further transportation to San Diego, California where I would receive basic training at the San Diego Naval Training Station.

20.

IN THE NAVY

Well there I was, Paul Miller... or rather, John Miller on a bus to the airport for my very first plane ride. Who would have guessed just seven months before when I was leaving Dad in California, that I'd be coming back this way as a U.S. Navy sailor? Boy, how things could change so fast.

I acted like a little kid on that flight, I was so excited. I'd look down at that ground and thought about how I'd traveled over that very land.

The adventure ahead of me was a lot bigger than hitchhiking across the country. It scared me something awful. I knew the Navy would feed me, clothe me, give me all the medical and dental attention I needed. But I was worried there were things I was supposed to know (or not know).

The plane landed in San Diego early in the morning. We were met by Navy personnel and directed to a bus that had U.S. Navy printed on its side. We had ten minutes to go to the restroom, which I took advantage of. The restroom was full of Navy and Marine Corp. recruits going home for their first leave. They looked so awfully young with their shaved heads and spanking new uniforms. I pointed this out to one of the guys in our group. He turned to me, looked me up and down and said, "What the hell are you? Old?" We both laughed.

We boarded the bus and headed off. During the ride, our sailor guide told us, "What time you hit the sack tonight depends on how fast you react today. If you don't learn and act fast, you may not get to bed at all."

One of the fellas in our group shouted out at him, "You mean we don't get to take a nap after our long trip?" The bus filled with laughter and the sailor smiled.

He said, "Nope. Sorry, no naps."

The 'Recruit Debarkation Area' was made up of lines of cold cement picnic tables standing blind and fierce. We were instructed to empty our

215

suitcases and bags of all our belongings, lay them out in the open air. I realized as I emptied my pockets that this was an exercise in letting go and welcomed it. But I looked over to the boy I'd laughed with who was hesitating before putting down a pocketknife. We were interviewed to make sure we were who we said we were, and then we were shipped off to the barbershop, little lambs all in a row.

Like the others before me, I was seated in the barber chair, an apron wrenched around my neck. One sailor kicked the chair into a spin while another held the electric clippers in one spot. Ninety seconds later I was blinking in the mirror at the cue ball of my head.

Next, we were handed a form that listed all the items we were going to be issued and a measuring tape. Our job was to write down all our measurements in the appropriate spots. Next we were sent to an area where a sailor filled all the items according to the sizes you'd written down. Then we were directed to a table, where we were handed a stencil with our names and serial number on it, and a white paint stick. They instructed us where and how to apply the stencil. We were told that we'd better get it right the first time because that ink didn't come off.

We were all very busy stenciling our clothes when an officious voice rang through the room; "Why you stupid son-of-a-bitches. Have you no f——— brains? You people are really dumber than you look. I guess you'll have to wear his clothes and he'll have to wear your clothes. But I don't see any f——— way that can be, because you must weight 225 pounds and are 6'2" and you are 130 pounds and are 5'5". Now you two glorious wonder boys, tell little ol' me just what the hell you're going to do to solve this little mess you got yourselves into?"

The rest of us were frozen in place, our attention fixed on those two poor guys. They stood there, humiliated. The little one started to cry. Not the right thing to do in a training station.

The instructor laid into him with remarks that would have flushed the cheeks of John Wayne. When he was done he turned to the rest of us and screamed, "What are you jockey asses looking at? You think destroying taxpayers good money on this clothing through stupidity is funny? Or are you just a little jealous that you're not getting all this attention?" The rest of us went back to stenciling our clothes, making triple sure we weren't making any stupid mistakes.

Next we were led to our barracks. Bunk beds lined each side with lockers at the foot of each and three feet between them. Mattresses were rolled in half at the head of the bed.

As we entered, the instructor told us which bunk to take. "And that better be the only bunk you ever, ever sleep on during your pleasant, short stay here with us. You all got that?" A couple of people mumbled something, and he screamed back at us, "You people don't talk very loud. I can't hear a damn thing you say. I asked you a question and I want an answer, did you hear me?" Several loud shouts of yea, yea we heard you, okay, got it. Then, he really started screaming. "That is not the way you respond in the Navy. You don't say *yea*, or *okay*, or *I got it*. No. You respond, *Yes Sir*. Now let's try it, nice and loud and together. Do you hear me?"

All out of sync, with no commitment, we mumbled one over top of the other, "Yes sir." It was pitiful.

Sarcasm intended, he said to us, "Oh, that was so sweet. Y'all sound like a bunch of giggling girls at a dress up party."

For the next twenty minutes he drilled us until we could say, "Yes Sir," in unison.

Next, it was time to take a shower. "Throw all your civilian belongings in the box given to you and mail the cruddy, stinking things back to Mama. When you're done showering, put on a pair of skivvies, a pair of dungarees, a work shirt, a white hat, your pretty new black boots and come outside." Then he added, "Oh, and by the way, you have exactly thirty minutes to accomplish this task. Now, hit it, you jackasses!"

I was done in twenty minutes and was the third one out there. When we arrived, the instructor told us that if we smoked, we could go ahead and light up. We watched as the instructor stood with his arm solid in front of him, staring at his watch. At the end of thirty minutes, only about half of the company was outside. His arm lowered quickly, and he started to yell.

Most of those left came running out the door so fast that three of them got stuck in the doorway, screaming at each other. There were four stragglers left.

At that point the instructor charged into the building and ripped into them, "I'm so sorry Mommy's not here to help you get dressed. And I'm sure as hell not going to help you. So, tonight, after everyone is nicely tucked into their bed, you four can practice, undressing, shaving, taking a shower, putting your dirty, filthy civilian clothes in the box, getting dressed in Navy issued gear, getting outside at attention in the allotted 30 minute time span. And let me see, I want you four imbeciles to do that little program, hmmmm, three times?"

One of the four screeched out, "What?"

"Oh, not enough? Okay, make it four times."

A recruit from the group that was finished started laughing. The instructor charged over to him and asked him, "Do you think that was funny Mister? If you think it's that funny, then you can stand outside here tonight and keep track of their times for each try they do. You can write can't you?"

"Yes, sir."

"Good, the faster you make them go, the faster you can crawl into your nice little bed. Understand, Mister?"

They took us back to the barracks and that's when they introduced us to our Company Commander, G. W. Rodgers, Gunners Mate Chief, and his assistant, R.W. Porter, Machinist Mate Chief.

Chief Rodgers was a burly man, ruddy complexion, 5'10", 200 pounds, balding, about 45 years old. He'd been in the Navy for 23 years.

Chief Porter was a short, pudgy man who wore rimless glasses, 5'5", 180 pounds, about 40 years. He'd been in the Navy for 19 years. He had a distinct shrill piercing voice. The madder he got, the louder he'd get and the shriller his voice would become. So if he started to dress you down it could get really funny. But our company learned early on not to laugh at him. The consequences were not worth the chuckle.

On one occasion, he was getting on strong with recruit B. G. Holbrook who was 6'2", 200 pounds. The Chief worked himself into a fierce rage. You could tell he thought that recruit Holbrook was not getting the full force of it because he had to look up at him. So Porter ran into the barracks and came back with a stool, stood on it so he could look Holbrook eye to eye, and finished chewing him out. Afterward each of us agreed that it took just about every muscle in our bodies to keep from laughing. Needless to say, ever after that day, during all of our training period, all you had to do to get a laugh out of the rest of the company was grab a stool and stand on it.

Boot camp was an exercise in humiliation. Each and every one of us got our turn, including me. On the drill field one day the Company Commander was running us through a rifle drill. For this drill, called 'The 16 Count Manual,' each of us held a rifle. We were to perform twirls and steps, turning left then right, in complete unison. Somehow, I got out of sync with everyone else. As they were going up, I was coming down and vice-a-versa. The Chief came running at me, his face so close I could see the red blood vessels in the whites of his eyes, yelling so hard his breath nearly knocked me down. "You're the dumbest sailor in the entire Navy. What the hell do you think you're doing? Why are you out of line, you stupid idiot?" I felt the eyes of the others, the searing regret for the act of one brief moment, now passed, wishing

I could go back and erase it. I was so humiliated I could have crawled under his shoes. But, I never got out of sync again.

You learned later that the idea was to make sure everyone got the treatment once. It broke you down, made you take everything they taught you with great seriousness and made the company bond in a way that was deeper than friendship.

The Navy was proving good for me. I resented authority, but in the Navy I couldn't fight it. I had to accept authority and it was that acceptance that helped me to grow up. I guess in a way you can't get respect until you give it. And until you give respect to others, how can you respect yourself?

Porter and Commander Rodgers were both excellent men. They taught us so well our Company, Company 301, was the Honor Company at the graduation ceremonies on Saturday, 30 January 1954. Both our Commanders and Teddy C. Davis, SR, our Company Chief Petty Officer, won the Brigade Award. We were very proud of our ability to perform the maneuvers after only being in the Navy for ten weeks. (Teddy C. Davis, SR., was one of those sailors who stenciled his clothes wrong on that very first day.)

After graduation, we asked the Chief about the stool incident. He said that he'd done it before, that it was part of the training. He said he used it to see who could control their emotions.

With boot camp done, the Navy took on a whole different feeling. The rough talking, humiliation, degradation and rigid rules ceased. You were treated like a human being again and life took on a more normal routine. We got our first pay in over two months and had our first liberty in San Diego.

It felt good to walk around a town with money in my pocket, knowing I had a warm bed and a meal waiting for me. If I got sick, there was a doctor with no appointment necessary. I liked knowing exactly where, when, how, and why I had to do something. Finally my life had some structure.

Shortly after graduation, we received orders for our first assignments. Our company was spread in all directions. I was assigned to the U.S.S. LSMR-536, based out of San Diego.

I remember wanting nothing more than a ship to be proud of. Well, the sea taxi was just about to pass this small thing when one of the taxi crewmen said, "There she blows. That's your ship." My jaw dropped. It wasn't much bigger than a fairy boat. It was 204 feet long, 36-foot berth and flat bottom. If the ship were anchored in a calm bay, the wake from a 16-foot boat would make it rock. That was the hardest thing to get used to, and the ship rocked all the time.

On February 10, 1954 our ship left San Diego for Yokuska, Japan. Three days out to sea, the weather turned nasty. Monster waves as high as 30 to 35 feet loomed like walls of water over our heads and came splashing down. The ship rocked back and forth, like a cork in a giant bathtub.

The second day of the storm I found myself standing with my arms wrapped tight around a gun support on the fantail of the ship with the dry heaves. When the ship's bow broke a wave, the fantail would sink into the ocean. The water would come up around my waist, but I didn't care. Several times I even thought about jumping in. All I wanted was the sickness to stop. When the wave would go under the ship and reach the stern, the bow would go under water and the ship's propellers would come out of the water. With all the creaking and bending, you'd swear the ship was about to break in half.

On the third night of the storm, it got so bad the Captain made everyone put life jackets on and get above decks. The ship was listing 40-plus degrees, and he was afraid we were about to capsize. But on the fourth day the weather turned and the rest of the trip was fine.

We spent one weekend in Hawaii then left for Midway Island, which could not be seen until you were almost on top of it. It was a flat just about sea level. There was nothing there but a Navy supply depot, and gooney birds.

Now, the gooney birds were the dumbest and funniest looking birds I'd ever seen. They reminded me of Noah's description of God's first attempt at making a land animal, the Moose. This must have been God's first attempt at making a bird. It would start to flap its wings real fast, rise up, like it was going to take off almost vertically, run like crazy for 15-20 feet, then crash on its belly. But the gooney bird would always pick itself up, shake itself off, and most times, try again. That's why they called them 'Gooney Birds'.

We spent just enough time at Midway to refuel, re-supply and walk on solid ground for a while. Then we departed for Japan.

The weather was rainy, cold and cloudy with choppy seas for the balance of the trip. We arrived in Yokuska, Japan on a cold, rainy afternoon, 30 days from the date we left San Diego. The ship docked for a few days and then left for Sasebo, which is on the southern tip of Japan. We docked in Sasebo for 2 weeks and then went on a good will tour of Japanese cities.

I asked Birdwell what a good will tour was. It meant we were going to visit ports of call and become a visible presence there. Our job was to spend money, be on our best behavior, and show the world that Americans are good and generous people. We weren't the enemy anymore. The Captain told us we were ambassadors for the United States. Not a bad job, I must say.

Our good will tour took us to the cities of Beppu, Nagasaki, Osaka, Tokyo and some very small ports. We even had the opportunity to go fishing in the mountains for a long weekend. I liked Japan. The odor that would hang in the evening air reminded me of the incense burned in the Catholic Church on Ash Wednesday. The people were friendly and liked to barter on price.

Orders came for the ship to set course for North Korea immediately. We were to take over a coastal patrol mission from a destroyer until relieved.

One cold, windy night during our assignment, I was on watch, looking out over a black sea, waves barely discernible in the darkness. I heard the Officer on the Bridge call down for the Captain. A minute later, the call to battle stations went off. As my mates raced along the ship to stations, I looked out into the blackness, looking for the threat, but couldn't see anything.

Chief Gunner, Johnny Hall, appeared by my side, handed me an M1 rifle and said to keep my eyes peeled for a submarine.

"Okay, Chief. But what the hell is I suppose to do? Shoot at it?"

"Yea, dummy, and try to sink it. Subs release divers who try to attach explosives to the ship. So if you see one, shoot the son-of-a-bitch."

"Okay, Chief. I'll do that."

I looked down into the lilting black waves. The depths were just as dark and mysterious as they had been before. I never saw anything and didn't have to make that decision, thank God. It was scary, to think that we could be sunk by a submarine out here in this cold black night. That wasn't quite the ending I had in mind.

Our ship participated in several naval operations in Taiwan, Okinawa, Korea and Japan. We simulated battle conditions and island invasions and even once were told a nuclear weapon hit us and were all-dead. We had to actually lie down and play dead.

I was lying on the Conning Tower Deck. An evaluation officer came by and I looked at him. He said, "Sailor, you're dead, what the hell you doing with your eyes open?" I didn't answer him nor move. He repeated the question. Again, I didn't respond. He walked away. Later I was told I did well, because people do die with their eyes open, but they can't answer questions. I should have had my eyes closed. But if I had answered questions, I would have been in a whole lot of trouble.

In mid August we set sail for Hong Kong. The route took us through the China Sea where it was hot. There was not a breeze or a ripple on the water, making it look like a piece of glass. Old sailors on sailing vessels long ago, used to call these conditions, 'the dol-drums'. The temperature reached 130-degree heat during the day and to make matters worse, one of our evaporators that produced fresh water, broke down. So the Captain put us on water rations, and no showers. 85 men in 130-degree heat with no bathing facilities don't make for a pleasant environment.

The heat started to get to us and we got testy. The mood on the ship was filled with a dark intensity. You couldn't think straight sometimes. It was like it was madness or a gauze that slipped on and off your common sense. Someone just getting in your way could make you feel a rage so fierce you wanted to lash out.

On the fourth day, the Captain stopped ship and we were allowed to go swimming. I dove off the deck and the water was nice and cool. You could see for 100 feet or more through the clear blue water. I swam about 50 feet from the ship and looked around thinking to myself, "I sure wouldn't want to be stranded out here by myself."

The swim was great, but then after we got underway, everyone wanted to take a shower to get the salt off. The Captain allowed us to enter the shower, turn the water on, get wet, turn the water off, soap down, turn the water on for one minute to rinse off and out. They put two guards at each shower to pull you out, whether you were done or not. But the swim and shower made all of our spirits rise and the dark mood disappeared like it had never been there.

Just about the whole crew was sleeping on deck because it was too hot below. We brought our mattresses up, threw them down and slept in ours skivvies under clear skies, which were loaded with stars from horizon to horizon. It was the most beautiful night sky I'd ever seen. The sight had an effect that was quite tranquilizing.

I was lying there staring at those stars one night when I realized that I'd never been so contented in all my life. More startling, I liked myself again.

I hadn't realized I'd been hating myself, but I had been. Sometimes there's a blindness you can have to how you feel. You think you've dealt with each challenge, but all you've really done is set it to the side. Looking back over the years, I narrowed the starting point down to that day I was told we were putting the house up for sale.

Making the decision to take control of my life, to share love instead of hate, and sticking to that decision, had been my salvation. It was like someone opened a door to the future for me. In the process, the Navy had become my family. Where I belonged.

I blinked at the stars.

I belonged?

I blinked again.

Yes, I did.

I thought I might explode with joy. There I was, in the middle of the night, in the middle of the China Sea, and I finally felt like I belonged.

You can't belong somewhere until you commit yourself to something. To find what's right you have to keep pushing that dang stone up the hill, no matter how many times it rolls back on you, no matter how bleak, how bad, how ugly, how depressed, how much you hurt. Perseverance will help you find your place. Sure, other people can do horrible things to you, put you in positions you may not deserve. But it's still up to you to find something — a calling, a community, a career, and a service — where you can belong, if but for enough time to find your bearings. It's your stone, your hill; no one else can climb it.

I looked up at those beautiful stars and tears streamed down my cheeks. Noah smiled at me from every little twinkle. The comforting rumble of his laughter echoed in memory.

"Thank you, Noah," I whispered. "Thank you, God, big buddy."

A sudden thought struck me. I sat up, looked around. It was August 22, 1954. It was my birthday. It was Paul Miller's 17th birthday. And nobody but me knew it.

For the briefest of moments I considered running up to the bow of the ship, screaming to the whole, wide world, "Hey, world! My name is Paul Miller, not John Miller! It's my birthday and I found a place to belong!" But instead I just walked back to the fantail where I could be alone and look out over those lonesome waves.

As the ship gently tossed and the water lapped and sucked, for the first time in my life I was really me, Paul Miller. Perhaps I hadn't found forgiveness — that process would take years — but somehow my heart was no longer severed in two. I wasn't alone. Out of all this strife I'd found a solid base from where I could launch a life and open up to love. And really, what else do you need?

21.

EPILOGUE

APRIL 2005

I turned onto a bumpy dirt road and pulled into the drive way of the "cottage," as the State of Michigan called it, bewildered as to why it was so remote. It wasn't a "cottage" at all. More like a modular home that had been added onto several times. The front yard had a small cement patio with a round black table, two chairs, a basketball hoop to one side and a few feet off the cement was a glider with a canopy. I thought, "How quaint."

I was apprehensive as I approached the front door. What would I find in this cottage? And worse, what would or could I do about it?

Two ladies were standing at the door awaiting my arrival.

"Hello. Are you Paul Miller?"

"Yes I am. I called a few minutes ago about visiting my brother."

The lady nodded and introduced herself as Doris and then asked to see some identification. She explained that they don't get very many visitors and they have to be cautious about who they allow in. I didn't mind at all. I pulled my wallet from my back pocket, dug out my Georgia's driver's license and handed it to her. She studied it carefully then handed the license back.

I immediately saw a man and one of the attendants sitting at a dining room table. I glanced into the living room and could see one man sitting in a high back chair, one on a couch below the front window and then I spotted Johnny napping on a leather lounge chair. Doris walked over to Johnny and nudged him.

"Johnny, your brother Paul is here to see you. Do you know your brother Paul?"

"Hi Johnny. I'm Paul, your brother," I said. "Do you remember me?"

Johnny looked at me, squinted and picked up his flat yellow plastic perforated board and started weaving a yellow piece of yarn through the holes.

The staff explained that he sits for hours and weaves this yarn in and out of that yellow board.

Doris asked Johnny if he knew me again. Johnny would look at me, turn his head away, look back at me, look away and with each turn to me the stare would get longer and longer.

Doris giggled. "He knows you," she said.

"How do you know?" I asked.

"Because Johnny only looks at strangers one time and then dismisses them. But keeps looking back at you, staring longer and longer."

Laughing louder now, Doris repeated with excitement, "He knows who you are! He knows! He knows!"

Doris stood in front of Johnny and with a gentle voice said, "Oh Johnny, you're going to smile!"

With that, Johnny turned his head and a smile crossed his face. I sat down next to him, reached out and touched his arm. He didn't like that and abruptly pulled his arm away.

"He doesn't like people touching him," Doris said. "He just likes to be left alone."

As I sat close to him, he would look at me and pull his head back as far as the chair would allow.

"I'm Paul. I'm your brother, Paul. Remember me? Paul?"

I repeated myself several times, until I got sick of hearing it. I thought I sounded like an idiot!

After a few minutes of this jabbering, all Johnny wanted to do was weave his yarn in and out of the yellow plastic board. So I decided to leave him be for now.

Doris took me for a tour of the "cottage." I followed her into the kitchen, the dining room, down the hall to view the two bathrooms and five bedrooms. The bedrooms were small with two beds, one on each opposite wall and one dresser at the foot of each bed, a table with a Small TV and some knick-knacks spread throughout the room. Although the place was small, it was neat, clean and orderly. I was impressed and satisfied. If I wasn't, I didn't know what I was going to do anyway, so I was very glad it was to my satisfaction. Whew, was I glad.

Oh, so glad!

I inundated Doris with questions, which she answered freely. How do you get them to the bathroom, how do they sleep, what do you feed them, what hours do they sleep, what time do you put them to bed and on and on.

I went back and sat next to Johnny and sort of modified my routine. He didn't respond in any way. After several minutes, I could feel the staff getting uncomfortable, I was getting uncomfortable and Johnny was getting bored. I decided to leave. I told Johnny I had to go now and I said goodbye. He turned his head away from me and his eyelids started to flutter very rapidly. I could see moisture building up in his eyes. No tears fell nor a sound came from him. He would not look at me again.

I started to think; does he understand, but cannot communicate back? In his head, does he know what's going on around him but lacks the motor skills to respond? Oh God, I hope not! That would be, for sure, hell on earth. A totally isolated prisoner in your own head.

As I drove down the dirt road, a horrible guilty feeling crept over me. Oh, God, have we all abandoned this boy for 45+ years because of a repulsive picture that has been implanted in our mind? Oh, Lord, please forgive me.

The staff told me Johnny likes to browse through magazines and look at the pictures. I have given him a subscription to National Geographic and will buy and send him clothes periodically. Johnny is now, and always will be, in my prayers. I ask for his forgiveness and hope to visit him again.

Paul Miller
December, 2002

Boot Camp – San Diego, Ca. December 1953

Boot Camp – San Diego, Ca. December 1953

Boot Camp – San Diego, Ca. December 1953

Hong Kong – September 9, 1954 – Just turned 17

Aboard ship – July 1954

My Ship
U.S.S. White River (LSMR-536)

Navy Pictures

Pers-E344-PML:shm
971 93 25
28 Sep 1956

From: Chief of Naval Personnel

To: Commanding Officer
        U. S. Naval Receiving Station
        Washington 25, D. C.

Subj: MILLER, John, Jr., 971 93 25, YN3, USN
        Correction of record

Ref: (a) Subject man's request of 6 Sep 1956 with encls. and forwarding
            endorsements
        (b) BuPers Instruction 1001.8

1. In accordance with the evidence submitted by reference (a), the records
of the Bureau have been changed to show subject man's true name to be Paul
Miller and his true date of birth to be 22 August 1937 and the date of expiration of his enlistment as 21 August 1958. Authority is granted to
change your records accordingly.

2. Due to the fact that Miller enlisted to serve during minority, the
evidence establishing his date of birth as 22 August 1937 automatically
changes the expiration date of his enlistment to 21 August 1958. There-
fore, in order for him to obtain the benefits of a completed enlistment,
it will be necessary for his to serve as a member of the Regular Navy
until that date. It has been held by the Judge Advocate General of the
Navy, however, that under such circumstances it would be proper to discharge a minor on the date of expiration of enlistment as originally
contained in the Shipping Articles provided he so requests.

3. Accordingly, obtain a signed statement on page 13 of the subject man's
service record, as to whether he desires early separation on the date
originally contained in the Enlistment Contract. If he elects early separation, effect his transfer to the U. S. Naval Reserve on the proper date and
release him to inactive duty without further reference to this Bureau. In
this regard, it is noted that Miller is an 8 year obligor as set forth on
reference (b).

4. The foregoing action is not intended to preclude his being discharged
upon expiration of enlistment in order to immediately reenlist in the
Regular Navy should he so desire and is qualified for reenlistment.

                                        G. W. TIMBERLAKE
                                        By direction

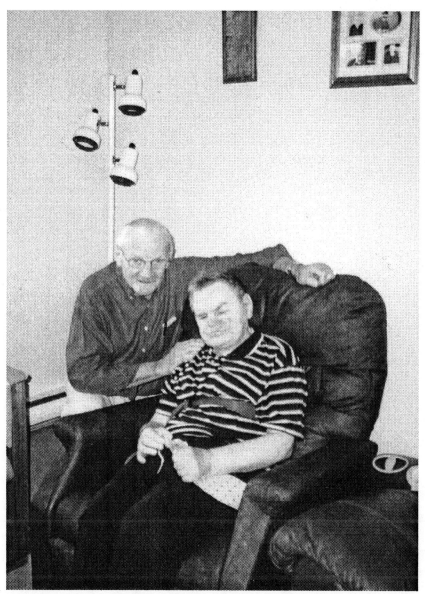

Paul and Johnny - April 2005

Printed in the United States
55137LVS00004B/169-219

9 781420 887877